THE CAVE AND THE HOUSEBOAT

THE ENDLESS WORLD BOOK ONE

MOOSE SHOEMAKER

Copyright © 2023 by Moose Shoemaker

All rights reserved.

No part of this publication may be reproduced, distributed, or transmitted in any form or by any means, including photocopying, recording, or other electronic or mechanical methods, without the prior written permission of the publisher, except as permitted by U.S. copyright law. For permission requests, contact [include publisher/author contact info].

The story, all names, characters, and incidents portrayed in this production are fictitious. No identification with actual persons (living or deceased), places, buildings, and products is intended or should be inferred.

Edited by Michael Matheson

Beta read by Nikki Mentges

Typography by GetCovers.com

Cover Art by Moose Shoemaker

First Edition 2023

To Mrs. Hunninghake, who suffered through years of tutoring the disorganized, binder-destroying, homework-forgetting nuisance that I was.

Thank you for believing in me.

1

GREEN SUN

Then__

A burst of purple sand hits my eyes as I step from the Judiciary building; scratched corneas and searing pain. My head snaps back just before the crack and sting begins. Sweaty hands pull at my neck as someone yells, "Devil! Devil Mace!"

Thirty, maybe forty people are yelling. They're everywhere, with their blistering red faces and spittle flying; with rolls of paper in their hand and fists armed with sand. A paper slides past my face, its crisp edge skittering on my cheek stubble. Spit hits my forehead above my burning eyes.

Security pushes me toward the waiting car. Someone opens the door, pulls me in. The car smells like the same products they used to clean the cells. My heart is thundering in my ears.

A heavy hand lands on my shoulder, shaking me. "Fabulous day, Devin. Ready to put this trauma behind us, aren't we? You're free, boy. After four years, you're free."

I nod, ears too hot to thread the words together. Outside, the crowd slams against the car, calling for my death.

Now__

I felt for my neck as Talsion and Rogard doubled over laughing. At my feet dropped the wad of paper trash Talsion had thrown in my direction.

"Devin can barely make it in the front door without getting hit in the face," Rogard gasped on a laugh.

The room seemed brighter, louder, vibrating. My coworkers rushed about, answering phones and yelling commands at each other, passing files and slamming hands on desks.

"What's going on?" I asked, scanning the room. Calls rang over excited chatter.

"Mess, this idiot doesn't even know who broke out of prison!"

Talsion threw a pointed finger toward the far end of the station and that's when I caught sight of her. Lit up on the wallscreen: a pale, pink face; lavender circles under hazel eyes; gaunt cheekbones and an uneasy scowl on dry lips; stick-straight hair, red like autumn amaranth. A high collar, inmate-blue, shielding a thin neck.

Mina Harker.

"But she's only been in a few months," I said, staring.

"Have you not turned on a screen in the last eight hours? What is wrong with you?" The two Batifban laughed as someone handed me a stack of paperwork. "Get cracking, kid. You'll be here late with a load like that."

I barely registered my coworkers, the shaking of their heads, throwing insults about my scuffed, government-issued work shoes. I couldn't take my eyes off the screen. My chest held tight, clenching, throbbing. Terror. Was it terror?

By the time I made it to my ill-lit desk in Accounts and Reports, I'd gathered more news. Mina had gone missing from her cell between midnight and 1 AM. It was another silent slip; the cageblock's surveillance failed for seven minutes; one minute she was lounging on the bench, seven later and she was gone. The entire floor's workforce was under investigation for collusion with a violent criminal.

There was a sliver of torn, blue fabric stuck inside the grey water outflow a few feet from Mina's cage. Nothing else to go on.

Within the first hour of my shift, my stack of papers grew. I read through each tip-line correspondence and transferred the documents into Station databanks. Four out of the fifty tips detailed reports of a Limits child gone missing in West Bend. The other forty-six read the same; fuel pump fire on Suttles Road, close to the 9-6. Half of them swore they saw Mina Harker dashing from the fire, lit up herself.

But everyone knew Mina wasn't a Firewalker, and she couldn't Suntap. She wasn't on the Limits registry, and her flesh test had come back negative. Mina was without Limits, just like me. Just like most people. She was your average lunatic, like any other crazed monster. She didn't need a special gift to cause impossible damage.

As for the missing child, my mind hardly paused on the incident.

Limits kids went missing all the time; it was their curse — you don't live long if you've got an energy-draining power. Their bodies, overridden by some primal instinct, sought death in lonesome places. Wooded areas, the banks of inner-city creeks. Somewhere peaceful; a soft, animalistic death. Terrible and true.

I bit into the inside of my cheek and thanked the Undergods for skipping my family when they doled out powers. We had enough pain as it was.

Instead, my focus was elsewhere: the day's villain; the horrid things she would do. My imagination didn't need more than a nudge to get going, and before long my chest muscles cramped again. Beads of sweat formed behind my ears and on the planes of my face. I blinked away what welled in the rims of my narrow eyes.

I always was a sensitive one.

Years ago, surveillance cameras caught Mina Harker on a dinner yacht, flinging a detached hand with four remaining fingers. She moved like the water below, the severed wrist spattering red rain above her. They hadn't caught her that night, or any night, for months after. They hadn't found the body either.

Now she was on the loose again. Had she stayed in Hashvest? That's where Necros' Universal Institute for Tyrants was; NUIT for short. The complexly guarded prison unit had housed Mina for just nine months. Far shorter than her life sentence, but longer than her usual stint.

The Station was swarming with hot tempers and bad feelings. Calls for extra hands on the phone lines, for less work in Evidence so the captain could headcount and take another team to Hashvest. New recruits welcome! *I* wasn't included; never was. A bruise on society like me wasn't much help in a time of crisis.

Mina Harker was out, for Mess sake. Hold yourself together, man.

"Last call for the shuttle. The rest of you, work like your life depends on it," the captain hollered from the front of the room.

Rogard had to get one last jab in. "You're not coming, Mace? We could really use you!"

The new recruits snickered, and I kept the emotion from leaking out. I knew what I was. Devin Mace, Station paperboy. Criminal deviant in a past life, colossal loser now.

It started again, the tremors beneath my muscles.

Was she close by? Would they capture her tonight? Maybe Mina had set that fuel pump on fire. There was a car on fire, too. The Batifban investigated that, right? What if the new team was ambushed?

She was an unknown, a government runaway. Like an MMP, a Melodic Mechanical Person, but with no shut-off code. She was cruel, sick — a long list of terrible things.

I lifted my eyes to her image on the screen and felt that familiar flicker in my chest. That uncontrollable clenching in my stomach. The sloshing of digesting fluids in my intestines, squeezing and gurgling as her round, wheat-stock irises watched me from the Station wallscreen.

My fingers drew up around the filigreed bars on the windows. The words *Spirits and Sours Fine Liquor* evolved in the metal and familiar, grievous thoughts chased my conscience. I would never set foot in a liquor store again. The grief resettled every day.

The white sun set on Pwero Ver as I walked home, painting the sky a mossy evening green. A long, grueling day, and my mind couldn't halt thoughts of jealousy. Jealousy for the fresh recruits, spending their first field day at NUIT, uncovering mysteries around Mina Harker's escape. Jealousy for the other five o'clockers entering *Spirits and Sours Fine Liquors* while I stood outside the store petting the barred windows. Jealousy for the mariners on the harbor whose ships could be heard docking a half-K away. Something about living at sea, about drinking after your shift, about escaping prison. Jealousy for freedom.

I wasn't free. The constant judgment of those around me dogged my ears like the pages of an old book. A prisoner in my own life, a life I didn't *want*. A life filled to bursting with my mistakes, missteps that followed me from city to city, job to job.

My home sat on the purple-sand flats of Pwero Ver's Harbor District. Lines of stark, sun-bleached houses homed dock workers and ship crew. Mine was government-issued, just like my work shoes, the car I never drove, my pocketscreen, my job. To the right side lived a middle-aged

Quaran couple who weren't too fond of each other. To the left, a deserted single-story.

I imagined the lives of these houses, before the sea-trade economy tanked. Maybe a family had lived in that forgotten home, children playing in the yard, that sort of thing. Now, the roof was close to caving.

A typical Tuesday comprised mindless scrolling, a box meal, and a call from my brothers. I punched in a minute-thirty on the microwave and waited for my dinner to heat. I turned on the screen and watched the news as I ate my meal; rootmash with a 'special brown sauce.' Maybe someday I'd have the budget for produce.

A golden-skinned Channic woman with metallic eye-frames swirled her cup as she spoke conspiratorially. "The Batifban swears they are doing their absolute best, but it's clear that isn't so. As far as we know, they knew about her escape plans before it even happened! Could the Batifban be working with Mina Harker?"

I tapped my pocketscreen to change the channel, searching for something with real information.

"Disturbed dirt near the greywater outflow points to the original theory—"

"But she would have had to pull up the flooring to get into that grate!"

The two newscasters argued over theories, scales raised in anger. The blue one kept on, "We've seen Mina Harker escape from more trying situations."

"Alright, so you think she *somehow* blanked the security system, jigged open her cage, pulled up the flooring and squeezed into a greywater pipe? In less than seven minutes? I don't see how that's possible," the grey and green Turret said, fixing her shirtsleeves, head held high.

"I think it's entirely possible. We always doubted NUIT could contain her for long."

"Impossible. And what of the tire scuffs on the street east of NUIT? Was that her, too?"

The blue Turret shook their head. "No, I doubt it."

The other Turret scoffed, "What, you believe Harker escaped through a cramped, wet pipe, but she couldn't have caused the scuff marks? If everything else is possible, why couldn't she have had a car waiting for her?"

"No, no. Mina Harker works alone. This we know from *years* of reporting on her."

I sighed, changing the channel again.

Everything was Harker-related, which, don't get me wrong, I expected. But the beings on screen were dramatic, and I wanted clear-cut information. Instead, I got salacious gossip and conspiracy theories.

They spoke about a strange call-in to a radio station from an untraceable number, where someone who sounded eerily similar to Mina Harker requested they play Kastute's *Wax Bits* for her. The station didn't even play music.

This was a subject of interest to me; Harker painted her victims' faces with hot wax. Sometimes complete with bits of hair or smudged lipstick, sometimes much worse. I wondered how she had the time to paint the faces of her victims with freshly melted wax. How did she melt the wax? Painting wasn't an especially portable hobby.

I muted the news when they rolled Mina's famous yacht video; the one with the severed hand. In my mind, the video never ended. Harker's odd dance moves, her scratchy cackle as she flung about the disembodied hand over her head. I read the captions as the reporters argued over who she could have been talking to, who she was dancing for.

As if someone couldn't possibly dance for themselves.

The room around me felt dark, expansive and so very quiet. The tapping of water in the sink echoed like a trickle in a cave. A tinny sound came from in the wall vent, and I bristled, nerves pricking at my spine. I was being watched.

I clicked the screen off just as I read the captions of Mina yelling at the surveillance cam, "*You did this!*" before shooting it out. The phrase repeated like wind in my ears.

The phone rang, and I promptly spilled rootmash and 'special brown sauce' on myself.

"Fuck — hold on," I answered the phone, tearing my pants off and tossing them into the hallway. The couch fabric scratched my thighs when I fell back onto it. "Ok, I'm here."

"What's happening over there?" Caulder answered, already laughing. All he seemed to do was laugh, the only Mace brother with a functional sense of humor.

"I feel like Mina Harker is in my wallpaper," I said as I rubbed at the sauce on my work shirt.

Caulder's voice was muffled. "Donnie! Devin skinned Mina Harker and tacked her up on the wall!"

I laid back onto the couch, eyeing the wall vent. "Don't tell him that; he'll believe you."

"C'mon flip, where's the joy? You high?"

"Don't tempt me," I replied, the lovely, memorized sting of icetar waltzing behind my eyelids.

"I'll come visit you if you keep up the sobriety! A whole month up there—"

A voice cut in from the other side. "No you won't, we don't have any money."

I couldn't help but roll my eyes. After a moment, I caved to say, "Tell Donnie I say hi."

Caulder laughed. "He's already gone. Can't spend more than a few seconds away from his precious packing."

"It's school season already?"

"They leave Friday."

We both went silent. I wasn't sure what to say; this subject had always been a point of contention between the younger siblings. Caulder stayed at the Landornian Monastery in Suradelphia while the other two went off to a fancy school on another layer.

"You could go with them, you know."

Caulder sighed. "I have to stay back. Someone's got to keep Elle and the monks sharp. This place would be such a bore without me. And, you know — I might not see you much, but at least we're on the same layer." Before I could reply, Caulder changed the subject. "So, Mina Harker is in your wallpaper? Let's talk more about that."

"I'm just hearing things. NUIT is near my Station. Not that I get to actually work on her case. My coworkers threw every single non-Harker related report my way."

"Hmm, it's almost like they don't trust you," Caulder said with a smile to his voice.

"Ha-ha, you're *very* clever. They talk about Harker in Sura?"

"She's all over Suradelphia One; Elle told me I wasn't allowed to watch for the rest of the day. Like he can tell me what to watch! Messer, I'm twenty. But Elle's sensitive about this stuff, I guess. She *is* pretty disturbing. The video of her on that boat with the hand. You know that one?"

"Yeah, I know it. Imagine living here with her breathing down your neck. I swear she's around every corner." I could practically see her eyes glinting out from the shadows. Ice pinched at my shoulders, making me twitch all over. I stood and went to the kitchen to shut the blinds. Goosebumps spotted my bare legs.

Caulder let out an awkward breath before channel-changing again. "I haven't seen Seth since Saturday."

"Ah. Well... Is he ready for school, then?"

"Doubt it. He's just gone, always gone. I wonder where he goes?"

Silence loomed. There was nothing I could do. I'd already done so much, right? So much damage.

Finally, I said, "He could be at the monastery right now and you wouldn't even know it."

Caulder's laugh turned into a whine. "There was an incident last week. Seth had a temperature spike, a big one. It hasn't happened in a while, and Donnie took him to the ER."

"What? Why the hell did he do that?" I flicked a dried piece of something off the green cupboards.

"I know! Insane. I couldn't even believe Seth was wearing his temp tracker in the first place. Donnie way overreacted. Seth skipped out after that." Caulder took a shaky, halting breath. "I'm always afraid he'll be... gone for good, you know?"

I pried my ashen fingertips from the counter edge. "Yeah, I know."

While my fellow recruits scouted all of Hashvest for clues, I was stuck on tipline reports again. Today, however, nearly every tip was Harker-related. They couldn't have stopped me from working on her case if they tried.

The Station hummed with the voices of my coworkers, stressed and tossing insults at each other. I was outcast enough to skirt the abuse, especially with Talsion and Rogard out of the office. I didn't *want* them to get ambushed by Harker, or fall into a deadly pit-trap, but I wouldn't have lost sleep if they did.

No two tips were the same. A group of teenagers saw Mina Harker on the Northbound in a red car, weaving into traffic erratically. A houseless woman saw Harker leaving a Smartlite grocery with two jugs of pear glace. One guy swore Harker was on the tram with a small dog, wearing a big puffy coat.

In the afternoon, the place got unnervingly quiet.

When someone at the Station flipped on the wallscreen, Harker was top news again. This time, a real development.

It was right downtown in Pwero Ver's entertainment and governing district, at the center of the famous Vervassia Fountain, directly in front of the governor's townhome, hanging on the district flagpole like a national emblem: Mina Harker's prison uniform.

I laughed and laughed. I could hardly catch my breath. While my coworkers scattered to their stations and yelled at each other for letting her crawl up the flagpole in the first place, I just laughed. It was too much.

I was glued to my living room screen post-work, staring at a collection of Harker's mugshots. Her face was striking. Not in a healthy way, definitely not. Was Mina Harker sickly looking? Sure. Were her cheekbones a little too pointy? Absolutely. Was she a serial murderer? Well, yes. The woman was completely insane. Terrifying. Uncontrollable.

But I couldn't deny Mina was... skillful. She was mysterious and deadly smart. And she did what she wanted, no matter the cost. Maybe I was romanticizing things, but Mina Harker was free, even when she was stuck in a 400-volt cage.

Having been out a full 24 hours, the news circled around her origin story, because it was about as salacious as they get. A young government agent, pulled from the depths of poverty and prostitution. At seventeen, Mina helped the feds nail the Mayor of Asala in the trafficking case of the century. She was so good that they had to have her. Regardless of her questionable mental health report.

The same golden woman on the TV spoke in a raspy hum, narrow eyes glinting with excitement, "But she got bored, didn't she? Helping the innocent citizens of Asala would never be enough for someone hiding such an *evil*. And now she's the vile, incomprehensible monster we all know and fear."

Someone knocked on the entry window. I froze in place, seeing the shape of a bulky figure through my curtains.

I made sure I zipped my fly before opening the door. "I'd forgotten what day it was. Thought Mina Harker was knocking."

Batif Naut attempted a smile. "On all our minds, isn't it? Can I come in?"

"Of course, sorry. Like I said, I'm not thinking straight." I moved aside to let Batif Naut in.

The Batif rounded the living room, pulling out his pocketscreen and beginning his sweep notes. Naut had been my parole Batif from the beginning; he'd seen five years of me, from panicked, paranoid criminal in NUIT to a free man, steadily working and paying bills. I might not have overcome my issues, but I was working toward it.

Batif Naut scanned my furniture with ease, pocketscreen emitting a steady pulse. He wouldn't find anything unsavory. I had yet to surprise him, beyond the initial shock of how well I'd handled parole. By the time they had relocated me to Pwero Ver, I was too nervous to break the rules.

"So, Devin, how's this last week been for you? I imagine your station is overwhelmed."

"Not great, I'm not taking news of Harker well. People won't stop calling the station. And these people have so many crazy ideas. I have to log every one, no matter how unlikely it is. I had one today that Harker had opened up a magical hole in the Gatespace down in the suburbs."

Naut laughed for real this time, slipping through the kitchen and hardly scanning anything. He moved to my bedroom when his pocketscreen buzzed and an attendant's metallic voice rang out, "Alert 89, repeat, alert 89. Calling all Batifban in Harbour district, all Batifban in Harbour—"

Naut threw his screen to his ear while making for the door. He was halfway down the porch steps when he remembered me. "I have to take this — it's in this district. We'll reschedule, okay? And, Devin, lock your doors." Seconds later he was in his vehicle, pulling down the silent street.

I stood on my porch and stared into the night. The colored lights of Batif vehicles throbbed to the beat of my overactive heart. Blue, white, pink.

Mina Harker had been out of prison a whole 36 hours and she'd already killed someone. The video surveillance leaked before the Batif announced the news. And because I had fallen into a Harker net-forum, I saw the video before they wiped it from the web.

At fourteen past eight, a body fell from a third-story window to the doorstop of my favorite, filigree-barred liquor store, *Spirits and Sours Fine Liquors.* The surveillance video had no sound, but I didn't need to hear it to know what the wet splat of torn flesh sounded like, falling three floors onto grey cobble. Something was *very wrong* with the man's neck, being that there wasn't much neck left. His wet, grey shirt blended into the cobble stone, splotches of red bright against the collar. His left hand splayed under him, mangled and raw.

Something blue covered his cheeks.

Before I could look away, another body fell, this time very alive. Mina landed on top of the body — I jolted in my seat, feeling the man's bones crush under the weight of the drop. Stick straight, red hair hung down over her shoulders, grazing her fingers along the wax-blue cheeks. She pulled some of the wax up with her fingernails and slipped it into her pants pocket. Her eyes darted into the liquor store and she stood, kicking the body under her.

Mina Harker walked into *Spirits and Sours Fine Liquors*, bloody footprints following her. She grabbed a bottle of glace and headed to the counter. The cashier, face gone pale, reached beneath the counter. Mina swung up and ripped a gun from their hands, snapping it open and throwing the bullets behind her. She dropped a fiver on the counter and ran out the door without forgetting her jug of overpriced water.

The video paused on the body outside, lying in a lake of blood.

What would your reaction be if you knew a violent criminal had just been in your area? Likely was *still in your area.*

In my previous life, I'd had a lot of practice marinating in fear. Before my conviction, before my stint in Hyme prison, when I sold my body for a sniff of icetar. When death followed me into the streets, and into my room at the Night Palace. And after my conviction was overturned, when they'd decided I wasn't guilty of murder. When I wasn't sure which fanatical letter was to be taken seriously. When the death threats got so loud in my ears that I debated moving again, leaving the layer of Dedocia.

There had to be a fulfilling life somewhere, right? Was freedom of self really so unattainable?

This night was different. I had said I wasn't afraid of dying because I'd met Loyal Death before, but I was lying to myself. And I also knew how bad my luck seemed to be. If Mina Harker was in Harbour District, she was coming to my home, and she was going to rip me to *shreds*.

And when I called him in my panic, my youngest brother Seth didn't answer the phone, so I couldn't even say goodbye.

I survived the night and was called into work for an extra shift the next morning.

I stretched my legs under the desk, praying for a few seconds' worth of a break. The break didn't come. Harbour District Station was slammed with damage control and crowd settlement. News broke that Harker had killed someone famous in that apartment above *Spirits and Sours Fine Liquors*; someone important. Civilian unrest shot to the boiling white sun.

The man Harker shot — his name was Kit Lambnoc, and he was the son of the governor of Pwero Ver. The very man whose house Harker had hung her prison uniform in front of.

This was supposed to be my free and easy day; laundry and consuming television or reading mindlessly. Instead, I was barring the door from frightened, angry citizens. I wasn't made for work like this. Lounging and sleeping and listening to the quiet birdsongs of dusk? That's what I was made for.

Not that I'd ever really done those things. But a delicate soul could dream.

That evening, I received a message from Batif Naut asking me to visit his Station in the morning to complete my parole visit. Once again, I couldn't enjoy an entire day to myself.

Eastbend Station was on the other side of town, and my under-used car needed a long charge to refill its battery. If I drove more often, I would have saved up for a newer car powered with paphador, the bioluminescent, naturally charged mineral that powered much of Dedocia.

To treat myself before the twenty-minute charge my car would need, I pulled into the Drybrews pickup line and ordered a gigantic paper seidel of rootbrew. I pulled away from the cafe, testing the warmth of the cup against my grey fingers.

My side mirror hit a cement planter. Hot root brew went flying. The delicious scent of cinnamon bark and cardal hit my nose as the scalding liquid hit my thighs.

I suffered all the way to a charging lot and plugged in. I headed to the bathroom, where I stood pantless, rinsing my trousers in the sink. My thighs were a furious shade of purple.

When I arrived at Eastbend Station, I was nearly a half-hour late. Wet splotches decorated my groin. I lifted my eyes to the front-desk clerk just as they caught sight of the mess. My nerves lit a fuse.

"Devin Mace, here to see Batif Naut," my voice cracked.

The clerk answered shortly, "Yeah, I remember you. But you're late."

"Yes, well…" I motioned to my pants.

A blank look transformed to appalled curiosity. "And what is that supposed to mean? You know what? No, I don't want to know. You'll have to sit down because Naut is in a meeting now."

I froze. "But — how long will it be?"

The clerk motioned me away as they answered the phone.

Sighing, I flopped down on a bench in the Station lobby and watched the minutes of my free-day slip away. Two thoughtless paintings of floral motifs disappeared into the whitewashed walls.

I could have been at home, without root brew on my pants, watching the Harker coverage and eating takeout. Or taken a walk to the hook market down the block and bought some mushrooms, maybe some salpice beans and thick-sliced bread.

I cupped my forehead in my hands.

At my periphery, copper, peach, blue spread across glossy paper. On the side table sat a magazine with Harker's face on the cover like she'd won criminal of the year. I picked it up and read the cover: *Notorious Killer Mina Harker gives her first interview in years!*

Twitmass Magazine: I didn't know what that meant, but I didn't like it. I flipped through the thing, so very uninterested in what Mina Harker could possibly have to say. And there she was, in a blue inmate's shirt, staring straight into the camera. No expression. The clarity of the photo zeroed in on her eyes; russet wrapped around golden-brown, framed with clean lashes. Her left eye had a strip of dark freckles running through the iris.

There was no meanness in her bored expression, in those clear eyes. Different from the woman whom I had seen pick dried wax off the body of the governor's son. The only hint of evil rested against her neck; a heavy metal bar clamped around her, bolted to the safety chair she sat on.

The length of the article was disappointing, barely taking up a two-page spread.

According to the statbox, Mina was thirty-three, five foot eleven, and had murdered dozens of people in the country of Besel alone. Her species was a fluid mix of genetic material; equal parts Vauveric and Eivian, with traces of Darkling. After she'd helped take down Asala's mayor, the feds had unleashed her on the sludge of the Beselian's criminal enterprise.

Mina spent her late teens and early twenties bettering the layer until her quick descent to madness.

I recognized the interviewer's name; I had seen him on the screen before. Ericson Blath had a catlike face and blond hair on his cheeks; Ingoriat or Bask, I wasn't certain which. He often commentated on national crime for Dedocia Nightly. For the interview, Blath visited Mina in NUIT prison a few weeks before her escape.

Blath had begun with the most basic question: "We at Twitmass Magazine are honored you chose us to run your story; as someone who's been housed in a variety of Beselian prisons, what is life like here at NUIT?"

"Unproductive," answered Harker.

"Can you elaborate on that for me?" Blath asked.

"I'm not sure what you want me to say. They treat me fine."

"Miss Harker, you're a serial murderer. If our laws rolled back a mere fifty years, you'd have been put to death. And the workers at NUIT treat you *fine*?"

According to the article, Harker sneered before replying, "They keep me fed, they stretch my legs for me. That's what your tax dollars pay for, yes? Keep me healthy so I can break out and disappoint you again."

Mr. Blath took a moment to write in great detail the shivers down his spine, the stick-straight hairs on his arms. According to him, the reaction was animal, like prey faced with a predator. He made sure we knew just how uncomfortable he was, while Mina sat straight-backed in her restraint.

My stomach rolled, either hunger or nerves. I could empathize with Blath's terror of Mina. And with his fascination.

"Are you planning to attempt escape soon?" he'd gone on to ask.

"I can't imagine why you'd think I would tell you that," Harker answered.

"Fine, fine, play coy if you want. But as you've said, it's you who's doing the disappointing. It seems that you've always lived above the law. And yet, your career in Besel started with law enforcement. We all know the story of Friedran Bore, once mayor of Asala, but I'd like to hear it in your own words."

"I was 17, a prostitute. Mayor Bore visited me often. I found his methods crude and unsavory, so I worked with local law enforcement to ruin his life."

Blath said, "But there's so much more to tell! Bringing down such a man at just seventeen!"

"He was a common pervert. I won't take credit for his downfall, just as he wouldn't take credit for mine."

"The government put you through years of schooling and you showed such promise. Why did you throw all of that away?"

Mina outright laughed. "What exactly have I thrown away? A stuffy paperwork job at a downtown investigation firm? I'm doing what I love. That's what parents tell young ones: find something you love and make it your future. Have you ever felt someone's veins collapse between your fingertips? Or the hot drip of wax on fading skin? You'd be hard-pressed to take that future away from me."

The interview ended with one final question.

"Do you feel any empathy for your victims?" Blath asked.

The killer turned away from him to glance at the clock before answering, "Not for my victims, no."

I sunk deeply into my chair and held the magazine up to the light, looking over Harker's photo once more. I counted the freckles in her left eye: one, two, three, four. The fourth was bigger than the rest, like the brightest star in a constellation.

On the wallscreen, a Turrisian news anchor stood before *Spirits and Sours Fine Liquors*, the dark brown splotch of Kit Lambnoc's blood still staining the cobble. "Governor Lambnoc has not yet released an official statement, but we are sure he and his family would like privacy to mourn this sudden, unexpected loss."

The TV went silent. I looked up to see the desk clerk scowling, setting the remote back on the counter.

I stormed up to the counter. "How much longer is it going to be?"

"I don't know, an hour?"

"Fine, you know what? Tell Naut I'll come back tomorrow," I said.

As I made my way to the exit, the glossy cover of Twitmass Magazine caught my eye. I tore off the cover of the magazine and shoved it in my pocket before bolting out the door.

My car smelled like stale root brew, musty and sweet. I relived my daydream of luxurious ingredients from a local hook market. My meandering thoughts drove me off the side street and into the diverse and unfamiliar district of Eastbend.

The district was sprawled with the city's art houses and innovative companies, where older stone buildings were interwoven with reflective surfaces and luscious green space. I rolled down the car windows, catching muffled voices of pedestrians eating at sidewalk cafes and traffic lulling by. Turrisian park musicians played soft, tinny notes on metal pipes as children chased each other through the tallgrass.

The crinkle of the magazine cover scratched in my pocket as I shifted in my seat.

I turned onto a street called Pollip to find myself in a crisp neighborhood of sloping high-rises. Woven meshwork floated above the street, copper and red, like branches of the nara trees which used to grow here. And bless the Messer, there it was; the *Green Sun Hook Market*.

The *Green Sun* was small, delicate, and shoved between shapeless blobs of modern architecture. Pristine vines laced up the façade, red-framed windows peeking from behind. The door was propped open and chimes sang in the wind. The smell of charred herbs wafted through. I had no choice but to stop.

I pulled in between a beetle-green sport scar and a yellow smudge of a vehicle that made my grey two-door feel new. My car rumbled as I perked up my shoulders and shook off nervous zaps in my spine. With Mina Harker's photo whispering in my pocket, I pulled open the door and forced my way to the shop.

A deep clang sounded from a circle-bell as I entered. The clerk nodded in my direction as they leafed through a print. They were elderly, spined, with iridescent scaling and a sharp smile.

"I'm looking for salpice beans and mushrooms," I said, humming with energy.

The clerk waved toward the back of the store. "Middle and end of the center aisle."

I walked among the cluttered shelves, touching things as I went. The circle-bell clanged and in waltzed a woman dressed in purple and fur.

"Can't believe I have to do this myself," she muttered as she rushed past.

I clutched at the bags of bread in the first aisle, reading labels and imagining myself as a sourceboy for the purple-and-fur woman. I would buy her groceries, only the best of the best. I'd be the most competent sourceboy she'd ever had.

At the back of the hook market, atop mounds of humid compost, grew a spread of fresh mushrooms. I picked three large trumpets and put them in an offered cloth bag. I could see the woman in purple checking out at the counter. Her pulled-back hair bounced as she walked out. It made me smile, although I wasn't sure why. If I asked her if she was hiring, would she sneer at me and stomp off? Or would she smile and tell me she'd keep me in mind? It's not like I couldn't leave my government-issue job, right?

"Excuse me," another woman slid past. I hadn't noticed her in my wall-staring, and jumped out of the way. She turned the corner as I apologized, unbothered by my rudeness. Her short, dark hair danced about her chin as she moved.

I pondered the high price of canned salpice beans and talked myself into juiced scally instead.

I crouched to take in the variety of flavors of glace the Green Sun offered. They had astria fruit, spiteberry, even lumpgrass. The dark-haired girl was there too, loading a jar of pear glace into her handcart. She wore a tailored black coat, eyelids shadowed in black. I stood aside as she moved to a locked case on the North wall and, with a key, opened it and pulled out a bottle of something clear.

With the way she moved so gracefully, I wondered if I could be her sourceboy too. Maybe she was a famous dancer. *They* hired servants, didn't they?

Back at the bread, I chose a crusty loaf and made my way to the counter. In front of me was the dark-haired dancer. I watched her booted feet slide silently on the tile with effortless grace. I pushed my foot around on the floor and smiled at the irritating squeaks. How could shoes make such an interesting, painful sound? I didn't notice the looks from the other customers. I didn't notice much of *anything*, period.

So, when the girl turned to glare at me, something uncharacteristic happened.

I noticed.

I noticed her eyes; that melodic russet and gold, with a line of dark freckles across one iris; one, two, three, four. I noticed her bored, thin lips and sharp cheekbones. And I knew her, *I knew her*.

As the woman stiffened, I felt for the crushed magazine cover in my pocket. The two of us watched each other as I unfurled the photo and held it up.

It was her. Mina Harker.

2

DELICATE SOUL

I was no delicate soul. I prided myself on my lack of delicacy; my irreverence, my fearlessness. So, when I felt the warmth of a hand hover over my bare shoulder, I didn't stop myself from grabbing said hand and twisting it.

"Whoa — Mayli, geez. Let go." my eldest brother Tom, thirteen years my senior, pulled his wrist from my grasp, shaking it off. "I wasn't expecting to see you, especially not here." He motioned to the outdoor bar I was hunched over.

I held up my drink. "It's legal." To be honest, I didn't know what I was drinking. It very possibly wasn't legal for someone my age. But it was my birthday, right? I was seventeen now, and this party was for me. "You look very nice," I said, sarcasm swelling. The great paphador stones hanging above us glowed, cooling his sweater to a vibrant turquoise.

He ran his hands through thick, dust-colored hair. Tom was so unlike the rest of us; red, blonde, pale, pink. But Tom was in the middle ground, always — in looks and in life. Brown hair, beige skin, nondescript. Maybe he was adopted.

"Is the sweater too much?"

"It's not enough," I said. I pressed my finger into the squishy middle of the palmpod strapped to my hand and waited for my father to reply. Nothing.

"Have you seen the doctor?" I did an unchecked spin to the ambient beat blaring around us.

"Haven't seen *dad* for a while. Why?"

"He was supposed to find me. We're … looking for somebody. But maybe you can help me out."

Tom's face went sour. "Is this a training exercise?"

"My last night of freedom is what it is."

Looking startlingly like my father, Tom put his head in his hands and scratched at his eyes, reluctant. "Well, what do you need?"

"Dad's got me looking for Harot Rubio. He's the one that wears the overdone jackets. Likes red. Insect eyes."

"Yeah, I know who Rubio is. He was in the back with the stage guys a while ago, and dad was *with him*, so I'm not sure what you could accomplish that he couldn't." Tom turned away from me and looked into the crowd. His tongue wet his lips. "There's no reason for you to go after Rubio."

I dug my dirty nails into my knees. "Yeah, well, get this. Turns out Rubio hasn't been as helpful as we thought, and the doctor thinks I can do it. Kinda pisses me off that you don't."

He shook his head. "Why can't you just enjoy this damn birthday party? Mom put this thing together for *you* and Nathali. Let dad clean up his mess. There's no reason for him to put you in that kind of situation."

That prickly, peckish feeling nipped at my neck. I tucked my chin to my chest and frowned; it was coming, I could feel it in the air.

"Besides, you should be helping people, not hurting them."

My eyes pulled shut before the wetness could escape. Suddenly, I was very small, and the brick pavilion beneath me was quaking, bloating. Someday, I would fall right through it. Or maybe I would get over the fact that I was given the wrong gift.

Tom's hand rubbed a wide circle on my back. His calluses snagged at the mesh of my top. "Go find someone to lure into that yarn trap you made earlier. Yeah, I saw it. Would have missed it if the yarn wasn't *red*."

My head snapped up. "Hey, that's all I had!"

We shared a smile and Tom's guard dropped with the tenseness of his shoulders. I hopped off my seat, downing my unknown beverage, reveling in the waver of the ground beneath my platform boots. The dizziness was unsettling and exciting.

"Mieda's hair will be absolutely ruined when I'm done with her," I said, smacking his arm and getting away from him before he could grab me.

Tom grinned, letting me go. He probably knew — I would, if I was watching — that I wasn't heading to the prank I'd set up that morning.

Weaving between gyrating, sweating bodies, I made the mistake of glancing toward the makeshift stage. My twin sister, Nathali, stepped toward the center, looking glamorous in a traditional Eivian dress that she'd cut off to sway at her glistening thighs. Her hair and her dress, both pale gold, reflected sickly in the glowing green paphador draped in lines above the stage. The pinkness of her cheeks radiated as she bounced on her silver-plated toes.

"Has anyone seen Mayli?" she called into the crowd, her voice twisting with subtle anxiety. I ducked away, whispering a plea to Slight Hands. The humid stink of the crowd swelled in my nostrils, but I got through unnoticed.

In the expanse of Monount Valley's pavilion, the glittering dance floor looked out of place. Crammed behind the stage, stone buildings and black and white wooden homes stacked nearly on top of each other. The contrast between weather-worn architecture and glittering, strobing party fare was stark. It was my mother's doing, of course. She couldn't pass up the opportunity for a party if her life depended on it.

Sitting on amp cases and smoking packs, a group of beings wearing matching shirts howled into the night. In the mix was Harot Rubio, my target, a criminal in our midst. It was my job to nail him to the wall. And I was going to do it, no matter what Tom said. I could do it.

I took a deep breath and slid behind the stones of a building corner.

The stagehands broke into raucous laughter, something about a girl who worked Backstage. I used the moment to shuffle my way to the line of cars parked in the alley. Three traveler vehicles and a red vintage with a tag reading *Ruby*.

"Self-centered ass," I said, lifting myself onto the hood of Rubio's car, the metal creaking beneath my weight. My tights caught on his hood ornament, tearing a big hole in the knee. I ripped myself away and kicked the ornament clear off the car.

I peeked through the yellowed apartment window Rubio's car was parked in front of. I gripped the edge and pulled, hissing an expletive when it didn't budge. I searched in my boot pocket and retrieved a keycard. It was smooth, metal, with two shiny datastrips and a grey jelly button on one side. I pushed my thumbnail into the flexible button, watching the liquid squeeze and divide.

The window unlocked with a satisfying click.

Adrenalin thrummed in my cheeks. I nudged the window open and whispered a prayer: "Slight Hands, crownless Divine, may I borrow one of your gloves? Any color will do, if the hand draws it."

With a steadying breath, I pulled myself up.

My wide hips squeezed against the wooden frame. I twisted, reaching for the nearby couch; stained, dirty. The apartment smelled of burnt plastic and cologne. Dark, shiny, ever-living bugs scattered up the wall from behind the couch.

I pushed myself through the window with one last shove. I fell to the floor, feeling the crunchy squish of ever-livers beneath me. I crawled onto the couch, panting, pulling their round, wet bodies from my hip. A shallow, red cut skittered across my thigh. Splinters stuck out of my forearm.

The apartment was sparse, with textured, white walls. The unarmed keypad next to the door blinked. I stumbled over, definitely *not* limping, and stopped to recenter. The wall was cool on the backs of my arms. I closed my eyes, breathing through my nose at a count of six. Eyes open, I raised a brow at the art hanging above the keypad. A pastel painting of a waterfall, caked with dust and bordered with a heavy, oversized frame.

"Ready?" I nodded to myself. "Ready."

I hit my fist against the keypad and ignored the warning message — *too many incorrect entries will result in an alarm.*

The alarm started up, blisteringly loud.

"Damn, you weren't joking," I said to the keypad before ducking into the bedroom.

Before long, Rubio's flat voice came from the other side of the door. "Stupid fucking alarm."

The front door creaked open. Rubio thundered around, growling in various tones of testosterone as he switched the alarm off.

I slunk low to move behind him, thanking Slight Hands for my luck.

"Excuse me, sir?"

He shot up, hitting his head on his precious waterfall art. Rubio fell forward, crying out, his hands racing to coddle the top of his head. My hand reached around, placing my fingertips to the wet line of his mouth. He opened up to yelp as I pushed the clear capsule in. It burst on contact with his saliva.

I grinned with my hand over his face until he stopped moving. He dropped to the floor as I stepped away.

Rubio wasn't a huge guy, but I wasn't exactly in top shape. I didn't know what Rubio had done; Dr. Harker hadn't given me that much. But I knew he needed to be taken care of. So, with my hands clamped beneath his armpits, I dragged him further into the apartment. His face squeaked across the wood floor with an awful squeal. I left him next to the dining table in search of ideas.

In the silverware drawer was a roll of fabric tape, a syringe, and an expensive-looking watch.

"Fabric tape? That's pretty strong, isn't it?" I asked myself. My fingers pressed the center button of my palmpod over and over. My internal earpiece remained quiet. The doctor wasn't there to walk me through it, but—

I didn't need him, anyway. I could tie up some loser.

Pushing my shoulders back, I slammed the roll of tape on the table. I tipped a dining chair onto its back next to Rubio's motionless form. I nudged the back of the chair beneath Rubio before hauling his legs up, forcing him into a sitting position on the chair.

I stretched the tape out in long strips, fastening his ankles to the chair legs. I taped his wrists together and bound his middle to the chair back for good measure. His facial exo-plating was cracked, and he had a seeping friction burn on the fleshy part of his cheek.

"Should I ... clean that?" Specks of dirt stuck to Rubio's friction-burned face. I plucked the leg of an ever-living bug off the tip of his nose.

Rubio shifted in his nightmarish sleep. I shuddered and backed away.

The rumble of music from the birthday party rattled the windowpanes. My palmpod sat quietly, strapped to my hand. No word from my father. No word from anyone.

"What the hell am I doing?" I mumbled, lowering myself onto the edge of the red couch, legs bouncing.

As Rubio stirred, I became very impatient with my father. I was just supposed to wait? Why hadn't we gone over this in more detail?

"What—" Rubio coughed, gasped in a breath, "What the fuck?" He tried to move his hands and legs, but I'd taped him down tight. He locked onto me with dripping, bloodshot eyes. "How'd you get in here?"

"Just ... stay there," I said, pulling my dress down over my knees.

He laughed gravely. "Listen, I'm not into this kinky shit, so why don't you just cut the crap and get out of here before I get George involved."

"Right," I scoffed. "*Trust me,* creep, I'm harboring no attraction for you. You're sick, man. Turns out you've been informing our checkbook, so it's my job to bust you." My stomach flopped at my choice of words.

Harot Rubio tossed his head back and groaned, "What are you talking about? Your dad set this up?"

"Yeah. I'm just waiting for him to tell me what to do with you."

My palmpod hadn't made a single tone since the evening had begun, but I tried to signal the doctor again. The silence thundered in my ears.

"Oh, I see. Another Harker girl who likes getting her hands dirty?"

"Would you stop talking?" I sighed, tapping my foot.

"Just like the last one with red hair. You know, I hung around her a bit. Back at school. You know what she did at school, don't you?"

The need pulsed within me, the need to *know*, but I pushed my shoulders back to refuse. "Is this really what you want to talk about before you get sent to Substage?"

"You leave for school tomorrow, don't you? I bet you'll turn out just like her." Rubio shuffled in his chair, pulling his arms, straining against the tape. His silvery overshirt was dampened with sweat.

"I've heard this all before, man. I'm bad, just like her and every other *bad person* in the Endless World. It's in my veins, the *bad*. Yeah, I know. I know every little line of gossip about me on this layer and I know it's all a load of pigsludge. I'm not her."

"Then why can't you say her name? *Mina*. You even look like her. A short, fat version."

The laugh ripped out of me, and the wide smile followed. Fantastic. I was the short, fat double in the play. The idea bloomed in me; the hilarity of it. I folded into myself, shoulders hunched to my ears, cackling.

"You think it's funny? George has made his perfect little girl out of you. He already had one of those; yeah, Mina. And look at what happened to *her*. You're doing your dad's dirty work, and he doesn't get even a smudge on his *pristine pink hands*."

Too far.

The breath sucked out of me, something untouched rising in waves of heat up my neck.

"Who the fuck are you, man?" I swung at Rubio's face. The heavy ring on my middle finger ripped into his red cheek. I pushed his chair backward, kicking his neck. He clattered to the floor, sputtering and coughing as I held my boot to his throat.

"Think you can talk about my dad like you know anything about him," I yelled at the floor, angry spit hitting the man beneath me.

"Mayli." Someone grabbed at me from behind. "Mayli, stop."

Tom was there, pulling me to the window. Rubio gasped on the floor. I wanted to throw him from the top of the building, drop him into a pit of ever-livers, stuff his bones into a plastic bag.

Tom turned me around toward him. "May, calm down." He looked at me; his eyes were big and brown and helped me catch my breath.

I squeezed my way through the window, Tom right behind me. He lifted me up onto Rubio's car hood and put his hands on my shoulders, panting.

"Dad got pulled away at the party; sent me to find you. He was worried. I was too."

The way he stood over me, shoulders wide in his white sweater, Tom could have been an angel. If I squinted, I could see the pearl-feathered wings sprout from his back, tapping against the sky.

"I wanted to kill him," I said, eying him sideways.

"He's not a good person. That's why he's going Substage, and you'll never have to see him again." He swiped at a bug before shaking his head. "I can't believe dad sent you after him."

My brother pulled himself onto the hood of the car and leaned into me. Above us, sweetly perfumed smoke rose into the sky from the party, glowing a hazy green in the paphador light. Far-off stars flickered, white and orange and pale yellow. Inside the apartment behind us, Rubio coughed until he threw up.

And tomorrow, I was going to leave this paradise behind.

The scent of madgeflower wafted in through the window in my attic bedroom. The flowers grew in rolling clumps on the pink mountains just south. Growing season closed with a burst of late blooms, to be drowned out by the first downpour of the rainy season. Monount Valley was my home, my beautiful birthplace, and here I was, packing my bags.

It was personal treason.

I crawled to the circle window over my bed to peer at the town below. The city center was littered with party mess; baskets overflowing with compostables, chairs strewn, a line of paphador lights hanging broken. At least I wouldn't have to deal with that.

The strange, small town perched beneath the cliff that housed my family home, Brigmot, and four other manors. This home, the others and the city below, were built by my grandparents and their peculiar troupe of refugees. Underground, in a luxuriously smooth cavern lay their bodies, encased in lifelike portraits of stone. I would be buried down there too; we all would.

From the floor beneath, my mother's voice carried up the stairs. "Two hours, child! You must be in your father's car in two hours!"

My beautiful Eivian mother, Narien, with flowing blonde locks and a voice like screeching needles. I pushed one of my packed bags down the stairs in response.

"I beg you take better care of the things we've given you," mom called in her Eivian timbre. "There are people on the other layers with nothing of their own. You'd do well to remember that."

I continued pushing piles of rumpled, black clothing into my second bag of luggage. There was no way all of my stuff was going to fit. "Yeah, and that's terrible, but I'm not going to a different layer," I said, peering down at her from the top step.

Her muddy blue eyes frosted like glass. "Many of your classmates will have gone through more hardship than you can imagine. Try to fake some empathy." She flashed me a cold smile and left, the silky peach of her dressing gown reflecting the intravenous fluid flowing into the port in her chest, her self-driving IV pole trailing behind her.

"I have empathy," I said, scowling at myself in the bedside mirror. The dark red and green of my hair clashed against my inflamed cheeks.

When my last bag was packed, I tipped it down the stairs and followed behind, heading to Nathali's room. I knocked, and she bid me inside. My twin was on her bed, staring at a hand-written list in front of her. The sunlight from the floor-length windows bathed her in warmth and gleamed off the golden, arched patterns on her walls.

"I know I'm forgetting something," she said as she leaned over the paper before her.

I sat on the floor cushions near her bookcase. "At least mom hasn't accused you of having no empathy. She hasn't, right?"

"She's probably just worried about you. I know Mieda is."

"Why?" I asked, riled.

Her pale eyes rolled to the ceiling. "Well, you know — you dress weird. And you do things without thinking. She just wants you to fit in."

"Wow," I fell back into the cushions and saw movement outside the door. "Hey, Mieda, come in here."

My twenty-year-old sister, Mieda, was the unstained example of what a good Harker could be. She took care of her outward appearance with an intensity much like our mother. Her clear skin and bouncy, straw-colored curls reflected the light like a tumbled agate. She carried a basket of clean laundry, heading to her own space down the hall.

She reluctantly obeyed. "What?" She set the basket on Thali's bed and it toppled over. Mieda huffed as she refolded the bundles of pastel. "What do you want?"

"So, what's the deal with you being worried about my wellbeing? That doesn't sound like you."

"I'm trying to get ready; can we argue about your wellbeing later?"

Nathali intervened. "Tell us about Voltenstraus."

Our older sister looked between us with narrowed eyes. "It's a school. What else do you want to know?" My twin and I nodded, eyes wide with expectation, and Mieda pulled up the desk chair. "Fine, but we don't have a lot of time."

"How does dad find students?" Nathali asked.

"He has a colleague who's a Whister, probably a Non-Eater, too. Idrissa — but I've never seen sae."

"Wait, a Whister, a Non-Eater *and* a samale? That's, like, the holy trinity," I said, head cocked to the side like a puppy.

"Yes, well, Voltenstraus has one. Idrissa Whists for troubled youth and comes back with a list of contacts for dad to follow up on. And because Idrissa is likely a Non-Eater, sae has enough power to search every layer."

I scoffed. "If everyone at Voltenstraus is troubled youth, what does that make us?"

Mieda raised a blonde eyebrow. "I wouldn't say we're undisturbed. And when you walk through the door and start dredging up fights, our reputation will only get worse."

"Why does everyone think I'm going to start fights? I never start fights!"

My sisters' expressions told me otherwise.

"You can't help yourself. Someone will push on one of your bizarre values and you'll have to get involved. Just like always," Mieda said.

I leaned forward. "Is this about that gallyhorse last week? Because that harness was way too tight on that thing's neck."

"That is but one fine example."

"Guys, come on. I want to know about the school," Nathali said. "Things have to be pretty bad to move a kid from their home layer."

"Most of the students are removed from dangerous situations. Some have family members who went there and live in Nepa now."

"What about your lover?" I asked, curling my mouth into a sick grin.

Mieda stood, flipping her hair and lifting the laundry basket from the bed. "Donnie is well-adjusted and kind. He's at Voltenstraus because he has an unhinged brother who can't function in the real world. I'm going to put these things away and start loading the car." And with that, she slinked down the hallway to her immaculate blue and silver-dusted chamber of a bedroom.

I couldn't understand why we were driving through three layers to get to a school on our very own homeworld of Nessa. The Doctor swore we needed the full Voltenstraus experience, complete with days of driving, three gate jumps, and a secret underground tram-ride to our final destination. Students who lived with their families in the off-season traveled four days before the school semester started. But we lived just a few hours' drive away, making this road trip vastly unnecessary.

Also, the car was cramped.

Tom stood outside my passenger-side window, shuffling on his feet. "You'll be safe," he said, like it was my own option. I smiled widely and waved to our mother behind him. She stood at the Brigmot's entryway, magnificently overdressed, with her IV tubing trailing into the house. My father was kissing her cheeks, one after the other, kissing her shoulders, her neck, until she shoved him off and told him to get a move on.

And so, now you meet George Harker; my father, my doctor, my Undergod. He stepped away from my mother, straightening his sport coat and scratching at his red beard. He was both refined and rough, civilized and libertine, controlled and quick as a hummingbird. Also, he was the president of Voltenstraus, my new school.

George hopped into the driver's seat and said in his graceful tone, "Everyone ready? Two days of close quarters; I hope we survive."

He cleaned his glasses with a fabric square and readjusted his collar. Always one to overdress, just like his gorgeous princess of a wife. Meanwhile, I picked at the hole stretched tightly across my knee.

Just outside of town, we came to our first stop: Lythia's Gate. A gate named for my grandmother, found by my relatives, and unknown to all but a handful of beings in the Endless World. My father got out and opened his hands wide upon the dark, rusted surface of the gate's doors. A single, hollow tone emanated and the monstrosity unlocked. George hoisted the doors open and pushed them into the shaded, grassy slope on either side, scraping the gravel beneath.

Dad drove us through as the doors closed behind us, shrouding the car in a depth of blackness. The silence pushed us forward. Within seconds we were through to the other side, on another world completely.

"Disappointed I didn't get to see the abyss," I said, sighing.

"The Indigo Abyss is hard to catch without trained eyes and ears," George replied.

"I heard it," Mieda said.

Nathali and I cut in with unbelieving scoffs.

"I did! It was quite loud; I can't believe you missed it. Every melodic note in existence played all at once. I'm not sure how the Undergods can stand it."

"It's supposed to be beautiful," Nathali said.

George answered, "It is chaotic, like all beautiful things. I'm proud of you, Mieda. You've worked hard to tune your spiritual perception, and it's certainly paid off."

In the mirror, I saw my older sister preen as she ran fingers through her hair. Praise like that was top shelf quality.

"Did Mina ever find a Gate?"

Mieda's confidence turned to outrage. "Why would you ask that?"

I moved the mirror so I wouldn't have to look at her anymore.

"I just wanted to know! She's a Gate Reader, right? I'd take full advantage of a Limit like that."

"Yes, well — I'm glad you aren't capable of such a thing; opening up portals to who knows where." George stretched his hands above the steering wheel before shifting to auto. The car lurched forward in the change of power, and I couldn't fathom why we hadn't invested in a newer vehicle. "You have gifts of your own."

My fingers pulled at the hole in my leggings, ripping them further. Nathali glanced at me in the mirror, shaking her head. She knew what words like that did to me.

"This takes me to a subject I've been unsure of how to broach. At Voltenstraus, it will be best for you not to associate yourself with your oldest sister. I recognize that nothing is black and white, but as you can imagine, Mina is not held in high regard in such a place. Some students have witnessed her cruelty in person. Distance yourself from her actions and do not speak of her, no matter how tempting."

Nathali piped up from the back seat. "What about you? Have you distanced yourself from her?"

I pushed a silent breath from my nose and waited for the blowback.

"What sort of question is that?" Our father bristled like a wild hog.

"Let's not do this," I started.

"I just want to know if dear old dad has been able to distance himself from the serial murderer in our family," Nathali pushed, chin tipped up.

"I have complete faith in *your* ability to detach yourself from Mina; it's Mayli I'm worried about."

"What? Why am I being thrown into this?"

Mieda jumped in too. "Well, you were the one to bring her up."

"I'm still trying to find out if dad has distanced himself from Mina," Nathali said, picking at her nails.

"Enough. We are going to enjoy this trip. Take in the magnificent scenery around us. We won't be on Ahk long," my father said, effectively ending the conversation.

Ahk was beautiful. Truly, it was. But the jutting, red stones and boiling, cliff-side springs were not enough to distract me from the questions left hanging between us.

We stopped in Noravel for lunch, a cliff-side city stacked with tiny, elaborate homes set into the rock wall. Our pathetic car couldn't self-drive much of the steep slopes, so the Doctor let Mieda drive for practice. She took us to an outdoor café, perched in the space between the dry, sand-colored trees clinging to the cliff. A beautiful Turret with large, crystalline eyes and delicately twisted antennae served us battered vash and greens. We joked about how mother and Tom would survive for the school year, just the two of them.

As the closer of the two suns sank to the horizon, we reached the arid, seaside metropolis of Desolation. This time of year, the far sun never set, so even the nighttime glowed with dim warmth. We parked at the shore near our hotel and spent the evening outside.

Nathali and Mieda ran up and down the beach, splashing in the tide. I sat on my jacket in the sand, my stomach rolling every time their bare feet touched the water. Dad took pictures of them with his pocketscreen, then wrapped his arm around my shoulder and snapped a photo of us too. I did my best to fake contentment while wetness sloshed at my sisters' legs.

Early the next morning, we made our way to Traveler's Sea Pass, the Supernal gate connecting the planet of Ahk to the planet of Dedocia. We drove onto a ferryboat at the first light of the close sun, white rays reflecting off the water around us. Tossed about at sea, I kept my eyes up to catch sight of the gate.

Shallow waves splashed at the structure. Two stone spires came into view, their connection concealed far above by heavy clouds. Fog settled thickly at the gate's entrance, rolling and tumbling in big knots. The Gatespace between was liquid, mirrored. We watched our ferry approach the arch.

The boat was pulled into darkness and pushed into a new ocean, with purple clouds roving over swaths of stars in a magnificent night sky. The air hummed with nightbird song.

How could anyone see the Indigo Abyss in the millisecond they stayed in the Gatespace? It didn't make sense.

I turned to my father. "Can you see the Abyss?"

The corners of his mouth turned up despite his attempt to stifle it. "Dear, I've told you before. It takes years of practice."

"Ok, great, but can you see it?"

"I have seen it before. Even I am not skilled enough to experience the Abyss every time." He turned toward the dark sea and breathed in the cool air. "If you do the work, you'll see it someday too."

We drove through the night. In the afternoon, we reached the doeboa fields surrounding our destination. Miles and miles of green tufts lined up in long, thin rows. Every few leagues, a workhouse would break the horizon. The land was flat and shined a bright orange in the low, white sun.

My sister, the one I wasn't allowed to talk about, lived on this layer. She lived a country away, in Besel, while we drove through Lacause. I'd never been this close to her before. She had left my family's home before my mother gave birth to my twin and I. I wondered what she was doing, who she was, why she was. My parents had divulged bits of their mistakes in raising her, but it couldn't have been that bad.

The town of Purvock Village jutted severely out of the shapeless landscape. We made our way to an inn and parked the car across the street. The inn was trimmed in thick, carved wood and stone. Dim paphador streetlamps began to heat up as the sun dipped lower, casting a green hue over the hot streets.

"Is it always this crowded?" I asked.

My father glanced at the host of cars around us. "It's the last tram before school starts. I assume we'll see students in the inn."

Dad turned off the car and sprung from his seat. "Everyone out. I'm only here for a short time tonight, so we'll need to bring your luggage in now."

I grabbed my bags and followed my father into the inn while Mieda and Nathali stayed back to gather their things.

The lobby was packed full of students. Around the hearth, fifteen or so kids sat on couches and on the floor socializing. They watched the Doctor and I with curious eyes, whispering to each other. My father pulled me up to the front desk with him. He made small talk with the attendant, someone he seemed to know well. I was introduced as his youngest, brightest, most impossible child.

The attendant said, "It's wonderful to meet you, miss Mayli. I'm sure the school needs a few more Harkers."

"I'm not sure that's what anyone needs," I replied. Dad put a soft hand on my back.

Mieda held the door open as Nathali stumbled in, carrying too many things at once. My father ran off to help them up the stairs, leaving me to stand at the front desk. I glanced around the room, pushing my shoulders back as I eyed the other students.

The entrance door opened, and a stiff breeze moved through the lobby. The cold zapped straight to my marrow and my lungs failed. Behind the breeze, two young men entered. The first was a thin, stony boy wearing black from head to foot, with short, dark hair and longer green bangs. Behind him was another boy; older, more muscular and with a healthy, grey complexion.

The room shifted in discomfort as the skinny boy stomped through, dripping in teen angst. He climbed the stairs and disappeared, taking with him the tangible chill.

The older one threw his hand out to the desk attendant. "The title suite, please." He grabbed the key, stopping for a second to look at me with utter confusion, then ran up the stairs.

A collective sigh of relief moved through the room.

"Mess, those people looked fun," I said, my words trailing off.

The desk attendant shrugged. "All I know is that every year the school books those boys the title suite, and every year the school pays for the repairs."

"Repairs?"

She lifted her hands in surrender. "Something always ends up broken. I don't want any part in it, so I leave it alone. I don't get paid enough to care."

I slid my luggage through the heavy, wooden door of our rented room. Nathali stood on the balcony with the Doctor, arguing under her breath. The white sun had just sunk below the sharp buildings of the horizon.

Mieda was running a bath in the big copper tub. There were two beds, small and piled high with thick quilting, unnecessary in the hot climate. I filed through a tin of beverage cards with little luck for something cool. I found a single card for a Quarran iced lolly. It would have to do.

I put the card in the slot and listened to the drink-maker churn behind the walls. Three mint-green ice cubes tumbled into a glass flute, the same shade of green that was streaked through that sullen teenager's hair; the one who'd stomped into the inn and effectively shut down every conversation in the room.

"Hey, dad," I called, watching green foam drop into my glass and fill to the brim. It smelled like candied pine needles.

He stepped back from Nathali, removing his hand from her shoulder. She tipped her head back and grumbled. Dad eyed the pastel beverage in my hand and forced a smile.

"There was a guy that came into the inn after you went upstairs. Skinny, angry, black and green hair. Know him?"

A laugh barked from his throat and transformed into a violent cough. He schooled himself and stepped into the room. "Yes, I know him."

"He seemed like an ass."

"Pure poetry, my love. Imagine the tales you could spin with a full vocabulary," he said, taking his turn with the drink-maker.

"Everyone stopped talking when he came in."

A white mug was pushed out of the dispenser and warm, orange liquid poured in. My father picked up the mug and inhaled the spicy scent. He took a drink, "Ahh, not as good as your mother's." His eyes would not meet mine. "He's a bit of a pariah, that one. Nothing to worry yourself with. Focus on your schoolwork and make some friends before you invest in disrupting the social order."

"Why does everyone think I'm going to start fights?" I said, throwing my hands in the air.

"Odd, isn't it?" He strode off, sipping his drink.

The doctor left us on our own that night. He didn't want to "taint our experience." I didn't understand it. Why drive for days only to drive all the way back? A waste of time.

Early in the morning, we shuffled out into the still streets of Purvock Village with a group of other students. I stopped to pull my short, straight hair out of my face and run my fingers through my bangs, fully aware that they were sticking in all directions. Dark green hair dye still stained my fingertips and I couldn't think back to the last time I'd washed my hands. Maybe back at home, after the birthday party? That couldn't be true, could it?

The group made their way to a tiny shed behind a tall, ornate building with thick columns. The shed had an electrical warning sign on the door. An older student of Veldian descent placed their webbed hand on a metal pad next to the door and it unlocked. They went inside and each student followed behind, placing their hands on the device in single file.

I splayed my hand on the metal and it was warm, almost oily.

"Oh, Mayli — your fingernails. You need to scrub your hands," Mieda said, peering over my shoulder.

"Oh, Mieda, sweet Mieda. I hope they put us in the same dorm room so you can tell me what to do all the time."

At the back of the small room was a stairwell. I followed the others down, holding onto the slick railing. My stomach churned with discomfort. The air smelled old, stale, dry, like I was breathing in the dust of an ancient catacomb. If I closed my eyes, I could see dead bits of skin floating through the air.

The tram needed a desperate upgrade, with worn metal paneling and thick, clouded windows. Its subterranean track creaked as each student boarded. A light flickered above me and I felt the pressure of being underground, the weight of it.

Nathali put her hand at my back and pushed me onward. "You're not going to start any fights."

I blew out a huff of air. "Yeah, of course not." I glanced around, cataloging the other students. Most of them had magnificent scaling, elaborate markings on smooth skin, or soft, patterned fur. I was stuck in a body of pink flesh, like that of a maggot. Not a single interesting spot on me.

"Look at these people. Nothing to fight about anyway; they're all miserable."

"You're the only person who's miserable," Nathali noted, and she was right. Everyone was chatting, bouncing and glowing with excitement. "You can do this."

She took my hand and squeezed. We stepped onto the tram together.

3

THE HOUSEBOAT

I dropped my handcart and groceries went flying. A shocking crack split my thoughts as my spiteberry glace bottle shattered. Mina tossed something at the clerk and they caught it; a key, maybe. She took off running, holding an unbroken bottle of glace beneath her armpit. Outside, the sickly yellow car parked next to mine roared up.

Mina Harker, disguised in a dark wig and coat, was pulling out onto Pollip street, in the middle of East Bend Pwero Ver.

It didn't take more than a second for me to reach my car, groceries forgotten on the floor of the Green Sun. I backed up and shot down the street, cursing myself. What the hell was I doing? Following Mina Harker? *What the hell was I doing?*

Mina knew this part of town much better than I did. She turned left, right, left again, skidding onto a sidewalk, nearly killing a family of four.

I fumbled for my pocketscreen. "Call Batif Naut," I yelled as I turned the car, skidding toward the 9-6.

Mina's car frothed at the tailpipe, spitting something foamy onto the street. It was an old car, and I swerved to the other side of the freeway to avoid the spew — right into oncoming traffic, just as East Bend station's damned desk-clerk answered the call, drawling a bored greeting.

"Naut! Get me Batif Naut!" I gasped into the screen, pulling myself from the brink of an unrailed overpass. The yellow car blared forward, loud and fuming.

"Who is this?" the clerk asked, weary.

"It — fuck, it doesn't matter, this is an emergency! Get Naut!"

"Then you should have called *Emergency.*"

"It's Devin Mace, get Naut! Fuck, oh no, what's—"

My car, my government issued, under-used little car, spun. Thick lines of rubber pulled from beneath me, tossing themselves on the ground like black confetti. My pocketscreen flew from my hand and smacked against the passenger window.

"Shit, shit." I reached for my head, vaguely concerned it was no longer attached to my neck. Had I hit something? The numbness of doom throbbed in my belly. Mina's car was upon me now, yellow and vibrant and stinking of exhaust. The woman inside leapt out, her fitted black coat slapping in the wind.

Dazedly, I saw her stomp up and pull open my car door. I sagged out, my body's weight held up by my safety belt, unaware that I'd been clinging to the handle.

Her long-fingered hand, red at the knuckles, rose into the air and came down on my face. I didn't feel it. It should have hurt, but I didn't feel it. Nothing but the sound of wind and racing cars.

"Wake up, idiot! Who are you?" Mina pulled off her wig, red hair snagging beneath it.

I looked up at her. There were those eye freckles; one, two, three—

She hit me again, this time on the mouth. I gaped and sucked in a breath, pulling myself back. Mina snarled, leaning over and unhooking my safety belt. She grabbed onto my arms and dragged me from the car.

The pavement was cool on the heels of my palms. I curled on all fours and gasped, head tucked to my chest.

"Who are you? Tell me, damnit!" When I didn't answer, she kicked my ribs and I fell to my side, covering my head with pleading hands. Cars zagged around us, horns blaring.

With my eyes squeezed shut, I felt her circle me, pacing. The steps stilled and I listened for the cock of a gun. Nothing.

I peaked, just one eye opening to the grey sky above. The color felt *wrong*.

"Get up."

I whispered, "*No.*"

"Get the fuck up before I kill you right here on the 9-6."

A pathetic sound drew from my lips, an aggravating little whimper. I rolled onto my belly and got my knees beneath me. Shakily, I rose.

The woman loomed over me. Her hair lashed in the wind, knotted and wild. In her outdrawn hands, she held a gun; not a big one, but still a gun. It was pointed right at me.

Mina pushed the gun to my chest and thrust, sending me into the side of my car with a thud. She kneeled, gun pointing unwaveringly at me, and pulled a thin, metal card from inside her boot. She thumbed at it, running one finger along the edge, before pressing into it. Behind me, my car locked.

"Come on, with me." Mina slipped the card back into her boot and pushed the gun to my head.

"*No,*" I said again, this time louder. "I... *can't.*"

"You heard me, get in the car." She yanked me forward by the shirt, opened her driver-side door, and manhandled me toward it.

"What are you gonna do to me?" I said, my voice cracking with adolescent fear.

"Just get in the car, kid."

With the barrel of her handgun now pressed to my neck, I got into the car.

The car was musty, stinking of dust and dry rot. The old fabric seats grabbed at my pants like sandpaper. The radio was on; a scratchy voice complained about fringe conspiracies involving Bright White Energy.

Mina Harker rounded the car, never once breaking eye contact with me, and slid into the passenger seat.

"Turn it on," she said, voice hard.

My hands wouldn't move. I *couldn't* move, even as I tried. It had been a long time since someone had pulled a gun on me. It had been a long time since I was around a serial killer, too.

"Use your hands, gutbag," the killer knocked into my arm with the barrel of her gun. It was cold. My teeth began to chatter. Overhead, the clouds darkened to an odd, nut-brown grey. There was a mirror attached to the ceiling of the car. I caught sight of myself in it; my eyes were bright, overly so. Orange, rimmed in raw redness.

Mina's hand came down onto the dashboard in a loud smack, and I flinched, drawing further into myself. I brought my hands up, trembling, and took hold of the steering wheel. I turned the scrap of metal in the ignition. The beast roared to life, shaking in jerky bounces on the asphalt.

"Turn us around. We're going west. *Drive.*"

I turned the car, unable to move my head enough to check for oncoming traffic. Horns blared angrily as drivers veered and shook their clenched fists at us. Did no one notice the devil in the passenger seat? No one was bothered by the gun pointed at my head?

It felt all too familiar.

"If you try to kill us again, I'll stick you in the trunk," Mina snarled, tapping my temple with the gun. "Drive west, towards the Kajiun. Forty minutes, tops."

I'd only seen the Kajiun forest once, on my charter ride from Suradelphia to my new home in Pwero Ver. I'd mostly ignored the ancient forest, or what was left of it; I had so much time left to enjoy the worlds now that I was out of prison. I told myself that I would bring Seth here when my travel restrictions lifted. We'd go on one of those plant tours; he'd always liked plants.

Cold metal tapped at my temple again. "Pay attention, you're veering.'

A full-body shiver rocked through me, sending my head jostling sideways toward the killer. Our eyes locked. There were those freckles. One, two, three, four.

She was just a person, and I wouldn't be told to *pay attention* to her. I was done being told to pay attention.

I swerved the car off the road, body jumping as we collided with gravel and high grass. A blasting pop sounded, and a bullet flew past my face, bursting through the driver-side window. My hands flew into the air in submission. A second shot came, followed by a caving sort of heat in my left hand. A hole bloomed there, circled in red.

"You *shot* me!" I yelled, pulling the bloody hand to my chest. Red spread on the white of my shirt.

Mina exited the car, ignoring my yowling. She ran to the driver's side and pulled me out of the car by the hair. I pushed against her with my shoulder, knocking her back, but I was unsteady on my feet. I tumbled onto the ground, horrified. This was not going well.

"Look at what you fucking did!" Mina stepped over me, surveying the damage to her car. "You think you're some fucking hero?"

Fingers wove back into my scalp and grasped, pulling me with them. I skittered up, sneezing on gravel dust. Mina pulled me to the passenger side and shoved me in. I struggled, squirming against her spidery arms, my bloodied hand swiping across her face as I pressed her away. She spit my blood from her mouth and reached for her boot. Something long, black — it was a blade, with holes in it — she grabbed my uninjured hand, placed it on the dash and —

"Fuck, no, no," I gasped, cried out.

The knife went through my hand, stabbing into the dashboard with a splintering, wooden thud.

"Oh, gods, my *god* what am I — fuck, fuck," I sobbed, flexing my hand. Metacarpal bones scraped against the knife. My torn skin knit around the blade, pushing against it in rebellion.

Mina slammed the car door shut with maddening force. The vibration of it jolted my stuck palm. I leaned forward into myself and cried.

The killer drove after that.

My skin wasn't normal, and twenty minutes into our drive of terror, I feared Mina had noticed.

Once her fits of angered breathing and finger-clenching lessened, she began to side eye my hands. The wound on my left hand, the gunshot, had woven back together in a raw circle of muscle. Pus gleamed against the blade pinning my other hand to the car, welling up in great clear bubbles. The skin had begun to search upward for a way to close the wound.

"What species are you?" Mina asked, breaking the long silence.

"Dedocian," I said, baring my teeth in a snarl.

"I didn't think Dedocians came in grey." Her voice was flat.

"We come in every color."

The brown sky shifted to a feeble yellow, and white clouds peeled away like shedding skin. The Kajiun forest snuck ever closer on the horizon. To the side of the road, a clump of leaning, thin grain towers clung to the wet soil. Buggish children chased an animal around them, laughing, careless. The radio shifted and crackled, losing the station. Only the rumbling of the car motor was left.

Today, I would find out if I could die.

The Kajiun grew out of the ground like a living wall. Hyssia saplings crowded at the front of the line like toddlers, branches reaching up to their parents with needy demands. At a crossroads right at the edge of the trees, a big, haphazard welcome sign drifted by. *Welcome to Frasier*, it said in chipped, blue letters, barely legible through the dusting of lime-green powder covering the thing.

Mina turned the opposite direction, left and parallel to the trees. She turned again at a lopsided mailbox, crusted with lichen. *240 Arm* was the address. I almost let a laugh out from the sheer absurdity of it. Arm Street? How many arms had Mina removed from bodies here? She pulled the car into a circle of trees and parked next to a big, rusted dumpster. Was it filled with arms? How many? Two hundred and forty arms? What the hell was I doing?

She shut off the car and stalked out and around to my side. Mina grabbed at the knife in my hand and wiggled it free. We watched the skin on the back of my hand fall and pool into the fresh hole with gelatinous ease.

"Get out," she said, disgusted.

I grunted, pulling myself from the seat.

Mina stepped behind me and pressed her gun between my shoulder blades. "Walk. *Go.*"

I stumbled into the wet leaves underfoot and trudged forward. My hands pulsed with blood. "Where are we going?"

"West, to the water. You'll see it."

With Mina at my back, I headed into the deep green woods, passing between heavy, slick trunks of ancient Hyssia trees. Midges swarmed around us, begging for a taste of the pus hardening on my hands.

Through the trees, water glinted dimly in the cloud-hazy daylight. A lake, green and placid, twisting like a serpent. Rocks lined the shore; glittering grey things with sharp edges. I stopped at the edge of the water, my shoes filling with water in a gash of peaty mud.

At the North edge, a few hundred yards from us, there was a boat, makeshift and decrepit, with planks of redwood nailed haphazardly to the façade. Crisp, dry leaves piled upon the tiny deck, fluttering in the wind. A windowed door mirrored the algae and lichens attached to the wooden sides.

I wasn't going to die on a boat, for Mess sake.

Mina pressed the gun into my back again. "Don't do anything stupid."

A sound squeezed from my throat, a laugh maybe, and I lunged myself into the rocks. I pried one up from the mud, skidding as Mina kicked one of my legs out from under me. I grabbed her arm, pulling her down with me, throwing the rock into her face.

Time slowed. A red scratch dotted Mina's jaw. I watched a single drop of blood slide down her neck and into her shirt.

Mina's eyes darted to my hands, narrowing. She pointed the gun to my chest and fired.

4

Grey Face, Green Hair

We hurtled along underground at great speed, swaying slightly with every turn. I sat on a cushioned bench in one of the three student rooms, staking my claim for the next two nights. Twelve sleeping spots lined the room, with dark blue sheets and woven multicolor blankets. With my feet perched atop my luggage, I watched the students around me.

Next to me, another group played some sort of maddening game. The girl to my left laid on the bench with her arms crossed over her face. On the fleshy part of her forearm, just beneath thick scales of bronze, purple and blue, patterns of a tattoo contrasted with the warm depth of her skin. The ink was still peeling.

She groaned and rolled to face the wall. Maybe she was hungover.

A group of four, each of a different species, lounged on the floor with schoolbooks open in their laps. One of them, Orcorne with dainty copper horns and red flesh, tossed her pen into the air. She flicked her hand without a second thought and the pen froze. It hovered above her shoulder, buzzing with energy.

I tucked my hands behind my elbows and cleared my throat. I shut my eyes for a moment to watch the swirling colors hidden in the darkness.

"May, hey. Found a spot to sleep?"

Nathali stood before me, glancing around the room.

"Yeah, seems fine." I watched people pass the arched door in the hallway. Mieda looked in and narrowed her eyes at me.

"Have you talked to anyone?"

"No. I've looked, though."

She scoffed, "I'm sure."

"What the fuck is Mieda doing?" I pointed to her peering at us from her perch in the doorway.

Nathali turned and waved her in. Our older sister huffed and traipsed to us, curls bouncing with every step.

"What are you two doing?" Mieda asked, lips pressed flat.

"What are *you* doing?" I asked.

She stood taller, chest thrust out with her arms crossed. "I was seeing what you were doing!"

"We're not *doing* anything. I was asking Mayli if she'd made any friends yet," Nathali answered.

"Yeah, so you can stop your patrol, batif," I said, pulling my knees to my chest.

Mieda closed the gap between us to fully join the conversation. "Well, have you made any friends?"

"We just got on this thing!"

"Have you even tried? Do you even know how to make friends?"

Nathali put her hand up, cutting Mieda off. "You have to jump in headfirst, you know? Be more outgoing or something," Nathali said.

"Or something," I replied.

Mieda added, "Acting kind goes a long way. Kind and *civil*."

"Civil." I stared at the rust-spotted ceiling. "Thanks for the tips, guys."

The tramcar was tube-shaped, with a curved ceiling. Convex windows lined the hallway, thick and greyed with scratches. Our path underground didn't have much of a view, but every few feet a wall-mounted bulb lit up the tunnel.

I stood at the window, eyes following holes in the metal mesh containing the dirt walls. "This place is going to cave in."

A cheery voice startled me. "That would be something, wouldn't it!"

Leaning against the wall behind me was a man so void of color that I swear I could see right through him. Sithnic, without a doubt, with skin like snow and eyes like marble.

"Thought I was talking to myself." I forced a smile.

His smile was genuine. "In close quarters like this? Hardly possible. You're new?"

I nodded. "Yeah, you're not?"

"Not even a bit. I'm Saren Vite. I teach Literature at the school; I'll likely have you in class. Are you ... excuse my guess, but are you Dr. Harker's daughter?"

"The hair gave it away?"

"Not just the hair." His pearly teeth formed little fangs at the edge of his smile. "Dr. Harker gave us a heads up that his twins were joining Voltenstraus this year. What's your name?"

"Mayli. Nathali is around here somewhere." I dropped to the floor and settled across from the window.

Saren sat down too and held out a hand. "Well, nice to meet you, Mayli Harker. I enjoy your hair, by the way."

I smoothed down my bangs. "Yeah? Thanks."

We spoke about Voltenstraus, about how the school was built into a cave under a massive waterfall, and how the place was magnificent. Saren said it was the best place in the entire Endless World, and I wanted to believe him. He was easy to talk to and had a soft, powdery voice. I let him speak well into the evening.

Every whisper, every creak of the tram on the rails beneath, every swerving turn woke me that night. The cushioned bench wasn't cushioned nearly enough.

Nathali found me early in the morning, freshly showered and wearing butter yellow.

"Two more days to go. Did you sleep?" she asked, pulling a brush through her wet hair.

"How long have you been up? You look perfect." I sat up in my blankets and pulled them around me.

"Just got up. But you didn't answer my question."

The taste of nerves pooled in my throat. "I didn't sleep at all. The motion."

"Oh. I actually slept okay! Have you made any friends yet?" She settled in next to me on the bench.

"Just one guy—"

"A guy? Is he attractive?"

"He's a teacher."

"Oh, well. Better not to seduce him, then," she said, smiling. "Breakfast is good today! You want me to walk down to the dining car with you?"

The food cart was filled with sliced fruits, flakey rolls, and cooked grains with syrup on top. Nathali sat at one of the tiny tables, surrounded by other social butterflies. She waved at me as I stood in the line.

Behind me, a fluffy, white kitten of a boy bounced impatiently. "Any day now, folks! I *will* starve." He heard my laugh and said, "Oh, you're the other Harker twin, aren't you. I can tell. My brother spent the day with you yesterday. He says you're funny."

"Ah, thanks. To him. For thinking I'm funny." I closed my eyes and shook my head to shut myself up.

His smile grew. "See, that was funny, in an awkward sort of way! I'm Aeshra. We're the same age, you and I. And my cousin, Riolyn. She's not up yet, I think." He peered easily over the students around us, "Nope, not yet. You can't miss her, she's gorgeous. Into chicks too, so you might have a chance." He winked at me. "You're a chick, right?"

"I guess," I said, because what else does a person say?

After breakfast, I snuck away from my twin's group to change my clothes. I pulled off my night shirt at lightspeed and replaced it with a clean one. For makeup, I drew big, yellow circles on my cheeks. It seemed like a good idea.

Saren's translucent, white face peeked in through the doorway and I waved him over from my spot on the bench.

"I see you've met my cousin!" he said, motioning to the girl laying on the bench behind me; the one with multicolored scales and tattoos over dark skin.

"I, uh — no," I said, raising an eyebrow.

"What? You slept next to each other!"

The girl rolled over and leaned up on one arm. Her wild, chestnut hair was shaved close in some parts. Her broad nose grounded her facial features. Prismatic scales on her cheeks and forehead glittered in the overhead light.

By contrast, I had two ill-drawn circles on my face.

The girl opened her mouth. "She just took off her shirt in front of everyone."

My mouth opened too. "Ok, well, I *thought* no one was looking."

The girl rolled her reptilian eyes.

Saren cleared his throat. "Mayli, this is Riolyn."

"I'm not in the mood," Riolyn said before turning her eyes on me. "Also, what's up with the circles? They look dumb. I'll pass."

"*Whoa*, alright psycho. I didn't exactly ask for your opinion!" My face heated to a boil.

Saren grabbed at my arm. "Ok, that's enough for now — Mayli, hallway please?" He tugged me to the windows beyond the room.

Blotches of purple stress stained his cheeks. He leaned forward onto the glass as the tram swerved underground.

"Please, go easy on her," he said.

"I mean, that was uncalled for! Who just tells a stranger they look—"

Aeshra pranced into the hallway. "Hey, guys!"

"Riolyn just told Mayli that her face looked dumb."

Aeshra halted. "Yeesh, tough stuff. Good luck with that." He turned back around to flee.

Saren caught him by the shirt. "Oh no you don't. You're going to help whether you like it or not."

"What am I supposed to do about it?" Aeshra whined.

As the brothers argued, I snuck a peek at their cousin. She laid on the bench, not moving, maybe not breathing. I said, "She's not wrong. I guarantee my makeup looks dumb. What's going on with her?"

Like mirror images the brothers closed their eyes and took a deep breath. Two white ghosts in an ill-lit hallway.

Saren answered, "I don't want to give away her business, but it was bad. We thought she was dead."

Aeshra's head bobbed in a nod. "We've got to kind of re-domesticate the girl."

I watched her again. Riolyn was separate from our peers; as they laughed, studied, smacked at each other playfully, she lay on the bench, arms crossing her face like a shroud. I swallowed the pang of understanding in my chest and grumbled, "Alright. No promises, though."

Aeshra jumped into the air, clapping like a seal. His big pastel sneakers smacked on the wooden floor when he came down. It made me smile.

"Ugh, you *poor thing,* your first class ever with Saren! It's cruel, really."

"Give me that." Saren pulled my school schedule from his younger brother's hands. He looked it over with parted lips. "Dwavasc Storytelling is a great class, I'm sure you'll love it. This history of the fables alone will amaze you. And we've a fascinating research assignment in the second quarter, it's my favorite to grade."

I sat back and grinned. "Careful, you might get me excited about school."

"Just wait. He's a dreadful teacher, always forgetting *everything*," Aeshra sniped. He bounced on the floor, endlessly moving. His limbs sprawled like a child that had been stretched to 6 and a half feet tall before their body was ready.

"Are there any classes about Develtic?" I asked.

Saren nodded. "A few. Eichi teaches Develtic anthrohistory, and I know Drucilla goes into detail about the Develtic rebellions in her classes."

"Don't you mean *Madam Adord*?" Aeshra asked with his lips pursed like a smushweed.

"Adord?" I cocked my head to the side. "Like, the judges?"

Aeshra answered, "Mhm, we've got one. And she thinks she's real important, too. Won't let you forget it."

"Is she on my schedule?" I peered over Saren's shoulder to look.

"She's on everyone's schedule," Aeshra said.

A grumbling voice came from behind me. "I'd rather die." Riolyn lifted from her spot on the bench, bending into the air like a scaly cat.

"If you stay quiet and focus on what she's teaching, you'll be fine. Oh, look; you two have her class together. *Post-Gate Rebellions* on Tuesdays."

I glanced sideways at Riolyn, and our eyes locked. Something uncomfortable tightened in my chest. There was a fight brewing. I just wasn't sure *who* I would be fighting.

Hours later, Saren had gone to make his rounds and check on the other students. It was getting close to lights out.

"Now that he's gone, we can get to the juicy stuff," Aeshra said, scooting closer. "Tell us about your dad, Mayli."

Riolyn shifted in her seat.

Aeshra turned to her. "You've met him. He's President of Voltenstraus, and now I have a ticket to his good side." He waggled his eyebrows.

"I don't really get what he does here. He keeps work and home separate. Doesn't talk about school much. He does admission, right? And mental health care."

Riolyn spoke up with a hard voice. "He came to Quar to interview me."

"Yeah, well, he admitted Seth Mace too, so he doesn't always make good decisions," Aeshra laughed.

"Who?" Riolyn and I said in unison.

With a whole-body gasp, he leaned forward to answer. "Seth Mace. Saren swears he's just a kid, nice once you get to know him. But I say no way — he's got a temper and he's scary if you ask me."

"Is he the other kid with green hair?" I pushed my green streaks behind my ears.

A student nearby interrupted our conversation. "You guys can keep talking about him if you want, but let me advise you"—her voice dropped to a whisper—"every time someone badmouths Seth it ends badly. You guys are endangering the entire student body."

I leaned into her space. "He's that bad, huh? That twig of a guy?"

She glared at me. "It won't be so funny when he's running the tram off the rails."

Aeshra leaned back on his elbows, eyes gleaming. "He's bad. Not as bad as your oldest sister though." When Riolyn's eyebrows knit together, he added, "Oh, come on. The psycho-killer on Dedocia? Mina Harker? Everyone knows about her."

The groan ripped from my chest was like a burnt-out car engine attempting startup. Our peers glanced to see if I'd died.

Riolyn cast cold eyes on me. "And you called me a psycho earlier? When it seems to run in your family?"

I glared back. "I've been advised not to talk about her."

"Probably a good idea," she said flatly. I rolled my eyes and escaped to the bathroom.

Sometime in the night, the tram surfaced on Nessa. I knew this because, just past 2:00 AM, I was pulled from sleep by rumbling vibration. It must have been the gate-jump. The pale pink Nessian moon hung low in the clouds, casting purple light into the tram windows. I smiled and smelled the air. It didn't smell like my world, yet.

A quick slam jolted the tram. The following swerve was nausea-inducing. I squeezed my eyes shut and tossed silent prayers from my lips on instinct. I didn't feel like I was home. I felt like I was stuck in a metal tube about to fly off its track.

A blast of noise shook the windows. A deep, guttural sound rumbled down the hall. I sat up, prodding my toes into Riolyn's leg. She awoke in confusion. When the tram squealed and swerved, someone in the room shrieked.

I turned to the girl behind me. Her face was drained of color. "What is going on?" I bent over to ask.

She put a silencing finger to her lips, then pointed out the door, shaking her head. "You shouldn't have talked about him."

Riolyn's feet were already on the floor when I slid from beneath my blankets. We exchanged a confirming look and headed into the hallway.

The tram quaked under our feet. Metal rattled in walls like the thing was being pulled apart. I wrapped my arms around my shoulders and shivered. My bare feet were purple in the moonlight. Another growl erupted, hollow and wooden.

"Is that an animal?" Riolyn asked. We stumbled down the hall together toward the operator's car.

"An MMP, maybe. Sounds like a living machine."

A pinch of light leaked from the farthest door. Muffled voices hissed inside, pressing against each other in short bursts. Riolyn's gleaming scales raised on her shoulders. I took a steadying breath before peaking in.

Inside, a group of teachers huddled around two students. Saren was in there, glowing in the dim light. Next to him stood a woman, a head taller than the rest, with her hand on the shoulder of someone younger and muscular.

At the center of the group was the boy I'd seen in Purvock Village; Seth Mace. He crouched with one hand flat on the ground, a sick-looking boy with no body fat. His long, mint bangs hung in wet strings around face. He let out a violent whine, and the tram seemed to ripple around him.

"Something is wrong, something is going on!" He slammed his fist on the floor.

Under, the rails creaked in terror.

"You have to stop this immediately. Someone is going to get hurt," a teacher said, standing over the kid having the tantrum on the floor.

Another teacher flailed. "Don't we have a tranquilizer?"

"That is *not* how we operate!" another gasped.

The other student pressed his hand to Seth's forehead. "He's cold as ice."

Seth pushed his brother away and a rude growl erupted from his belly, "Don't touch me, you're not — If you would just *listen* to me," his voice cracked and the tram tipped, rearing to its side. It slammed back onto the rails and I lost balance, hitting the doorframe. The door swung open to Riolyn and I eavesdropping. My eyelids stretched to their widest limit.

Saren stepped forward. "Mayli, Riolyn, go back to bed!" But something pulled him back and he gasped.

Seth, grey like a corpse, stood in front of me, breathing cold air on my face. Violent energy rolled off him and turned my stomach. I lurched forward, gagging on it, gasping.

Riolyn stepped up next to me. Her boiling heat clashed with Seth, pushing him back. I forced a breath from my clenching lungs and said, "What is going on in here?"

"Seth, just calm down. You're scaring people," the other boy said, reaching for Seth's shoulder. When his grey fingertips touched him, Seth kicked him in the stomach. He fell back with a thud.

"What the fuck, man?" I said, outraged.

Turning back to me, Seth spoke in a hard whisper, "Do what your teacher says. Go back to bed." A shadow of energy surrounded him like he was the devil himself.

Unimpressed, I punched him in the face.

5

MUD AND INJECTIONS

The smell of fruit wafted into my nostrils. I laid somewhere, swaying, smiling. What fruit did I buy from the Hook Market?

I rolled onto my side and breathed in the sweet scent. Astria fruit, or maybe pear, and a hint of something musty. I cradled myself, curled against the cool air nipping at my ankles. Thank Mess I'd left my shoes on — it was so cold in here. I felt for my blankets, nestling my face into the scratchy fabric beneath me. The room rocked sedately, side to side. Was the tide so far up the coast this morning?

My eyes shot open. A white glare blasted through windows across the room. *Not* my room.

I felt for my chest, grasping at the hole there. I stretched my hands out, tracking the dried blood crusting beneath my fingernails and around closed wounds.

Mina Harker had stabbed me. Mina Harker had *shot* me. Twice.

I froze, listening for signs of life. The room continued to rock back and forth. I had to be on that boat near where she'd shot me. I'd thrown a stone at her, right? And she shot me for it.

A snap blew from under the windows and I tucked into cover, hiding beneath a couch cushion.

An anxious voice was in the room, *"A body has been found in the Halstock district of Massia. The victim has not been identified and the batifban have yet to comment, but our reporter on the scene has gotten wind of wax on the victim's face. We expect this to be a Harker killing."*

I peeked out from my pillow and spied the TV as it snapped and went dark again. The boat was silent.

"She went to Massia?" I whispered, drawing myself up. I was wearing my clothes from the day before, stiff and bloodied. The smell of stale sweat rolled off me. I flexed my toes, pruney in my wet socks. I slipped onto the floor and crawled on all fours to the windows across the room. A plume of dust rose with every shuffle forward.

Beneath the windows sat a flatscreen atop a black, wired-up box with three lights; red, orange, green. The orange one was blinking.

A vine with crackling, dry leaves crept into the window frame. I peered out to find a wash of green. The lake slept calmly against the wide trunks of the ancient Kajiun forest. Something moved through the trees.

"Fuck," I spat, watching the killer weave her way out of the brush. Her eyes snapped up to mine; she couldn't see me, right? She *could.* We stared at each other, predator and prey.

I scanned the room, looking for a way out. There was an open door with a circular window to my right and I ran for it, tripping and thudding against the wooden wall. I reached for the window and pulled at the curved sash lock. It sprung free and popped open. With two hands on the sill, I pressed a foot to the wall and climbed. My head dipped into the open air and I let out a laughing breath.

I squeezed my shoulders through the circle, feet slipping against the wooden wall as I looked up.

Mina Harker stood at the edge of the water with her chin jutting out and her arms crossed. In one hand, she held a gun; in the other, a freshly bitten pear. The sun glowed behind her like a halo. She watched me probingly, audience to my present failure.

My feet slipped on the paneling and I tumbled back through the window, chin cracking against the frame on my way down. I scrambled across the floor in a daze. My eyes caught the glow of another window. I slid into the room, digging my fingernails into the grouted floor. I crawled onto the toilet and frantically dug against the window sash.

A door shut somewhere and the boat rocked.

"Fuck, oh fuck," I stuttered, jamming my fingers in a space between windowpane and frame. Red smeared across the glass.

The hairs stood on my spine and I looked over my shoulder.

"I'll shoot you again. I'll do it every day if I have to."

The killer loomed in the doorway. She held her gun out, aimed and ready. Behind her, the circle window streamed golden light through her crown of red hair.

I slumped onto the toilet and wept.

"You will not leave," Mina said from her perch on the dusty armchair. I sat on the couch, legs bouncing uncontrollably. "You will sleep on that couch. You will only get up to relieve yourself. In the bathroom, not in here like some feral animal. If you try to escape, I will know. If you try to trick me, hide a weapon or something, I will know. So go ahead and try it. You will not enjoy the outcome."

The screen behind Mina snapped on again. She squeezed her eyes shut and let out a low, groaning breath. I sunk deep into the couch and focused on the news.

The same reporter from before, with her shocking pink hair and flat, Dedocian nose, held herself against the wind. *We have a development in the Massia killing. We can now confirm that Mina Harker has indeed taken another life in Besel. The victim has been identified as Dr. Cassick Edmund, lead psychologist at Necros Universal Institute for Tyrants. Edmund worked closely with Mina Harker during her recent stay at NUIT. Dr. Edmund leaves behind his wife, Celian Banks of the Edmund-Banks Co., along with their two children, ages six and eight.*

"Furthermore, today would have been Kit Lambnoc's fortieth birthday. We at Suradelphia One wish his father, Governor Herse Lambnoc, luck and health in this trying time and hope to hear an update from him soon."

Mind scoffed. "That crusty boar is in hiding. He knows I'm coming for him next."

She stretched her legs out and put her arms behind her head. Her pink flesh was mottled with purple in the cold living room of the houseboat.

"What's your Limit, kid?"

My voice cracked, "My, um — my what?"

"Your Limit."

"I don't, it's — I don't have one."

"Bullshit, don't lie to me. You heal faster than anyone I've met. Are you a Palm Lifter?" She sat forward with her elbows on her bony knees.

I shook my head, eyes flitting around the room for something, *anything* to focus on. "No, it's not that. I'm not anything."

Her stare was relentless. The killer didn't move, poised to attack. The screen behind her began flipping through channels, stopping only for a clip of Harker news to finish before hurtling to a new one. We sat in silence while news of Mina's most recent murder nattered on in the background.

"What's your name, kid?"

We made eye contact, just long enough to send the ghost of a gunshot ripping through my chest.

"What?"

"Are you always this dumb? Use your fucking words. What is your name?"

On the couch, folded on the armrest, was a pile of towels. I ran my fingers over the top one; it was blue, faded, threadbare. A little stiff, like it had dried on a line and been left in a drawer for a year. "Devin Mace."

I let myself side-glance at her. Mina hunched forward, sniffing the stale air like a dog. I lifted the towel to my nose and breathed it in; it smelled just as I thought it would; nine months of dust. If Mina had the mind that I thought she did, she would recall my name. Devin Mace, The Devil of Suradelphia. I'd cleaned up so nicely since then; I wasn't that power-hungry drug addict anymore. But she didn't have to know that.

Mina was more of a devil than I'd ever be.

She twisted away, body slipping through the room like an eel. She knelt on the floor in front of the screen and splayed her hands on the metal surface of the black, wired-up box; a keyboard surfaced. She began typing.

"Where are you from, Devin Mace?"

"Pwero Ver."

"The city of Dedocian Innocence," she said. "Now we'll get to see if there's any news reports about you. Maybe they'll interview your family. I'm sure they'll be *heartbroken* to know you've disappeared."

After, when she strolled from the room and shut herself away in a back room, I imagined picking up the massive potted fern next to the screen and dropping it on her head. Maybe, if I threw it hard enough, Mina's brain would seep from her skull like silken pudding.

I snuck to the bathroom halfway through the day, and that's when I first heard it. The double-click and following hiss of a lighter. The rapid boil of fluid in a thin-stemmed glass. The gulp and quiet gasp of a first drink. The sounds of my youth.

Mina Harker was drinking the fire.

The Batifban called it Viadin; a watery chemical concoction that turned to gas when boiled. A user held a flame to the stem of a fluted jar and gulped the noxious gas before it cooled. The high that followed was a slow, burning sort of melancholy. They say the sizzle in your throat scorched away thoughts of self-doubt and self-loathing.

I had always preferred icetar, myself.

I stood at the sink in the bathroom and listened to Mina enjoy herself. She would be swallowing now, over and over, trying to coat her burning throat with saliva. The comfort would never come, and so — yep, there it was. She was lighting up again.

The cracked mirror above the sink split my face in half. My polka-dot shirt was stained with blood, my skin was grey, my hair was black. I was still me. Still a recovered addict with a job I hated and a family I never saw. If I got out of this alive, I'd change two of the three.

It was night, but the screen lit up the room in jumping colors. I had muted the thing, sick of hearing the same reports told with varying levels of excitement and disgust.

Mina yelled at someone on her pocketscreen, pacing the length of the boat in long strides, "And tell me why most of my plants are dead? You had a very short list of tasks—" she popped the lid off a greenish bottle of pear glace and sniffed, "Even my fridge is empty. I gave you a week to get this place ready. What exactly have you been doing?"

The mumbling on the other end of the line did nothing to quell her frustration.

"Oh yes, I'm sure it's been terrible without me. With all of your training, you'd think my number one could handle it. But leave it to me to put people on a pedestal they do not deserve!"

She stomped into the living room like a tantruming child with the phone still to her ear, and spoke to me, "I'm leaving. If you do fucking *anything*, I will know about it. Do not try me."

Within seconds, a door slammed shut.

I sat listening. The boat rocked as Mina jumped from it, still yelling on her pocketscreen. I stood and watched from the window as she disappeared into the woods, hidden by moonless shadows.

"*Food,*" I groaned. The kitchen joined the living room by a thin space between, crowded with a round table, three chairs, and a host of dying potted plants. Their crispy leaves looked black in the dark room.

The refrigerator hummed with the glorious promise of food.

Inside was only disappointment, and an ungodly amount of fruit. Mina had two crisper drawers filled to the brim with pears and two jugs of pear glace. That was it. Pears.

I bit into a browning pear and watched varmints chase each other on the dark bank outside. The subtle rocking of the boat lulled my sick stomach.

On the wall behind me was an old box phone. I picked it up. There were no numbers to dial, only three buttons: red, orange, and green. Just like the box beneath the living room screen.

I decided not to push my luck. Not tonight. Nor the next morning.

I huddled over the sink in the bathroom, shirtless and cold. I scrubbed my white polka-dot shirt with my fingernails, willing the stiff bloodstains to lift. In the corner of the bathroom was a wall-mounted hose with a drain on the floor beneath. A parched wooden shelf clung to the wall, barely holding up the weight of a jug of bleach and four different soaps.

Eventually, I gave in and bleached the shirt.

It was midday and Mina hadn't yet returned. Who had she been talking with on the phone? Her '*number one*,' she'd said. So, the killer was working with someone. More than one someones, if she had a number two, number three... How many people? Did they pull names from a chip bag to help her decide which random stranger she'd murder next?

Was *I* going to be next?

I rinsed the shirt again, letting the water chill my hands to a dull throbbing. The water was clear, fresh, like it gushed straight from a highland spring. I rang the shirt out and hung it next to a towel. My hands absently traced the gunshot scar on my chest, following ripples of flesh. My mirror reflection's eyes glazed over, lulling between sleep and waking. If I didn't get out, I would be next.

I dried my hands on the musty towel and tore through the houseboat.

I skidded through the kitchen and out the door; it wasn't even locked. The boat deck was slick with a layer of soggy, fallen leaves. I jumped off the boat, my knees landing on the rocky shore. The sun shone through heavy clouds above. I took off running, adrenaline buzzing under my skin.

Silence clogged my ears. Green forest floor, green tree trunks, green leaves. I felt my way along, hands gripping at patches of moss. My body slowed, weaving through the trees.

"Keep going," I hissed to myself. "Get to the street."

My feet picked themselves up, *shlick, shlick,* on the wet ground. I ran.

I stumbled into the clearing by the road, the one with the dumpster. Mina's mailbox waited menacingly, perched on the side of the road. A car zoomed past, kicking up dust. I jumped into the street, hollering, waving my arms. The car kept on, too far to care now.

My knees buckled and I bent over, gasping. My lungs shuddered, breathless. In the distance, traffic came and went on the intersection.

A lulling hum whispered above me in the trees like a mechanical bird. There, roosting in the limbs of a young hyssia, sat a green and grey mechanism, eyeing me with its single lens.

"Mess," I hissed, staring at the camera. How many did she have in the forest?

A yellow car roared up the road.

I took off across the street and into the field beyond. Skeletons of dried summer tallgrass scratched against my bare chest. I heaved myself forward, jumping, scrambling.

The car squealed behind me. I dropped into the grass. My heart thrashed in my ribcage.

"Devin, oh *Devin*," Mina's voice sang. She sounded out of breath. "What are you doing, Devin?" Dry grass swished and crunched. Her purring voice moved closer. "I told you not to fuck with me."

Terrible little bugs stepped over my hands in confused lines. I shuffled forward on my belly, cringing at the cold dirt on my stomach.

"Did you think I wouldn't come get you? Did you think you could get away?" She was right behind me now.

I sucked in a breath and blew it out through my mouth.

When I stood up, the killer was only a few feet from me. I glared at her, ignoring the gun pointed at my bare chest.

"Get back to the boat."

"No."

Mina pulled the trigger.

Naked on the couch, wrapped in a warm, pink quilt, I sipped on hot tea and slipped into the soft folds of insanity. My toes curled in the cold. My head ached like it was filled with rocks. Blood wasn't circulating, and I was, without a doubt, going to lose all of my extremities. *All* of them. At the center of my chest, just off-center from the last one, was a fresh new gunshot wound.

My hypochondria paused when the screen turned on and a devastatingly bad photo of myself lit up.

Ericson Blath, the man who'd interviewed Mina for *Twitmass*, was on *Dedocia Nightly*.

"Have you seen this man? Devin Mace has been missing since last Tuesday. Mace is an ex-convict with a violent criminal history and could be dangerous. If you see Devin Mace, please call Emergency or the missing persons' hotline. Do not make contact with Mace, as he is likely armed and unwell."

Great. I was the victim of an abduction and they were painting me as a vicious criminal on the loose. Not sure what I had expected, but it wasn't this. And all the while, the killer was out doing Baheeba knows what. For all I knew, she could be roasting children and eating their flesh.

The fabric of the old couch scratched at my bare ass as I shifted in my blanket.

Mina came into the living room the next morning with a dangerous look on her face. Her neck was red and scratched, and she smelled like burnt chemicals.

My life was out of my hands, so I said, "You're back early."

She sat on the tattered chair across from the couch and glared at the wall. She was upset about something and I couldn't care less. I stood, walking to the bathroom.

"I wasn't done talking to you," Mina hissed. "You think you can do whatever you want, don't you?"

I turned my narrow eyes on her. "I can't *leave*."

When I got back from the bathroom, Mina was gone.

I turned on the screen and watched whatever I wanted. I went to the fridge and ate an entire half-loaf of bread and two pears. I even went outside and sat on the boat deck, watching varmints fight over seed pods. I did whatever I wanted to do. Everything but leave.

As the days continued, my courage built. Who did Mina have contact with? I searched the house for clues. The kitchen cupboards were bare but for a few pans, a bag of garden soil, and broken pottery. Mina had three yellow plates with white trim, matching drinking glasses, two forks, and *one knife*. What serial murderer kept only one kitchen knife? And a dull one at that.

There were no body parts in the freezer — only a grand selection of rock hard, frozen pears and a few opaque jars labeled with colors: red ochre, cerulean, limonite oxide.

A big hole cracked one dining room wall, and a reddish-brown swipe skittered across another. The table was made from old, dry wood and none of the chairs matched. Two rugs laid beneath, one patterned and blue, the other orange with brown tassels around the edges.

Mina had spent time coaxing life back into her dying plants. Big ferns and wide-leafed tropicals lined the windows, sprouting new greenery. Ivy clung to the ceiling, trailing into the living room. A small, cracked pot centered the dining table, a single white bloom popping from its center.

Beneath the living room windows, Mina had a book for everything; electrical engineering, ancient Dwavasc puzzles, Misanthrope Theory. I thumbed through a delicate, velvet-sleeved hardback about painter Narien Evroldengaud. The woman used pigmented wax to create sweeping, foggy landscapes and portraits. Two of Narien's paintings were on display in Parsells, Coesha; a landscape of the Cospyre hills and an after-death portrait of an elderly man.

A square leaf of cardstock marked a middle page, on which was written, *For MUBS, my eldest treasure. May this find you in times of boundless abundance.* Beside the note was a penned sketch of a woman kissing a round-cheeked toddler.

I slammed the book shut and never opened it again.

On my eighth day of captivity, I wandered into Mina's bedroom. She had not been home in two days.

Mina's bedroom was vastly normal. It curved against the boat's stern with a bed, a side table with a locked drawer, and a pipe with clothes hanging neatly from it. No art, no plants, nothing to boast personality.

The bed was hard as I sat on it.

But as I sat on Mina Harker's bed, my mind wandered into the dark. How many nights had Mina come back to the boat and sunk into this very bed, exhausted after a long night of murder, the DNA of her freshest victim sloughing onto the covers? How many microscopic pieces of dead flesh were in this bed? How many bodies drifted through the air like common dust?

I let a single tear well in my eyes before retreating back to my couch.

On day nine, Mina killed Celien Edmund-Banks, Cassick Edmund's wife.

Mina poisoned her in her corner-office at Edmund Banks Co., the MMP development firm, right in downtown Massia. Not even the robots Celien helped design had detected Mina. She and Cassick had two children. The children had lost their father just a week earlier. Now their mother was gone.

The screen was on well into the night. Multiple stations played at the same time, splitting the frame.

The newscasts played the same: *Celien was a mother. A beautiful being with heart. Celien was a wife. Celien was a great businessman. A great boss. A Mother — Wife — Daughter — CEO — Kind — Genuine — Personable—*

Innocent.

My tears had dried into parched lines on my face. I found myself hiding behind the couch, pressed tightly between the wall and the coarse pink and blue fabric. I barely remembered crawling back there, wet with tears and cold sweat. Days of bread and pears must have curled my mind at the edges, because — Mina wouldn't find me here — no, she'd forget about me. I'd starve to death, maybe. Or, if things panned out, I could escape. Just soak into the floor and become one with the lake beneath.

Something on the TV changed. The cacophony of voices narrowed into one, and they weren't talking about Mina Harker at all.

I peeked over the couch and was faced with a lovely, glowing image of Alexander Bergoin, billionaire philanthropist extraordinaire. Bergoin was the second-generation CEO of *Boister Energies*, and champion of the *Godsend Award* for six years running. With his honey-green complexion and pristine, white fangs jutting from his gentle smile, Alexander Bergoin was the kind of person my mother would have *loved* me to bring home.

I could think of absolutely nothing Mina Harker would want with him. Nothing good, at least.

The door in the kitchen clicked open, and I dug myself back behind the couch.

"Have you eaten yet?" her voice was much too cheery. "Where *are* you?"

I shuffled behind the couch. "Why did you have to kill that woman?"

Mina stepped up to the couch and peered down at me. "What are you doing?"

"She had two children!"

Mina grabbed a fistful of my hair and dragged me out. I shrieked, throwing my hands up in surrender. She shoved me onto the couch cushions.

"The kids are far better off without those two psychos for parents," Mina said, dropping into the worn chair.

I wiped the wetness from my cheeks, snarling, "What happened to make you so fucking awful?"

Mina heaved from the chair and charged. Red hair, green suit, thin bones flashing toward me. Mina's hand went up into the air and, before it came down, I smacked her away. Hard.

A frozen moment. Labored breathing. The room swam, but I refused to cower.

Mina leaned in. Her hand gripped at my jaw, fingernails digging into my skin. Her eyes narrowed into dark slits; her cheeks flushed peach.

"And you're going to kill Alexander Bergoin next," I said, chin jutting out in defiance.

Mina's eyebrows knit together. "What?"

"The TV — it's recording stuff about Bergoin now. He's next, isn't he?"

She shook her head, "What? No. Leave Alex out of this." She swung herself back into the chair.

I puffed up like a showdog. "So, you're on a first name basis with him now? You are so smug. I know you're going to kill him next, and there's nothing I can do about it. *Nothing.* So, will you please just kill *me*? Just get it over with. I'm ready to be done."

From the battered armchair, she eyed me. I couldn't care less. The numb throb in my belly had taken over the rest of me. When she pulled the gun from inside the chair cushion and pointed it at me, I let out a callous laugh.

"Fuck you, asshole. Let's do it now," she said.

My eyes didn't leave hers. "Aim for my head, this time."

A beat passed. She stood up and fit the gun in the waist of her pants. "No. I have much bigger plans for you."

I walked into the kitchen. The killer was on the phone with a gravelly voiced someone. My captor was dressed professionally in stark white, and her hair was pulled back, sleek and low. Her neck was scratched and red. My mind lit with the desire for icetar.

She hung up the phone. "I'm going out. Big day today."

I opened the fridge door and hid behind it to block her out.

"I shouldn't be too late. You like Turrisian food? I'll bring something back for dinner." Her tone was too light, too easy.

Body shoved into the chill of the fridge, I mumbled a quick goodbye. The cold rested lightly on my forehead. She was going to kill someone else today, wasn't she? Busy murdering Alexander Bergoin, then. How far was the run to the end of the field? If I ran to the intersection, someone would recognize me, with my picture plastered all over the news stations. I didn't want to go back to prison, but if I could lead the Batif to Mina's boat...

Mina was silent for a moment. Then, the keys clanked in her hand and she sighed, "Alright, bye."

I didn't allow myself to ponder the disappointment in her voice.

It was evening time. I wasn't waiting for Mina to come home; I wasn't. But I was hungry, and she had mentioned Turrisian food. So, when the kitchen door banged open, I closed my eyes in relief.

Thudding sounds, a shallow grunt, and then—

"Shit." A gasp, a clank, and then the sound of water pouring, trickling onto the floor. "Shit, shit."

Mina's pocketscreen rang in clipping chirps.

I strained to hear before smacking my hands over my ears to block out the retching sounds coming from the other room.

The pocketscreen stopped ringing.

"I — yeah, it's bad. Shut the fuck up, let me think — No, don't you dare," Mina snapped and retched again.

I ran my hands over my face.

"Med-kit? Fuck you. I'd rather die. He can die too, for all I care."

My eyebrows raised another inch, because — was she talking about me? Slipping, wet sounds came from the kitchen. Vomit? Piss? Blood? I stood up and flexed my shoulders.

When I rounded the corner, the metal scent hit me. My stomach turned, heaving.

"No — get out," Mina said, but I could hardly hear her. I pressed my sweaty palms into my eye sockets and willed the vision gone.

Mina was hunched against the kitchen counter, absolutely covered in blood. Her once-white pants dripped with it. She was pouring water from a glace jar over her left leg. Blood and water swirled together on the floor beneath her.

"What happened?" I squeaked, hugging myself with tight arms.

"Got ... sshhot," she hissed, eyes rolling back in her skull. Mina buckled and slipped. The pocketscreen fell as she gripped at the counter edge. She dropped weakly to the floor, gasping for breath.

The pocketscreen blinked at my feet with someone yelling on the other line. I picked it up. "Uh, hello?"

A voice of a woman gasped. "Hello? Is this Devin?"

"... Yeah." I watched in a daze as Mina tried to pull herself back up, slipping in her own blood on the laminate floor.

"Devin, my name is Matey. I'm a doctor. Can you help, please? I can walk you through it." She had the voice of a little angel.

"Help?"

I'd never seen a seriously injured person before. Not in real life. I curled in on myself, retching again.

Mina clunked her head back on the cabinet and closed her eyes. Her skin was stark white.

"Devin? It's very important that we do this quickly. Mina has a med-kit in her kitchen; can you see it? Grey metal box — I think it's near the box phone. Can you see it?"

My head turned around the room without my permission. Did I see it?

"Yeah, I see it."

"Open it. Please hurry."

I grabbed the box; it was cold. I popped the tabs and the lid sprung open.

On the floor, Mina cried out in pain.

"It's open," I told the girl on the phone.

"Great! Attached to the lid should be three syringes. Do you see them? Good — they're called Cryonac injections. Pull them from the lid and set them on the counter."

The syringes were white and preloaded with blue liquid. I tipped one to the side and watched a single bubble bob around inside the chamber.

Mina wrapped her hand around my bare ankle. Her voice had turned to gravel, "I'll kill you if you—"

I shoved her off with my foot. "Hey lady, why am I doing this?"

"Because you're a good person," the doctor answered. "Aren't you?"

"Am I?" I wondered aloud.

Mina rolled over and hugged one knee to her chest, moaning. Her neck was still red from drinking the fire this morning. She looked like any common addict, strung out and bleeding from a trip-fight.

"Please, take the syringe labeled 'one' and — listen carefully, if the doses are administered incorrectly Mina's leg will paralyze. Take syringe one and—"

"What happens if I don't give her the meds?"

"She'll die."

"From getting shot in the leg?"

"It's a Sinnia State bullet."

I nodded, even if I had no clue what that meant.

"Where does number one go?"

The doctor let out a single happy sigh before answering, "Inject syringe one into the spot two inches above the bullet entry wound. Syringe two goes into her neck, either side. Syringe three goes two inches below the entry wound. Please hurry."

"Why are you helping her?" I asked, kicking Mina's hand away from me again.

"Because she is very important to me. Now please, hurry."

"You know she's shot me three times, right? In a week," I said as I pushed syringe one around on the countertop with my finger.

"Devin. Do it now. Injection one above the wound. Injection two in her neck. Injection three below the wound."

I set the pocketscreen down and watched Mina writhe below me. I popped the caps off the three syringes. I sunk to the floor at Mina's feet; the fabric around my knees soaked up her blood in thin, inky smears.

"I hate you," I said, quietly at first. Then louder: "I hate you."

She tried to slither away from me. Her voice grated, "Don't you fucking touch me."

I grabbed her ankle and pulled her back in place. "I hate you." She kicked at me, so I crawled over her and let my bodyweight keep her still. She was burning hot beneath my thighs.

"I'll kill you — shit," she gasped, struggling.

My hand pressed down over her mouth and held her face. Her eyes were wide. Tears pooled at the edges.

My other hand grabbed the three syringes and set them on the floor next to us. Mina moved away, so I squeezed her face harder. "Stop moving," I spat.

I plunged the first syringe into her upper thigh as hard as I could, growling out, "I hate you too." Mina bucked her hips against my backside, trying to push me off.

Syringe two. "I hate you." I stabbed into her neck. Her eyes fluttered and rolled.

I struck syringe three above her knee.

"I hate you," I said once more. Her mouth went slack behind my hand.

Just before she went into convulsions, a strange emotion flashed over her glassy eyes. Was it anger? Shock?

It was terror.

6

THE CAVE

Non-Eater:

A being who has transcended Worldliness and now resides with Loyal Death in the space between. Non-Eaters commune with both Worldly beings and the Undergods.

My knuckles collided with Seth's cheekbone. His skin was wet and icy, like someone trapped in snow. His head snapped back in slow motion, twisting, cracking. Color bloomed on his cheeks, flushing purple.

"*Fuck,*" Riolyn croaked behind me.

Seth and I locked eyes.

Riolyn gripped the back of my shirt and pulled as the door slammed in our faces.

I fell back on top of her, splayed on the floor together like clumsy criminals.

"Oh, *fuck.* You hit him," she said.

I turned to see a grizzly smile ripping across her face. I crawled onto my hands and knees and pressed my forehead to the old carpet, squeezing my eyes shut.

She cackled. "You are *insane!*"

I was going to be in so much trouble.

The red sun broke through the fog, glazing the rocky hillsides just as the tram slowed to a stop. It was early morning. Riolyn and I sat on our benches, glumly watching the other students pack up their things to disembark. Nathali stood at the door, waiting for me to hurry up. I didn't.

"You're going to have to leave sometime," she yelled across the room.

I pulled in a breath and held it for a count. Beside me, Riolyn slung her luggage over her shoulder. She grumbled all the way to the door and parked next to my sister.

I had no choice but to go.

"Mieda tells me you committed assault," Nathali said, smiling impishly.

"Assault? Really? And how does she even know?"

Riolyn trailed behind us as we stepped out of the tram and into the wet underground air. The three of us made it up the stairwell and into the haze. It smelled of fresh rain and evergreen, thin shrubs dotted along the sloping hills, peeking out from between slices of rock. Past the road was a lake, silvery and placid, butting up against a wall of cliffs. The red sun reflected peachy lines across the water.

"You're going to tell me what happened," Nathali said.

"Where is this school?" I said, ignoring her. "Aren't we here for *school*?"

"It's under the waterfall," Riolyn said, pointing to the thundering monstrosity, dumping water over the cliff face and into the grey lake.

"Answer me, May."

My hands flew up in dramatics. "The guy came outta nowhere! I had no choice but to defend myself!"

"Eh, not accurate," Riolyn hummed. "But he did kick a guy in the stomach."

"On the tram?"

"Yeah — the spooky kid. Kicking people, growling like an animal, etcetera. Didn't you notice the tram literally tipping over? He did that. I don't know how. Real case, that one."

We headed up the path, following those in front of us. Aeshra caught up to talk to Riolyn, so I listened to the chatter from nameless students around us.

"She punched him square in the jaw. I can't even imagine the look on his face."

"She and that Reptile were eavesdropping. What kind of person would do that?"

"She's new. She doesn't know what she's doing."

"She put the rest of us in danger."

"I heard Seth barely even taunted her."

"Well, you know who her sister is, don't you?"

It was going to be a rough year.

The falls loomed, slamming into the surface of the lake beneath. I stuck to the rock wall to keep dry. We trudged single file behind the waterfall into the shadows beyond. The massive cave was carved deeply with swooping, organic shapes, and soft rounds of glowing paphador swelled out like the eyes of giant amphibians. Moss clung to the ceiling, green and dripping. I swerved between droplets for dear life.

At the back wall was a door, hollowed out from the stone and made of tarnished metal. The ancient door groaned as it heaved open.

"This place is very wet," I said, eyeing a thin line of water seeping from the cave wall.

Nathali rolled her eyes. "You'll be okay."

"What's the opposite of validation?

"*In*validation?"

"Yeah, that. That's what I'm getting from you," I said as we moved through the doorway into a smooth stone cavern, student's footsteps echoing through the space.

Two grand staircases curved up the sides of the circular room, with a large balcony above. Carved patterns curved around us; gorgeous shapes with images of nature, so large you had to stand far back to get any idea of what they were. Colored pigment hid deep in the cracks of the ceiling. Turquoise crystals of paphador hung in ornate, twisted metal, casting a blue glow over our heads.

I turned to my sister as she gaped at the sight. "Wet ... and cold. Like a tomb."

Riolyn hummed in agreement.

A chill snuck up my shoulders and my eyes were drawn to the entrance. That beast of a boy entered; the one I'd "assaulted." The surrounding students scattered like roaches. He sunk into a dark corner and disappeared from sight.

In the bright absence of Seth Mace, noise came from above; three floors of balconies flooded with the faces of students. Faces of teenagers from every layer, every species, crowding together. At the center stepped a booming woman of Kajiun heritage, with soft, coppery fur dusting her face.

"Welcome home from your holidays, all," she purred like a great cat. "I'm sure, for many of you, it was a much-needed time off. "For those of you new to Voltenstraus, I am Varali Garima, Vice Advisory."

She pulled forward two older students. "New students will follow our volunteers to the top floor Dossier to get acclimated. Tomorrow is orientation day, and I need not remind you of the importance of attending. Last year was a good year, and you did exceptional work. Let's hope that this year is one of the same."

My peers hollered and cheered, but my eyes were locked with the Vice Advisory. She stared down at me, brows pushed together in concentration. The blood began to thump against my breastbone and I stretched my fingers at my sides to find relief.

At my side, Riolyn followed my gaze and whispered a harsh, "*Fuck.*"

"Yeah. Fuck."

We moved up the stairs with the group. I ran my clammy palms along the cold, rounded stone and focused on my breathing.

Varali Garima was at the top, waiting for us.

"Miss Harker, Miss Vite; with me, please. Dr. Harker has asked to see you." She stepped aside from the horde with us.

I couldn't shut up. "Been here for fifteen minutes and we're already in trouble."

"The trouble started long before you got to Voltenstraus. Seems there was an incident on the tram, yes?" Her gaze flickered between the two of us. "I'm not surprised you've already found each other." Varali led us through the smooth stone hallways, curving behind numbered classrooms.

"Why?" Riolyn asked.

Varali's lips curved in a knowing smile. "The troublemakers always do."

We rounded a tight curve and started up a yellow-lit stairwell. My worn sneakers flapped against the stone steps. After a whopping five flights of stairs, we stepped onto a bright landing. I doubled over, gulping air to fill my lungs. My belly hung as a reminder; I wasn't cut out for this.

"How do people in wheelers get around this place?" I growled, massaging the stitch in my side.

Varali looked me over. "Elevators, dear. *Only* for those who need them, of course."

I stumbled after Riolyn and the Vice Advisory into a bright space and slumped onto a half-wall. It enclosed a wide circle cut through the floor. Each floor beneath mimicked with its own cutout, and at the bottom, the stone of the main entry glowed greenish blue. I swayed with vertigo against the depth of the bioluminescent cave.

A great archway swooped through the stone behind us, where students stood at desks, glancing around in blundering newness. I scoffed and pushed my shoulders back.

"This is the Dossier. Once you're done with Dr. Harker, proceed to finish any outstanding paperwork. I hope he won't take too long, as it's already late in the day." Her spotted ears flickered in annoyance. "And *please*, do take care not to fight. Let's maintain peace, shall we?"

We followed her around the hole in the floor to a tarnished metal door. The plaque read *Dr. George A. W. Harker.*

The Vice Advisory smiled weakly and knocked once. The door flew open.

My father's pale fingers snatched the collar of my shirt, "Maysolpheta Ann Isis—"

Varali's hand slapped my father's, and he dropped me like he'd been burned.

"Doctor, behave yourself." Her nose twitched in disapproval. "Mayli is a *student* now, as is Miss Vite here. She and Mayli had a confrontation with Mr. Mace on the tram last night, as I'm sure you've heard. It could have been much worse."

The Doctor pressed a pale hand to his chest and smoothed down his wrinkle-free dress shirt.

"And remember, they need to be by the Dossier before nine." Varali bowed her head, turned and left us.

The Doctor ushered us past the door. "Do come in. Sit, please," he said.

George's office was regal, much like the one hidden at the back of our home library. Red walls, dark flooring, rich wooden furniture and a tufted green rug, with a heavy desk at the center. There were two red sitting chairs facing his desk, and another against the wall, between shelves of books. A stately, encaustic self portrait of my mother hung in magnificence over the fireplace.

We sat at his desk, waiting for him to begin berating us.

"I must say, Riolyn; I'm surprised to see you at my daughter's side. She normally commits these sorts of disorderly acts on her own." He peered over his tortoiseshell glasses at the two of us. "Care to explain?"

Her face remained blank as she answered: "The tram was shaking, like it was breaking down. We followed the noises and the door was open, so we watched. Seth was angry over something, and violent. He threatened Mayli, so she punched him. I would have punched him myself."

"Yeah, he was literally going to crash the thing. How was he doing that? And — he felt just ... *sick*. I don't know. It was bad."

Riolyn's eyes darted to me and I shut my mouth.

The Doctor crossed his arms over his chest. His face had settled to a bored pinch.

He sighed, stood and took to the right side of the room. He pointed up at the grand portrait of my mother. "Do you see this woman? Her name is Narien Evroldengaud, and she is my wife. She is my pride and joy. This woman is my life. I strive every day to exhibit her most positive qualities, and if you knew her like I did, you would too.

"The problem is, Mayli, you *do* know this woman; she is your mother. And yet you are acting quite the opposite of her. You are throwing a lead blanket over the reputation she has created. If I had a right mind, I would send you back home immediately. These actions are unacceptable — attacking a stranger!"

My eyes rolled as far back as they could. "Total garbage."

His nostrils flared. "Excuse me?"

"Mom's no Non-Eater and you know it. She's punched plenty of people, including you. At least *I* don't have to get drunk to punch a dirtbag."

George gripped the edge of the fireplace with tense fingers. "Damnit, Mayli. I specifically remember in Purvock Village telling you to *leave him alone.*"

"I know. I'm sorry," I sighed.

Riolyn cleared her throat. "Seth did calm down after Mayli punched him."

"Tram went back to normal and all that. What were we supposed to do?"

The doctor flopped back in his desk chair. "From now on, you will do as I ask. You will leave Seth Mace alone. Both of you. No more vigilante activity."

Riolyn and I nodded.

"Now, get to the Dossier before dinner time or Varali will behead me."

We stood and shuffled to the door.

"I have a question," Riolyn said.

"Yes?"

"I want to be dorm mates with Mayli."

A vein surfaced in the doctor's forehead. "That's not a question."

I stepped back against the door as Riolyn's scales fired up to a bright blue. George pushed his shoulders up, puffing up like a great bird.

"Can I be dorm mates with Mayli?" She asked.

"You are rooming with your cousin, Aeshra."

"I don't want to spend that much time with him."

The doctor's forehead vein throbbed. "Fine. But we have a protocol for these things. Plans have been made, paperwork has been filed."

My voice broke through the tense fog, "What's the big deal, man?"

"The *big deal* ... is that Benjamin will have a fit. And, what of Aeshra? He'd be alone."

"Who's Benjamin?" I asked.

"Aeshra was alone last year," Riolyn said.

The doctor darted glances between the both of us, his cheeks mottled with peach, "I will allow it. But any issue, any whiff of trouble and there will be consequences. Do not disappoint me."

When I dared a glance at Riolyn, her lips were pulled back over her teeth in a wide grin. Her smile was worth suffering the discomfort crackling in the room.

We signed dormmate release forms while hunched over the Dossier counter. The guy behind the desk handed us paper maps. I folded the corners, running my fingernail along the new edges.

"There are five dormitory halls; Ivorton East and Ivorton West flank the medical ward on floor five. Illiad North and Illiad South are on the third floor, behind classrooms and the gymnasium. Eldrid is on the basement level."

He circled our dorm on the map. "You're in Eldrid #14. The stairwell to the basement is located here, under the western entry stairs." He drew red arrows to point our way.

"Do you think the basement floods?" I scrubbed at my neck.

"Not really, no," he answered in an afterthought.

"Right. Cool," I said, forcing a smile.

Running my hands along the sloping stone, we searched for the Eldrid dorms. Each level of the cave was much like the others; rock walls carved with organic patterns, tiny fountains trickling from the rock every so often, spurting out of the abstract mouths of stone creatures, or dripping down the veins of sculpted leaves. The school ran on paphador, and used the gemstone in as many forms as it could. It hung from the ceiling like glowing raindrops; peeked out from cracks in the walls; inlaid in long strips along the floor. The cave glowed green and blue in every corner.

Riolyn readjusted her overshirt and said, "So, your sister."

My stomach dropped. I said, "One of the many topics I don't know how to talk about."

"She killed someone?"

A laugh escaped my throat, "You could say that. She's what they call a *serial killer*."

"Whoa. That's ... fuck. When was the last time you saw her?"

"I think I saw her once when I was little. Could have been a dream, though. She was climbing out of my brother's window."

Riolyn stopped at the top of our last staircase. "Wait, you've never met her?"

"She left the house before we were born. She's fifteen years older than us. The only one that really knew her was Tom, my brother. He doesn't talk about it much. She went to Voltenstraus. Not for long, though. Got kicked out."

"Killed someone?" Riolyn scoffed.

"That does seem to be her weak spot," I said, looking away. I didn't want it to be true.

Our luggage was set in the main entry, some of the last to remain. Riolyn's single bag was crisp and new, and clashed with her in every way. A pair of exhausted combat boots hung by the laces from the shoulder strap.

Drops of water plinked and trickled from the seeping cave walls. I shuddered at the sound.

"Why's it gotta be so wet?" I growled, pulling one of my bags around my neck.

"Why's it matter?" Riolyn's eyes raked over the tall, metal doors of the entry.

My lips curled in distracted disgust, "It doesn't matter—"

A single, heavy drop of water fell from above. My eyes zeroed in on it as it splashed onto my forearm. It welled and burst, peeling into wormy streams, sliding around my arm hair. I gasped and jumped, grabbing a handful of shirt to wipe it away.

"Doesn't matter, huh?"

I narrowed my eyes at Riolyn. Her eyebrows rose to hide behind chopped bangs.

"Let's pretend it doesn't matter."

It was the first in a long line of *understandings* between Riolyn and I.

At the edge of the entry hall, a stairwell descended into the unknown. A fount spewed up clear water on the top stair, and it trickled into the basement via a paphador channel edging the wall. Riolyn marched down the steps without a second thought. I dragged my luggage, eyeing the stream.

Wide, wooden doors flanked an open space, with a stone arch between; the plaque above the arch read *Eldrid*. The humid, cool air of the lowest level hummed against my bare arms. I hugged myself.

"In there?" I nodded toward the arch.

Riolyn nodded and stepped into the dark tunnel.

The passage beyond was more like a cave than what I'd seen of my new home so far. Rough walls were broken apart by thin, yellowed veins of paphador. Pale, moist fuzz grew in deep cracks. I stopped to look at the fungus. It smelled like damn paper.

Riolyn disappeared into the adjoining room.

Through the second arch was a space lit by a lonely lamp; the Eldrid lounge, according to my crumpled map.

No one was in sight.

A few couches spotted the room, and floor pillows were scattered in front of a gaming unit. Books were strewn about on coffee tables. Deskscreens glowed at the back of the room. Portraits of past students hung on the walls; the Bergoin triplets, my brother Tom, many others I didn't know. The frames covered swooping carvings.

"Covering ancient Nepatin art with *photographs*, for Mess sake," I growled.

Riolyn strolled through the room, "You think they're Nepatin?" She disappeared into a hallway and said, "Number fourteen is down here."

I followed, dragging my bags. "Yeah, definitely. I mean, that's what my dad says at least."

Our dorm, number fourteen, marked the end of the hall. Riolyn placed her hand on the scanner inlaid into the wall and the door clicked open.

"Where's the gate to Develtic, then?" She pushed the door open and stepped inside.

I would have answered, but I was struck dumb with a punch of realization. The room was much too big to have to myself, which was the original plan. The doctor's plan. The last thing I wanted was special treatment from my father. Also, there were two beds, which didn't make any sense. Why would I have needed a huge room with *two beds* to myself?

Heavy, black curtains covered the back wall. A faint turquoise glow poked out from the edges. I pulled back the velvet to reveal an entire wall of paphador. It was beautiful.

"Saren told me the entire back of the school is lined with paphador," Riolyn stayed at the door, still. Her flesh was green in the glowing light.

My hand found the wall. It was cool and smooth like tumbled stone. A jolt of pleasure rushed down my arm and to my spinal cord.

A low bookcase curved along the front of the paphador wall. I leaned against it, toeing my bags toward the nearest bed.

Riolyn opened a door opposite me and flipped on a light, "Bathroom. We get a bathtub." She walked to the far wall and slid the doors open. "Closets."

Someone knocked on the doorframe. Aeshra bounced into our room, smiling, "What happened to my roommate?"

Riolyn shrugged her shoulders and continued exploring.

"You'd be unimpressed with my room, anyway. It's smaller. Also, no glowing wall. I've always wanted this room." Aeshra pressed the side of his face to the paphador and sighed, "It's so nice. I already saw Nathali's room; she's up in Illiad North."

"Is she by herself?" I asked, pulling pajamas out of my bag.

"No, not even close. They do three-roomers up there. She's with Natso Horn and a new guy. Natso is a loudmouth so I'm not sure how that's going to go." Aeshra ran his hands over the wall, hypnotized. "Your dad must really like you to put you in here by yourself."

Riolyn bid Aeshra goodnight and went into the bathroom while I sat on my new bed to think. Why did the doctor want me in this room? It didn't make *sense*. I couldn't find a reason.

And with Dr. George A. W. Harker, everything had a reason.

We sat in the lounge, Riolyn, Aeshra and I, with fellow students dispersed around us. Riolyn was a steady, neutral vibration; a comfortable grounding. Having Aeshra around was a relief, too; he let his emotions bubble up from him like candy foam. They both thought I was funny, which didn't hurt. I could hide behind them or jump in front if I needed attention.

Sometimes, I needed attention.

A girl with dust-colored curls stood at the front of the room and rang a small bell.

"Really, a bell? What sort of debutante cult *is* this?"

Aeshra gave me a look, as stern as he could manage. Riolyn laughed under her breath.

The girl picked up some papers, flattening the front of her skirt, "Good morning, everyone. My name is Oesh." Her voice sounded like a bell, too. "We've got three newbies this year! I will be your go-to from here on out. You will live in Eldrid for the remainder of your time at Voltenstraus. I'm here for two more years so you'll be seeing a bit of me around. Today I'm your guide for orientation.

"Please wave when I call your name. Siddrum Gast?"

Everyone's heads spun around to see the first new kid. He was standing against the wall, looking smug. Brownish-purple tinted his sleek scales; a Margrev, like Riolyn. He was lean and athletic. I didn't stare; didn't want to give him the attention.

"Welcome, Siddrum! You're in room nine with Jeniss." Oesh motioned to an annoyed Turret with well-oiled, blue exo-plating.

"Mayli Harker? I hope it's okay I used your shortened name," Oesh smiled at me.

I raised an eyebrow and let out a lopsided smile. I wasn't sure what version of myself to be. "Mayli is good," I said.

"Some of you might recognize Mayli's last name. She's Dr. Harker's daughter. If you need to get in good with the doctor, maybe you can go to Mayli first." Oesh smiled.

I shook my head. "I have no sway with him."

"Mayli is in dorm fourteen at the end of the hall," Oesh looked back down at her paper. Then called out: "Riolyn Vite?"

Aeshra popped up and pointed to Riolyn with both hands, "Right here! My cousin!"

Riolyn was blank-faced and rigid. Aeshra sat back down with force, knocking into her and her shoulder scales raised.

"Thank you Aeshra! It's nice to meet you, Riolyn. And you are in room twelve with Aeshra."

Aeshra wiggled in his seat. "Actually, she left me for Mayli." He put on a baby face. Riolyn's cheeks burst with warmth and she looked away. I enjoyed Aeshra, but his fizzy, kitten-bursts of energy could be overwhelming.

"Oh! I don't have that in my notes. You did clear this with an authority, correct?"

"Yeah," I said. "Doctor Harker."

"So, you do have some sway with him!" Oesh winked at me.

I sat back onto the couch, calling up my wall of confidence, widening my legs like a pack leader and denying myself the pleasure of poisoning everyone in the room. Everyone in the building.

Riolyn's hackles lowered as we continued through the morning. The entire student body had breakfast in the dining hall.

Nathali greeted me as we waited in the breakfast line. "So, what do you think?" She grabbed a toasted seed bun.

"Not sure. The building is fascinating, but most of the people aren't." I grabbed a seed bun too and loaded it up with dark syrup.

"Maybe I can swing by your dorm tonight and meet your new friends. I want to see where dad put you, especially since you've got the room to yourself."

"Actually," I reached for a jammed slice, "I have a roommate now."

"Should I say congrats or sorry?"

"It's all good, we asked to room together."

"Is it Riolyn? She's cute, yeah?" She winked at me and headed back to wherever she came from.

I rolled my eyes.

The fourth floor opened into a magnificent library with glowing fireplaces and spiraling columns, tables lined with supplies for studying, and rows of deskscreens. At the center of the room, bright lights perched over a forest of plants. And of course, the books. Books from every layer, in every language, on every subject.

The librarian gave us a brief lesson on the history of the cave; the Nepatin species created the dwelling to live and work with the earliest MMPs. Both races were lab-races and essentially servants to their Dwavasc creators. When the gate between Develtics and Nessa was permanently closed, the cave and entire layer were lost for centuries.

"How was the layer found again?" someone asked.

"Terrance and Lythia Harker stumbled across it, so they say," the librarian answered, a glint in their eyes.

Aeshra moved in to whisper in my ear, but I didn't hear what he said. An electric chill sliced through my skin and my eyes followed the feeling to the corner of the room. There he was; tiny, angry, grey-faced. Seth Mace.

Riolyn shivered and said, "I don't trust that guy at all."

"You felt that too?"

The neck of his black sweater was pulled up around his cheeks like he could disappear into it. He skimmed the edge of the room and vanished into an aisle of books, heaviness trailing after him. The discomfort left my body as fast as it had arrived.

After an extensive tour of the school, we suffered meeting the entire staff. We were shuffled into the largest classroom, Keshack auditorium on the second floor, and made to wait. The crowd of students grew steadily louder at the minutes wore on, chatter turning to raucous laughter and yelling and nonsensical school chants.

I sat with silent Riolyn and Aeshra, who purred salacious commentary into our ears. Nathali was across the auditorium with a hoard of luxuriously dressed teenagers who'd welcomed her into their fold. I pulled on my coat of not-caring, my confidence wall, and scowled. When the teachers made their little speeches, Saren blustered through his in the most endearing way.

Varali Garima and the Doctor sat on the platform with a middle-aged Dedocian man wearing ill-fitting clothes. The unknown man stepped up to the podium first, introducing himself as Benjamin Plunk, the school's Advisory. I guess that meant he was in charge. His speech was long and boring, and I didn't listen to a word of it. I *can* tell you that he looked overwhelmed.

Varali spoke about extra curriculars, clubs, and the exciting possibility of visiting the town of Nepa in our off time.

"If you are a new student and have a Limit, expect a visit from me in the next few days. Limits class is held on weekends so as to not interfere with your education."

The muscles in my stomach held on for dear life as I sipped on rootbrew. My eyes bored into the stage, refusing to meet my twin's gaze. I knew she was sitting with a group of Limits kids she'd already befriended. She was going to have special-person class with them, while I was stuck in Nepa getting in fights with other unblessed idiots. Because that's what I did, right? I got in fights. And — I might have had a Limit too, but it was the wrong one.

Doctor Harker was at the podium now, running a hand over his beard.

"I've met you all, of course, but let me introduce myself again. I am Doctor Harker, president of Voltenstraus. I work behind the scenes to make sure our students, our school, our layer is a place of safety and calm. Over the next weeks, I will meet with every student at Voltenstraus. It's my job to look after the mental health and wellbeing of our student body. I also secure funding, and will gladly take requests for monetary needs. Lastly, but most importantly: if you have concerns that involve the security of our school, you come directly to me.

"To our newest students, thank you for enduring this long day."

My eyes drifted over the room, cataloging the people around me. That's when I saw him. Seth was at the back, hovering against the stone like a gargoyle. He watched my father speak, and no one knew he was there; no one felt him. Could he turn that awful feeling off?

And then he was looking at me. Both of us diverted as soon as our eyes met, but it was too late. My eyes watered as I clutched my abdomen. It was like I'd caught the shards of glass right in my gut. My limbs burned with electricity.

"That slime! What a creep — he was looking at me," I hissed. No one had the right to affect me so strongly.

"Who?" Riolyn shot her eyes around the place.

"Seth Mace! He's against the back wall."

Riolyn turned back to me, "He's not there. You sure?"

I looked back. "What the heck — he was there! Where does he go?"

She scoffed at my side, "He must have a Limit to move that fast."

Dr. Harker was still talking, and I strained to listen.

"This school is not like any other you might have attended. All of our students have colorful pasts, some of which they are trying to escape. You will be expected to know someone not for their past, but for their future. Know one another, not as what they have done, but who they are and what they can do. An open mind is critically important. Voltenstraus is a safe space for everyone, no matter what they came from."

He continued with, "Benjamin and I live behind the Dossier, and Varali lives on the first floor beyond the kitchens. If you have needs after hours, you are to call one of the three of us with the wallscreen in your dorm room." George ran his hands over the front of his tweed vest, rippling with quiet energy.

"Attached to our quarters is Idrissa's home." He paused and my ears perked up. "Previous to coming here, you should have been briefed on Idrissa's wearabouts. Sae is not to be bothered, and is incredibly private. It is probable that you will go through years of schooling here and never see Idrissa. We are gifted with the presence of sae's wisdom. It's a rare opportunity to have such a being in our midst."

A student called out, "Is Idrissa a Non-Eater?"

My father released a breath, "I'm sure all of you have a wealth of questions about Idrissa. Today is not the day for those questions. Let this day be about exploring your new lives here at Voltenstraus. This place is full of secrets to uncover, but Idrissa is not the egg to crack."

Dr. Harker locked eyes with me, green irises behind tortoiseshell glasses. We raised single eyebrows at each other before he turned and disappeared behind the adjoining door.

What egg was I not supposed to crack? Seth Mace? Idrissa?

"I'm gonna crack the shit outta that egg."

Riolyn's sharp laughter pulled a smile from me.

7

CORNER OF THE SKY

A man was outside, just beyond the shore, stringing a navy-blue wire from tree to tree. He wrapped the cord around each trunk twice, pulling it taut before moving to the next. My eyes tracked the wire from the spool in the man's large fingers where it was knotted to the boat deck.

I was being contained.

My left sock stuck to a big smear of dried blood on the laminate. I shivered, pulling my foot from the floor. The last thing I wanted to do was clean up the blood of my captor.

Mina had been carted off by two bumbling fools, one of which was outside imprisoning me with motion-detection stun-wire. This one called himself Fruit, of all things, but his stained shirt did not smell like fruit. He chewed spitgrass, shoving dry handfuls onto his tongue every half hour. Sallow lines of long-term addiction wrinkled around his mouth, aging him.

The other fool was called Squeem, but he hadn't been back around. He had the nerve to tell me he was sorry I was stuck here, and that he didn't agree with Mina's methods. Then he hobbled away and locked up the boat while Fruit carried Mina's dead weight into the forest.

Mina hadn't died, of course. Because I was such a *good person*.

When Mina returned, I was crouched over, scrubbing blood from the kitchen floor. My hands were tinted red.

"You're still here?" she set her angry glare on me. She was paler than usual, with her hair in a ratted nest at the top of her head.

I shook off and continued scrubbing. "Where was I supposed to go? Your cronies fenced me in with that razor wire."

"Yeah, but — you don't get hurt! Just get past it!"

My fist squeezed around the bloody sponge. "I tried! It knocked me out before I could get across. Every time."

Mina threw her hands into the air and stomped from the room like a teenager.

"If you didn't want me here, you shouldn't have kidnapped me!" I yelled through the boat.

A door slammed.

In the days following, Mina continued on like I wasn't there. She watered her plants, cooked her pears, yelled on her pocketscreen. I ignored her too, sniping whatever I could from the fridge that wasn't a pear. I never wanted to eat another pear in my life.

The nights were bad. Mostly because Mina was gone, and if she was gone I could assume she was off killing people. It was only a matter of time before the news picked something up.

The news ran my story once a day, always during prime-time locals. I was a criminal on the loose, a bad seed who'd gotten away with murder in my twenties. They painted me as a psychopath who'd spent the last five years conning the local Batifban into thinking I was reformed. Talsion and Rogard, my coworkers, even went on the record to state that they: "Always pegged me as a sicko."

What would they think if they knew I'd been abducted by Mina Harker? That I'd been shot and stabbed by her? Knocked out by electrified wires and imprisoned on a rotting houseboat?

What would they think if they knew I'd crawled on top of her dying body and brought her back to life?

I was no better than the villain they believed me to be.

Then__

I'm slinking around the monastery, twenty-four years old and fresh off my shift at the Night Palace. My feet make no sound in the bricked hallway.

My youngest brother catches me as I try to sneak past his bedroom. I'm amazed, as always, that he heard me coming, because his room is equipped with padded walls and a solid steel door. He needs that sort of protection. We all do.

"Where were you?" Seth asks, squinting up at me in the dim light. The strips of white hair around his face reflect the moonlight in the windows behind me. His soft jaw clenches. "You were supposed to take me to Dr. Galvantia."

My first reaction is defense, "I was working! You know I can't just skip work—"

"Working? That's what you call it?"

"Yes, working. And besides, Elle should take you to those things. He's not bringing in money like I do."

"Where's the money, then? If you've got money, you should help pay the bills."

I scratch at my dry, plaque-covered arms. I know what I look like; a strung-out piece of trash. "The congregation pays them. You're twelve; What do you know about bills?"

"Damnit, Devin—" Seth crouches over and coughs. Specks of black spit dot the floor. He slams his hand on the steel door. The sound echoes in the cavernous wing. "I'm thirteen now. You missed that day, too."

I put my hands up. He's normally not violent, but I'm paranoid. Too many grabby johns over the last few weeks.

"I wanted to be home, I did, but — I have a life outside of here, too. I can't be dragging you to appointments when I — you know. I have things to do."

Seth backs into his room, wetness rimming his cold eyes. The door shuts in my face.

With an eyeroll, I step over the drops of black on the floor. I pull out a fresh baggie of icetar I'd stolen from one of my patrons earlier that night and watch the icy stones shift in the bag.

What's one more missed appointment? One more lifesaving appointment for a kid who can't be saved.

Now__

Mina dropped into the old armchair. "Why are you still here?"

The look on my face should have been answer enough.

"I gave you *three days* to get out of here. I sat in Matey's damn chair for three days, stuck with pins and tubes like a fucking robot, and you're still here. Tell me why."

I sat forward. "Why do you kill people?"

Mina's head tipped to the side as she watched me. I wrapped my arms around myself in protection. Her fingers ran over the embroidery on the chair's arms, picking at threadbare flowers. Her nails were short and clean. No blood, no graveyard dirt, no dead body dust.

"There are few good excuses for killing." She pulled a green string from the chair and watched it snap. "I was always meant to be a weapon. I was trained that way, and what a success it was; I'm nothing if not lethal," she scoffed dangerously. "They made a lot of mistakes with me."

"They?" I asked.

Mina nodded. "Family. My father, mostly. He was a good teacher; taught me to hunt, to set traps. Turned me into an ... actress, you could say. I was good at it, loved it even. Made it my life, as you can see." Mina motioned to the knife sheathed against her hip.

"He taught you to *hunt people*? That's child abuse," I said, tugging the pink blanket around my shoulders.

She sat forward with hard eyes. "My father is no abuser. I owe everything I am to him."

"But he—"

"I've already told you too much," she snapped.

"Did you do this when you were a *kid*?"

Mina's mouth stretched into a proud smile. "I killed a rapist when I was fifteen. That was my first real accomplishment." Her fingers wrapped around the handle of her knife absently. "My father is not a perfect man, but I owe him my life."

She stood and walked to the kitchen, leaving me nauseated on the couch. Mina's *family* had done this to her. What kind of person could teach their child to hurt people?

I followed after her. "Wait, just wait."

She stood over the counter, hands grasping at a wide-leafed plant in the sink. Her eyebrows raised in annoyance.

"I have to get off this boat. Take me somewhere. Even if it's the last thing I see."

Mina ran her hand along the leaves' transparent stems, appraising them. "And if I say no?"

"Don't say no."

I watched as she turned on the faucet, letting out a steady flow of lake water. She pulled a heap of moss from the pot and held it under the stream. Green water and soil dripped from her fingers.

"Maybe tomorrow."

I woke to the smell of pear.

"Eat this, and here." Mina pulled a cloth bag from behind her and shoved it toward me. "Wear these. Hurry up."

I sat up, swimming in pink blanket, and took a bite of the brown and green pear. It was soft, fragrant, perfect. It tasted like possibility.

I unfolded the clothes and took a look. A black shirt, a fuzzy coat and a pair of dark pants, nice quality. Striped socks, fresh underwear, new oxfords.

"Is this part of your ritual? Dressing me up to kill me?"

Her pale hands danced over the back of the armchair. "Do you want to leave or not? I'll be waiting outside."

With Mina safely gone, I ran my fingers through my hair, pulling at tangles. I peeled off layers of grimy clothes, slipping on the buttons of my bleached polka dot shirt, and raised my new clothes to my nose. Clean cotton, with a hint of posh fragrance; the kind they diffused in upscale offices.

I put on the shoes and took one last look at the room. I wouldn't miss the couch, plants, the Mina-tracking wallscreen. The fear that so often simmered at the surface didn't bother to rise. If I died today, at least I'd die looking and smelling like corporate royalty.

Mina leaned against the houseboat. She tossed her keys up into the air and caught them. We jumped from the deck onto the shore, taking bites of pear in unison as we stepped into the damp woods. The morning wind swept my hair up, and I laughed, reeling in my newfound freedom.

"Don't make me regret this," Mina shot me a serious look as we climbed into her car.

I had no plans of doing so.

I tapped my shackled wrists together to hear the different sounds they would make. We sat at the crossroads in Mina's car, waiting for the opposite side to pass. The *Welcome to Frasier* sign in the field beyond shuttered in the gusty wind.

Frasier was a quiet working-town surrounded by fields of frasiora fern. The dry season bruised the prairie with grey and brown, leaving behind large, broken plant skeletons. The fern's neon pollen, referred to as lime dust, covered the land. The dormant particles waited for spring.

The town was unremarkable. Abandoned houses on the margins were covered with more lime dust and graffiti, frasiora sprouting from wooden-shingled roofs. A derelict Shuttle Station sat on the left side of the main street. Two small children sat under the overhang, drawing in the pollen with sticks. They looked up and waved at us as we passed.

The tips of my toes tingled, and I stiffened. Mina wasn't wearing a disguise. Had those kids just knowingly waved at Mina Harker? Did they know she was a serial murderer?

The main street was as depressing as the rest. We passed through what you might call a neighborhood, but the spindly houses were devastated by poverty and many looked unoccupied. Dead plants dotted garden plots in the front lawns, and every few feet stood a gangly, leafless tree with water-catching jars hanging from the lower limbs.

Skinny, attached businesses with windowed storefronts mirrored on either side of the main street, many with broken windows and lime dust-covered signs. Troughs for water-catching sat beneath each window and rain grates were set in the concrete.

A deserted park square was strangled by weeds and still more plant skeletons. Central to the park was an ancient structure, fenced off and coated in a thousand layers of green pollen.

"What's that?" I motioned toward the crumbling, red monument.

"Kajiun shrine."

"Like the ancient ones?"

"I don't know, what do you think?" Mina snarled.

The car turned and, in a field beyond the heart of the town, stood the great, cement block of a building. Out of place in dilapidated Frasier, it cast a pink glare over the field of fern husks. The beige, poured concrete was smooth and soaked up the morning sun. It looked like a temple to modern emptiness.

At the front was a circle drive with a few dormant lantern trees, their pinkish trunks blending into the concrete. The front entrance was flanked by long lines of reflective copper windows. A single car was parked out front, black and beat up.

Light blue letters glowed above the entrance; *Boister Energies*.

Mina pulled to the side of the building, swerving recklessly to park by a line of garage doors. She got out of the car and stretched her long arms above her head, cracking her shoulders. She went around to my side of the car and opened the door.

"Come on! Let's go," she shouted.

My eyes drifted over the pink building. She was going to kill me *here*?

I followed her out of the car, stretching against my bonds. Mina pushed open a door, and we stepped into a large, shadowy space. My eyes were slow to adjust to the darkness.

Inside, two *Boister* maintenance vans parked side by side, as well as some technology I'd never seen. A low, drumming hum came from beyond the garage, vibrating the floor every few seconds. Thick cords ran the length of the room, trailing up the walls and into a room filled with blue screens. Fruit sat motionless, watching words scroll past.

A large door to our left burst open and Squeem limped in, cane scraping on the floor.

"Thank Mess you're here. I just got a message you aren't going to like." Squeem stopped, cocking his head. His eyes drifted over me and to my cuffed wrists. A crooked smile grew across his face. "You brought Devin!"

"What's the message?" Mina snapped.

Squeem threw his hands into the air and turned back through the door. Mina stalked after him and I followed like a good boy.

In the hallway, paphador stones glistened in the ceiling, casting blue shadows under us as we walked. I caught sight of other rooms: a windowed conference room, a courtyard with shapeless grass tufts and dead frasiora, a breakroom with a kitchenette, and a small room filled with books and a wallscreen playing news of Mina.

I followed them into the lobby. The sweet scent of corporate greed wafted up, and I stopped to catch my breath. An elaborate paphador chandelier draped across the cavernous ceiling. Mina's heels clicked on the slick black floors. Morning sunshine warmed the space while the windows were still fogged with dew.

"Up at the front desk," Mina waved me off. "That's where you'll work today."

Before I could reply, she and Squeem disappeared behind a far door. I stared as the door clicked shut.

"Well, come on then."

A woman with a heavy accent called from behind a half-moon counter. Her hair was clipped short and sleek, and she was middle-aged. She had the sort of brown-purple complexion they favored on Ma'dra.

At her side sat another woman. Her hair was bleached to burning, and she had just one eye. She was pretty, small, like a fairytale character. "Come sit with us," she said, and I knew her voice; the doctor on the phone.

I stood dumbly, unable to move my feet. The dizzy feeling thumping against my temples seemed to quicken.

"We're not all killers here," the dark-haired woman said with an intimidating smile. "My name is Taro, and this is Matey. You've talked to her, briefly, I've heard."

"It's nice to meet you in person, Devin." Matey stretched her dainty hand over the counter in a friendly gesture.

"Yeah," I replied, glancing around. "Why did Mina bring me here?"

"I doubt even Mina could answer that. It was only a matter of time, it seems." Taro sighed and tapped the counter again. "Matey, go find Mr. Devin a chair."

Matey smiled and leapt from the room. She might as well have had little glittery wings.

I stepped up to the counter, searching the room for any hint at who these people were. "You're from Ma'dra?" I asked Taro. "Your eyes glow like a predator."

"My, aren't you charming?" Taro said with sarcasm. "Matey is aware she has one eye, so no need to bring it to her attention."

"I'm sorry, I'm nervous." I wiped the sweat from my forehead. "Is she really a doctor?"

"One of the best."

Anxiety burned in my chest. Why had Mina brought me here? Was this a body-harvesting warehouse? Where were the corpses? The walk-in freezers?

Matey made her way back in with a chair that mismatched the others. "I'm so excited to have you here! I'm surprised Mina let you come in." She moved her damaged hair from her face, revealing dark makeup around her eye and eyeless socket. Exo-plating shifted underneath the shoulders of her dress.

"Because she's going to kill me?" I let out an anxious laugh.

"You don't really think she's going to kill you, right?"

Taro cut her off. "We don't know what will happen in this situation. But we are happy to see you here, Devin. Can I get those cuffs off you?"

"Really?" I jumped at the chance.

Taro motioned for my wrists. I brought them to the countertop and she peered at them. "Oh yes, easy." She grasped the center interface between two fingers and brought her other hand up. A transparent piece of something was wrapped around her palm. She pressed at it, tapping, and my shackles snapped open.

I gasped with relief, unaware of the building tension in my hands.

I sat behind the desk. Taped up behind the counter was a paper with the printed words, *"You are the face of the Guild!"* The desk was well-organized: pens in pen cups, two phones placed neatly next to two deskscreens.

Matey leaned forward, placed her chin in her hands and asked, "So what's it like, living on the boat?"

I laughed uncomfortably, unsure how to respond.

Matey went on, "You must be exhausted. Really, I want to know all about it. Mina doesn't say much about life outside of work, but she had us do some digging on you! You've led a *very* interesting life."

"Let him settle in before we burden him with our questioning," Taro said over the brim of her teacup.

I swiveled on my stool. These people worked for Mina Harker. I knew they couldn't be as lovingly innocent as they seemed.

One of the phones rang and Matey answered. She looked nothing like a doctor, with her white tights and pink shoes tapping on the floor. If she was a doctor, why was she also a secretary? For *Boister Energies*, of all places. Nothing made sense.

I turned to Taro. "Do you really work for Boister?"

Taro nodded. "In a way."

"But — you seem so normal. Why are you working with a monster?"

The woman tipped her face with a sad smile. She placed her hand on top of mine and said, "I want you to know that you're safe here. Eventually, your questions will be answered. Or you could choose to go right now. We wouldn't stop you. A shuttle still visits the station every afternoon. You could get on it and never turn back. Leave this place forever and not know any more than you do at this moment.

"But, regardless of what you choose, I need you to know this," her glowing eyes locked with mine, "Mina is not as evil as she seems."

"Well, I don't know — Mina is pretty evil," Matey interrupted, off the phone.

Taro's eyes shot disapproval. "Mina follows a dark path that leads to the light."

The words turned over in my mind. The spinning slowed and solidified into one giant question mark. "*What*?"

Matey said something about the *good of all beings*, but I couldn't focus. Was Mina the leader of a sacrificial cult? Had Mina brainwashed her followers into believing her murders were for the greater good?

And here I was, stuck in a corporate park with her mindless cult of psychos.

Standing up, I shook myself off and asked where the bathroom was. I proceeded to the toilet and threw up my breakfast.

I stayed in the bathroom for as long as I could before someone found me. Surprisingly, it was Squeem.

"Are you hiding in here?" His voice was scratchy. "Mina wants to see you in her office."

Dread settled in my stomach, but I followed Squeem out. In the hallway, I caught sight of the breakroom wallscreen. Mina was on and she was much younger, with a long, tight braid down her back. Dark bruising trailed down her neck; she showed the wounds off to the interviewer with a smile on her face.

"What is that video?" I motioned to the screen.

Squeem stopped to look. "Probably Nessuir, the trafficking governor. I don't remember his name." Squeem trailed off, watching the young Mina quietly. Then he added, "She looks high."

"Did you know her then?" I asked.

"She found me later, strung out and hacking bank accounts out of a booth in a blood club. That's when she roped me into all this. She'd come to terms with her purpose by then."

We stood in silence, watching young Mina drunkenly talk to the reporter. I tried to process what Squeem said. *Her purpose.* My cult story was checking out.

But Squeem seemed like such a genuine person, just like calming Taro and wide-eyed Matey. These people were strange, but I was finding it hard to believe they could be duped by sociopathic conspiracy theories or whatever ideals were stringing them together.

Mina's office was a blank slate of commercial dystopia. No windows, no plants, no rugs — none of the comforts of the houseboat. It was a cold, white space with slick black floors and paphador stones hanging from the ceiling. The only bit of life hung behind her desk; a long painting of a person laying on their back, white fabric draped over their body.

"Is that a Narien Evroldengaud?" I asked, pointing to the painting.

Mina eyed me, quietly ripping the flesh from my bones.

"It's nice," I added.

"Are you finding something to do out there, or are you just taking up space?"

"I'm not sure why these people like you. You're kind of mean."

Mina rolled her eyes. "You want me to work on my tact? Answer the question. What are you working on?"

I started to pace. "You dropped me out there without a word, and expected me to know what to do. Well, I don't, and Taro and Matey aren't sure what to do with me either. I don't even know what goes on here!"

Sitting back in her fancy desk chair, Mina pulled a knee to her chest, dropping her CEO of Hell act in a matter of seconds. She nearly *smiled*.

"I don't get you." I shook my head.

"Why would I tell you what's going on here? Why would I trust you?" Mischief gleamed in her eyes. She was egging me on.

"I'm not doing this with you. I'm not your little brother to torment."

Her grin only widened. Mina stood and passed me through the door, beckoning me to follow. "You might be surprised to know that I never tormented my younger brother."

She took me to the front desk and said to Taro and Matey, "Put him on wordsearch. Something meaningless." She thought for a moment, snapped her fingers and said, "Amnea Station; that's a good one."

"What's wordsearch?" I asked, but Mina was already disappearing back into her lair.

Taro turned to Matey. "We could give him a pocketscreen."

Matey stilled at her keyboard. "Without Mina's permission?"

"She put us in charge of him, didn't she? I'll have Squeem get him one with limited capabilities." Taro left through the hallway, and Matey shrugged her shoulder at me.

When Taro came back, she handed me a small screen. She opened an app and swiped around. "Here, it's ready for you."

She tapped a word on the screen before handing it to me. Lines scrolled passed in quick, highlighted flashes.

"It's searching for the term Amnea Station within company coms, and other places. Just keep watch to see if anything pops up. With a new term, it could take a day."

I sat and watched it fly through files, hypnotized as it scanned each document, email, call transcription, contract for Boister Energies. Two hours later and it was still scanning.

Boister Energies came and went, followed by something new.

"Hey, what is the Dight Actors Guild?" I asked.

Taro and Matey stopped clicking away on their keyboards and exchanged looks.

"What? What is it?" I pushed.

Taro sighed in resignation, head in her hands, as Matey answered. "It's us, Devin."

"You?"

"*We* are the Dight Actors Guild," she motioned to space around her. "Mina, Squeem, Fruit — a lot of people, really." She turned to a grumbling Taro. "What? You're the one who gave him a screen!"

"Is that the name of your murder cult? Murder *guild,*" I asked incredulously.

Taro stood and snatched up her coat. "It's the end of the day. If Mina wants you to know what's going on, she can tell you herself. It's not our place." Taro placed an angry finger on the keypad's number 1 and snarled in her thick accent, "Come get your hostage. It's 5 and I'm going home."

Mina opened her office door. "Whoa, Devin, what did you do to my employees? Has he pissed you off, ladies?"

Taro swung her body toward Mina like a rhino readying for battle, "No, but *you* have! For dropping him here and giving him not an *ounce* of information. You need to take this more seriously. Your carelessness has torn this man from his life and I would say he is taking it very well. Show him some respect and figure out what the hell you are doing with him! It's just not *right,* Mina."

I waited for Mina to explode in Taro's face. Maybe she'd throw a knife at her, or pull a gun from her waist. But it didn't happen. Taro grabbed me in an abrupt handshake before stomping from the room.

Mina was unbothered, watching me with narrowed eyes, "You sure are good at looking dumb. Come on, let's go."

I trudged behind Mina through the strange building and out into the parking lot in a daze. Behind the smooth *Boister Energies* building loomed a huge Kajiun temple, peeking out from the afternoon fog. Its pink paint was chipped, and the roof was covered in a thick coating of lime dust. I took a deep breath, smelling decades of frasiora pollen and musty old car, and something magnificent happened to me. I *smiled.*

8

THE FEAR OF WATER

At the door of room 322, I sucked air into my over-exerted lungs. The stairs were going to be an issue.

"Um, Mayli," Saren said, tapping on my shoulder. "There's one desk left if you'd like to take a seat."

"I would not like to do that, thank you." I inhaled into my hands one last time.

The entire class was watching me, of course. They looked like a bunch of nervous geese.

I strolled in, acting cool. I kicked my bag under the seat and slid into the chair. Seated next to me was a girl with bushy eyebrows and boring clothing. She smiled at me when I sat down. Behind her was an Orcorne boy with a big scar where his top lip should have been. Interesting bunch.

Saren stood next to a desk covered with pink and yellow breakfast cakes. His grey sweater had a wet splotch on it.

He flipped on his desk screen. "Now that everyone is here; Welcome to Dwavasc Storytelling, your new favorite literature class! You'll notice I have cakes. But first!" He waved a halting finger in the air. "Let's introduce ourselves to the new faces in class."

Feet shuffled under desks and a classmate or two groaned.

"Now, now; let's show our new students some love. I'll go first. I am Saren Vite, originally from Quar. I finished at the University of Nepa three years ago, specializing in layer mythologies. I am a history buff and avid reader. And, before anyone dares make the joke, while I might be the palest man you've ever met, my last name is indeed *Vite*, not *White*." He raised his arms to the class like he expected us to fake-laugh along with him. The corners of my mouth twitched despite myself.

Classmates began to introduce themselves; Something-something Lagenstrauh from Ahk, a Vauvire from Votia whose name started with a B, and so on. My attention waned immediately.

The girl next to me was named Magbel Hathcreet, and she was from Kist, a country on the layer of Ma'dra. She was new this year, which explained why she wasn't afraid to look me in the eye.

I sat back with wide legs, entering my go-to confidence pose. "Yeah, Mayli Harker. From here. New this year."

Someone scoffed behind me.

I turned and shot a nasty glance around the room. "Somehow I've already made enemies."

Saren jumped in, "Mayli, tell us something about yourself so we can get to know you. How do you like to spend your time?" He smiled encouragingly at me.

My face contorted into something wild as I searched for an answer. "Well, I'm into art, books, eating...bugs. Oh, and music, of course."

A voice from the back of the room interrupted me. "Wait, did you say you eat bugs?"

The class erupted in laughter, but I wasn't going down without a fight. "Oh, it's possible. In fact, your mom told me she *loves* to eat bugs."

Saren jumped at the front of the room, a pink pastry in hand, "How about we eat some cake? I have a feeling this year's gonna be a long one."

Riolyn, Aeshra and I sat on the floor, tossing bits of lunch into the air to catch it in our mouths. Riolyn never missed. Most of my food ended up on the floor. Whenever someone walked by, I cocked my head to look cool and disengaged, but kept forgetting my act and smiling at strangers.

In instances like this, Tom would say, "*Just be yourself, dove,*" and I would reply, "*I am. I am both versions.*"

Pendants of glowing stone hung from the ceiling, swaying with each gust of air from the wall grates. Organic shapes were cut into the cave walls, revealing paphador beneath. The bioluminescent mineral illuminated the space with green, blue and yellow. It was hard to hate Voltenstraus with its magnificent scenery.

Aeshra snagged Riolyn's schedule with a lengthy groan. "Oh, no. You've got Tallis next!"

"We both do," I said, scanning my paper.

"He's going to *hate* you."

"What? Why?"

Aeshra leaned forward, dropping his voice conspiratorially. "Grant Tallis *hates* Harkers. All of you. I had a defense class with Mieda and he was ruthless with her. It's something that goes back to"—Aeshra dropped his voice even lower— "your *older siblings*, I think."

Now Riolyn was interested. "You mean Mina?"

Aeshra's glance flew around the room, shushing us. "I can't hang out with you guys if you're going to be dropping her name all the time! Unnecessary attention, you know?"

The Pit was a circular, stone auditorium with sport lines painted on the waxed floor. Layer flags fluttered from the ceiling and the room smelled like my mother's painting studio.

A man in his thirties kicked floor cushions into a line. He glanced at students as they entered and told us to open up the wall compartments and each get out a springboard. Riolyn and I set ours up and leaned against the edge of the pit.

The man edged along, sizing up students as they picked spots around the circle. He was stocky, with dark blond hair, golden tan skin, bright, wide-set eyes, full lips. Definitely a Channic, the supposed cherubs of Ma'dra.

He didn't seem much like a cherub to me.

"Today we will be attempting springboard kicks. Place your cushion behind you, your springboard in front. Take a gentle hop onto the springboard and back onto the ground. Do this twenty times."

Students glanced around with mild confusion. I knew what he was talking about, but I sure as hell wasn't going to be the first to start jumping.

The teacher walked up and down the line, grunting approval and disapproval.

"This class is an introductory level defense class. I quite dislike introductory classes." He stopped to glare at two boys pretending to kick each other. "And that is why I despise introductory classes. Intro students are clueless, easily distracted children."

He went on, cracking his shoulders in a stretch. "Nevertheless, introductions are necessary. I am Grant Tallis, director of the Athletics and Defense program at Voltenstraus. This department is without a doubt the most important one you can immerse yourself in. Difficult situations have and will continue to affect you. Knowing the difference between a good decision and a bad one will save your life in an instant. That is where I come in."

Riolyn and I rolled our eyes at each other. We jumped on and off in unison, counting to twenty. My endurance was mediocre but my form wasn't bad; this was something I'd learned at eight years old. I did a few jump kicks.

Grant Tallis took one look at me and transformed into a snarling dog.

"If I wanted the class to start kicks, *I would have asked*." His words spit like venom. "If you cannot follow my instruction, you have no place in my class."

Throughout the class, Grant Tallis threw jabs at me in between his corrections and compliments. The lesson went on for another full hour before the clock struck three.

Tallis bid the class farewell with a bored tone. "Practice your calf stretches and toe lifts. I expect improvement by next week."

Students began to put their springboards back into the wall storage.

"Harker, you will stay back for a word."

Riolyn and I looked at each other with worried expressions. It was hard not to notice how little our new teacher respected me. As the class left, I stood there awkwardly, waiting for whatever misfortune was coming at me.

Tallis took his time locking up cabinets and flipping off lights while I chewed the inside of my cheek. He met me at the doorway and stopped.

"Let me be straight with you. I do not enjoy your family. You are irreverent know-it-alls who flirt with evil. The longer I have to deal with classless, brutish Harkers, the less patience I have. So, I will only say this once; you will not be a show-off in my class. In fact, you will not speak if I can help it. I am well aware that your father thinks he has taught you everything you need to know about defense, and I am not interested in his methods. Forget them in my class or do not show up."

My eyes were round and glossy. I stood motionless, unsure how to respond.

Tallis motioned irritably toward the entrance. "Now, please go."

Riolyn was waiting outside the door. She mouthed, "What the fuck?"

I didn't want to cry, so I just shook my head.

"That chick was *hot*," Riolyn groaned as we dropped our bags by two seats in a middle row of the auditorium.

"You mean Dr. Valentine, our *teacher*?" I feigned shock.

Green, gold and blue fabric hung around the walls, billowing as cool air moved around the space. An ornate fixture hung at the center of the room, filled with hundreds of glowing stones.

Riolyn thumbed through the textbook on her desk tray; *A History of Activism in Post-Gate Society* pictured an elaborate gate adorned with golden roses on its slick cover.

"Yeah, our teacher. It's the big curly hair; I love girls with big hair."

"I'm glad it's not the red hair you liked. I don't want to fight you off," I said, flipping my hair. Dr. Squidzy Valentine was not your average doctor, with violently red hair, falling in springy curls over her exo-plated shoulders. She wore bright blush on her cheeks like a Rastian doll. "The surgical bots in the med-lab were cool."

"I was looking at the teacher too much to notice. I'll be volunteering for everything I can in that class. What was it called again?"

"First Response Medicine. Might actually learn something real-world useful."

Riolyn flashed me a cocky smile. "If I can pay attention long enough."

At the central stage of the auditorium, a young woman wearing religious garb hurried, readying materials. When the door at the back opened, she fumbled, knocking something over. A bowl of polished stones tipped, thudding to the floor in loud plunks.

Another woman entered, shoving a stack of papers into the assistant's hands.

"What's all this?" she muttered, flipping her wrists toward the Gnastorian scrying stones rolling on the floor. The stones froze at the woman's gesture. The assistant raced to tidy them up, scooping the stones into her apron and vanishing through the door.

Our teacher, older and brutish, was wearing an ornate garment. Gold and copper beading trailed the hem of her head covering. A robe of indigo covered her mustard undergown. She was over-saturated, like a bright screen in a dark room. The blue of her flesh seemed to radiate.

Riolyn leaned into me and whispered, "Is she Hoodash?"

"You're from Quar, aren't you? You should know."

"And she's wearing Adord Judge getup," Riolyn said with slits for eyes.

Our teacher lifted her hands into the air and the doors of the auditorium slammed shut. Students jumped in their seats.

"I am Drucilla Laverick," her voice boomed. "You are to call me Madame Adord—*not* professor, *not* judge. You are to call my assistant Elandra," Drucilla whirled around, twisting her hand to throw open the back door. Elandra stood wide-eyed in the doorway.

I whispered, "Bet Elandra loves her job." Riolyn snickered beside me.

Drucilla began again. "With your textbooks in hand, we will begin." Circling the stage, Drucilla picked up a textbook. With a flick of her wrist, a picture of a cracked, glowing planet appeared on the screens.

Drucilla held up her textbook to the class, motioning to the cover. "This famous landmark, the Gate of Orsha, was the first Gate to be discovered. Can anyone tell me where this Supernal Gate is located?"

A few students lifted their hands into the air. I lifted mine too.

Drucilla motioned to someone in the front row, "What is your name, girl?"

"Mell Norvac, miss."

"You are to address me as Madame Adord. Not Miss, not Ma'am, not Professor. Do I make myself clear?"

Mell sat up straighter, "Yes, Madame Adord. The Gate of Orsha is on the Eivian layer, Madame Adord."

"And what is the proper name of the Eivian layer?" Drucilla cast her eyes down on the girl. Her head covering glittered in the paphador light.

"I'm sorry, Nirth is the correct name—"

"Do not apologize to me." Drucilla darted her gaze around the class as she swept to the center of her stage like an overdramatic cult leader. "Speak with confidence, certainty, conviction. Strength in tone gives strength to your words. Now, page seven is where we begin."

As the fluttering of pages filled the room, Drucilla waved her hand and the projections on the walls changed to a moving image of the Gate of Orsha. Manicured plants grew around it and bright sunlight caught the edges of its golden roses. At the gate's center, a deep, inky void shimmered like a vertical pool of water.

I opened to page seven; *Chapter 1: Tar Fire and the Beginning of Modern Vale.*

"We begin at the end of the Pre-Gate Era. Tar Fire has just erupted from the center of each layer planet, bubbling up and destroying civilizations. Most binary beings, male and female, do not survive, while non-binary beings and Samales are not harmed. Who can tell me the difference between a non-binary being and a Samale?" Drucilla looked about the class. She motioned to Siddrum Gast, the other new kid in the Eldrid dorms.

He spoke with complete confidence, "Non-binaries are outside the male and female gender binary, with male or female sex organs, while Samales could procreate with any sex."

Drucilla tensed. "Excuse me; Samales *could*?"

Siddrum nodded, chin thrust up. "Everyone knows that Samales no longer exist. It's probable that they never existed in the first place."

Drucilla crept closer, hunched like a storybook witch. Blue fire cast in her eyes.

She knelt down before Siddrum, staring directly into his eyes. "You dare come into my classroom to spread *dastardly lies* about the beings who gave life to your miserable self?" The words spat from her curled tongue. "Write this one's name down, Elandra. He will have extra work this weekend studying the vastness of truth that is the *Nasgolt Var*."

Siddrum shrunk into his seat as Elandra hurried a massive tome over to him. The sound of the book thudding onto his desk echoed in the cave.

Drucilla charged around her little stage and called to the top of the seats behind us, "Mr. Mace, can you tell us why the lower beings often believe Samales no longer exist?"

A quiet '*fuck*' issued from Riolyn's mouth. Seth Mace, the devil himself, was in our class. He was perched in the top row, closest to the door.

I leaned back and groaned. "Man, fuck this guy."

Seth didn't look up from his desk tray when he answered, "It's easier to follow the herd."

Drucilla nodded, "Precisely. In my class, you will learn to question what you've been taught. Without questioning our culture's ideals there can be no rebellion, and without rebellion there is no societal growth."

Drucilla Laverick, Adord Judge and bitchass extraordinaire, continued on with the lesson while Siddrum squirmed in his seat. The humiliation seeped from him like smog.

When class ended, my eyes darted to Seth's seat, but he was already gone.

The art room door was propped open to reveal a brightly lit space overlooking the atrium. Water outside echoed through the cave overhang, thundering behind the walls. I squeezed my hands inside my pockets.

At the center of the class, between easels and supply tabourets, my lovely twin sat on a table talking to the other students.

Nathali saw me and broke away from her group.

"Hey! So, I talked to Dad."

"Oh, Messer's balls," I sighed.

"And he seems to think you're having a rough time. Maybe getting into things you shouldn't be? What's up with that?" She put her hand on my shoulder.

"It's that damn Seth kid. I got into a fight with him and now everyone thinks I'm a degenerate." I rolled my eyes.

"Yeah, why did you do that?" Nathali pulled back her pale hair, twisting it up with a pencil and looking like a supermodel in the process.

"You would have done something too. It felt really bad in there."

Nathali's lips twisted in concern. "Bad how?"

"I don't know, murder bad!" I threw my hands into the air. "Everyone is terrified of him and I can't figure out why."

Nodding, Nathali responded, "People are going to be terrified of you, though. And that's a shame because they would love you if they knew you! But you really are terrible at first impressions."

"Yeah, yeah, don't get in fights, Mayli. I get it."

"I have astronomy with Seth and he was quiet the whole time."

"But you could feel him in the room, right? Bad energy. Something's up with that guy."

My twin tipped her head back and sighed. "Maybe so, but it's not your problem to fix. This isn't some school side-project, he's a person! And it's a hunch, anyway. You can care about his issues when you fix your own."

"Oh, like you have?"

Her eyebrows raised, "No. But I'm trying. That's the best we can do, right?"

I sunk into a seat and began opening drawers, pushing around the paint tubes inside. "I don't know what my deal is. I despise that kid and I don't even know why."

"Life is weird right now. Everything will even out."

"It's like you're capable of anything. No wonder you can talk to animals. If anyone deserves to be a Faunate, it's you."

Nathali sat in the station next to mine and kicked at my foot with hers. "And someday, you'll be healing people with your bare hands instead of wishing your own perfect gift away."

Riolyn's shoulders were raised and blue when I got back to the dorm. "He's in my Fables class with Saren! That Seth kid," she said, snarling.

"No way. Are they doing this to us on purpose?" I dropped onto my bed.

"He didn't talk the whole time, but get this — he left early. He just *walked out*. Saren didn't say a word," Riolyn sat on the floor, tugging off her shoes, "It's like I was the only one that noticed."

"Where does he go? We have to figure this out."

Riolyn kicked off her pants and reclined on the floor like a pantless starfish. "At this point, it's our duty."

I stared up at the ceiling and said, "Our *dark path to the light.*"

When I got downstairs, students were crowded around the auditorium door. I didn't see anyone I recognized, so I sat on the floor against the wall, waiting for the classroom door to open. I unfurled my deteriorating class schedule to make sure I was in the right place; Dedocian Anthrohistory, Dridyard Auditorium, Floor 0.

The teacher's aide propped open the door and students filed in.

I dragged my bag toward the door when I felt it again; an uneasy sickness in my bones. Everyone slowed down and looked at each other, shivering. The hairs on my limbs stood as I searched for the only person it could be: Seth Mace. He slinked into the auditorium, the last to enter, and shrunk into the seat nearest the door.

I found a seat where I could watch Seth from my periphery. He was wearing a dark, stretched-out t-shirt that was much too big for him, and the flesh around his narrow eyes was bruised with insomnia. Seth's heavy boots clung to his seedling-thin legs. How could anyone be scared of this snappable twig?

My classmates were watching Seth as well. When I caught a few glances in my direction, I pushed my chin up and shoulders back.

"The Mayli exhibit is closed; come back later," I snarled.

I'm sure class was fascinating, but my thoughts were focused singularly on Seth.

With a minute to go, Seth packed up his belongings and slipped out of the auditorium. I drummed my fingers on my desk, knees bouncing. As soon as class was dismissed, I shot out the door.

I ran up the stairs to the main floor, knowing he had to have gone up; there was nowhere to go in the basement but the Eldrid dorms.

Seth's massive t-shirt whipped around a corner into a maintenance tunnel behind the dining hall. I toed off my shoes to cut sound, just like when I was back home running "missions" for my father.

Like Riolyn had said: at this point, figuring Seth out was our duty.

There was a spiral staircase at the end of the tunnel. I took a deep breath and trudged up. Eventually, the stairs would get easier, right? How was Seth flying up them in such heavy-looking boots?

We were two floors up, in another maintenance hall, when I heard coughing. I stopped to listen, gauging how far ahead he was. When the silence returned, I continued on.

At the base of the fourth level of stairs, I slipped on something. I dropped to my knees. "Okay, okay — it's just wet, it's not a big deal — you'll be okay. Just get back up."

I pulled myself up and shook off like an over-stimulated animal. The dark, slick substance soaked through my tights. My skin tingled with discomfort.

I limped up the next spiral staircase, holding my breath to stay quiet.

A pale light filtered from beyond the curve of the hallway. I continued on, pushing forward against the heaviness of my body. My throbbing, wet legs prickled unnervingly.

"Maybe this was a bad idea," I said to myself.

What exactly did I expect to find at the end of this hallway? Was I going to catch Seth in the act of some heinous crime? Or was I about to see him perched on the seat of a very private toilet? Was I even following Seth anymore?

Thick black globs of something spattered the stone, trailing through the pale-lit door.

Staring into the light, I tried to make out shapes ahead. There was an archway and the bright, cool light came from within. The sound of water flowing and bubbling echoed. In the pale, white-green void, a figure crouched on the floor.

Seth's black-clad body rose and fell with silent breaths. He huddled at the edge of a pool, swirling one finger through the calm, iridescent ripples. A string of black gunk dripped from his mouth, dotting the back of his hand.

I was filled with a disgusting, voyeuristic feeling. My eyes would not leave his finger as it circled the liquid, coating it in multicolored wetness. The pain in my lungs grew, tightened, and I could not ease it.

Seth leaned forward. The tips of his green bangs floated on the surface like waterweeds. He took a single, hollow breath and dipped his face into the pool.

My knees hit the floor. Air wouldn't fill my lungs. The gurgling, bubbling, flowing wetness — My fingers clutched at my chest for something, anything to make it stop. His face, his mouth, his eyes, covered with water. He would die. I would die. I was dying.

Seth pulled his face from the pool. The silvery fluid dripped from his lashes.

He opened his eyes.

I slid on the stone, grasping at the doorframe. My nails snagged at the wall. Tremors jolted in my skin. An impossible energy thundered in the floors. Liquid sloshed from the sides of the pool onto Seth's hands.

A low growl stretched from his black-smeared mouth. The doors slammed shut in my face.

9

MURDER WISHLIST

"Where did she go? To kill someone?"

Dry grass scraped against the concrete exterior of the *Boister Energies* building, blowing in gusts of hot wind. With Mina gone, I'd been left to my own devices. I opted to learn what Fruit actually did at this place. So far, he'd spent the day staring at parking lot surveillance.

"Not to kill. Important meetings," Fruit replied, preoccupied with his parking lots. Absolutely nothing happened on the screen.

"Meetings? With who?" I prodded.

Fruit shook his head. "Important people. Can't tell you."

I groaned and spun in my chair. "But for how long?"

The man's eyes jumped from screen to screen. "Two weeks."

Mina had dropped me off at the *Boister* building with a bag of new clothes. She told me I'd be staying with Fruit and Squeem until she got back, and then she'd "Decide what to do with me." The dank cloud over me lifted as I watched her stupid yellow car drive away, replacing itself with candy floss.

Before she left, Mina gave the team a stern talking to. *"Devin's time here is not long-term nor permanent. He will not be joining our cause, so do not reveal sensitive information to him. If I find out people are telling*

Devin more than he needs to know, there will be serious consequences. Do you want to be the reason his life is cut short?"

Mina's lecture had slammed any and all possible doors shut. Taro was no more interested in telling me what they were doing than she was interested in eating her own toenails. They took Mina's warning seriously.

They must not have known that I couldn't die.

Fruit slammed a big, sausage-fingered hand onto the table. "There! There," he hollered.

"What? What is it?" I watched the screen; a blue car attempted to back into a space, albeit badly. Ordinary parking lot business.

"Nothing." Fruit waved me away as he pressed his desk keypad. "Hey, they're back."

Squeem radioed back, "Isn't Devin in there? He's gotta go. I'll be right there."

"Are you kidding me?" I said as Fruit rolled my chair toward the door. I stood outside, peering through the windowed wall as Squeem went inside. Squeem shook his head at me before the blinds clattered shut.

"I'm sick of being the loser around here," I swam in my self-pity at the front desk.

Matey sat to my right, counting individual packets of pills. "You heard Mina. We give you information and it's the death of you!"

The front door alert hummed and a new character entered *Boister Energies*: A sharp Orcorne man strutted in with a white leather duffle in hand. He had a honey-green complexion, sculpted hair and an angular nose.

He set his bag on the counter. "Is the beast still gone?"

Taro rolled her eyes. "You know she is. Why aren't you with her?"

"Good afternoon, *doctor*." He winked at Matey and she giggled. Taro grumbled at my side.

He continued, dancing his manicured fingers along the desk edge. "I received an invitation, but I decided it was best to not tempt fate. We all know how Mina gets when she's angry."

He *was* incredibly attractive. I watched him with awe as he completely disregarded my existence. There was something so alluring about being ignored.

The man's gaze settled on me. He scrunched his nose up. "Are we recruiting the local addicts now?"

"Cassius, this is Devin. Mina is — keeping him, remember?" Matey pawed at Cassius' arm like a kitten. "Be nice to him."

Cassius removed his arm with a sideways glance, then turned back to me. "So, this is Mina's little pet. I wonder what the Producer would think about that. I guess it's for the best that I didn't attend the meetings." He turned his nose up and looked down at me. "Think of me as a traveling salesman. I prefer to come by when Mina is not here. Such a tragedy it must be to *live* with her."

He walked off before I could reply.

Cassius set up his things in Mina's office. He left the office door open and turned on some low-brow binaural music. Cassius used Mina's screen, her phone. He rifled through her drawers. I even saw him go through her mail.

"This seems like a bad idea," I said under my breath.

Taro nodded. "He's just as bad as Mina is; there's no use in trying to control either of them. He's loyal to our cause, but he has to stir up a little war with her whenever he can."

I watched as Cassius sat back while on the phone, shiny dress shoes up on Mina's desk. His arrogance did remind me of Mina in a way; so lovely, and yet so unlikable.

"Why do they hate each other?" I asked.

Matey sighed and pushed her pill baggies into a storage container. She'd been at it all day.

Taro watched Cassius through the doorway and said, "It's personal."

Fruit and Squeem had a second-story apartment on Frasier's main street, perched above a closed-up bakery. It reminded me of my childhood home; the one I lived in before the Great Family Disaster that forced us into a Landornian monastery.

The apartment was drab, with faded walls and dingy flooring, but the gaming system was top notch. Fruit and Squeem played first-person shooters well into the night. Like my captor, they had a black box under their screen that recorded Mina's news segments.

"There's just one house rule," Squeem said, after he climbed the stairs with his cane in hand. "No work at home."

I asked him if I was allowed to try to figure out what their work actually was. He just laughed.

So far, my theories were lacking. They called themselves the *Dight Actors Guild*, or DAG. My wordsearching screen revealed some common code-words: *actor, crew, theater, production*. I'd concluded that the Director was, in fact, Mina Harker, and that the *Boister Theater* was the Boister Energies branch in Frasier. But who was the Producer? They seemed to be running DAG from *Backstage*. Was *Backstage* a real place?

On top of that, there were my wordsearches; Amnea Station, Luck of the Draw, and Teme'te.

Information about Amnea Station was nonexistent, but I stumbled upon Teme'te in a geographic dictionary in the breakroom. Teme'te was a rural Gate connecting Nirth and Votia. The two layers were constantly at war, but this Gate was less traveled. What about this insignificant, worlds-away Gate could be important to Mina's secret society of psychos?

Luck of the Draw was a term I knew; slang for an unexpected gift, an unforeseen event that brought good fortune. Less than a miracle, more than an accident. Gifts like these were often associated with Slight Hands, the most mysterious Undergod. The triangle-faced, many-gloved shadow seemed to spring up once a century to give someone the Trick; the gift of everlasting life.

But Slight Hands gave the Trick to a single being, not an entire family. That counted me out.

I wasn't missing Mina, no. But I was missing someone to hate, because I adored everyone else at Boister.

The night before Mina got back, I was invited to a cookout in Taro's backyard; she lived in a misshapen duplex in town. Taro and Fruit cooked a big Dedocian dinner of grilled whisp, salpice beans, rootmash, and Sorvian gravy. Squeem and Cassius drank malted beer while I sipped on homemade vinegar tea. Matey played with Taro's hounds on the patio next to us.

"Why don't we do these sorts of things more often? I'm having fun," Matey said, pulling one of the dogs into her lap. He licked across her face and took off across the yard, baying at the moon.

Taro replied from the grill, "Because Mina always gets too loaded to function and starts fights with everyone."

A slow nod of agreement moved through the group.

Cassius poured another beer into his stemmed glass and turned to me. "Devin, pet. Tell me what it's like to live with Mina. My dear brother was the only one I've ever met who could survive that kind of torture, but you seem to doing rather well." He swirled his beer, appraising me like an overpriced, second-hand object.

My eyes were fogged with exhaustion. I tilted my head back and tried to make out a coherent statement, "Live with Mina? She's not too nice, that one." A wide smile crawled across my face, and I wasn't sure why.

Cassius raised an eyebrow. "Are you a glutton for punishment, my friend?"

Squeem laughed, nodding fervently. "Devin has been *lost* without her!"

"Squeem doesn't know anything." I smacked him on the arm. Much too loudly, I asked, "You have a brother?"

Squeem and Cassius lost their smiles. Taro's mouth was pursed up in a strange shape. Fruit watched from afar. Silence cast a shadow over the patio, with only the tug-of-war growls coming from Taro's hounds.

Cassius stood and cleared his throat, tipping his glass of beer into the drought-bruised plants lining the patio. He fixed his collar in strict movements, then headed into Taro's house, not to be seen again.

Hours later, I sat on the worn sofa in the apartment. Squeem was in bed; he'd gotten pretty hammered. Fruit sat next to me, playing a first-person RPG through tired eyes. The game's dark city setting and neon signage reminded me of Suradelphia.

"Fruit, are you drunk?"

"No. I don't drink." He talked slowly while his fingers moved fast on the controller.

I sighed. "You wouldn't lie to me, would you?"

"Only if I had to."

"Who is Cassius' brother?"

"Oh," Fruit's character jumped into a car. Fruit's body swerved as the virtual vehicle moved with smooth speed. "Calix. He was Mina's spouse. He died."

"Oh." I wiped my sweaty palms on my pants.

"It was very bad." Fruit demolished an enemy car with some sort of flaming bottle. "They had a kid; it died also. Very bad time."

The colors of Fruit's game seemed to dull. The longer I stared, the less I saw.

Mina turned up the next day in a terribly good mood. She wore a thick sweater, much too hot for the warmth outside. A glowing tan glazed her cheeks and forehead.

"After so many hot nights on the beaches of Quar, Frasier feels like a tundra." Mina pulled her sweater up around her neck in a dramatic flourish. "Of all the places to build our main theater, why did it have to be *Frasier*?"

Squeem rolled his eyes. "You know why." He leaned against Mina's office door; I stood next to him, unable to stop wringing my hands.

Mina ignored Squeem and I from her desk chair, scrolling through her pocketscreen. Cassius sat on the edge of Mina's desk, flicking crumbs from yesterday's biscuit at her. She ignored him too until she didn't.

Mina snarled at Cassius, "Why are you here? Have you been using my office? It smells like you."

He flicked another crumb at her, "What do you think? You have the only worthwhile space in this entire complex. I think the Producer spoils you."

Mina scoffed, "I'm the Director, of course I have a nice office. Aren't you a traveling ticket salesman? That thing you drive is *much* too nice for you. You should be taking a shuttle."

Squeem cleared his throat. "Any news you want to relay to us?"

Before I'd thought better to stop myself, I added, "How did your meetings go?"

I backed into the door and it smacked against the wall with a thud. Mina's eyes darted over me. She lifted her feet onto her desk and leaned back, her straight hair bunching up on the seatback.

"The arguments were lively, the location was exciting, and everyone lived. That's more than I can say for some meetings." She stretched her arms in the air, popping her shoulders. Cassius made a disgusted noise, and she kicked him off her desk with her socked feet. "I have a new list and it's a long one. I plan to get started immediately. Is everything in order?"

"Things ran smoothly while you were gone. A few hitches in Lansche according to the Sarif actors, but we can go over that later. Also, Fruit and I have been playing with a new hounding device that I'd like to show you." Squeem's frailty seemed to vanish when he spoke to Mina. I wondered if I would ever have a backbone like that.

"How was our dear Headliner?" Cassius licked a biscuit crumb off his index finger. "Did the two of you drink cocktails and make love on golden beaches, waves crashing at your toes? I see you have *quite* the tan."

Mina shot back without hesitation, "I have no interest in frivolous sex with the Headliner so stick someone else with your voyeuristic fantasies."

"And what of the Producer?" He had a mischievous look.

At this, she leaned forward on the desk to shift a stack of paper, avoiding eye contact. She took a long, calculated drink from her rootbrew before answering, "The Producer did a lot of watching and not a lot of partaking."

"And you think *I'm* the voyeur," Cassius said.

"But he was interested in some of our ideas — well, other people's ideas. I seemed to have gotten myself into some trouble when I divulged our little prisoner situation."

It was quiet for a moment and I looked around; everyone's eyes were on me, "Oh! I'm the prisoner." Squeem patted my shoulder and left his hand there.

Cassius barked with laughter, "And here I thought it would be *me* giving your little pet-secret away! How I wish I would have accepted my invitation. I would have loved to see the verbal thrashing you received. Ah, well, there's always next year."

"The Producer knows you have me?" I couldn't keep my damn mouth shut.

"I assured everyone that you wouldn't be a problem for much longer."

Squeem's cold hand squeezed my shoulder as he sighed. "Oh, Mina."

She scoffed, "What, you pity Devin now?"

"No, I pity *you*."

My captor walked in on Squeem, Fruit, Matey and I cleaning up after dinner in the breakroom. She washed her hands in the sink, watching us from the corner of her eye, and said, "What did you work on today?"

"Coms," Matey said. "We had activity in Farelawn."

Squeem shot me a nervous glance. "Well, I was on Devin duty. We repaired some old casping devices."

Mina tipped her head to the side. "Devin shows promise with repairs?"

Squeem replied, "Well, no. Devin is lousy with repairs. But he can watch."

I wanted to disintegrate.

"So, what can he do? What has he been doing? I was gone for two weeks and he still hasn't proven himself?"

Fruit said, "Devin's nice."

She didn't like that answer at all. Mina hung the hand towel on its hook. "Of all the people I could have stolen, it had to be you."

Squeem spoke up, "Devin is great at interpersonal relations. He has good ideas sometimes. And his trains of thought are ... interesting to follow. He's creative."

My thoughts drifted to the pop of a gun, a hole at the center of my polka-dot shirt, red spilling from my chest. My hand, pierced clean through, stuck to the dashboard of a car. Mina's car.

Squeem's ragged voice broke through the haze. "So, what should we do with Devin, then?"

"I don't know, hound someone? Do whatever you want; it doesn't matter. He's going to die, anyway."

Mina turned toward the door, stopped, and reached for the utensils on the breakroom counter. Her hand grasped the handle of a kitchen knife like it was made of silk. One second, the knife was draped over her palm like a silver ribbon. In the next, the blade was soaring through the air. It flew past my nose and struck the wall, tip lodging into painted plaster. It swayed in the silence.

When Mina walked out of the room, Fruit's eyebrows were pushed together in concern. "Is she serious?"

Squeem scratched his forehead, and sighed. "I don't know."

Fruit and Squeem weren't ready to abandon me to the knife.

Fruit's office was alight with pink and blue in the rosy, night-vision glow of the surveillance screens. As the white sun hung low in Besel's sky, I settled in for my first Dight Actors Guild lesson.

"So, hounding," Squeem began. "It's how we watch people. It's like catching their scent and following it."

"Who are you watching? Or, hounding, I guess."

"Here, let's show him," Squeem said.

Fruit scrolled through a gallery of thumbnails and clicked on someone. Every screen in the room began to flicker as they siphoned through camera angles. Within seconds, the man Fruit selected was on screen. He was walking down a quiet sidewalk in Pwero Ver's Harbour District.

"I know that place! That's on Raspa street, by the best delicatessen in Pwero Ver. Who is he?"

"Probably nobody, but he was on the new list. He's one of the only ones with a signature so far."

"Wait, is Mina going to kill this guy?" There he was, minding his business, walking down the street. Just a stranger to me, but surely he had a life that was worth keeping. I swallowed the metallic taste in my throat.

Squeem put his hand on my arm and squeezed. "We're just watching him, that's all. This is just a test run to show you what we do."

I let myself feel the weight of his hand and counted out two breaths.

"Anyway, this man," Squeem leaned into the database screen, "Tenor Rubark, thirty-nine, Dedocian, Pwero Ver. Works for Macton Corp. He has a hounding signature, so we can locate and follow him with our system. Fruit, do you want to explain the signature system?"

Fruit pushed a handful of spitgrass onto his tongue. The sweet, rough scent permeated the room.

"Neurochemical signatures. Cassius tags the list. We find them if they're in range."

"Exactly. Every person has a unique neurochemical signature. Once it's in our system, we can find them." Squeem said.

"So, Cassius isn't a traveling salesman?" I said, nodding to myself. That guy was much too suave to be selling tickets.

Squeem answered, "He gets a list from higher up and tracks down the people on it. It's a huge job for one person, but Cassius is damn good at it. He scans them with a short-wave OBR and logs it. Once he logs someone, we can hound them. We have hounds going at all times; hundreds, DAG-wide."

"Am I in there?"

Fruit answered this time. "We all are." He clicked around until his own office popped up. The three of us looked like computer rats, scrunching over the keyboard, blue light on our faces. I might have thought it troubling if I wasn't so overwhelmed with comradery. Were these people my friends?

"And Mina's in there?" I asked.

"Especially Mina. We need to know where she is at all times. That was the original point." Squeem waved awkwardly at the camera before Fruit turned Tenor Rubark back on.

I watched the man as he entered a corner store, just blocks from my government-issued home in Pwero Ver. The screen switched to an interior shot of Rubark. He grabbed a terribly unhealthy lunch and scrolled on his pocketscreen in the payline. It felt entirely too personal, watching someone like this. Yet I couldn't look away.

"These cameras, are you hacking into them?"

Fruit shrugged. "They use Boister regulated energy systems. We have full access."

"There are dead zones, though," Squeem added. "The places that run on *Bright White Energy*; mainly the big corporations and high-end neighborhoods. You know, those who can afford *Bright White*. If we need to see inside a dead zone, we send in an actor. A crew if it's a big job."

"So, you can practically see the whole city of Pwero Ver?"

"Devin. We can see everywhere, not just Pwero."

"What? The entire layer?"

"No. *Every layer.* Every open layer, at least. Our crew sticks to Dedocia, mostly, but sometimes we get to follow someone through Gates." Squeem noticed my expression and began to laugh.

Fruit tapped Squeem's shoulder. "Rubark is an idiot."

We devolved into fits of laughter as Sir Tenor Rubark argued with a particularly witty Batifban. The Batif, a woman with wide hips and a wider vocabulary, had stopped him for a parking violation. She was winning the argument, without a doubt, verbally cutting Rubark to bits. But Rubark, the poor fool, would not back down.

The lights in the room were off, casting pink and blue shadows from the variety of screens. The room smelled heavily of spitgrass and stonefruit cider. It penetrated the whole room, leaving me dizzy. I had unbuttoned my top few buttons like a schoolboy caught in a bar. We were eating fried succulents from the Turrisian restaurant in town. It was nearly 10 PM. At this point we were just hanging out, putting off going back to the apartment.

Behind us, someone cleared their throat. We spun to look, shocked. Squeem attempted to cover up the cider, but that just led to more giggling from Fruit and I.

Mina leaned against the door frame with her sweater pulled up to her chin. "I'm a little annoyed I wasn't invited to this gathering. Devin, are you ready to go?"

I looked around at Fruit and Squeem. "Go where?"

"Home? I'm done working."

"You want me to go back to the houseboat with you?" Heat crept up my face.

"Yes, *obviously*. Hurry up, I'm ready to go. Do you have your clothes bag?" But before I could answer, she said, "Good, let's go."

"Why are you bringing me back to the boat?" I asked in the dark, street-lamp lit car. The radio played a low, scratchy tune.

"Because it's where you live now. I'm surprised a concept this simple evades you, but I'm sure your brain is in overdrive from all the *difficult work* you've been doing."

"But I was staying with Fruit and Squeem."

She slammed on the brakes at a stop sign. "Why does this concern you anyway? This isn't vacation, Devin. You're a hostage — you don't get to pick where you're imprisoned."

I kicked my feet up on the dashboard like an angry teenager. "What exactly do you want from me?"

Mina snorted and the car lurched forward. I didn't want to look at her, didn't want to notice that she'd put her hair up or that she was shivering under her massive sweater, her shoulders scrunched up to her ears.

"Answer me. What do you want from me?"

Mina drew an alarmingly sizable blade from her car door and stuck it hard into the center console between us. She said through gritted teeth, "Do not speak to me again."

In the moonlight, Mina's pale hand pushed open the door. The boat rocked as we stepped into the musty kitchen. She pulled an overripe pear from a bowl on the counter and sunk her teeth in with a wet squelch. I looked away.

In the shadowy living room, I pulled a pair of boxers from the plastic bag I kept my clothes in. The TV was recording soundless stories of Mina, casting fast-moving lights around the room. I sat on the couch and stared at the screen.

It was unreal that I was back at the houseboat. In the short twelve days Mina had been gone, I tasted freedom. I had some friends who enjoyed my company, my bad jokes, and my constant barrage of questions. Squeem, Fruit, Matey, Taro; they were intelligent, caring, generous people. Hell, even Cassius had redeeming qualities. Why did they fall in line with someone like Mina Harker?

The screen showed footage of Mina jumping on the shoulders of a woman. They dropped to the ground and struggled before Mina dragged her through the shadows of an open door. I wondered if Fruit had watched this happen in real time from his Boister Energies office. The thought made me shudder.

Mina, the real one, stepped in front of the screen and fell into the armchair. My eyes broke from the flashing lights to refocus on her. She pushed the hair out of her eyes, pulling her luxurious sweater into her palms, squeezing the fabric. Her ankles crossed under her. She looked like a normal, mid-thirties woman; exhausted, a little frayed at the edges, cold in a warm room.

I spoke before I could stop myself, "So, your meetings didn't go well?"

"Not especially." Mina threw her head back against the chair and sighed. "I should have kept this situation quiet. I don't know why I told him. He gets *everything* out of me."

"The Producer?"

She cursed. The screen brightened behind her, shrinking her into a dark silhouette.

"He doesn't know *who* you are, just that I captured some guy and decided to try him out. He was angry. Would hardly speak to me the entire time he was there. But if he finds out you have a criminal history, he'll..." Mina's voice wavered, "He puts his faith in me to do this right."

The screen switched off and we plunged into darkness. I leaned to pull on the lamp cord. Mina's eyes were closed, eyelids lined with jagged veins. Her eyelashes cast shadows over her cheeks.

"What are you afraid of?" I asked.

She dragged her eyes open. "What the fuck kind of question is that?"

In a fog of sleep, Mina pulled herself from the chair and stalked to her bedroom, slamming the door behind her. She was holding onto her anger by a thread, and eventually it would snap.

In the coming days, Mina shut herself away in her office, and her mood mirrored her stress. Everything seemed more dire after Mina returned. Every job, every little task, felt urgent in its completion. And the most important task was, without a doubt, the new "wishlist" from her Very Important Meetings on Quar.

I couldn't fathom who was having murder meetings on the pale, sunny beaches of Quar. Mina was infamous, so why wasn't she lounging in a bathing suit all over the news right now? Someone would have seen.

When I happened upon the lunchtime news in the breakroom, a piece of the puzzle slotted into place. Beautiful beast Alexander Bergoin, CEO of Boister Energies and Loveliest Being Alive, was seen exiting his hovercar after a two-week getaway to his private Quaran island. The newscaster waved a mic in his nose, asking if he'd spent the holiday with a special lady. She blushed as he evaded her question with a gentle wink.

Alexander Bergoin, *billionaire philanthropist good-boy*, was somehow involved with Mina Harker, *homicidal maniac*. They were having week-long meetings on his private island, compiling lists of people to stalk.

Mina was likely killing people on these lists, some of them high-profile; almost as high-profile as Alexander Bergoin. Where were the connections? I didn't have the brain power to figure out a conspiracy this deep.

So instead, I sat in Fruit's office, hounding Tenor Rubark. It was nostalgic, watching someone fumble their way through a boring life. Almost like I was back home in Pwero.

Fruit hounded others at my side, always with a mouthful of spitgrass. When Cassius sent in a new signature, he'd add it to the queue. Squeem dropped in every once in a while to show Fruit a mechanism he was working on, but they went so far over my head I didn't pay attention.

I watched as Rubark passed through town in his brand-new vehicle. He lived in a posh sublet on the edge of Harbour District. He dated a chubby nightclub owner, but their schedules were so opposite that they hardly saw each other. Rubark worked at Macton Corp, a cyber security firm in downtown Pwero; Macton Corp was a Bright White deadzone, but the parking lots adjacent were Boister compliant.

Tenor Rubark was a programmer. Fruit had tried to explain the details of his job, but I didn't quite get it. Something about abstract problems and coding.

A few days into watching Rubark, I noticed some interesting behaviors.

First, he kept a radically strict routine. Up at 6 AM, pre-made breakfast, work out, drive to Macton Corp via the same route, walk down the street for lunch, leave work at exactly 4:15, quick errands, home by 6 PM, bed by 10 PM. He didn't leave his house once he got home, he spent all day on the computer and all night on his pocketscreen.

A few days a week, his partner would visit in the morning, but they seemed to be on the outs.

Second, Rubark rarely deviated from his routine, and when he did he was extremely agitated. I'd only seen it a few times; once, he left work a whopping ten minutes late. Afterwards, he fumbled through the grocery store, checking his watch constantly, breaking speed limits on the drive home to get there at exactly 6 PM. I couldn't decide if he was just particularly precise or if there were actual consequences to his lateness.

My mind wandered to a vision of Rubark getting home late to find Mina waiting patiently in his living room with a very large knife and wax melting on the stove.

Because I'd mentally logged Tenor Rubark's obsessive routine, I noticed rather starkly when he stayed forty minutes late at work. And after clocking out, Rubark stood at the backdoor and scrolled on his pocketscreen for a few more minutes. Then, much to my surprise, a short man with a snappy suit and short-brimmed hat strolled up to the door and walked through it as Rubark held it open. They nodded to each other, and Rubark headed home like nothing out of the ordinary had happened.

This strange display happened three more times in the month I watched Rubark. Always at 4:55, always the same door, always Tenor Rubark and the snappy dresser.

Mina worked late into the night in the weeks after her trip. Sometimes, she'd have Squeem and Fruit drop me off at the boat. On the nights when she did make it home, I would catch the sounds of a lighter hiss, of crackling inside of glass; a wrestle with drug paraphernalia. It stirred the deep shiver of addiction in me. But I had to hold on. This was not the time to slide back into my vices.

The phones at the front desk rang more often, message pings popped at rapid fire, and even my wordsearch screen had a few notifications as the days progressed. Suffice to say, *Teme'te* was becoming a popular term among the coastal elite. Whatever that meant.

I shuffled back and forth from Fruit's office to the front desk, dividing my time between the two. It was with great displeasure that I'd chosen the front desk on the day that a striking woman with translucent eyes and dark, pulled back hair swanned into the lobby. Echoes of her high heels clicked through the space and grabbed everyone's attention. The woman was wearing a tight, black suit and a sullen expression.

"Where is Mina? I need to see her." The woman's voice cracked as she spoke.

"She's probably on her way here right now, she's been gone a while," Matey answered, not bothering with pleasantries.

"Do you need us to contact her?" Taro asked.

The woman nodded. She began to pace.

"Bana, is everything alright?" Squeem walked into the lobby. The woman trotted over to him.

"I've got sketchy things happening and I don't think I can handle it much longer without your help." The woman was clearly scared. "I caught people watching my last few job sites. It feels like something bad is happening; I don't know who they are."

Taro interrupted to say that Mina was on her way.

Squeem took Bana to the seating arrangement near the front windows. She spoke in terrified whispers, "Yesterday, my number two came in late and he was — not himself. He could barely look at me. He had a nervous breakdown or something. I know they did something to him."

An anxious clench in my stomach took hold.

Mina clanged the doors open as she stomped inside. She was in a prickly mood and wanted everyone to know it. Her hair was down and windblown and she had dirt on her suit jacket.

"Please, get started. I left in the middle of a very important errand and I'm under time constraints."

Bana's face fell, "I have people watching my job sites. I've repeatedly asked for them to be tailed but I'm having an impossible time getting ahold of the Massia actors—"

"We don't have actors in Massia right now, I told you *months* ago," Mina sniped.

"You think I wouldn't remember that? You never once mentioned that to me!"

"I know I told you. I'll find the emails."

"Damnit, Mina. I am constantly watching my back out there, putting my life on the line to get you this scrap. I have a family; did you know that? Kids. Did you ever bother to learn that information about me? I'm not going to rip off a site for your scrap wire just to have the Massia crew disappear when I need them. This is dangerous work I'm doing!"

Squeem piped up. "We can reinstate Massia; you are important to us and we want you to feel protected."

Bana rolled her head back with a joyless laugh, "This honestly hurts, Squeem. Because I believe in this cause. I've always felt good about being a part of it. But I'm not throwing myself and my children in the fire anymore, not for you, Mina. I believe in the cause, but I don't believe you can lead us anymore."

Mina was rolling her sleeves up, ready for a fight. "You've *got* to be kidding me! How much of a coward are you? All because people are 'watching your job sites'? Fucking pathetic. If you would have paid attention to my correspondence, you would have known to contact us directly and not your precious Massia crew."

Bana shook her head. "Your disrespect doesn't even shock me anymore. Come on Mina, you've become lazy. You're held up here in Frasier with your little office and your joyride killing and your fucking Viadin addiction. Good luck finding someone else to provide your wire. You've burnt this bridge to a fucking crisp. I'm done."

With that, Bana was clicking her heels right out the glossy front doors. Mina had the gall to throw a half-full styro of hot rootbrew in her direction, spraying at her feet. Bana ignored her and the door slammed shut in her wake.

Silence.

I was too afraid to look at anyone. Mina marched to the counter and shoved Matey's deskscreen onto the floor with an angry growl. Matey's chair spun as she cleared away.

Squeem's voice rose over the clatter, "She came here to ask for help, and left *quitting*! She is never coming back!"

"Good, we don't need her." Mina hunched over, squeezing her thighs with red hands.

"Yes, we do! That woman oversaw every corporate renovation site in the entire city of Suradelphia. Every bit of wire we use comes from Bana Vastro. That is *gone* now." His cane punched the floor as he walked over to her. He could have been her sibling, with the pink flesh and angular nose. "And I know what you're going to do. You're going to put it all on me to fix this situation. And I will, because I don't have much of a choice, do I?"

Mina puffed up to speak, but he cut her off.

"So, I'll sit down and shut up and do my job in my dark fucking office while you lounge about and throw things. But I need you to understand that *YOU* fucked this up, Mina." He jammed a finger into her chest. "This one is *all on you.* Bana isn't wrong when she says you've gotten lazy."

"Oh, fuck you, Squeem!" Mina yelled, towering over him. Her ears burned red, poking out of her copper hair.

"What are you going to do, kill me?" he taunted. "Yeah, great idea, Mina. I'm sure that'd make your life so much easier."

Squeem stalked out of the room, back to his dark office.

10

FOUL BULLIES

A soft ringing sound woke me from a restless sleep. A square of white light glowed in the dark dorm. I stumbled from my bed to shut it up.

Please see Doctor Harker in his office immediately.

I tapped my finger on the screen and grumbled.

Riolyn was still sleeping when I hit the halls. The cave was quiet. A few students chattered in the breakfast room, but the halls were cold and abandoned. I skipped around, scraping my fingers along the walls and dancing as I hummed to myself.

I'd maintain eye contact. Ask George about his trip. If I played it cool, maybe I'd get away with walking in on Seth's bizarre ritual. I mean, maybe he just wanted to tell me about his travels? Yeah, right.

I knocked on the doctor's office door after climbing every stair in the damn building.

George motioned me into the room. "Sit."

I sat, out of breath, and tried to assess his mood. My father was at his desk with his head in his hands, fingers combing through his red hair.

"How was the trip?"

White teeth gleamed in a joyless smile. "Not well in the slightest. My business partner has put our entire operation in minor peril. Alas, their irresponsibility continues to surprise me. It seems I have no control over my employees." He unclenched his fists, stretching his long fingers.

I had a hunch who he was talking about, but didn't dare say the words.

"I looked forward to being back here. Voltenstraus is a place of comfort for me, and until very recently I had a meaningful amount of control here. *Sometimes*, I enjoy when my ventures go according to plan. And yet," George seared me with eye contact, "since I've gotten back, Mr. Mace has refused to come to our therapy sessions."

A little rumble of nerves rolled around in my stomach.

The good doctor smelled my fear. "And I have an inkling that it has something to do with you."

I stared at him, trying to maintain composure. "Huh."

My father mocked me, "*Huh*. Strange. Did anything happen while I was gone? Anything at all?"

"There might have been an uncomfortable moment while you were gone," I said. I knew a lie would be fruitless.

George set his glasses on the table and rubbed at his tired eyes. "Please, tell me what happened."

"I followed him, but—"

"You followed him. Where? When?"

"To some weird room with green water—"

He held his pointer finger up to stop me. His voice climbed from a hiss to a yell, "You mean to tell me that you followed Seth to the fifth floor, through back access hallways, where no student should go?"

George started pacing his office in a fit of madness.

I jumped up. "You're the one who taught me to be like this! To watch people I don't trust, to listen to my intuition, to 'solve the puzzles around me.' Yeah, well, something fucked up is going on with that guy and I'm going to figure it out!"

My father whirled, his breath hot on my face. "And what did you find on the fifth floor? Did it answer all of your questions?"

"No, it didn't answer any of my questions! I had a panic attack! Now get out of my face." I knocked my knuckles against his chest.

George faltered. His tone dared to dip fatherly. "You saw the ritual."

I didn't want to look at him.

"Did you do your thought mapping? Grounding exercises?"

"Kind of hard to ground yourself when you're sliding around in black gunk. What was that?"

My father turned toward the dark fireplace, leaving me to stare at his back. "You are dismantling years of progress, Maysolpheta. And there could be dire consequences for your actions. I cannot allow this to continue." He opened his office door. "Go wait outside Benjamin's office; I need to speak to him."

George adjusted his tidy, plaid sport coat. "He is in charge of discipline, and I don't have time to deal with you."

My ears strained against sounds reverberating through the cave as I tried to hear the muffled conversation in Benjamin's office. I was sweating through the armpits of my neon orange jacket. Sure, I acted like a lawless punk-bandit around people my own age, but let's be honest: I hated disappointing people. My father, the one I looked up to most, was definitely disappointed in me. Now this Benjamin guy would be, too.

According to my father, Benjamin was a "wishy-washy, incompetent dullard." So, if I played it cool with him—

The office door opened and there stood the man himself; a bland, middle-aged man who could be anyone's sad uncle. He wore brown from head to toe. Thick glasses shelled exhausted eyes. Too much time in the cave had given his skin a sallow sheen. The man exuded joylessness.

Benjamin's office was strikingly different to my father's: light colors and not an ounce of velvet. A fake picture window took up most of the back wall, revealing a serene beach, complete with shingled palms and sitting stones.

"Nice," I nodded to the window. I sat across from him.

"Thank you. I don't like caves." Benjamin was shuffling through a cabinet. "Doctor Harker filled me in." Benjamin pulled out a folder full of papers and a chipcase. He inserted the chip into his screen. "Seems you're a headache for him."

I sneered. "He's always loved that about me."

Benjamin agreed absentmindedly as he scrolled.

"What's it say about me on there?" I leaned forward, lifting an eyebrow. "Does it mention my curious nature? Spirited creativity? What about marvelous good looks?"

"I'm not sure what you are trying to do, but please stop," Benjamin sighed, still scrolling.

I rolled my eyes, absolutely thrilled. Anyone who preferred a placid beach to this magnificent, ancient cave-dwelling was beyond my help. I sat there in his mediocre office and moped.

"I see your father in you, which must be why you're so hard for him to control."

This took me back a bit. "I don't think he wants to control me."

"I'm sure he'd say the same," Benjamin mumbled as he pulled sheets from my file. He placed a beautiful paper, embossed in green and gold, before me. Something I hadn't seen in years; something filed away and forgotten. Something I didn't allow myself to think about.

My body slid back in the chair, as far from the desk as I could get.

"So, Miss Harker. Seth Mace isn't one to mess with. Frankly, Seth shouldn't be at Voltenstraus in the first place. But that decision is not up to me. No, that would be Doctor Harker, who wants me to punish you. No one wants to hear my opinion on the matter."

Benjamin's annoyance was not missed as he read over my Limits Registration.

"I think you are bored and need a new challenge. You wouldn't heed my punishment even if I tried. Instead, you will be enrolled in Limits lessons."

Heat burned my cheeks. I let my chin drop to my chest to hide the wetness in my eyes.

"You are a Palm Lifter and should be honing that gift. It's shocking to me that you aren't already."

The gold edges of the page distorted to glistening blurs "I don't think..." I started, but my trembling teeth stopped me.

"Whatever you might think doesn't apply here. Every Saturday morning, you will meet with the other Limits students. Three hours with Vice Advisory Varali Garima and the others for the rest of your time here. I will notify her today and she will send you the important information."

He stood and went to the door. I swiped a tissue from his desk and turned away, blotting my face. The sun rose over the faux beach on the wall.

Benjamin stopped me at the door before I could escape. "This will be good for you. Now, please, go enjoy your Sunday, and stop breaking every rule you come in contact with. I will have to punish you next time."

Drucilla Laverick — excuse me, *Madame Adord* — swished around the auditorium stage, barking orders at her assistant.

Riolyn leaned over to whisper. "No sign of the beast yet."

I nodded, eyes glued forward.

Drucilla had noticed too; she glanced in the direction of Seth's empty seat with frown lines cutting her forehead.

My mind wandered to home as Drucilla snapped at a student tapping their pen on the desk. In just a few days, I would be forced to sit in a room full of Limits kids and pretend I was one of them. Nathali would be there, whispering loving phrases to the dust mites. Would Drucilla be there? She was a Limit, with her magical hand waving. Firewalkers could do that, I guess. Shut doors with their hands.

Palm Lifters — the real ones — could lift disease from someone's blood. They could heal sickness and stitch bones back together. Could I do that? Fuck no.

"Miss Harker!"

I shot up straight in my chair. "Sorry, what?"

"*I said*," Drucilla's lips curls in distaste. "Please tell the class the location of the Sanguine Road."

"Ah. Well, uh. The Sanguine Road? It's the Gate — the closed gate — between Develtic, and, oh, I know this," I stuttered, searching for the words.

"If you cannot pay attention in class, you will be *removed*. I have heard great things about you, Miss Harker, and I am waiting to be impressed. The Sanguine Road connected Develtic and Ahk. Who can tell me when this Supernal gate was closed?"

Riolyn gave me a sidelong look. My face grew hot as I shrugged.

That evening in the dining hall, Riolyn spoke with her mouth full. "Dude, some of these people really don't like you."

"What, me? People love me!" Aeshra shrieked with a hand pressed to his chest. Purple glitter sparkled in his hair.

"Obviously not you." I gave him a shove. "Drucilla came for me in class today. Said she was '*Waiting to be impressed.*'"

"Don't worry about Drucilla Laverick," Saren replied. "She doesn't like anyone."

"That's the truth!" Aeshra laughed, stretching his long legs out before him and touching his toes.

"She loves creepy Mr. Mace."

"Of course she does; Seth is special. He's strange and different and *'full of potential,'* as she would say. Don't take it personally. I guarantee Drucilla will verbally abuse every student in your class before Veishrin," said Saren.

Riolyn swallowed a mouthful and raised her eyebrows at Saren. "Seth wasn't in our Old-World Fables class today. You okay with that?"

"Nothing to worry about. He misses class sometimes."

My voice raised over the dining hall clatter, "Ok but, who else gets to skip whenever they want? Why does he get days off?"

"I am not at liberty to say," Saren said, with an air of mystery, as he finished his cream-filled londi roll in one bite.

An unsympathetic thunderstorm pounded beyond the cave for three days straight. Deep, rumbling thunder echoed through the school. Every bolt of lightning ignited our dorm's paphador wall with an eerie blue flash. Even with the black curtains drawn, the flares of light kept me up. Riolyn, naturally, had no problem sleeping.

The night before my first Limits class, in shallow moments of sleep, I had strange dreams. I dreamt of iridescent, greenish rivers gliding their way through hollow spaces in the sky; the sweet scent of frasiora fern wafting through the darkness; a soft tug between inner peace and despair; a thick, black liquid dripping in big spots onto my palms. And a man, somewhat like me, but older and quieter and stricken by an overwhelming guilt.

I woke with tears in my eyes, without knowing why.

The rain poured in waves over the grey lake, pounding on the clifftop above. Nessa was entering the rainy season, but this rain was so different from the thunderstorms of home.

"Here I go, my first lesson in how to save the world," I harmonized from the bathroom, dragging eyeliner on my lids. Acid green everything, just the way I like it.

Riolyn rolled her eyes, watching me from her desk chair. "I can't tell if you're being sarcastic or not. Do you actually have an ability?"

"No. I mean, I've got one, but I can't use it. Tried a few times as a kid and it didn't go well, if you know what I mean."

"No, I don't," my roommate glared at me with cold, reptilian eyes.

"It just wasn't for me, I guess."

Riolyn sunk into silence, watching me. A pan of lime eyeshadow fumbled in my fingers and broke apart in the sink.

"You seem agitated now."

"Dude, no. I just — look, I'm running so late. Can't skip breakfast or I'll be a wreck later."

I tripped out the door, still trying to lace my combat boots.

I set my breakfast dish at a table with a loud clank. Mieda's face shot up, pinching with annoyance at the sight of me. She was curled into the defined chest of a man with dark hair. It had to be her fabled boyfriend.

But when the man set his eyes on me, I just about disintegrated into the air. It was the guy Seth had kicked in the stomach on the tram; Seth Mace's damn brother.

"Can I help you?" Mieda snapped, pulling on a ringlet of her strawberry curls.

I pretended to not be utterly horrified. "Is this the boyfriend? Nice to meet you."

I held out my hand in a satirical greeting and he took it. He was built for running, jumping, climbing; a little underwhelming in originality, but he made up for it with exquisite, narrow, golden eyes and full, coral lips against grey flesh. He wore a close-knit sweater and his hair was thoughtfully unkempt.

And that smile, *wow*. Mieda knew what she was doing.

"My name is Donnie. I believe we've already met, in a way," he smiled crookedly. Sadness tugged on his upper lip.

"Yes, Mayli is one of many family embarrassments," Mieda said, waving me off. "I'm trying to maintain a wee bit of harmony here, May."

Donnie smiled again. "It's alright, she was just standing her ground. We can move on from it."

"If you would quit starting fights with innocent bystanders, we'd be fine. There are so many other questionable things you can do."

I rolled my eyes. "Oh please, you fight with anyone you can. You love an argument."

"This isn't an argument we are talking about!" Mieda cut me off, voice rising. Other students shifted their eyes to the table. "You are overstepping boundaries because of your self-absorbed, inconsiderate moral compass. Work on your *schoolwork*, sharpen your *throwing knives*, question the powers that be! I don't know. Just stop harassing people!"

Donnie ever-so-gently put his hand on Mieda's back and whispered, "Dear, I think she has had enough verbal whipping."

Mieda held her breath and glanced around the room. Anger was red on her dewy, flushed cheeks.

"So, self-absorbed, inconsiderate moral compass, huh? Damn." I chuckled, scratching my neck.

"I'm sick of being the family maid. Quit making messes that I have to clean up."

Donnie brushed Mieda's curls out of her face so she'd stop fidgeting with them. Mieda's round eyes gazed up at her magnetic, graceful boyfriend through her lashes. The lovers breathed at each other in romantic-comedy-level synthesis. It was nice to see Mieda with someone that evened her out. Such a shame that he was the brother of my nemesis.

I pushed Voltenstraus' ancient, metal door open and stepped into a wall of sound. Wind from the storm sprayed mist over my face. With an involuntary twitch, I flung myself back against the cave wall, pulling my jacket up to shield myself. I heaved forward along the stone. Limits class was out here?

I felt along, unseeing, and slow-motion collided with a person.

Was it a person? She practically absorbed my shockwaves, like velvet foam against my body. Long whips of braided black hair whirled around us, brushing my face. She seemed like an unfathomable, luminescent shadow-being.

I pried my eyes out of the protective jacket to see.

She took a deep breath. Her black skin flushed deep scarlet. Her glossy cheekbones caught the light that filtered through the waterfall above us. Her eyes, her glowing pale eyes, stopped on mine. And then she turned away without a word, her delicately beaded, black jacket swaying with her steps.

Standing there like a dumb brick, I watched her place her hand on a small, wooden door in the side of the cliff. The door vibrated with a sonorous tone and opened. The girl disappeared inside, enveloped by the soft turquoise light of paphador.

The door was holey with wood rot, slick and coated with fungus and dark moss. The center of the door repelled water in a hand-like shape. The word *limits* hid in the curves of the soft wood.

I placed my hand where so many others had and immediately felt an electrifying vibration sweep through my body. The low, lovely tone followed and the door opened for me.

I smirked to myself, letting myself be swept up in emotion. Hopefully, they wouldn't kick me out too soon.

As I stepped beyond the door, I was bathed in paphador light. I followed the claustrophobically close path. The rock walls of grey stone and paphador were worn smooth at my height, sharper and more jagged above. I skidded past streams of rainwater that trickled down the walls, gurgling into mossy floor grates below.

Subtle curves arched into a cavernous room. Light bounced around the room by a series of mirrors and sun tunnels. Strips of green paphador veined the polished walls. Charts and beautifully drawn diagrams hung from the walls, covering subjects from light-casting to gem-dusting to plant identification. Quiet chimes echoed through the room. The ambiance was beautiful, almost ironically so. I couldn't help but laugh at the over-the-top mood of the place. I thought I was here to learn to harness my inner power, not relax myself into a mystical, dreamless sleep.

"You think you're in the wrong place?" a voice called to me.

I stepped into the room and lifted my Limits class sheet for all to see. "I don't know, I have this paper with directions to get here. Weird, huh?"

They didn't skip a beat. "Ok, but classes are already weeks in, so why are you just showing up?" The person talking at me had pale blue flesh and way too many arms; a Nian, and combative, to say the least.

"Benjamin gave me this class as a punishment, and now I can see why."

"May?" Nathali bounded into the room and wrapped a hand around my arm. "What's up?"

"Students, please." Varali Garima swept over. Her magenta slippers tapped against the floor. "Mayli has joined us late, but we will welcome her because we embody unity in this class."

The Nian scoffed, their extra arms resting lazily about their head. "She's just as bad as the Ghost."

"Sheirsh, enough. I will not tolerate that sort of talk, and I *won't* remind you again."

Nathali pulled me onto the floor with her and gushed, "Did dad set this up?"

I laughed. "No, I don't think he even knows. Benjamin enrolled me. Said I was getting in trouble because I was bored."

"So, he's not as dumb as Dad thinks he is." She sat back onto a floor cushion and wrapped her hand around my wrist, holding onto like I'd slip away. "Speaking of Dad..."

"Yeah. He's going to lose it."

"Did you — tell Benjamin?"

"Tell him what, exactly? What was I supposed to say? *Hey, Benny boy, turns out I'm a fraud, so let's not waste everyone's time.*"

My twin groaned and rolled onto her side. More students streamed in from the archway. Raindrops clung to the edge of the stone, falling in quiet trickles onto the grated floor outside. The warm smell of incense was dampened by the rain.

Nathali's pearly fingernails walked along my knuckles. She scraped a nail across the buildup of purpled, dead skin. A dry, white line was left behind. She turned my hand over and examined my palm.

"You're right, there's nothing to tell. Dad's reasoning never made much sense to me, anyway."

Varali sat front and center on a thin cushion, tapping on a metal plate with a pen. Students sat on the floor around us, quiet in the cavernous room.

"Mayli, dear, welcome to Limits lessons. You round the class out to ten, which makes partnering much easier. We're glad to have you," the Vice Advisory smiled. "We have an array of abilities in this class. I myself am a Fire-Walker and Suntap. As you get to know the others, you will learn about the energies within all of us, and how those energies manifest different outcomes. But first, we must learn to access that energy. I assume you don't have experience in this?"

Murmurs shifted through the class as I shook my head *no*.

"Very well, that is where we begin every class, and today is no different. I will lead the *dwam*," Varali dimmed the lights with a wave of her clawed hand.

We were told to lie on our backs. I settled onto the woven rug beside my sister. Blue paphador reflected in her eyes as she squeezed my hand.

"Pick a spot on the ceiling and focus your eyes. Notice the texture of the rock above. How would it feel to run your hand along it? Would it be smooth? Jagged? Would the cracks run deep, or shallow like the veins of a young tree?"

Deep.

"Breathe deeply. Open your lungs. Would your spot of stone feel cold or very hot? Wet or dry? If you scraped it with metal, would the rock crumble? Turn to sand? Or would it form lines of a drawing? What shape would you draw?"

Circle.

A distant crack of thunder pulsed the paphador lighting. Sounds of rain seemed to grow louder from my spot on the floor. Was the person near the door getting wet? I tipped my head up to look — the doorway was far away. No one was over there. No one was wet. I wasn't wet.

My eyes caught Varali Garima. She sat perched like a cat surveying her domain, ears flicking with interest. She was looking right at me.

"Is your spot of stone porous? If you painted it, would the pigment seep in? Would it lay on the surface and drip onto the floor? What color would you choose?"

Red.

"Now, close your eyes. What do you feel in your fingers, your toes? Are they cold, like the grey lake outside? Are your fingers hot, like the flame of a candle?"

Cold.

"Feel your energy in the tips of your toes and fingers. You might not feel it yet, but it's there. Imagining is the next best thing."

I forced my eyes to shut and squeezed them tightly. My internal organs moved up and down with each breath; My brain opened and tightly packed secrets floated to the surface.

Breathe, breathe, breathe. It wasn't a big deal.

"Your arms and legs should be straight but loose at the joints. Keep breathing deeply, slowly."

I tried to imagine something, anything, going on in my toes and fingers. What would this energy feel like? Tingling? A dull pulse? Vibration? Maybe just warmth. If I tried, I could feel it; a singeing, slow burn of delicate power in my fingers. My toes didn't feel anything, but my fingers? Yeah, maybe there was something there.

"Follow your body's whims. Do you need to cross your feet at the ankles? Place your hands on your belly? Be loose and flexible. Release the tension in your shoulders. Let the energy move through you if it wants to. No need to control your power just yet."

I looked around at what the class was doing. They were practically breathing in unison. Was I a part of a cult, now?

"Deep breaths. Know your power. Feel it pool at the base of your skull."

I audibly gasped. I could feel it; energy building on the back of my neck. It was hot, like there was a candle burning an inch away.

I could feel the student next to me glance over and I looked at them too, flushing with embarrassment at my verbal response. The soft, black fur on their nose twisted into patterns of gold on sharp cheekbones. They looked away as quickly as I did.

On the other side of me laid the equally stunning girl I'd collided with before class. Her eyes rested closed like she was sleeping. Something about her was indefinably different.

"Toes, flex and spread; fingers, flex and spread. Deep breath. Relax and see your energy move through your joints, flowing like pure lights in the tips of your fingers, toes, and base of the skull. What color is your energy?" Varali was silent for a few seconds. Then: "Feel the light of your energy in your spine. Feel it in your pelvis, in your elbows. Everywhere."

I closed my eyes and saw this energy in my body, fluent and red hot; broiling steam nipping at my hands. And I felt it in my *palms*, burning in the most pleasant way possible.

I'd never been able to get there before. I'd only experienced my own internal power once, and it had been a disaster. But here I was, the very first day of Limits class, and it was coursing through me like it was dying to get out. Like it had always been there, just under the surface. If only I'd listened for it.

Riolyn and Aeshra met me on the pale, rocky shore of the lake after class. The heavy clouds drifted over the red sun as my boots sunk into the soggy gravel path. Puddles formed in low spots around us. I pulled my plastic hood down over my brows.

"You still up for heading into town?" Aeshra bounced at the chance for an excursion.

I nodded, shifting from foot to foot. "I didn't get any cash from my dad though."

Aeshra laughed, sprinting toward the port in the pouring rain, "I doubt you'll need cash; your dad practically owns this place!"

"*That's* embarrassing," I grumbled, following behind.

A few of the Limits kids stepped onto the boat behind us, including the glorious Baskian with black and gold fur. Shivers rocketed through my chest.

We stowed away in a three-seater in the boat's main compartment.

"How was your class?" Riolyn asked. Her wet raincoat squeaked against the plastic bench.

I used two fingers to pry the wet jacket off and shook it with an outstretched arm. Water flew and dripped in great drops. "Strange. Incredible. I don't know."

A horn sounded, and the ferry swerved away from the dock. Water sloshed up, splashing our window.

"So, you hated it?"

"Obviously she didn't *hate* it, Ry. I'm honestly so jealous." Aeshra's pointy teeth poked at his bottom lip as he grinned. He relaxed back with his hands behind his head, "I mean, you have power! I *wish*."

I held back a smile. "Yeah, I guess. I felt the energy for the first time today."

He gasped and squealed with excitement.

"How many kids are in the class?" Riolyn tipped into the center aisle and shook the rain from her hair. It stuck up in every direction.

Counting my fingers, I responded, "Ten, with me," then, lowering my voice, "Some of them are on the boat with us." I nodded around to the Baske kid, the two blue Nian twins, one of whom had said I was "as bad as the ghost" in class, and a Vauveric boy who hung his arms out the open window, feeling the rain. The wetness dotted his hands. I twitched.

Aeshra had no shame. "Yeah, I know most of them! Hey Corin, Uyentra!"

"Which one is which?" I whispered to Aeshra.

He laughed loud enough for anyone to hear, "Corin is the pale one. Uyentra is the cat."

I nodded, internalizing a scream as Uyentra, beautiful black and gold Uyentra, smiled at me. It felt like my uterus had been unzipped and joyous little bells danced within.

Nepa rose on the shore, waves licking the sides of the ferry as we inched closer. The coastal town was shrouded in rain. Pillars of green paphador peeked along the shore in ghostly lines. The ferry hit the dock with a soft bounce.

Riolyn stepped off the boat first, pulling me up with her. Aeshra jumped off, running and laughing. We chased him down the boardwalk like kids on a field trip. My combat boots slid on the wet wood and I tumbled onto shore on my hands and knees. The panic welled up — the water on my hands, on my clothes—

A hand descended, offering to pull me up. Long, gold-painted nails grew from stark black fingers. Uyentra stood over me, tall and imposing.

"Your outfit is lovely," they said as they pulled me up.

I stood there speechless, looking down at my splotchy, acid green dress, as Uyentra walked off. Rain pelted at their back. I grounded myself, then took off running after my friends.

My friends.

We ran through the streets of Nepa, Aeshra twirling and stomping in puddles.

Skidding into a little diner with a view of the port, we sat down to get some lunch. The place was called Caster's. A waiter made his way to us, scowling when he saw Aeshra at the table. He was short, stocky, with large hands and glasses.

Aeshra greeted him with a mischievous tone. "Hey, Roz."

Roz set down some water glasses. "I'd hoped it was Saren, he owes me some grass." Then he added reluctantly, "Who are your friends?"

Riolyn ignored him, looking over the menu, but I nodded at the waiter. "I'm Mayli, this is Riolyn."

"They're new this year! Riolyn is my cousin, Mayli is *George Harker's* daughter," Aeshra explained with a glint in his eye.

Roz's expression changed a bit. "Oh, nice to meet you. Are you the twin?"

I scoffed, "I am. Have you already met the other one?"

Nodding, Roz tried to hide a smile. "Nathali has been in town every weekend so far. She's fun."

"Wow, yeah, *fun*. I wouldn't know fun if it hit me in the face."

"False!" Aeshra shrieked, "Mayli is so much fun. She really is."

"Are we going to order food or what?" Riolyn peered at us over her menu.

Halfway through our lunch, Saren entered the diner. He had dirt under his fingernails and on his shirt. He joined us at our table. Roz came over and opened his hand out like he expected Saren to drop something in it.

"Alright, alright," Saren said as he pulled a little bag from his pants pocket. "You *could* just grow it yourself."

Roz snatched the bag out of his hands and pulled it open to sniff. The smell of spitgrass wafted over the table.

Saren waved Roz off, something about a *bad influence,* and said to the table, "I've been up at the greenhouse with Seth."

Riolyn and I glanced at each other.

She smacked her menu down on the table. "Why are you hanging out with that Seth guy? He's a tramp."

Saren sighed, "Seth is not the Devil. He's a fine guy if you like slow, intense conversation. Which I do. If you start putting in the work now, you might get to know him within the next ten years."

Roz set plates of food in front of us.

"So, why is everyone so terrified of him?" I asked, swirling a fork through my rootmash.

The cook started to answer, but Saren shook his head.

"Seth's done some stuff in the past, and you know how people are! They can't get over anything. Once you make a bad impression, it's hard to move on," Aeshra answered, "What — did I say too much?

Saren shook his head and sighed again. "No, you're right. Seth is just misunderstood."

There was a party at an abandoned house on the beach. Aeshra said he *"Wasn't one to deny getting shitfaced."* So Riolyn and I sat outside and growled at people as they walked in. It wasn't a great way to make friends, but it *was* a great way to maintain our social-outcast labels.

We ended the night by burning some stuff out on the misty street in front of the party; Riolyn's idea. She sat on the wet ground next to the fire, while I hovered on a patch of concrete.

Riolyn stared into the fire and said, "I think I'm going to seduce Valentine."

Saren choked on his spitgrass. "Your teacher?"

"Yeah, of course our teacher. She's my ideal woman, I've decided."

The outspoken Nian kid from my Limits class flipped Riolyn off as she shot them with an imaginary shotgun. Riolyn sneered. "Fuck, I want to burn this place to the ground some days."

After weeks of his absence, I was shocked to find Seth Mace sitting at the back of Post-Gate Rebellions class. Drucilla doted on him, giving him extra time to settle in before she started class. The uncomfortable feeling emanating from him thrummed at the back of my skull, in the same place where I'd first felt my energy. Was that a coincidence? Hell fucking no, it wasn't.

We were still focused on the opening of the Supernal Gates. But when the class shifted into a tangential discussion of the Nepatin species, Drucilla tried to reel her students in with a line of ethics questions. Things devolved quickly after that.

"The Undergods were wrong to allow experimental species," Corin Verner said from the front of the class. He was a Limits kid; Vauveric, with rose-colored skin like mine, and dark hair coifed into fashionable waves.

"And why do you think that?" Drucilla asked.

"Without the lab-races, we would have avoided our cultures' biggest wars. The Nepatin species are the sole reason the Develtic layer was cut off from the rest of us."

"*Whoa*," I said from my seat. "Bold statement."

Corin nodded, "Who knows what evil exists there, now."

A tremor shook the room. Students shrieked.

Seth stood at the top of the auditorium, stance wide and ready for a fight. "We don't know *anything* about what happened to the Nepatin people."

Corin raised his waxed brows. "Really, Seth? Because I have seen the library shelf, and it's full. Maybe *you* don't know, but the rest of us do."

"Now, students," Drucilla held her hands up to the class.

"You weren't there, you don't know—" Seth's fists clenched at his sides, grey little balls of fury.

"Oh, and you were?" Corin spat from his seat. "Or did Idrissa tell you all the secrets of the Endless World? Mess knows sae gives you everything you want."

Students gasped. The paphador light fixture shuddered over Drucilla. She shouted, red-faced, at Corin to sit down. Seth was shoving books into this backpack and leaving. At the door, everyone watching him, Seth turned to look into the room. His eyes shot right to me. His nostrils flared and then he was gone.

But Drucilla wasn't.

"Mayli Harker, what do you have to say for yourself?"

I shuddered, "Wha — what?"

"Two class periods in a row now that you've refused to partake in discussion. I can only assume you've not done any of the readings and therefore have nothing to add. But, when the class enter into an argument, you place yourself *front and center*! So, what do you have to say for yourself?"

Shaking my head, dumbfounded, I tried to reply, "I'm sorry, what does this have to do with me?"

Riolyn leaned forward, muscles flexed, staring daggers at Drucilla.

"Detention, now. Both of you. Tell your father that I won't have you disrupting my class any longer. He can deal with your insubordination."

I looked at Riolyn, shocked and confused. "What the hell did we do?"

Drucilla started yelling, throwing the doors open behind us. "Go! You have one minute to get out of my classroom before I have you forcibly removed. Get out!"

We flew from the room with our classwork in hand and raced up the stairs to Doctor Harker's office.

I banged on his door and it squeaked open, revealing an empty office. The double doors at the back of the room were ajar.

I sat my bag on his desk, "I think that's his living quarters. Haven't actually checked it out."

Riolyn nodded. "Saren's room is behind his office too. I haven't seen it. Should you go back there, or should we just leave?"

"You think Drucilla is going to stomp up here after class to see to it that we're properly punished?"

Scoffing, Riolyn shrugged.

The doctor's voice drifted through the doors, "I'm not sure what more we can do that we haven't tried already."

"You don't understand!" a brittle cry interrupted him. "It's getting worse every day. I'm not going to be able to hold it in."

The doors opened. Seth Mace stood in the doorway with my father. Seth's eyes were wide and wild. He stiffened like a dead tree at the sight of us.

I flung my head back and howled, "Oh my *god*, this is tiring."

Seth punched the wooden frame before storming back through doors and slamming them shut behind him.

My father took a deep breath and tugged off his glasses to wipe his eyes. He leaned back on the doors in utter exhaustion.

"This is proving to be much harder than I anticipated."

George sat on his desktop, all pretense of proper decorum gone. He untied his bowtie and draped it over his shoulder before undoing his shirt's top button.

"Ok, I'll start," I said. "We literally did nothing, and Drucilla sent us up here for detention."

"Oh, Mayli." My father squeezed the bridge of his nose. "Tell me more about this *nothing* you did."

Riolyn answered, "It's true, Mister, uh — sir. Seth was arguing with Corin Verner in class. He made eye contact with us, that's it. And Drucilla blamed it on us."

A loud crash came from behind the double doors and we all jumped. The doctor sighed, "Oh my, wonder what he's destroyed now."

"Why is he in your room?" Riolyn asked.

George sifted through a pile of thin papers on his desk with lazy hands, "Seth lives with Idrissa, and our quarters are connected. Benjamin's rooms are back there as well. Quite a happy family we are."

I said, "I didn't know you *lived* with him!"

"No, no. We stick to our separate areas. Benjamin in his sad little closet of a room, I in mine, and Idrissa and Seth in theirs. A student named Moonie lives with them as well."

A thump of angry knocking sounded for the doctor's door. When he opened it, his jaw set into a hard clench.

"Madame Adord, to what do I owe this visit?"

Drucilla snarled, "You are looking rather casual." She peaked her head around the door and narrowed her eyes. "Are you undressing in front of students now?"

"No, I am not, but thank you for your concern."

Drucilla took up the center of the office as she stomped and whirled, "Once again, your vast inability to remain unbiased has revealed itself. I sent these two nuisances to you for punishment and," she looked us over with revulsion, "I see they are receiving no such thing. When will you begin doing your job? Obviously, your self-interest knows no bounds."

"My dear Madam Adord," Doctor Harker's voice dripped with sarcasm, "I only just began talking to these two *nuisances* because I was preoccupied with another certain student whose concerns dominate all others."

"And do you know what provoked him into such unease?"

"I have a feeling you're going to tell me."

"Because your daughter and her little friend love nothing more than harassing their classmates. They are foul bullies, and it must stop!"

"Come on, now," I said. Both Drucilla and Doctor Harker threw a flat, halting hand up as they glared daggers at each other.

Drucilla's long skirt billowed as she cut through the room to the door, "Deal with this, George Harker. Or I *will*."

As Drucilla left, my father stooped over to his man-sized fireplace to gaze at my mother's portrait. He stared at it a long while. Riolyn and I attempted to converse through facial expressions.

"I don't want to believe that you are — what did she say? Foul bullies? But I do think you are swimming into some very dark waters."

"Dude we literally did *nothing* today. I mean, we're not perfect, but that woman has got it out for us."

"I have no doubt Drucilla dislikes you. *That woman* has a startling amount of blackmail on me; she's been holding onto it for some time, just waiting for the perfect moment. I'm sure she has something on us all. But, that's beside the point."

He knelt down in front of my chair and pleaded, "Mayli, this is serious. Not Drucilla, not the blackmail. Seth. Remember what I said? Leave Seth alone. *Leave it alone*."

We got off without detention, but Doctor Harker's stark warning was enough. I had seen the honesty in him; I'd felt his exhaustion, his unease. It made me feel uneasy too.

So, in the turquoise glow of our cave dorm room, Riolyn and I vowed to forget Seth Mace existed. If others mentioned him, our ears would close. If we saw him, we'd act like he wasn't there. If our eyes met, we'd look right through him.

I was a good actress, and now seemed like a good time to prove it.

11

NIGHT, DAY, GREY

Mina threw herself against Fruit, pounding her fists against his chest. "Give me the list, Fruit! Do it now!"

He placed one big hand up to stop her. "No. You're not you."

I scrambled back to avoid her blows, wedging myself in the corner of Fruit's office. The killer's eyes were bloodshot. She slammed her hands onto the desk. The smell of burnt Viadin clung to her clothes.

"I'm right here, you *useless coward*!" She clawed at her throat. Great, raw scratches followed her fingernails.

Squeem stumbled in, unsteady without his cane. He wrapped his hands around Mina's arm and pulled her toward the door, "You're not getting the list when you're like this." She smacked him, backhand, across the cheek. Squeem shook it off, eyes wet, but didn't slow. "Please, stop this — you aren't right in the head."

"You are *nothing* to me. Give me the list, now; I won't ask again!"

Fruit's stringy hair waved as he shook his head *no*.

Mina panted, eyes wild as she snarled, "You are going to regret this."

She wheeled out of the parking lot before the three of us caught our breath.

Squeem leaned his head against the office door and said, "This is not good." A palm-sized mark blossomed on his cheek.

By the time our hounding devices found Mina in range, she'd made it to Burr, a suburb of Pwero Ver.

Taro poured four large glasses of the stonefruit cider.

"Mess, she's not even wearing a disguise," Squeem said.

Mina flew down the highway at top speed, swerving around other cars. We watched silently. She drove up onto a median, gouging tire-marks into the flowerbeds, and turned onto a main street.

Matey popped her head in, nerves in her voice, and asked, "What's going on?"

"Mina's high off her ass in the suburbs. We're in for a rough night. You guys should probably close the place down. I don't think we'll be going anywhere for a while." Squeem scratched at the bridge of his nose. His pink skin had taken on a yellow tinge.

The five of us watched as Mina's car squealed into a parking spot in front of a disco bar. She jumped out of the car and across the hood, sliding down it like a carefree, drunken teenager. A line of people stood at the door, waiting to get in. Their glittering costumes flickered in the neon as they scattered like roaches at the sight of the serial killer.

Squeem turned to Matey. "Actually, will you take Devin to your place? He doesn't need to see this."

Matey's apartment was down the street from Fruit and Squeem's. She had a cushy white couch and two cushy white dogs.

As I settled onto her couch, I asked, "How did you lose your eye?"

"That's a rude thing to ask, you know?"

Matey didn't have a black box, so the screen wasn't on all night. But Mina had made quite the spectacle of herself. In the morning, video evidence was splashed on every channel in Besel.

The DAG crew and I watched the news from the conference room at *Boister Energies*.

Mina yelled and howled at walls, at strangers, at the moon. Absolutely deranged. She pushed her way into the neon-lit bar and smashed bottles of alcohol on the dance floor. She threatened terrified partiers with shards of broken glass, waving them in their faces. And when two burly men attempted to jump her, she'd beaten one of them unconscious. She dragged his sleeping body out onto the pavement and erupted to the sky, *"Do you want me to sacrifice him? Is that what you want? Just tell me what you want!"*

"I have never seen such a display of insanity in my life," Taro said into her teacup.

"I have," I grumbled, wringing my hands beneath the table. I had been that pained before, that destroyed. And it landed me on the news as well. Mina's inebriated tailspin was a vicious reminder of days before my trial. When I was so scared and alone that I would settle for whatever drug I could nab.

The news was rife with theories about Mina's breakdown. And the public called for the resignation of the region's Batif Commander. The Batifban had pulled up just as Mina skidded off to the highway. They lost her within minutes. It was all too convenient.

The car was found abandoned on a dirt road, halfway across the country, wiped clean.

When I asked Matey and Taro how she'd gotten home, Taro rolled her eyes. "Squeem would do anything for Mina."

The news interviewed bar patrons, gleefully catching any detail of the horror they survived on their greedy tongues. Because, for the first time in history, there were survivors. Mina had gone of a drunken killing spree, and *no one died*. Was Mina Harker getting soft?

But the news didn't know what I knew. That guy wasn't on the *list*. Mina was too afraid of the Producer to go on a real killing spree. She feared consequences the rest of the world couldn't see.

Good news came on the same day Mina showed back up at work. She acted as though nothing had happened, but her hands were wrapped in bandages and bruises crept up her wrists under her shirtsleeves. She gave us all sugary sweet, mocking smiles as she entered her office and closed the door behind her.

Squeem was still angry with her, so he put off telling Mina the good news until the absolute last minute.

"I think I've found someone to take over Bana's job."

"Who?" Mina checked over her bandaged knuckles, avoiding Squeem's eyes.

"His name is Merchant. He worked with Bana a few times. Owns a bank and the majority of stock in a construction company out of Lansche; he's trustworthy, according to the Sarif crew. Likes his stacks thick and constant." Squeem couldn't hide his excitement.

Irritation on Mina's tongue, she replied, "So, we have to pay him. I'm not looking for a hired thug. We've been down that road before."

He tossed his hands into the air. "I'm doing the best that I can here! I'm not the one who royally fucked us, remember? That was *you.*"

"Fine, interview this Merchant person," Mina started to push the back door open but Squeem stopped her again.

"Also, Bana Vastro wants protection, or, preferably, relocation."

Mina wheeled around, smacking one of her banged up hands on the door frame. She yelped in pain, "Fuck, I'm not some babysitter! She left us!"

"People are driving by her house and watching her drop her kids off at school. Come on, Mina. Think of the children."

"And where does she expect us to move her?"

"She asked to relocate her family to Brunock Island."

"Oh, for Mess sake! We don't even have a theater there!"

"She wants a break from DAG work, and I don't blame her! Come on. Do you really want Bana Vastro to get nabbed and tortured for information? She hates you so much now, I guarantee she'd fold easy. So, can I send the request?"

"Fine, Mess, do whatever you want. I don't care. Move Bana and her entire neighborhood. To Brunock Island, good gods. For the children."

That evening, when Mina and I got back to 240 Arm, there was a stack of letters in Mina's mailbox.

When I set the letters on the table, I caught sight of two strange postage addresses; two with the address Forty Mark Ten MV, and three with the address Forty-Two Mark Nineteen V. I'd never seen anything like them. Mina impulsively ripped up both of the Forty Mark Ten letters, then sat on the floor and taped the pieces back together.

I was banished to the couch when she caught me peeking over her shoulder.

While my coworkers dined at the local Turrisian spot in Frasier, I clicked around on the main computer between bites of cold soup. I'd seen Fruit do enough to fumble my way around the hounding program without breaking the thing. With a full view of the restaurant and Boister enterances on screen, I could snoop freely until the crew got back.

First, Tenor Rubark. He was at work, if today was like every weekday, so it was a good test run. The cameras showed his car and the side entrance at Macton Corp.

Next, I typed in Squeem.

There he was, a strange little thumbnail of him with long bangs waxed into thin points on his forehead, too-big glasses and the same sickly yellow-pink he'd been when Mina had her public meltdown. He looked much younger and very under-the-influence.

Name: Merscha Rodag'riel, Stage name: Squeem, Age: 35, Species: Vauveric, Job title: Lead Set Designer, Actor, Theater: Frasier, Clearance level: 9

The humble, kind inventor, creating devious devices for his murderous overlord.

Next, I typed in Fruit.

Name: Fruit, Stage name: Fruit, Age: 35, Species: Vauveric, Job title: Lead Spotlight Operator, Theater: Frasier, Clearance level: 9

I wondered if Fruit and Squeem had always been a package deal.

Name: Taro Leifer, Stage name: Rhonnia, Age: 48, Species: Darkling, Noxte clan, Job title: Actor, Stage Manager, Theater: Frasier, Clearance level: 8

Name: Matsil Valentine, Stage name: Matey, Age: 40, Species: Dedocian, Job title: Physician, Box Office Attendant, Theater: Frasier, Clearance level: 8

Name: Mina Urchin Bindi Sulfana Harker, Stage name: Mina, Age: 33, Species: Vauveric and Eivian, Job title: Director, Theater: Frasier, Clearance level: 11

Name: Devin Alo-Ellosa Cemet Mace, Stage name: Devin Age: 32, Species: Unknown, Job title: Understudy, Theater: Frasier, Clearance level: 1

Understudy?

"What does *that* mean?" I said into the empty office.

I scratched at my internal earpiece, adjusting it again.

On screen, Squeem cleared his throat and shot a look at the surveillance camera above him.

"It's loud when you do that," Fruit said.

Taro and Squeem sat at a table for three in a high-end restaurant in Lansche, waiting for Merchant to join them. Fruit and I watched the whole thing from Boister Energies. Taro sent us code tones through something called a palmpod; surely one of Squeem's inventions.

My ears flexed up and down to move my earpiece into a more comfortable position. It didn't help.

Taro cleaned up rather nicely. She wore a turtleneck dress and a long coat with big, expensive glasses perched on her nose. She'd trimmed her bangs blunt to sit right over her eyes. She looked like the more reliable of the two, considering Squeem had no business being in button-down shirt and slacks. He seemed wholly out of place in the glittering, gaudy restaurant. He'd slicked his hair back. The grown-out streaks of bleach lined the top of his head like pavement markings.

Two long tones sounded in the office.

"Was that the palmpod?" I asked.

Fruit nodded. "Two long means alert. Merchant's there."

Squeem stood while Taro remained seated with her nose upturned.

Merchant was a big man. His wide shoulders stretched the fabric of his clean, pressed suit. He resembled a highland boar; the bridge of his nose was broad and the whiskers on his chin were bristly and cut short. He had thick, manicured eyebrows and a mustache sharply cut around the corners of his mouth. He wore thin glasses with wired temples that snaked inside his ear. Tech like that was for the wealthiest of the wealthy.

The man grabbed Squeem's hand in a rough handshake. "I was expecting to meet with your Head of Operations today. I take it she couldn't make it?" He had a grating voice.

Taro's eyes were narrowed shrewdly. When she spoke, her classic Darkling accent was replaced with a Lacausian twang. "Our Head will not be meeting with you today. We hardly know a thing about you. This is a preliminary meeting so we can get a feel for you and understand what you bring to our operation."

Merchant's booming laugh shook the table. "I should have known! Caution is afforded these days. Allow me to introduce myself. I am Mard Merchant Sr., owner of Terrion Banks in Lansche. We are a union bank, dealing in local and Beselian businesses. We specialize in large loans and accounts.

"But, what I assume you're most interested in — I am chair of the board for Merchant & Kin Construction. It's a family business I have considerable part in. That company would be the basis of our agreement."

The man laid his napkin on his lap and ordered a Vilent, neat, the best they had, from the waiter. "And now, may I ask who you are? I like to know who I'm doing business with."

Taro held out her right hand to the man. Merchant took it and kissed her knuckles. Her lips turned up in a discreet smile, "My name is Rhonnia, I work directly under our Head. I charge the regional business agreements. This is Merscha; Merscha works under me. I trust his judgment."

I looked at Fruit. "So, we're going with fake identities now?"

Fruit nodded, "These are their—" He paused, thinking. "These are their characters."

"Oh right, Dight *Actors* Guild."

Taro transformed before our eyes; Her voice, her word patterns, her body language. She told Squeem to refill her water, get the waiter and ask for new silverware, she even ordered for him. Juiced scally and a half-shell of mallowcrab. Squeem took the place of a fearful sourceboy with skill. No one would expect this mumbling, shivering man was a tech genius who stood up to Mina Harker on the daily.

Over steaming appetizers, Merchant declared himself an expert replacement for Bana Vastro. He'd worked with her to recruit for a big job outside of Suradelphia and found "covert work" both exciting and well-paying. He gushed about the opportunity to get his construction company into the under-the-table scrap trade.

"And, need I not remind you, I have access to loyal, hardworking labor. If the price is right, of course."

Taro surveyed Merchant with hard eyes. "We have hired out before and found turnover to be regrettable. The industry is sensitive to change, especially with the kind of information we retain. Some of that turnover has been forced. We aren't in the business of mass killings. However, a job site accident has been known to happen. Sometimes, we must remove those who need to be removed. Including those whom we deal directly."

I whispered in Fruit's space, "Is she serious?"

But Merchant didn't miss a beat. "I am aware of your business practices, Miss Rhonnia. I have found that hiring the right labor makes all the difference. I have a list ready to go. Many of them have worked with your Sarif crew. You can check with Sarif on their reliability, and mine as well."

Merchant's glasses flashed yellow as he sent over the list directly to Taro's pocketscreen.

Taro's gloved hand dipped under the table. A tonal sound resonated in the office. A mirror image of Taro's phone showed up. She took her time as she scrolled lazily over the list, wearing a flat face.

"Damn, Taro is good at this. She looks like a supervillain," I said.

A flush appeared on Taro's nose.

Taro turned to Squeem. "Merscha, dear, will you send this list to headquarters? And you haven't even touched your scally! This is why you're so thin. Eat up, we have a long trip home."

I watched Merchant while the other two talked. His eyes grazed over Taro with hunger. He focused in on her upturned hand; beneath the glove fabric, her palmpod glowed. My stomach did a disturbed flip.

At the end of the meal, Squeem stood and helped Taro with her coat while Merchant kissed her hand again.

"It was lovely meeting you, Rhonnia. I look forward to our future business ventures."

Lansche was on the other side of the country, eight hours from Frasier; Taro and Squeem wouldn't be back until late in the evening. They changed outfits on their first tram, before switching trams twice more. Taro's car was parked in a paid lot on the river port in Rasa Ver.

Fruit and I were tasked with hounding their journey home, in case they'd been tailed. It seemed that they'd gotten away unscathed.

"Is it always this high stakes, going in public like this?" I asked in a lull of boredom as Squeem and Taro drove silently down a two-lane highway.

Fruit answered, "We can't be followed."

I thought for a moment, "When Mina took me, I'd seen her in a hook market in Pwero Ver. She was wearing a disguise, but I knew it was her."

"How did you know?" Fruit asked.

"I, uh, I'd seen her picture a lot. I knew what she looked like."

Taro lifted up her hand and spoke into her palmpod, mirth behind her words. "Her disguises are the best we have."

Squeem grabbed Taro's hand, "Yeah, I seem to recall, you were carrying around a picture of her in your pocket."

Everyone laughed and laughed while my face heated up to a bright shade of purple.

Dry ferns thrashed against the conference room windows at *Boister Energies*. The Dight Actor's Guild crew and I sat at the table in expensive, rolling chairs with grey upholstery. On the copper wall opposite the windows, a long, waxy painting hung. An expanse of the iconic, soft hills of Nirth swelled across the painting; golden grasses and luminous, pink clouds.

"Is that a Narien Evroldengaud?" I motioned to the painting.

There was silence as everyone's eyebrows shot up. Squeem looked to Mina, and she responded nonchalantly with, "He reads my books."

Heads nodded around the room and they began their debriefing, ignoring my question. We watched a recording of the dinner with Merchant. There he sat, a predator among friends, using the tiniest spoon on the table to scoop sugar into his rootbrew. A few months ago, I was an ex-con paperboy working at Harbor District Station. Now, here I sat with a serial murderer and her crew of loyal subjects, debriefing after a day of subterfuge and lunch with a probable mob boss.

Merchant was a wealthy, pushy hog of a man. Something unsavory cast a blur behind his eyes. How much did his swishy, custom suits cost? How much did those glasses cost?

"Why don't we have cool glasses like that?" I asked out loud.

Mina slammed her hands onto the table. "Have you been paying attention at *all*?"

I cleared my throat. "Sorry. I will pay attention. Just ... Merchant had those screen glasses that connect to your neural network. We don't have stuff like that."

"We?" Mina said. Her silhouette was outlined by the white glare of the wall projection.

Squeem put a hand on Mina's arm before she could destroy me. "We can't use mass-market tech; it's all traceable. But the tech we have doesn't even exist in the outside world. We have the upper hand on that front."

"Yes, thanks to Squeem." Mina pulled her arm from under Squeem's grasp. "Devin, what did you think of Merchant? Other than his *cool glasses*."

I thought for a moment. What did I think? Everyone stared at me in the dark. My mind couldn't seem to focus on the question.

"Well?"

"He looked at Taro like he wanted to eat her," I said. Taro sat in front of the painting. It was *definitely* a Narien Evroldengaud.

"So, no one likes Merchant. Good. Let's hire him and maybe we'll find out *why*."

Mina began to clean up her side of the table. We'd gotten Turrisian takeout, and it was delicious, as always. She looked up at the glances of unease being cast in her direction. "Does someone have a better idea?"

No one did.

It was just past midnight. Soft, misty rain fogged the windshield of Mina's new car. It reminded me of my time at Hyme Prison; the constant pattering of rain on the glass. Grey cell walls, grey tile on the floor, grey bars caging me in, and a view of never-ending grey through my thin window. Night, day, grey.

Then__

It's Gleaning Day.

I haven't slept in weeks. The horrors I've uncovered are too much to close my eyes peacefully. My face is plastered on every newsprint; video footage of my arrest is on every screen. When they book me in, I am on the station screen, pleading with a journalist outside of the Night Palace: *Please, I was lying! I didn't do it! Tell them I didn't do it!* Wet mascara runs down my cheeks.

There is no end to it.

I haven't smoked any icetar since my arrest. Coming down from that is like having the undersides of your feet slowly, delicately flayed with a citrusy razor. Every surface I touch aches beneath my skin; every noise grates my eardrums. Every embarrassing thought rattles around in my head.

So, when a janitorial figure stands behind the bars and offers me some questionable pills in exchange for a tongue bath, I gracelessly oblige. When the pills kick in, I scream foul obscenities from my cell between bouts of hysterical crying.

"Filthy, evil monster Devil Mace, murdering your husbands! Slicing your brothers to bits! Feeding your fathers to the street rats!"

I bang my head on the bars until I black out. I flood my sink with newspaper, sliding and rolling around in the water like a beached fish. I claw and bite the rubber arms of the nurses who sedate me.

The next day, it's on the news; the surveillance footage of my meltdown. Every living soul watched with bated breath as I coined the name myself; Devil Mace, the Devil of Suradelphia.

In the glorious land of Dedocia, the fall of a villain is top entertainment. My publicized trial is streamed at top numbers; businesses and schools shut down to watch. The bruises on my forehead become a symbol of the sterilization of Evil.

Now__

I sat on the boat deck under the overhang, and closed my eyes against the gentle murmur of mist. I was so tired that I was past sleeping. Night birds glided on the water, searching for amphibians to snack on. Crisp leaves rustled under animal feet on the shore.

When the first light of dawn burned orange between tree trucks, I finally went inside. Mina was sitting at the dining table with her head in her hands, a glass of pear glace tipped over and dripping to the floor. I was shocked to see her.

Her harsh eyes held the possibility of tears.

She tossed me an open letter. "Look at this. What the hell am I supposed to do with this?"

MUBS

The daft bastard put the help on leave for my health. FOR MY HEALTH! He thinks I need to do something with my time. He's not here enough to know what I need. Vile, spineless ratkiller! If he had eyes for anyone but himself, he'd know that I am long past saving.

May I be dead by Veishrin. You can visit my corpse when you make the time for me.

Your Dying, Wingless Tyrna

I read the letter twice. It was written in a sloppy, slanted script on fine paper. *Tyrna* — a title given to Eivian queens.

I slid into the dining chair next to her, chewing on the inside of my cheek.

She held up another letter. "Oh look, another one." She opened the letter with a quick slice of the blade. It was written on the same exquisitely pressed paper. "Here's the next day's apology."

Mina spoke with an Eivian accent as she read it. *"I can't imagine what I'd sent to you yesterday, but I'm certain it was regrettable. Please accept my apology. I hope to see you in the warmer months."* She crumbled the letter in her fist. "Fucking unbelievable."

Sunlight glistened on the water outside. I stayed at the table as Mina opened letters and tossed them aside. I didn't try to read over her shoulder this time.

"Can I ask you something? It's personal, I think."

Mina didn't look up from her letters as she answered, "I guess."

"We had a cookout at Taro's before you got back from Quar. Cassius mentioned his brother having lived with you, and I asked who his brother was. It definitely killed the mood."

Locks of red hair slid from Mina's shoulder and covered half of face. She didn't respond.

"Fruit told me you were married before."

"So, what's your question, then? If Fruit told you all about it."

"Can you just — tell me what happened?"

Mina sat back, scoffing, "Why exactly do you care about this?"

I shifted in my chair, glancing around at the array of houseplants in the room. Well-cared-for, little green bits of life in the home of a killer. The contradictions were hard to ignore.

"I just want to understand."

"I was young and dumb, thinking I'd ever have a chance at normalcy. I married Calix when I was nineteen. A few years later, we tried to have a kid. It was going rather well until I got them both killed by the very people I spend my days and nights hunting. They are always one step ahead, no matter what."

She spread her hands flat on the table and added, "Pregnancy made me weak and lovesick. It was foolish of me to think I could protect us."

"But he knew, right? He knew what you were wrapped up in?"

"Don't pull that shit on me, Devin. I know the game and I won't fall for it." Mina looked like a feral cat, ears back and eyes wide. "I thought I was invincible, and I didn't stop to think about those around me. Cassius will never forgive me for it."

The deep, sickening silence crept between us. Mina stabbed at the mail on the table. I stared at her shaking hands, her long, thin fingers pressed red around the knife.

Words began to roll off Mina's tongue. "Calix, Cassius, they were like family to me. We grew up together. They were raised like I was; to be little weapons. I, of course, was the worst off. But Calix was a complex person; gentle and kind, and so smart. He and I were the perfect team. I'm not sure why someone so calm and respectable could stand someone like me. But he did. It was more than I deserved.

"I was eight months along when it happened. Maybe it was a Divine objection — a kid shouldn't have to live like this." She trailed off, cutting bits of paper off with her overly sharp knife. She dropped the tiny pieces into the nearest potted plant like confetti. We watched the paper settle.

Her voice broke me from a trance I didn't know I was in. "What are your parents like, Devin?"

"Oh." I ran my hands through my hair, which had grown to my chin by now. "They died when I was thirteen"

"Both of them?"

"Ma died in childbirth. My dad died on the way to the hospital; bus accident."

"What the fuck?"

"Yeah. I suddenly went from having two parents and two siblings to no parents and three siblings to watch over. I wasn't ready for that kind of responsibility."

Mina's brows pushed together into a jagged line. "What were they like?"

"My father, Al, was quiet. He had this booming laugh that I'll never forget. Ma, Ana, looked like his twin; they were both so small, young too. She was stern, with a temper that seemed to only come out at night. They owned a resale shop, and we all lived in the tiny apartment above it. Ma and Dad were both so *grey,* with dark hair. They looked like living ghosts."

Mina let out a quiet laugh. "You kind of look like a living ghost."

I couldn't help but smile, "Yeah, no — I do. And so do my siblings. You'd like them. Caulder is so funny, he's a shot of sunshine." A sudden ache spread through my chest, and I couldn't continue.

Mina cursed under her breath. "I shouldn't have taken you."

I barely heard her shadow of an apology.

I kept my mind on hounding with Fruit during the days at Boister. All was quiet on the wordsearching front, and while I enjoyed Squeem's company, his work was so complex I had no chance of helping.

Hounding, I could do.

It was fun watching people, even if I didn't know why we were doing so. We hounded three Batifban, a realtor, even a judge, and one waitress. The rest were boring, desk job yawners.

Tenor Rubark was a boring, desk job yawner with one interesting quirk. He still met with the snappy dresser every other Wednesday evening at exactly 4:55 PM. Rubark would hold open the western back door for the short man. They'd nod at each other, and both be on their ways. It was odd, I had to admit, but I was still on this guy's side. He'd done nothing wrong as far as I could tell. Maybe the snappy dresser was the office supply manager. Maybe he always lost his keys and Rubark had helped him so many times that it was routine now. Maybe he was Rubark's cousin, and he felt obliged to say hello when the snappy dresser came in.

I had gotten used to seeing this strange exchange between Tenor Rubark and the snappy dresser that I was looking forward to the following Wednesday. Squeem joined us for a pre-clock out chat and swig of stonefruit cider. The two of them were having an argument (Squeem spoke, Fruit mostly grunted disapproval) about the pronunciation of Votian words while I watched the screen, counting down the minutes until Tenor Rubark exited and waited for the snappy dresser.

It was a snowy day in Pwero Ver, rare in the coastal city. The snow never lasted, always turning to brown slush soon after. Watching the snow fall in my warm city made me homesick. I'd always gotten hot mulled pear juice on the coldest evenings after work at the Batif. If I imagined it, I could feel the warm styrocup in my hands.

I caught sight of a slender woman wearing a knit hat and thick snow boots lean against the wall where Rubark normally stood. She had a square, black bag slung over her shoulder. She scrolled on her pocketscreen, her long, thin fingers peeking out of her fingerless gloves.

"Oh no," I gasped. I knew those fingers.

Squeem snapped his head to me. "What?" Fruit and Squeem were next to me, watching the screen.

"Oh no," they both echoed.

Tenor Rubark walked out of the door, startled by the woman standing in his spot. She looked up nonchalantly, then moved aside and went back to her pocketscreen. Rubark tried to play it cool, standing as far from her as he could. They both scrolled on their pocketscreens in silence.

The snappy dresser walked up at exactly 4:55, like always. And as he nodded to Rubark, Mina sprang. She slammed the snappy dresser into the door with a hard push, kicking back at Rubark and sending him to the snowy, wet pavement. She shot the snappy dresser in the chest and turned, standing over Rubark as she did the same to him. It was fast, agile, impossible to expect. I couldn't look away.

Both men laid motionless as Mina crept over them, reaching into her square bag and retrieving one of the glass jars she kept in her freezer on the houseboat. With a lighter in hand, she took out a paintbrush and began heating the bristles. Dipping the brush into the jar, Mina painted thick, transparent wax over Rubark's face.

Suddenly I was on the floor, cradling my head in my hands. That man — I *knew* that man. I had watched him for weeks. He was just a nice, normal, boring man. He wasn't anything else. He had to be, right? Nice, normal, boring.

The flashing, moving glow from the hounding screens confused my eyes. I thought I could hear Squeem's voice, feel Fruit's hands on my shoulders. But the room was spinning and when I shut my eyes, I could only see the bright burst of red on snow at the back door of Macton Corp. Tenor Rubark was dead. The snappy dresser was dead. Mina was painting their faces with the jars of wax she kept in her freezer. *Our* freezer. I ate the little cups of iced cream she kept next to those jars. The jars that Mina painted the faces of her victims with.

After that thought, there was nothing but the blank, black space of unconsciousness.

12

Dinner and a Landquake

The stone beneath my cushion hummed with each clap of thunder, each burst of a monstrous wave on the shore outside. The Limits classroom was dimly lit, brightening in cracks of white through the sun-tunnels overhead. I imagined being calm, thoughtless, easily drifting from experience to experience without a care in the world. If I imagined hard enough, maybe I would achieve the meditative softness we were tasked with.

Varali swept around the room, buzzing with delight. It was distracting.

To my left sat Corin Verner. We had a few Vauverics like him at home; the ones that came from Votia, with wealth and power knit into their skin. Votian culture was like that, I guess. I wasn't sure what someone so soft and regal as Uyentra Vash saw in him, but they were nearly inseparable.

Corin was a Firewalker, like Madame Adord Drucilla Laverick. Firewalkers could safely exist in incompatible spaces by projecting their energy to manipulate the atmosphere. They could walk through fire, breathe underwater, be shot into space and survive. With practice, Firewalkers became theatrical show-offs, opening windows and turning off lights with their energy. Hence, Drucilla felt it acceptable to slam her classroom doors shut whenever tension was high.

There was one other Palm Lifter in the class; Moonie Devince, the magical being I'd knocked into my first day of class. Now, she sat across from me on the floor, meditating.

I snuck a peek at her. Moonie's pupils bobbed back and forth under her glossy eyelids like she was reading a book. Her lips rested softly in a straight line. Black skin, black hair, black clothes. In the dim room, she was a bottomless shadow.

The stillness made my mind wander to every corner of every layer. I drifted over the mountain ranges of Votia, over the Beselian sea. I beamed up to Noor and Hood, the sister planets. How long had it been since Drucilla had been home? Why did she still wear her Adord judge habit? Did Saren get in trouble for hanging out with students?

I sighed, "I am really terrible at this."

The shadow of Moonie replied, "We were too, once."

"We?" I asked.

Moonie stilled. Her hairless browbone pushed together, and she replied in unnatural roughness, "The class. No one is good at meditation at first."

I paused, certain she'd just fed me a lie. What could she be lying about?

Varali's voice lifted through the dark. "Children, where do your gifts come from?" Varali called us Children when she was feeling philosophical.

Crater, an Orcorne boy with serious arm muscles, called out in dramatics, "From within!"

Varali smiled, cat eyes flickering in the flashes of lightning. "Yes, from within. And who gave you your gifts?"

Crater threw his arms out. "Our souls!"

"You are putting on quite the show today." Varali pointed at him with the long strip of crystal she was holding. "But yes, you are correct. The soul chooses the gift. No one gave your Limits to you; you are indebted only to yourself. Never forget that."

Varali stood, waltzing between pairs of students, "Now, let's go over who created your gifts, as that is an important distinction. Each Limit was created by an Undergod. It is said that Baheeba created the two rarest gifts: Whisting and Gate Reading. As you know, our very own Idrissa is a Whister. Baheeba's gifts present in adulthood, unlike the others, so we have no Gate Reading or Whisting students at Voltenstraus.

"But, we have quite a mix of divine gifts in our class. So, please, if you will; Speak to your partners about your gift's creator and why you think they created it."

Varali moved around the room, lighting candles. The beads in Moonie's braided hair glistened in the flame light.

I cleared my throat, "So, Erytoa made Palm Lifting. Yeah?"

Moonie took a radically deep breath and finally opened her night-vision eyes. "Yes, she did."

"Yeah. Cool. So, why create Palm Lifters? I mean, it seems obvious that people would need healers. Injuries and all that."

Her eyes closed again. My knees bounced while I waited. Uyentra was behind her; their delicious voice swelled over the class like a lullaby. The tips of their ears were translucent in the candlelight. Jagged veins snaked beneath.

"Do you want to know the answer?"

"Uh—" I refocused on Moonie. "Is there a right answer?" Like she could know anyway. She stood out in this wretched place, but she wasn't a damn Non-Eater.

"To quote *The Contents*; Erytoa so loved Baheeba's creations, transcendent flesh a mortal being would never grasp. Her words touched their ears, planting seeds of peace in mortal minds, to burst forth and vine the mortal form."

"Ok, so — Erytoa couldn't touch people," I asked, unsure.

Moonie nodded. "She wasn't able to affect them physically. She could create plants with her fingers, and mend broken stems, but never heal a being's body or mind. So Erytoa wished Palm Lifters into existence to affect beings for her. We must touch those we heal because Erytoa cannot. That is the correct answer."

"Did Erytoa tell you that one herself?" I laughed.

"Have you seen your energy before?"

"Oh, mine? You mean, my own?" I stammered, "I'm a bit behind everyone."

"No, then?" Moonie brought her hands up, palms flat, level with my shoulders. "Let's try."

I forced against the urge to look around the room, and I joined my hands with Moonie, flat-palmed and rigid. Her warmth wrapped around my fingers.

"Close your eyes," she said.

In the blank space of my mind, colors shimmered — palest blue, like the moon on dark water.

I couldn't help but laugh. "Your name is perfect; Moonie."

She hummed. In my mind's eye, Moonie was there with me, looking over the water; two pairs of eyes drifting over a lake. Her light blue energy snaked over the water. It crackled and froze the surface. The red water crystalized, clinging to the blue like snow on the sole of a shoe.

"Why's the lake look like blood?" I grumbled.

Moonie hummed again, "Can you feel your energy?"

I scanned over myself; toes, fingertips, elbows, spine, hips — yes, there, simmering in my pelvic bowl. Mess, was I cooking something down there?

"It's stuck down low," I answered.

"Force some of it up. If you squeeze your hands, it will move. Press your fingernails into your palms — *oh!*"

Moonie gasped as a thick, red wave leapt from the lake, colliding with her own frosty light. Blood — *was it blood?* — sprayed, spattering the blackness with hot red. It steamed and sizzled before calm returned to the surface.

My heart pounded in my chest. I breathed through my mouth, pulling breath in and out like an overworked animal.

Around us, the rest of the class went on unaware.

"It would seem that your energy is a ... lake of blood."

"Is that normal?"

Moonie's eyes shifted back and forth, *left, right, left,* and slowed to a stop on me. "No. It's not."

We sat in silence. The room moved in quiet conversation, students' bodies lit in candlelight and lightning flashes. They explored the reason behind their abilities. They shared the color of their energies, the temperature, and how each power glowed with a different shade of light. Every single one of them, filled with light. And what was I filled with?

"Mayli."

I sprang back, cleared of fog and now hyperaware that the class was packing up. Uyentra Vash stood over me, smiling.

"I'd like to take you on a date."

The sound lengthened and snapped in my eardrums.

"A date? Like, romantically?"

Uyentra laughed; a luxurious sound. They said, "Yes, I guess so. I'm interested in you."

"Ok, I just — damn, you really come out swinging, don't you?" What was happening? Why was I still on the floor? "What do people do on dates?"

The most miraculous smile graced Uyentra's godlike face. "Are you going to agree, or do I need to give you the whole night's itinerary first?"

"No, wait, yeah, sorry, I don't know what's wrong with me. Yeah, let's go on a date."

"Alright. Are you free tomorrow? What dorm are you in?" They handed me my backpack, never once breaking eye contact.

I thought for a moment, looking away from Uyentra's intense gaze. Where did I live, again? "Oh, Eldrid, the basement. Number 14."

"Tomorrow, I will meet you in the Eldrid lounge at 7:30." And they were off, hand on Corin Verner's shoulder, leaving the classroom. I remained on the floor, staring at the door as Uyentra glided through. The most beautiful, intriguing, regal being on the entire layer having just asked me on a date.

Moonie's hand was at my side, offering to pull me up. "Uyentra must not be bothered by your bloody energy."

It took everything to keep the glee from spewing out of me.

My friends weren't shocked nearly enough that Uyentra had asked me out.

Aeshra sat on the thick rug in the Eldrid lounge, unable to keep still. "They look like they're headed to an opera every day! I'm so jealous. Plus, the cat can see your *soul*; that should feel pretty good!"

"What if this is just part of Uyentra's quarter-life crisis? Or Mess — what if they asked me to pull an intervention on me?" I dropped my voice a few octaves, "*Mayli, love, your soul is beyond repair, a dire cavern of evil.*"

"A *dire cavern*? Where do you come up with this stuff? Your soul is probably fine." Riolyn said, picking dirt off her combat boots.

"Are you going to clean all this dirt up or are you saving it for the maids?" I asked.

"We have maids?" Riolyn asked.

"No, dumbass. *We* are the maids. Where are your manners?" I smacked her on the thigh.

"Don't you want to get laid? Show off your butt! That's your asset," Riolyn hollered from the closet as I swirled red eyeshadow around my eyes in front of the mirror.

"I'm not trying to get laid, dude. Where would we do it, in *here*?"

She ignored my comment as she rifled through my clothes. "Wear the lightning pants; they're tight on your thighs. Uyentra deserves a little taste."

"Oh, please, man. No one wants to see that!"

I wore the lightning pants.

Uyentra wasn't the only one waiting for me as I stumbled into the Eldrid lounge.

Behind my date, Nathali stood hand in hand with Corin Verner. Was she dating him? A cold, hard lump sat in my stomach. I was going to be outshone by my damn sister. Again. This date would end with me, perpetually single, and Nathali with two lovers.

Uyentra took my hand, their nails glittering gold. They leaned down into my space and whispered, "I promise we won't be with them all night; just dinner."

"Yeah, it's fine. The more the merrier, right?" I could fake it.

Nathali bounced up beside me. "Sorry I haven't made it down to visit yet! This is the *saddest* of lounges. It's so gloomy down here! Perfect for you though, I'm sure." She had the audacity to wink at me. Nathali Rose Lien Harker, in pure white, like a fae in the morning dew. Utterly flawless.

Corin ignored me, glancing around our dingy lounge with a nauseated frown. It couldn't be *that* bad. Maybe the Eldrid kids just weren't snobs.

In the windy night, we headed toward Nepa on the ferryboat.

Uyentra sat across from me and watched as I looked everywhere but them. They had this infuriating, knowing smile on their face, and I wanted to kiss it off. Nathali commented on the strangeness of my outfit, *"It's a bit irreverent, May, but I guess that's your thing."* When Corin spoke, I wasn't sure if he was insulting me or not. I opted to keep the chatter to a minimum.

I could play the game when the stakes were low, but this was too real.

At the restaurant in Nepa, a grand little place called the *Silver Spout*, food tasted ill on my tongue. The clench in my stomach hadn't subsided. I was embarrassed by my outfit choice. And why hadn't I learned to talk like a normal person? Uyentra had to be in the thick of a quarter-life crisis to ask me on a date. I was a wreck.

"May, are you okay?" Nathali asked.

"Yeah, I'm good. How's your food?" I stabbed at the roast frasiora fern on my plate.

Nathali gave me a sidelong look. I mirrored it back to her, so she'd drop it.

Nathali's ethereal skirt whipped around her ankles as the four of us stood outside of the Silver Spout. Corin and Nathali were catching a small party in town, but Uyentra told them we were going to continue our date elsewhere. As the other two walked away, Nathali threw me a sly smile. I rolled my eyes at her but couldn't help but smile, too.

The mood turned awkward as Uyentra and I stood together, blowing in the wind. I tried not to scratch at my neck. I wasn't going to be an embarrassment. I wasn't.

"Do you like dessert?" Uyentra asked innocently.

I motioned to my chubby shape. "What do you think?"

Over flakey, sweet pie, Uyentra and I were able to unwind. I had been so unreasonably concerned with my own nervousness that I'd completely missed how nervous Uyentra was, mistaking their stiff body language at dinner for posh manners.

"Is the weather in Monount Valley as dismal as Nepa?" Uyentra wiped their mouth carefully on a paper napkin; they were out of place in the laid-back atmosphere of Caster's. The Silver Spout seemed second nature to Uyentra, but this was a place for peasants. I liked watching the regal cat stretch out in a place like this.

"It's higher up, greener, bright days and misty nights. Spring is out of control with flowers. Are we really talking about the weather now?"

Uyentra laughed.

"So, you know about Monount?" I asked.

Nodding, Uyentra cut off a slice of pie delicately. "That seems to be where the Limits move to. Taken as an honor, of course. No early deaths for us, here," Uyentra waved their fork in the air in sing-song glee. "I do find it odd that your father chose to keep you out of Limits training."

The waiter, Roz, refilled our waters as I answered, "Doctor Harker is hard to explain."

"You call your father Dr. Harker?" Mirth graced their lips.

"He is ... sort of a revolving character in my mind. Doctor, George, Father, Dad. We have a weird relationship. Do you have a weird family?"

"Not especially. I grew up in a children's home in Parcells, Coesha. It was state-run, so we had the best of everything. Corin was there as well."

"Mess, no wonder you're so posh. Votia is the most get-a-job layer there is," I joked.

"Yes, it was a strict upbringing. Worked out fine for me. Votia takes good care of their charity cases. The kids they know will die before puberty."

"So, how'd you make it here?"

Uyentra offered a delicate bite of pie to me. I opened my mouth, and they dipped the fork in. When I closed my lips around it, Uyentra's ears turned out in open interest.

"Well?" I asked, smiling.

They set the fork on the table. "Got into some trouble with Larcies, Corin, and I."

My eyes bulged, "*What*?"

Uyentra laughed softly and leaned back against the booth, "The way your soul alights when you're excited — it could become an addiction."

I followed their body, leaning forward, "Hey, one thing at a time. Did you say *Larcies*? Do you feel comfortable telling me about that?"

"Oh, yes, I'm an open book. Whatever you've heard is probably true. Two of them seemingly *popped* into existence and reached out with those — those *hands*. I'll never forget the hands. Black, like me, but artificial. Shiny, plastic, but pliable like flesh."

"Just their hands?"

"Yes. Otherwise, they looked like regular people. If they'd been walking on the street, no one would notice."

"Gloves?"

"I don't think so. However, it's been nine years since it happened. The mind slips lies into memories."

Uyentra's hands spread across the tabletop. Their golden fingernails reflected the lines of white neon outlining the diner's interior. I let one of my hands drop onto theirs. Uyentra's hand turned over; they scraped their nails across my sensitive palm. I shivered and turned away, holding my smile back for dear life.

"I remember an odorless vapor blowing into our faces. Corin dropped quicker than I, and one of the Larcies knelt over him. I remember thinking, '*Della won't be pleased about my getting snow on my pants.*' Della was our Minder at the home; a part-time parent, really." Uyentra brushed pie crumbs off my knuckles. "Then I saw Corin. His face was wet, oily, or covered in something yellow, like honey. I don't remember anything after that. Besides fear."

Our fingers wove together on the table. Theirs were so different to mine; dark, angular, with long, manicured nails, versus my mottled pink, callused fingers, with dirt beneath my nails.

"How did you get out of it?"

They pulled my hand up to their mouth and kissed the back of it, "We woke up in a lab. I remember the smell; sweet and metallic. An odd combination. Corin was up, sitting in a chair, eating bread. His face was normal again. And a huge woman with horns bent down and offered me some, too. The next day, we were on the tram to Voltenstraus."

Across the diner, the door dinged open. We swiveled to see three college-aged women stumble in. All three had puffy, reddened eyes.

Roz brought them to their table, passing us. One of them recognized my date, and spoke with a heavy voice, "Hey Uyentra, celebrating something?"

"Are you three well?" Uyentra asked.

The other two girls sat a few tables away and put their heads in their hands.

"I don't know. We were at the gardens, but left to get some dinner. Thought we were hungry, but I'm not sure. Everything is foggy now."

Uyentra squeezed my hand as they answered, "Odd. Maybe a nice meal is what you need. How were the gardens, otherwise?"

"It's mating season for those blue and white birds, whatever they are," she answered, paling to a dull grey in the passing seconds.

"Klaxsons," I said absentmindedly watching her ill friends.

"That's right, Klaxsons. Thanks," she paused, out of breath. "It was a nice day, except the Mace kid. He looks dead, even there. Something's wrong with that kid."

"Well, certainly eating something will help. Have Roz get you something nice," Uyentra said, waving Roz over.

The girl went back to her table and slouched with her friends. It was very strange; they looked like they'd just left a funeral.

After a long pause, I said, "They don't look so good."

Lines of worry cut across Uyentra's forehead. "Indeed."

"I don't get what the deal with Seth Mace is; everyone being afraid of him."

Uyentra cut the remainder of our cold pie into tiny bits with their dessert fork. "Ah, well, you weren't here a few years ago. Seth injured a few students. It just happened once, and I believe it was an accident, but it was enough to terrify everyone for life. He loses control in a scary way. I don't know what's changed, but whatever Idrissa and Dr. Harker are doing is helping."

I couldn't help but ask, "What does *his* soul feel like?"

Uyentra shook like an uncomfortable animal. "The best word I have for it is *confusing*. Turbulent. Crowded. It's uncomfortable to be near him; I don't know how Moonie does it."

"Moonie?"

But Uyentra didn't hear my question. They were running to help as one of the sick women upchucked all over the diner floor.

I laid on my bed, staring up at the ornate ceiling while Riolyn asked me endless questions about my date. Water-like forms swirled in the stone. If I tuned out my nosey friend, I could hear the rain hitting the lake outside, reverberating against the cave walls. It was well past midnight now, but neither of us could sleep.

"What was it like, holding hands with a furry?" Riolyn threw a sock at my head, and it hit my chin.

"Oh Mess, don't be racist. You don't like it when people call you a reptile. They were... soft. They take good care of their body," I mumbled, trying to remember. "There was a lot going on. I just remember feeling happy and nauseous."

"What did Uyentra smell like? They're so posh, I bet they have some of that fancy cologne." Riolyn tossed her pillow up in the air and caught it.

"Man, I don't know. Sweet? Might have been the pie. Will you quit throwing things?"

"How can you not remember what they smelled like? That just blows my mind. If they smell good, you can count on the sex being good."

"Does Squidzy Valentine smell good, then?" I shot her an arched eyebrow.

"Uh, *yeah*. Valentine smells damn good. Like candied lemons and rubber gloves," Riolyn smacked her hands together like she was about to dig into a tasty snack, "Patch me up, Dr. Valentine!"

"You are a disaster."

The little framed painting next to my bed shifted on the wall. We stopped to watch as the thing began to clatter and shake. Rumbling erupted from above us. Deep, low vibrations reverberated through the cave. The stone groaned like it was carrying a great weight.

"Is that a landquake?" Riolyn yelled, pulling me off the bed.

"Like on the tram—"

Tremors growled, shaking the floor. The bathroom mirror dislodged and fell, cracking over the sinks. It showered the floor in shards of glass.

We ran to the door and looked out; Aeshra was at his door too, and other students' heads were popping out.

"It sounds like it's above us!" I started out the door and Riolyn caught my hand.

"You really want to get smashed by falling rock up there?" She yelled over the rumbling.

"I'm sure as fuck not staying in the basement!" I pulled Riolyn with me. No one else dared emerge from their dorms.

Aeshra's eyes were wide with terror. He stood frozen in the doorway.

The vibrations stopped. An eerie silence settled.

Aeshra squeaked, "Is it over?"

Nothing.

And then — a head-splitting cry burst through the cave. The thunderous shaking began again.

"Maybe someone's hurt!" Riolyn took off running through the lounge.

I followed at her heels, my heart slamming against my breastbone. Any sort of natural disaster would be catastrophic at Voltenstraus; a cave *full of children*. I imagined their squashed bodies beneath fallen pillars of stone; blood pooling on the floor.

An unnerving quiet swelled as we fled up the stairs. The quaking stone had silenced. The blue and gold banners that hung from the grand staircases swayed. As though nothing had happened. As though we'd imagined it all.

Riolyn and I stepped into the cavernous entryway.

At the center of the room, a crack stretched across the floor. At its center, it opened a foot across. Wetness glistened in its depths. I crouched to look at it.

"Fuck," Riolyn hissed. "What is that?" She tiptoed up to the crack as if it would come alive and swallow her whole. "It's all over the place."

In the shadows of the cracked stone, black liquid churned. Round drops of it spattered the edges of the fissure. The same oily, blood-thick goo that dripped from the mouth of darkness himself.

"Looks like Devil Spit to me."

13

PLASTIC DRESS

Wetness. My socks stuck to a spot of wetness on the floor. Dark splotches on tiled floor — Mina's blood? The houseboat?

No.

Black. Thick, tarry. Medicinal smell. I was home in Suradelphia. The pounding on the door — the cops? Again? What had I done this time?

The sound reverberated around the room in hollow, metallic pangs. Small tools, clacking against the table. The group meal? What time was it?

"Devin."

I was sweeping the sidewalk now. Mother's frail hands were pulling the store shutters closed, slamming them against their wooden frames. How did she have such force so late into her pregnancy? How did she hold that huge belly up? When she finally gave birth, I would be expected to help with the baby.

"Devin, can you see?"

Could I?

"It's red," I answered.

Someone put a cold cloth on my forehead. I reached up and held it there, fearing some foul creature would take this small comfort from me.

"Is Seth alive?"

A clammy hand covered mine. "Devin. I'm so sorry. I didn't look at Mina's itinerary. I — I should have. I'm so sorry."

"Hmm?" I rolled onto my side. "Whose banging on the door?"

Someone scoffed, "Who do you think?"

The bright ceiling lights hung too close to my eyes. Two people stood over me, watching me like a zoo animal. Matey and Squeem. Maybe it was comforting to be taken care of. But at that moment, I just felt sick and embarrassed.

Matey held small, metal tweezers in one hand, and a clear thread in the other. She held up a tray of broken glass. "You fell onto a bottle of cider. I was going to patch you up, but ..."

"Hmm," I nodded, closing my eyes again. "Maybe Mina will off me now."

"Eventually, everyone sees Mina in operation. You're safe here." Her eye, overlined with blue, glistened with kindness.

"What did Rubark do?"

Squeem let air out through his crooked teeth. His cane scraped on the floor as he pulled a chair over to sit next to me. "Beedy, the man Tenor Rubark was working with, had direct ties to Governor Lambnoc. Mina's been following him for weeks trying to get intel on where Lambnoc is hiding. They are bad people, Devin. Even Rubark."

The space between my eyes throbbed. "No. I never saw him do anything wrong," I said.

"You weren't looking at his comms. He was in direct communication with Sinnia State bullet manufacturers. He placed the order for the bullets Mina was shot with those few weeks ago. Rubark led us to Beedy in the first place. We really need to get Lambnoc; he's a big player. These are *bad people*."

I rolled my eyes, pulling my body up to sit on the exam table. "A big player — what does that mean? You guys are shooting innocent people in the middle of the day because they might know something about — about some bullets? Some bullets that should have killed Mina, because she's a *murderer*? *You* are the bad people!"

Matey said, "Devin, please. I know this is confusing. You were thrown into this mess without your consent, and that's wrong." She pulled her gloves off with a snap. "We probably seem like monsters. And maybe we are, I don't know. But I can promise you, we are on the right side of this. The people Mina kills are dangerous, and not just to us. To everyone."

I put my head in my hands and tried to think, but there was nothing coherent in my head. Just red spats of blood on bright white snow. Mina, kneeling over someone I thought I knew, painting his face with a jar of wax.

Squeem squeezed my shoulder. "Let's take the evening off. Go do something to get your mind off this."

"No," I answered at once, "I need to be preoccupied with work. I want to use, and I *know* what Mina keeps in her desk."

"Even more reason to get out of Boister. We can do work in town. I have some line repairs you can help me with." Squeem smacked me on the back. He felt it more than I did.

Squeem and I crouched over a paphador line in a quiet, foggy neighborhood in Frasier. The lines glowed an eerie green in the fog, thin and snaking across the bare hills where frasiora ferns had been burned to a crispy nothing. It was quiet, apart from the mild breeze whipping the hair around my ears.

Squeem looked strange out in nature; he was not built for the outside world. His tan coveralls, splotched with grease, hung off his thin frame.

He used no cane out here, instead relying on a mechanical brace attached to his nerve-endings. It was an all-together uncomfortable object to put on.

"I don't expect you to remember how to do this, but if you did, that would be excellent." Squeem pulled a hefty tool from his belt. "This line links directly to the paphador chargers in Massia. If it went down, we'd lose all power. Mina says I need to check our lines weekly because they're *so important*, but really, she likes to put as much as possible on my plate. Keeps me on my feeble toes." Squeem used a clamping tool to test the charge of the wire. A snapping sound ensued.

"Says I should go to the gym. Like my lack of agility has ever affected my job," He scoffed. "Now we check the line all the way to the conduction tanker."

We walked slowly, Squeem holding some sort of reader over the wire all the way down. It beeped in agreement every few steps. The sun cast brilliant orange across the sky as it descended behind the far hills. It contrasted with the grey fog swirling around us in low places.

As we got closer to the bottom of the slope, the wooziness began. An aching nausea in my middle came in waves, slow at first, but building with every step.

"Shouldn't have eaten that hotwrap," I said. Squeem was busy trying to steady his steps on the mist-slick grass.

The conduction tanker was metallic silver, concealed by the fog if not for the yellow glowing '*Boister*' trailing along its screen. Squeem placed his hand on a white square and a low tone emanated. My skin was crawling. I let my legs drop and my head lull back. The sickness built; a cramp held onto my diaphragm and I heaved.

Squeem looked up. "Hey, what's happening? Are you okay?"

"The tanker, I think," I scooted further away in the wet grass. Another dry heave, and I let my lunch go.

Trotting like a lame horse, Squeem got to me and hoisted me up, my arm over his shoulders. "What's going on?"

The orange sky was grey now — everything blended together into grey. "I need to ... get back."

Squeem dragged me farther away from the conduction tanker and crouched in front of me, and watched me throw up again. He pulled out a water jar. He poured water onto his handkerchief and raised it to my mouth, wiping away sweat and vomit.

I sipped at the water and let myself breathe.

Squeem asked, "Was it the food?"

"The tanker. There's — sorite in there? Red water?"

He nodded. "We use red water to suppress the paphador charge. You have a reaction to it?"

"An allergy, maybe." I laid back onto the hillside. The soggy ground soaked into the fabric of my shirt and cooled my back.

"Allergic to sorite? I've never heard of such a thing. You look like a ghost." He forced out a smile, but I knew he was worried. "You are a strange man, Devin."

We leaned against each other like friends do. My panting began to subside.

"I don't know where it comes from; my whole family is allergic to the stuff. It hurts, makes me feel drained."

Squeem nodded, cracking a smile. "So, I guess you won't be doing repairs on conduction tankers. You *poor thing*."

He rubbed his callused palm across my forearm for a moment, drawing circles in the muscle, before abandoning me for the tanker to finish the job.

In the earliest hours of the morning, Mina woke me, toeing at my shoulder with her bare foot, "Get up. I made breakfast."

"I'm not hungry. You shouldn't be either," I whimpered into my pillow.

Mina pulled the warm, yarny blanket from me and I cursed as the cold air hit my back. It was frigid on Mina's damn boat. I sat up, snatching the blanket from her and wrapping myself in it like a baby bird burrowing into their mother's feathers.

The air smelled like cinnamon and butter; I licked my lips.

"What are you making? It's too early," I cursed as my senses betrayed me.

A devilish smile scrawled across Mina's face. "Toasted cinnamon. I want to see if I can eat it; I haven't drank the fire in two weeks. Today is a good day. Enjoy it with me or I'll throw you in the lake."

Mina practically skipped to the kitchen, leaving me huddled in my mountain of blankets. She was wearing something much too small and elegant for the chilly morning air. I couldn't stop myself from obeying her.

Mina flipped on a lamp as she swept into the kitchen. The moon's glow broke through the sheer curtains, lighting the dining table in strips of faint white. The slow swaying of the boat drifted me to the edge of sleep. I imagined the fantastical creatures that were active just before dawn. Big, hooved beasts that smacked their antlers against tree trunks to communicate. Clawed amphibians who pushed their soft bellies along the muddy bank. Night birds, humming low calls above and below the water.

"You know, I made this feast for you," Mina said, pushing a plate of cinnamon-dusted toast to me. She scraped a helping of roasted pears and welu seeds onto the side. Sugary, brown syrup spread across the plate.

"Is this poisoned?" Cinnamon was my favorite, but she didn't know that. We didn't talk about food; we didn't talk about *anything*.

Mina let out a gleeful laugh. "No! Of course not. You survived your first dress rehearsal! You made it through! You saw me kill someone, in real time, and you got through it. You've *made it*! This is exciting news."

A shiver ran down my neck to my pelvis, "But I didn't want to see that." I pushed the bread around with my fork. "How am I supposed to eat now?"

"No, I — this is a good thing." Mina brushed her slender fingers across my shoulder. I was used to Squeem being physical, but not Mina. I told myself to flinch away as I leaned into her touch.

"I watched Tenor Rubark *die,* with no warning. I wasn't ready for that."

Mina stood. I half-expected her to kick the table leg and heave our breakfast onto the floor.

"Tenor Rubark was an evil person."

The boat creaked as the wind picked up outside. I'd watched Rubark drive to and from work, obsessed with time, obsessed with his schedule. His deviations seemed so random at first, but maybe there was something there; something unsavory. But *evil*? Who had the right to measure evil? Mina Harker? Really?

"Your toast is getting cold," she reminded me.

It was. I sighed and took a bite, letting out a quiet groan as I did. The crisp, buttery crust melted on my tongue, cinnamon warming my tastebuds. Even at 4 AM, it was delicious. And beautiful Mina, watching me eat her treacherous breakfast. Her figure-hugging plastic dress pressed tightly across her breasts. The unforgiving fabric squeaked when she moved. Did she cook in that outfit? Bending over the hot stovetop with the blue plastic sticking to her thighs.

"I'm trying to persuade you with this food; is it working?"

I rolled my eyes. "I still hate you." *Did I?*

Mina chewed on her food, eyeing me like a curious animal. I pretended not to notice.

"I'm going to kill Governor Lambnoc today."

Nerves bubbled in my stomach. Her words might as well have been sorite. But I didn't look up at my captor. We ate in silence as every question possible ran through my head, one after the other, until I landed on the one that wouldn't go away. The question that sealed my future in this world.

"Are you going to kill me?"

Mina didn't hesitate. "No."

"Because Squeem told you not to?"

"No."

"Because the Producer told you not to?"

This time, hesitation. "...No."

Something stirred in me, but I left it for later. Instead, I asked, "What was your husband like?"

Mina's dress squeaked against the table edge. "Nothing like you."

Mina Harker killed Herse Lambnoc, Governor of Southern Besel, at noon.

I sat beside Fruit and Squeem as they hacked into Beselian news channels and broadcast the spectacle for all to see.

Mina wore the same elegant, plastic dress she'd worn that morning. The light caught and bounced off her body like oil on the surface of putrid water. Blood splashed the dress with each slash of the knife. It dripped off in lurid spots onto the floor of the commercial kitchen she'd infested.

When the deed was done — when the killer had pulled every hair from the man's chin, one-by-one; after he had begged for an end and she'd given him one — Mina crouched over Lambnoc's pallid, dead face, swiping a flat, wax-loaded paintbrush across his wounds. I snuck peaks through my fingers, my mouth agape and dry. Sickened. Horrified. Mesmerized.

The feeling of disgust at Mina's actions clashed with the feeling of privilege of being woken up by her, looking so lovely, that same morning. Self-loathing came in painful waves. Mina was evil. Mina was *brave*. What did that make me?

There was a big celebration that night. People I'd never seen before showed up at Boister for the party. I sat in the back office and watched from the surveillance cameras. I didn't fit into this world, but I sure as hell could never go back to the other one. I was stuck in between. I prayed to Loyal Death as I watched partygoers sing and dance like drunk teenagers.

A full 24 hours after Mina's breakfast feast, I surveyed the party from afar through dangerously heavy eyes. I'd stayed away, holding fast to any thread of sobriety. There was heavy drinking, and with Mina came the promise of hard drugs as well. I wouldn't fall back into that grave of life. I wouldn't.

I laid my head on Fruit's desk, looking up lazily at the surrounding screens. There was a live feed from the riots in Pwero Ver, where civilians called for Mina's head in loud chants and on picket signs. The feed from Lansche revealed much of the same. I'd turned off coverage of

Suradelphia, where my brother Caulder likely tried to sleep in his stiff monastery bed.

Did Caulder believe the news anchors? That I was an unhinged criminal on the loose?

Mina pushed open the door with a loud thud, giggling madly. Squeem, Fruit, and Matey stumbled up behind her; Squeem was the only one who looked rightly lucid. He gave me an apologetic look.

Holding a half-empty bottle of dark liquor, Mina fell into the other rolling chair. "Why are you hiding back here in the dark? We killed that crusty old king today!"

"We?" I murmured, desperate for sleep.

"Come on, Devin, I know you like to get fucked up!" She slammed the bottle down on the counter in front of my face.

The black liquor sloshed against the glass, sending opaque bubbles to the surface. I clenched my eyes shut.

"It's icetar you like, yeah? I bet I can find you some." Mina was too shitfaced to see what she was doing to me.

"Devin is in recovery, for fuck's sake!" Squeem growled, pushing Mina in her chair.

Mina spun in the chair, smiling. Her throat was violently red. After the morning's celebratory breakfast, she'd used again. And it would have been so easy for me to join her; I was exhausted and confused. Something to take the nervous, anxious edge off. Something sharp and splintery like icetar. Just one taste would send me into a quick oblivion.

"You know, Devin and I have *so* much in common." Mina said stagily, scratching hard at her throat, leaving long red marks. "Right, Devin? Both street tricks, addicted to *money* and *power*. You ran with that queer group in Sura — Squeem, you remember them, yeah? Tough ponies,"

Mina smiled fondly at the memory and took a long gulp from the bottle, missing the horrified look on my face.

Squeem didn't miss a thing, though. He put his hand on my shoulder and squeezed. Behind him, Matey slipped out of the room quietly. Fruit watched with as much interest as his overhigh brain could muster.

Mina went on, spinning and drinking and scratching at her neck like a flea-bitten rat. Her body glistened with sweat; it dripped down her chest beyond the sharp neckline of her plastic dress. She'd removed her shoes, and her holey tights were caught up in her toes. I could imagine she'd gotten a lot of business when she was a working girl. When Mina was high, she moved like a serpent.

"Of course, you killed more people in a matter of weeks than I did in *years* at that age. Fucking legend."

"That conviction was overturned," I defended myself. Sleeplessness was replaced with insecurity. So much for sleeping; I'd never sleep again.

She went on, unaware of the mood in the room, "But then who *did* kill all of your johns? Why'd you take the fall for them?" She crouched over me and put on the voice of a seasoned Batif. "Who are you protecting, Mr. Mace? Who was the *real* Devil of Suradelphia?"

I drove Mina back to the houseboat, teetering on the edge of sleep, while she slept beside me. In the dark, the first rays of dawn reflected off her dress, orange and mauve.

What a *legend* I was, ugh. The thought disgusted me. I knew I wasn't a good person. I might not have killed anyone, but I had abandoned my family to be a silly little *terrorist*. The shame was enough to send me right back into using. If I couldn't control my urges, I would be in big trouble.

Mina stirred as we neared 240 Arm. The sun glittered off the shiny, blue plastic of her dress. She smelled of sweat and alcohol, and cinnamon. Her cold fingertips danced over my leg.

"Devin, will you marry me?" Her sleep-clouded voice was like an angel's song.

"Maybe if you ask nicely," I grumbled.

14

ROOMMATE RELEASE FORM

Devil spit:

Popular slang for Hemacrux, *a solvent substance consisting of soul essence and phlegm from the respiratory system. Viscous, oily, sticky, and dark in color. Expelled by way of the mouth, nose and tear ducts.*

In the creaking silence of the cave, Riolyn and I bent over the crack in the entry floor. A foot below, oily blackness swirled against the rock. It bubbled at the edges.

"It smells like toothpaste," Riolyn said, peering down into the crevice. "You're telling me Seth did this?"

"This is what he coughed up over that ritual pool," I said.

"But — Devil Spit? *Really*? I thought that stuff was only in movies."

Noises clattered as someone flew down the stairs. Benjamin appeared, dressed in tan pajamas, with a mountaineer's cap pulled down over his ears. In one hand, he held a metal rod. He bumbled down the steps like a baby elephant, tripping on the last step.

"Out — before your father comes. Any second now." He waved us away, skittering to the edge of the crack. "Messer's sheet! What a mess — go, off to bed. Now!"

Riolyn rounded on Benjamin with her scales raised. "The hell we are! Someone was just screaming up here!"

Benjamin's words broke in panic. "Miss Vite, do not raise your voice to me! Idrissa is sorting it out, and *you* will—"

Scuffing sounds broke downstairs, and Benjamin groaned. Students from the Eldrid dorms peeked out from the stairwell. Above us, shiny-eyed teenagers peered over the stone barrier. Quiet murmurs drifted from above.

Benjamin, *Advisory of Voltenstraus*, stomped his foot on the ground and yelled, "All students to bed! Damages will be addressed in the morning! Go to bed!"

I leaned into his space and whispered, "What if someone's hurt?"

With a sharp breath, he yelled again: "If you are hurt, send a message to Valentine!"

"*Doctor* Valentine?" I added.

He growled and shouted, "*Doctor* Valentine! Now, go to bed!"

Back in our dorm, Riolyn and I picked up our shattered mirror in silence.

The missing information often held the answer. The quaking, shuttering cave had felt exactly like Seth's tram meltdown. The electric hum of uncontrolled power permeated every surface. The squealing of the tram on its tracks, and the stone above us, creaking and growling. The two situations were so alike, if I just could connect the dots.

"So, what's all this with Seth?" Riolyn slid down to the bathroom floor and finally asked. She had cut her arm on a piece of glass and was holding a washrag on the wound. "People don't cause land quakes."

"*Most* people don't," I said, sitting next to her.

"So, what then? Seth has Limits?"

"I don't know. It doesn't feel like a Limit. Limits don't feel so sick, even when someone uses them for evil. He's got some sketchy, dark power."

Riolyn checked her wound with a scowl. "Don't try to tell me that creep's a Non-Eater."

I shook my head, "No way. Non-Eaters are practically gods. A person doesn't transcend by scaring people to death."

We watched a line of dark blood run down Riolyn's arm, outlining her geometric scales. A single drip landed on the floor.

"That black stuff ... in the crack? It's the same stuff I saw when I followed Seth up to that weird room on the fifth floor. It was coming from his mouth."

Riolyn stretched her legs out and pressed her toes against the cold porcelain bathtub. Blue and orange scales topped her toes, while hair topped mine. She shook her head and focused on her bleeding forearm. I handed her another wash rag. Together, we sighed.

In the early hours of the morning, thinly veiled threats began to ping on our dorm screen.

Mayli Harker has been summoned to the office of Doctor George A. W. Harker, for a meeting to be held immediately. Click "seen" to record your response.

Mayli Harker has not yet responded to an emergency message from Doctor George A. W. Harker. Please click "seen" to record your response.

Response is expected after initial interaction with screen messages.

May it be known that called-on student has interacted with each prior screen message on the day of Monday, the 211th day of the 149th year of Nessa. Please click "seen" to record your response.

Mayli Harker, Eldrid dorm number fourteen, has been summoned to the office of Doctor George A. W. Harker immediately. If said student fails to respond by 6:45 AM, a physical call will be placed to said student's dorm room. Please click "seen" to record your response.

I knocked my elbow into the little yellow "seen" button, a bit too forcefully.

I heaved my body onto the final landing and leaned against the stone, panting.

"Oh Mayli, you really should get some exercise."

I squeezed my eyes shut. "So, it's a family meeting, then?"

Nathali and Mieda sat on a bench outside of our father's office. Mieda's hair was in full coif, with delicate, strawberry ringlets framing her round face. It clashed with her permanent scowl.

The door opened. Deep wrinkles cut across the doctor's dress shirt. His face was flushed beneath smudged glasses. He held a worn book in his hands.

"Rough night?" I asked.

"Come in. There is breakfast." He slammed the book shut and tossed it onto his desk as he walked past through the doors into his private quarters.

I snuck a glance at the book, *How to Navigate Unspeakable Disasters.* My inevitable laugh afforded a fiery glare from my father.

"No wonder you've kept me out of here! Everything is breakable," I said, running my finger along golden shelves bursting with books and emotional trinkets. A chaotically patterned rug laid beneath stiff furniture. I sat on a wooden pew, pushing aside the pillows. The paphador cutouts cast a green glow on my knees.

A big, silver pair of sheers sat menacingly on a side table, resting on a golden tray like an offering to the gods.

"Over here, Mayli."

George showed us to the dining table. Grating ambient tones played softly in the background as we sat for a breakfast of fruit and thin, crunchy pasty. My father poured himself a stiff drink before he sat down.

"Isn't it a little early for that?" Nathali said, watching him.

"What's one more before bed?" He smiled tightly, raising his glass.

I sat up and grabbed a pastry. "Nice place you got here, Dad. Mom did those?" I motioned to the six over-large paintings spanning the wall. One for each sibling, and a self-portrait of the Tyrna herself.

"They are recent works of hers, yes," he answered, fixating on cutting his fruit into microscopic squares.

I stared up at our portraits while the others picked at their strange breakfast. The paintings were moody, with pale pink faces surfacing from black shadows. We sat in velvet chairs, fabric draped over our bodies like funerary statues. The waxy paint gleamed plasticky in the dull light.

Mieda's painted expression was drawn and disconnected, while strangling weeds grew up around her, tight on her limbs. Nathali seemed to rest at the bottom of a lake, hazy and grey. I shuddered to think of it. Tom's bleeding fingers wrapped around a traditional Eivian scepter, held there by tight strips of duct tape. The golden vines tangled in his hair seemed to bore into his head.

My mother's self-portrait was regal, perfect, and so very ill. Tubes snaked out of her arms and her abdomen, and ghostly wings fluttered behind her. She held her IV stand like a scepter.

Mina, the sibling I'd never met, lounged in her velvet chair, drenched in red; the background, her hair, her blood-soaked dress. A large pair of scissors lay across her lap, just like the ones in my father's sitting room. Blood flooded the bottom half of the painting.

And in the next, I lounged too, while blood flowed from Mina's painting into mine. It swirled around my toes, not quite touching me. Blood poured over the stones behind me, dropping in thick splashes, while I danced my fingers over a plate of pastries, completely unaware.

I gasped down at the plate of pastries before me, shoving it away.

Nathali's arm rested on my hand. "It's alright. Mom needs help."

"That *is* her help," Dad sniped, spooning fruit in his mouth. "Now, onto the matters at hand. As you know, we had an incident last night. Everything is in order, but you might hear some frightening things over the next few days. I welcome your questions, but assure you, you are safe here. The three of you are trained in these sorts of situations."

"What kind of situations, exactly? Because that Seth kid is causing natural disasters now, and I don't remember being trained in *that*," I said.

George narrowed his eyes.

"He seems fine to me," Nathali answered, popping a big slice of melon into her mouth.

Mieda sighed, "Can I go, please? I know all of this already."

George slammed his fist on the table, our glasses of water clanking in fear. "Can we *not* just have breakfast together? This was supposed to be a simple meeting. I was forced to spend hours with disgruntled staff last night and an angry teenager and I would appreciate a moment of your obviously *very important* time. Being your Father, you think I would be *allotted such*."

I couldn't help myself. "Is this your hangover breakfast, or are you still drunk?"

My siblings sent me looks of disdain as our father thundered up from the table, knocking his chair against the wall.

"This is your fault; do you realize that?" He pointed at me, of course, but also at Nathali.

"Me?" Nathali cried, "I have been lying low, just like you said! I've made friends, I've had a good time, I've been nice to everyone!"

"That last part, *that's* the problem. You two have some strange energy that is interfering with years — yes, *years* of work," he paced back and forth, "Seth complains to me about how nice you are, he complains that you try to *talk* to him. Why can't you two just pretend he doesn't exist like everyone else?"

Mieda sighed, pushing her fruit around, "Honestly, father, you should have expected this. Mayli and Nathali have always gotten into things they weren't supposed to."

George let out a sarcastic laugh, "Don't get me started about you, Mieda dear. *You* are dating his brother, for Uyenl's sake! I don't know what you could possibly see in someone so thoughtless and unimaginative."

Mieda lost it.

She sprung from the table and rushed at our father, baring her teeth, transformed into a feral animal. "Don't you dare talk about Donnie that way. You know nothing about him! I'm sorry he's not fucked up enough to fit into your *sick values*, but he has saved my life far more than *you* ever have!" Mieda grabbed dad's fancy scissors and chucked them at her portrait. They clattered to the floor, leaving a gash across her waxy chest.

"Where's *your* portrait, father? Oh, that's right! Mother doesn't paint you!" Mieda ripped open the doors, slamming them against the wall, and was gone.

George took a deep breath and went to collect his scissors. He picked them up like an acolyte handles a holy object, running his fingers over them, checking for damage, feeling every surface with reverence. He set them delicately on their golden tray.

Nathali and I held a stimulating conversation with our eyebrows.

George came back to the table, slumping loudly into his chair. He sipped at his liquor with a flat face.

"I will beg if I need to. Leave Seth Mace alone. Do not speak to him, do not look at him. This is heading for disaster if we can't contain it," he said.

Nathali said, "Seth made the crack in the floor."

"Yes," the Doctor rasped from inside his drinking glass.

Nathali placed her hands on the table and stood. "If you invited us here to tell us nothing, there's no use in me staying. I've done everything I was supposed to, but still, you pass the blame." Nathali packed herself up and left more quietly than Mieda. "Mayli, come on."

I stilled, looking at her through my down-turned lashes. Across from me, Doctor Harker strangled the tablecloth in his right hand. Behind him, my portrait watched her plate of food restlessly, unaware of the familial blood she would soon drown in.

"I'll meet you downstairs," I said.

Nathali's sad eyes lingered on me before she left.

The doctor stared at his drink. Paphador green reflected in his glasses. I could see my silhouette there, too. He was more sober now, more exhausted. When the Good Doctor act slipped, his emotions were so easy to read. Disappointment bled from him like invisible sweat; he stunk of it.

My hand stretched across to him, reaching out. "You're hiding things from us. It doesn't feel good."

My father shook his head. "I don't mean to be deceitful. It's improper to give out confidential information from one student to another. Seth's case *is* confidential, and at any rate, it's under control now."

"Ok, I get the confidential thing. But, dude, there was a *cataclysmic event* last night, big enough to crack open the cave. And you're telling me it's under control, but it's not. You showed up for breakfast *drunk*, George. It's not under control."

With downcast eyes, he said, "I'm ashamed that you've seen me like this."

"That doesn't matter, we're family. I've seen you a lot of ways. But you are obviously stressed. Can I help you out?"

"I already ask so much of you. Soon it will be too much."

I raced to get to Dwavasc Storytelling on time. Saren stood at the classroom door, welcoming me with dark circles beneath his eyes. His forced smile was stretched and thin.

He started with an announcement, "You've all seen the main entry by now. I've been assured by Dr. Harker and Advisory Benjamin that everything is stable. If your dorm has been damaged, please send a notice to the Dossier and it will be fixed as soon as possible."

From there, Saren went on with class as though all was normal, but the constant note-passing and whispers were enough to remind me that it wasn't. No one bothered to hand me a note.

After a grueling Introductory Defense class, Riolyn, Aeshra and I stood over the crack in the floor. The black liquid was gone; not even a trace of residue was left.

"Are you sure you saw the black goo?" Aeshra asked.

"Yes!" Riolyn and I groaned together.

"Well, where is it now?"

Riolyn said, "What is Devil Spit, exactly?"

"Hemacrux. It's like ... soul blood. Or, I guess it's like, if you get a cut, pus leaks out to clean the wound."

"So, it's pus?" Aeshra asked.

"*No*, or, *maybe*? Fuck, I don't know. It cleans a wounded soul."

"Doesn't everyone get soul wounds?" Riolyn asked.

"Yeah, when we do something messed up and our soul is scratched. Devil Spit is the extreme version. When a soul is so damaged that the body flushes with Hemacrux to repair it."

Aeshra's brows knit together in confusion before widening, "You mean, Seth's soul is that messed up?"

I scoffed. "Why else would he feel like garbage to be around?"

Seth wasn't in Post-Gate Rebellions on Tuesday, which was less than shocking. But Drucilla did give me multiple, uncalled-for verbal lashings when I couldn't repeat facts verbatim from memory. After Riolyn called her out, Drucilla confessed that she couldn't stand students like us, who acted as though we "deserved preferential treatment." I scoffed loud enough for Drucilla to hear.

She yelled from her little stage, "If you would not have been so bothersome to Seth, this never would have happened!"

Elandra, the assistant, gasped behind her and Drucilla quickly ended class. The entire class gaped open-mouthed like beached whales.

The school week continued with a lot of "*Drucilla is right, you know*," from faceless students. Riolyn was always the first to knock them back, defending me to the death if she had to. Walking the school hallways was like watching a horror movie; their timid glances flitting to the corners of rooms for a sign of the Beast. I knew something unpleasant was coming, but wasn't sure what or when.

Seth wasn't to be seen the rest of the week, but I'd expected that. I couldn't imagine him ever showing his face in the halls of Voltenstraus after what had happened. Surely, he had to know everyone was whispering about him. I knew what that felt like, at least.

Uyentra popped by at dinner and asked me out on another date; Friday night.

On Friday morning, on my way to the library for study hall, I caught Nathali draped over Corin, laughing at an almost certainly laughless joke. She motioned toward me, and spoke into my ear, "Watch yourself, the Devil's out." She nodded toward the end of the hall, and I caught a glimpse of Seth turning the corner in his platform, lace-up boots. "Looks like he raided your closet, too."

I wanted to follow Seth, but ... I wasn't doing that anymore.

Uyentra met me in the main entry after dinner, wearing all black and standing over the crack in the floor like they owned it. They took me to a dark spot in Nepa with fancy drinks and soft music. Uyentra laughed at all my jokes, complimented me on my creative outfit choice and engaged me in abstract conversation. This time, I noticed their scent. Warm, green, peppery. We managed to not talk about Seth Mace at all.

"The Divine energy of this place has been tangled," Varali said as she held her hands to the polished vein of paphador snaking across the Limits classroom wall. "We must use our Limits with the utmost care."

I sat on the floor with the rest of the class, trying to harness my power. It seemed there wasn't a drop in me, and maybe there never had been. Which, to be honest, was possible. My parents had often reminded me of the trouble with my power; how it wasn't worth honing, because it wasn't *right*. And I had a lot of other gifts to honor the Vales with. Slight

Hands was pleased with my creativity; Uyenl with my wit. Erytoa had given me Palm Lifting by accident, or maybe she'd forced it on me out of spite (did Erytoa do stuff like that?). Either way, it *wasn't meant to be.* And that was fine.

But when my eyes opened out of my own spite, I realized that my fellow students were shifting and shuffling, not because they were filled to bursting with radiant, divine power, but because they couldn't find theirs either.

"Yes, this is troubling," Varali said. "It seems that Moonie is the only one with access to her energy today. Now, understand — this is a normal reaction to a radical energy discharge. Your powers will resurface, but in the meantime, Moonie will Palm Lift every one of you. After, you will know what it is to be affected by another's energy. And this will be good practice for Moonie as well."

Moonie knelt in front of each student, placing one flat hand across their clavicles. People gasped, or laughed, or cried when she was done with them. Uyentra sat next to me, close enough to feel their body heat on my arm. I wanted to burrow into them and disappear. When Moonie got to me, she'd see that there was nothing in me; nothing but guts and bones and broken power that flowed like blood.

And there she sat, vibrating with ghostly blue energy. She smiled and closed her moonstone eyes.

Moonie grasped my upper arm and laid her other hand on my collarbone. Her fingers parted and clenched down at the base of my neck. Immediately, the energy burst within me. I had shut my mouth to keep from groaning. Between my eyes, two points burned like tiny, ferocious flames pressing into my muscles. Red filled my mind, slamming against the blue ice entering my system. The red grew, and so did the blue, tracing and swirling together like a hurricane.

When Moonie pulled away, she was panting. So was I. Her hands glowed blood red. I cast my eyes downward, and my hands were lit up in cold blue.

Varali chirped over applause. "How wonderful! A successful unity of power! Very good, you two; this is the beginning of very advanced magic."

Heat flushed my face as my fellow students clapped for us.

Nathali pulled me into a hug, taking my blue hands in hers. Her nose was cold against my ear when she whispered, "Dad can't know about this."

Uyentra sat on the hearth of the largest fireplace in the library; the fire sparked and hissed behind them, casting orange on their fur. Saren and Aeshra bent forward, enthralled in Uyentra's dramatic retelling of Moonie and I "*lighting each other up*" in Limits class. Riolyn held a mug of rootbrew to her lips, covertly watching Dr. Valentine from across the library.

A student aide tapped on my shoulder, handing me a notice from Benjamin.

"Weird." Aeshra snatched the note up. "Teachers never ask students up on Saturdays. Especially Benjamin."

"Am I in trouble?" I looked to Saren for an answer.

He shrugged. "Have you done anything devious this weekend?"

"Not that I know of."

Riolyn raised an eyebrow over her mug. "That's not much of an answer."

When I got up to the sixth floor, the Dossier was dark. In the late weekend afternoon, workers fled Voltenstraus, escaping on the ferry back to their homes in Nepa. It was strange to be there, like I was breaking and entering. My footsteps echoed in the empty cave. Ever-present water tapped on a floor grate somewhere past the desks. I shivered.

Commotion sounded from Benjamin's office, and I couldn't stop myself from listening. A dull thrum of dark energy vibrated off the door. My stomach flipped.

A low growl came from beyond the door, and the hair on my back stood. I stepped back from the door.

Inside, Seth Mace's voice spoke lowly, "This is ridiculous, I've lived here for years. And now Idrissa wants me out?"

Benjamin said, "Please, calm down. We don't want another incident. This change will help you integrate with your classmates—"

"I don't want to integrate!" A burst of energy rumbled through the floor. "You saw what I did down there! Do you want to put the others in that sort of danger?"

A chair skidded across the floor in a clatter. I stepped back again, afraid the door would break open.

My father's smooth voice wafted through the air. "Idrissa is tired; you know this. You were doing so well, and the progress has been a gift to see. But something has changed, and Idrissa needs space for recovery."

"*Something* has changed? Really? I have enough guilt as it is."

Dad's voice cracked. "You are draining sae. You are *destroying* sae. There, does that make it easier for you? Do the honorable thing, Seth. This line, right here."

"We need your signature. It's the right thing to do," Benjamin said as papers rustled.

With eyes opened to their widest, I turned to slip away. I must have been called up by mistake. This was not a conversation I could be caught eavesdropping on.

"Where is she? Late again."

Well, shit.

My father opened the door, his face flat. His eyes hardened at the sight of me. Seth stood behind him, mumbling like an animated corpse. Bruised grey circled his humid, sunken eyes, and his hair was a ratted mess. He turned to the back door and hissed, "I won't be there when you come for me." The room's unsettling cold left with him.

George ran a taught hand over his eyes, scrubbing beneath his glasses. Benjamin slumped against the wall, sighing heavily.

"My, my," I said, snaking into the room. "You two look well-rested."

George clenched his jaw. He reached for my hand and held it up, squeezing it in an unnatural gesture. He turned to Benjamin and said, "I will leave this to you. I'm already late for a meeting in Nepa."

Benjamin's mouth gaped. "You're leaving? Now?"

My father pulled his coat from a chairback. "I won't be back until late tonight." His eyes snapped to mine. "Do not come looking for me."

The nervous whisper in my stomach grew to a howl.

Dr. Harker abandoned us with nothing more than a nod. Behind the door to Benjamin's quarters, a thunderous sound ruptured, and glass shattered. Benjamin and I stood alone in his office. Red with stress, Benjamin said, "You're lucky to have missed the first part of that exchange."

"I have no idea what I'm walking into."

The advisory stumbled to his desk and fell into the chair. "I looked for another solution — I did. I pulled for Donnie, Saren, even *Aeshra,* for Messer's sake." He shuffled his hands over the desk, muttering to himself. "George seems determined to force you into this. I don't understand his thinking, but of course, *he* has the final say."

"I need more information, man. What are you talking about?"

Benjamin smacked his blotchy hand on a paper and slid it toward me. I read the first line, *Roommate Release Form*. The bottom was signed by Benjamin, Idrissa, and my father. Two more lines had to be signed: one was blank, and the other had a red X scratched through it.

My brows shot to the ceiling. Benjamin and I stared at each other for a long, long moment. Water trickled down the cave wall behind him, dripping into a little, decorative basin with palm trees painted on it. I hated the man sitting before me.

"No, no, no." I slid my chair back and tripped away from the desk with my hands in the air. "I won't sign that."

"Please, I know — Mayli, you *must*. Idrissa is deathly ill, and Seth *must* be moved. Your father is — *Messer's ass*, why did he have to run off right *now*?" He hit the desktop with his pudgy fist; papers fluttered in the impact.

"Messer's ass is right! Seth is killing a Non-Eater and *I'm* the one you stick him with?! Who gets him when he starts killing *me*?"

"No, *no,* that won't happen. He doesn't affect the others in the same way. According to Dr. Harker, you have extensive knowledge in a variety of situations. You can handle yourself. He believes your personalities could work well together through the initial ... growing pains. Seth has no interaction with his peers outside of the classroom. He needs to be a teenager. He needs friends to have fun with—"

"Whoa, wait just a minute. Do you people have brains? I cannot stand that guy! How am I supposed to live with him? In the *same room*? Has everyone lost their minds?" I paced the beige office, nausea burning up my throat.

Benjamin picked up the blasted paper and shook it in the air. "You have no choice! The arrangements have been made, and I know your stubborn father will force it with or without your signature. Tomorrow afternoon, Riolyn will move in with Aeshra. Seth will move to Eldrid #14. Monday morning, it will be as if nothing happened. You will go to your classes; Seth will go to his. You will eat dinner, and Seth will eat dinner. The only thing changing is your roommate."

"Oh, right, just like any other day," I hissed. With a red pen in hand, I drew a sad face on the signature line. "My father always gets what he wants. At least I'm barred from 'looking for him.' I don't want to see his scruffy-bearded face for the rest of my life."

"That makes two of us," Benjamin said as the sun set in the beach-themed window behind him.

15

KICKING ROCKS, MULLING THOUGHTS

Mina stood over the kitchen sink, lurching and gagging. I watched from the dining table. My dress shirt felt like silk between my fingers; slick, soft, liquid. Vomit splattered on stainless steel like the sound of tires through mud.

She straightened and wiped her mouth with a rag. The scratch-lines on her throat had scabbed overnight after the Lambnoc death party. After she fell in her quest for sobriety. After she'd waved my sins before our friends, calling me a "fucking legend." After she'd prodded my leg and asked: *Devin, will you marry me?*

Mina's red eyes raked over me as she pulled a jar of pear glace from the fridge. "I don't remember last night much. But I know I said something that upset you. I'm sorry." She poured glace into a cup and sipped at it. "Also, I'm sorry for doing Viadin again. I don't know what happened."

"Why are you apologizing to me?"

Mina stepped back from me and sniffed. "Good question." She opened a drawer and pulled out her car keys, tossing them to me, and stomped through the house. Her bedroom door slammed shut.

When I pulled out of 240 Arm in her car, I realized something unfathomable: I'd hurt Mina's feelings.

The Frasier crew and I ate soft noodles in the breakroom. Cassius even joined us; he'd driven in overnight after hearing the *fantastic news* of Governor Lambnoc's murder. Most everyone was nursing a hangover.

Cassius gushed about his very exciting travels to the country of Nessuir in the next weeks. "I rarely have a hounding target in Nessuir, and this time I have *four*! Three of the four are in Empress Village and — well, of course, most of you haven't been there." He cast an upturned glance around. "The culture is purely Baskian; you know, *regal*. Those cats certainly have taste. I'll catch a Bough Ritual if I can. No matter that Mina will say it's *not in the budget*."

"Bough Ritual?" I asked.

Cassius let out a theatrical sigh. "Bough Rituals are the Baskian treetop dance; honoring Erytoa, of course. The dancers are quite *agile*. Oh, Devin, you haven't lived!"

Squeem gave me a Cassius-worthy eye roll. I covered my mouth to keep my giggling quiet.

"According to Mina, Devin's done plenty of living," Matey said into her bowl of noodles.

Taro gasped, "*Matey!*"

"*Oh*, do tell!" Cassius said.

Squeem stood from the table. "Enough, guys. We have work to do."

He latched onto my shoulder and practically dragged me from the room.

I sat with Squeem as he worked tediously on repairing a small, metallic object. Squeem mentioned that he hated the tedious repairs that other teams sent in; he much rather spent his days inventing more and better tools for DAG.

"I want to know how things work. I don't want to work on things. Does that make sense?" He mumbled as he snapped a thin disk in place. "Fruit is so much better at this part of the job than I am; he has that unbreakable focus."

"Why doesn't he do it, then?" I asked, staring up at the blinking surveillance camera at the top of the room.

"He did, at first, when it was just us three. I came up with designs and he built. Or I hacked into wherever, and he took over from there. His attention to detail is better spent on that sort of stuff. He doesn't get bored with it, doesn't need to channel surf like I do. Once I invented the hounding system, it's like he was made for it."

I was quiet for a while, imagining what this group had been like in the beginning. Just Mina, Fruit and Squeem. Doing what? Designing weird contraptions and killing people?

Next to me, Squeem belched loudly. We giggled like schoolboys.

Sometime after 3pm, I was padding around in my socks, processing existential feelings. Mina was a monster. Mina was a woman with a drug addiction. Mina hurt people for fun. Mina looked magnificent in blue plastic. In my pocket, my wordsearching screen pinged. I took the screen out and glanced over it.

Cassius opened the door with a loud click. We made eye contact. At the same time, I processed what was on my screen. Something to Merchant. Something mentioning *Amnea Station*. I looked back down at the hacked comm.

Lambnoc lost, Amnea Station closed through Veishrin, reroute packages.

My heart began beating at an alarming rate. A crazed smile cut across my face.

"Devin, are you quite alright? You look rather…" Cassius trailed off as I held my wordsearching screen up in his direction.

I didn't know what *Amnea Station* meant. But I did know that this pinned something on Merchant, that damned boar.

My mind stalled, thoughts dripping out like oil in an old car. Merchant was bad news. Would Mina kill him now? How did I feel about that? Good? Bad? Both?

Cassius grabbed my screen. He gave a low hum. "Ah, yes, this is good. Well done, friend." He turned out of the door with my screen still in hand.

I chased after him. "Wait! What are you doing?"

"Taking this to Squeem, obviously. Really, Devin, you need to be more proactive. I'm not sure who this *Merchant* character is, but they are in *deep.*"

Squeem's eyes went wide as he read the comm, "When did this come in? *Minutes* after Lambnoc died. Holy shit. This is brilliant." He pounded his fist on the intercom and yelled, "Everyone, conference room, *now!*"

Cassius rubbed his hands together. "I picked quite the day to drop by."

Squeem pressed some buttons and screens ascended from within the tabletop, one for each crew member. He screenshared the comm with the crew. Yelps and howls of excitement lit up the room.

"This comm was sent to Merchant right after Mina killed Lambnoc senior," Squeem said from his spot next to me at the table. "Merchant is high up on the food chain. We need this comm decrypted today. There are a few jobs I can divide up between you all. We monitor three communication systems connected to Merchant. So, who sent it, and from where? Which system received this comm? If we can answer these questions, we'll hit a gold mine."

"This makes it seem like Amnea station is a physical place," Matey said.

"I think we can assume it's an actual location. We can entertain theories about virtual reality, as well. These deliveries they mentioned could be physical or digital."

Taro cleared her throat heavily before raising her hand. "I have a question."

Squeem looked up at her. "Yes?"

"Should Devin be here? We are delving into secure information."

An ache clenched in my middle.

Squeem sighed. He pulled up the table-set keyboard and typed on the pink-lit keys. There, for all to see, popped up my old, messy mugshot from my felony days, with mascara running down my cheeks and a big knot of hair on the side of my head.

Name: Devin Alo-Ellosa Cemet Mace, *Stage name:* Devin *Age:* 32, *Species:* Unknown, *Job title:* Understudy, *Theater:* Frasier, *Clearance level:* 1

"See, it's official!" Squeem's face cracked open in glee.

"Cute picture, Mr. *Mace,*" Cassius laughed. My body sunk further into the chair.

"However," Squeem leaned into the screen, studying it. "I've never seen this glitch before; Fruit? It says his species is Unknown."

Fruit gave a soft grunt.

Squeem tapped on his keyboard, reversing the screen share. I watched as he searched for other *Species: Unknowns.* Five thumbnails popped up, four of which said *redacted: level 12* over red. The fifth was me, practically drooling icetar in my mugshot. He glanced at me with a frown. "We should have him scanned again. I doubt Mina would like knowing there's a glitch we haven't addressed."

Who else was an Unknown in there?

Matey spoke up, "Has anyone contacted Mina? Or Backstage?"

Squeem averted her eyes, digging deeper into my species glitch. He didn't answer her.

"I'll take that as a no. She's going to be angry." Matey glared at Squeem.

Squeem looked up at the table, groaning. I finally saw him clearly; Squeem was a sickly looking fellow on a good day, but today... I hadn't noticed before. I'd been too caught up in my own wallowing; my mugshot! It was so ugly! Everyone knew what I looked like on the come-down, now! But Squeem was living *right now*, and right now was very stressful for him.

"Let's give Mina one day of peace," Squeem said. "Today, we need to brief Devin on the Full Set."

And so, over the course of the next three hours, many things were unveiled to me.

Taro pushed her short, black hair behind her ears. "This should go without saying, but the Dight Actors Guild has nothing to do with theater. Our purpose is more than to be a troop of lawless actors."

I nodded, heat flushing to my cheeks.

"The first thing you need to understand is about Limits children. So, we should ask — have you known any Limits in your life?"

I squinted at the wall, thinking of my youngest brother and the razor-edge of magic he balanced on. "Not really, no."

Taro nodded, "Good. This information is traumatizing to anyone, but it would be much worse if you had lost a Limit." She stretched her arms as if readying herself for battle. "It is common knowledge throughout the six habitable layers that energy-imbued beings die at an early age. We've come to know this as "going away to die," when a Limit has used up their remaining essence and instinctively leaves their family home to die alone."

Matey shuffled in her chair, taking an unsteady breath.

"What you need to know first is that Limits children do not 'go away to die', as they say. It is not biologically normal for a twelve-year-old Firewalker to disappear into the woods, curl up and die. This is a lie we, and everyone else, have been fed from birth."

In the moments it took to catch my brain up, everyone sat forward in their seats and watched me with bated breath.

"I'm sorry, what?"

Squeem put a hand on my arm. "This is a lot to take in, so we'll go slow."

Taro continued, "Energy-imbued beings have the same lifespan as anyone else. In ancient times, they were killed out of fear. Then, they were worked to death by industrialist society. For hundreds of years, after the closing of the Supernal Gate to Develtic, Limits lived normal lives, aging into adulthood, having children of their own, and dying in old age.

"And then, three generations ago, they began disappearing. Sometimes, bodies were found, drained of their essence. It has been taught since that the sheer existence of divine energy in a person drains their lifeforce. And, when all the essence has dried up, they crawl off like dying cats. Due to some *base primordial instinct*," Taro scoffed at the fact I'd heard my entire life.

"We know this isn't true. All of us have witnessed children with Limits aging alongside us, honing their powers into something magnificent, and never 'running out of essence.' If the child is protected, they live."

"Then why are the rest of them dying?" I asked.

Squeem answered, "The Full Set takes them. And does Mess-knows-what with them."

Silence. My brain was stuck in a loop of confusion.

"I didn't believe it either, at first," Matey admitted. "I went to medical school; I'd been trained in the life cycles of Limits, and studied countless reports of Limits drained and dying. It's *common knowledge*. But, I ended up Backstage after my accident, and it's *full* of adults with Limits. Suntappers, Faunate, Palm Lifters, even a *Whister*. Elderly, happy, very much alive. And only because they are in a place that the Full Set can't get to."

"So, they just find someone on the registry and grab them off the street? People would *notice*," I said.

Pink light glowed around Fruit's fingers as he typed. An image of a person shared on each screen. The being's face was blurred by jagged squares. "Larcies."

Squeem nodded. "They use professional abductors. We call them Larcies. They wear these black gloves that do ... something to the victim." The image zoomed onto the person's hands.

I sucked in a breath. Black, shiny, hard and soft, rubber, or was it silicone? Or something else entirely. The smell of the humid summer traffic on Brunock Island overwhelmed my memory. The sound of floatcars blaring their horns at me, just fifteen and standing in the middle of the street. Donnie, seven years old, pushing his little fists into someone's chest; their black, plastic hands grabbing him by the shoulders, and then disappearing completely. Baby Seth, cradled in the arms of a hysterical nurse. The sudden blankness of a concussion as a car collided with me.

"My, my, Devin. Have you seen a Larcie?" Cassius purred.

"My brother — when he was born, maybe. I don't remember, I was outside, just ... saw it from a window. But my other brothers *swear* it. Gave them nightmares for years."

"Wow. That's unexpected. Your brothers are okay?" Squeem asked from my side. His hand pulled at mine with a rough squeeze.

I coughed up a sick laugh. "I don't know if I'd call them okay, but they're alive."

"That's extremely lucky. It's rare to escape a run in with a Larcie," Taro said. "We don't know why or where they take them. But the bodies that turn back up have no more essence in them. And contrary to popular thought, that is not a natural process."

Tears caught on the brims of my eyes. "So, my newborn brother was seconds away from having his essence drained by some secret society? Is that what you're telling me?"

Sad eyes met mine from around the room. I paused to let the horror settle in my stomach.

"Is that who Mina is killing? These Larcies? Because I can't imagine Governor Lambnoc being fit enough to grab some kid off the street."

Squeem laughed at the thought, "Our sole mission at the Frasier Theater is to track and kill Full Set members, whatever their connection to the group might be. Governor Lambnoc was dripping in Full Set money. His campaign funding was dark, and we were able to tie his son's company board to other known members. We know he was a prominent member in the Full Set, but it took a few years to get sound evidence; this stuff is incredibly hard to trace."

I wasn't one for conspiracy theories, and this one seemed beyond far-fetched. If special children were found to be missing, why wasn't it being reported on the news?

At the same time, the bit about Larcies strummed at my bones. It was too close to home.

"When the person tried to take my youngest brother, my other brothers fought back. The person with the black hands disappeared. I mean, *vanished*. Right there in front of everyone. I got hit by a car right after, and I assumed I was imagining it, but my brothers saw it too."

"Yes, they can disappear. We haven't learned how. It's rare to see, I'm surprised they did it so publicly."

I tapped my fingers on the table, thinking. "So, Cassick Edmund, Merchant, Kit Lambnoc? They're all caught up in stealing Limits kids? *Kit Lambnoc*? He seemed so normal."

"Why don't you show him the Kit video," Cassius said, sprawling wide-legged in his chair.

Groans sounded around the table. Matey even put her head in her hands, objecting with a long "*Nooo.*"

"He should see it," Fruit said.

Squeem sighed, scrolling through files until a video came up on our screens. "We're not watching the whole bloody thing. No one deserves that kind of punishment. Look away while I find the right part."

Everyone shielded their eyes except Fruit, who'd seen it all before. I peered through my fingers and regretted it. Whatever Mina was doing to that man — it was bad. When he finally stopped, I watched the unfolding scene.

Kit Lambnoc sat in an armchair in an abandoned apartment, kept there with some sort of black cord around his body. Warm light lit the room in soft bursts. It was shadowy, nighttime. Mina circled the bound man with an expression of frustration. Kit Lambnoc's hands were nothing but raw, bloody pulps.

Lambnoc, however, didn't look to be in pain at all. His eyes watched her smoothly, his nose turned up. The sight sent waves of unease to my stomach. It was clear that Kit Lambnoc was not the swiftly generous, easy-going man the news had labeled him as. No, something was very wrong with him.

Mina continued circling, waving her hands animatedly as she said, "You're a hard sell, Lambnoc, I'll give you that."

"I am trained for this, just as you are."

"I guess I'll be done with you, then. No use in dragging this out. I am disappointed, I won't lie. I thought we would have more of a rapport."

Mina walked over to a side table where her jars of wax were warming on a plug-in burner. As she ran her hands through her bristly-haired paintbrushes and readied her supplies, she spoke again, "It has been fun, tracking you down. You are great evidence of your father's involvement. He has been at the top of my list for a while now."

Kit faltered just a bit. He took three deep breaths, stretching what was left of his hands.

"I feel no remorse for my path. None of us do. Those children's sacrifices are honored for the good of all."

Mina's eyes squeezed shut, "Yes, *for the good of all*. I'm so fucking sick of hearing you bastards use that line on me." Mina ran her slender, pale fingers over a slender, pale knife. She held it in her hands like a holy object. "What do you think, knife?"

"Do savor it for me." Kit closed his eyes.

She set the knife back down. "On second thought," she picked up her heavy, orange pistol, "I think I'll give you a lazy death. You're no martyr."

Mina held the gun to his neck and pulled the trigger.

Right before the video stopped, Mina lurched forward. Kit's neck flowed with red. Her hand cupped under the faucet of blood with childlike wonder in her eyes. She *did* savor it; she practically bathed in it.

The room was silent. Matey had her head in her hands, breathing in short rasps. Taro stared out the window with a lost expression, rubbing slow circles on Matey's back. Cassius picked at his fingernails. Fruit pointedly picked up his pocketscreen from the table and left the room without a word.

Squeem sighed, casting weary eyes on me. "Maybe that wasn't a good idea." His eyes floated around the table. "None of us are comfortable with Mina's..." Squeem trailed off.

"Bloodlust?" I offered, my voice shaking. "I know she ... enjoys her work."

Matey scoffed and looked up, tears falling from her eye, makeup smudged. She and Taro packed up and left too.

Cassius pulled out his winning smile. "No fear, Devin boy. I won't leave you."

"I could have done without the last second of footage," I replied. "I'd thought her live airing of killing Lambnoc senior was bad, but this..."

"Mina dumbed that down for the school children!" Cassius laughed, standing. He went to the counter and popped open the cookie jar. He offered me one. "Snack?"

"Really, Cash?" Squeem said. *"Now?"*

"Merchant is a part of this Full Set?" I interrupted.

Squeem nodded. "Looks like it. If this wordsearch comm is to be trusted. We will need to dive in deeper to find more evidence, and you are invited to help us with that, if you'd take the offer."

My eyes bored into the wood of the table. It swirled; jagged lines cut by breakings in the woodgrain. I reached for my head, feeling for the spot that had never quite healed; the tender, mushy bone on my right side where I'd hit my head on the concrete. The person — Larcie — vanished, the world turned, and I was hit by a floatcar. Now, these occurrences seemed more than pure chance.

"Devin?"

"Yeah. I'll help."

I spent the evening on the lake shore, kicking rocks and mulling thoughts.

Kit Lambnoc, bound to a chair and bleeding all over. He wasn't even *bothered*. Maybe he was on something. Maybe he couldn't feel pain. Was Kit Lambnoc a Limit?

Even worse — the kids. An image flashed in my eyes; a two-line report I received on the day Mina broke out of prison. A Limits child had gone missing and I all but ignored it. Had that child been abducted? Had Kit Lambnoc been a part of that?

How could it be that a man with my life experiences — who'd grown up around religious do-gooders and swam my way in and out of law enforcement; first imprisoned, later employed — I'd never heard a single *drip* about Limits children being abducted. They went away to die, and that was that. What kind of world did we live in — blooming technology, power and an endless supply of wealth — that we couldn't keep the most innocent of us safe? Or at least fess up that there was a problem at all?

And the only person doing anything about it was sitting meters away from me in her boat of pears and weapons and wax. Probably looking up new, creative ways to drain the life from someone. Mina was the one saving these kids? *Mina?*

The killer stepped onto the boat deck and yelled across the water, "Do you want dinner?"

Her ashen voice was enough to drag me out of my thoughts.

"I will poison every piece of food in that refrigerator! I will remove your occipital lobes with a laser scalpel! I will drag your sinuses right out of your nostrils! I demand respect! Chain of command!"

No one took Mina seriously, of course. As she stomped around the lobby of *Boister Energies*, Squeem whispered into my ear, "This always happens when we wait to tell her big news. She'll come down by lunch time."

He was right.

In the break room, over Matey's favorite jazzy techno, Mina apologized for her verbal abuse.

"Now we can nail Merchant to the wall of this *Amnea Station*," she said, with pear juice running down her chin. She took another bite. The squelch of her teeth in the fleshy fruit sent a curling blaze to my middle. I wiped my hand across my chin.

Taro crossed her arms over her chest. "Oh Mina, we can't touch Amnea Station, and you know it. That's not our job."

Mina groaned, Squeem groaned, pretty much everyone groaned. I held my breath, watching a drop of pear juice slide down Mina's neck.

"It's been so long since we did anything else. Maybe the Producer will give us a break," Matey sighed.

"What is our crew's mission again?" Taro's eyes were hard. "Finding and killing Full Set players. *Finding* and *killing* Full Set players. That's it."

"Taro, I recant my apology to you." Mina reached across the table and took a longbean from my plate, snapping it in half with her teeth.

Squeem cast veiled eyes at me from under his shaggy bangs. All I could do was shrug.

Merchant turned out to be a very busy man. He swung back and forth from business to business, board meetings and charity events. He had his chain of banks, with four locations in Lansche. The flagship location was on the base level of a modern, twisting high-rise. Merchant's lovely and impossible-to-hound penthouse was perched at the top, 44 floors above.

There was also the construction company, Merchant & Kin Construction, which he helped manage for a pat on the back and little to no pay. Not fishy at all.

This was also the basis for our working agreement; Merchant would budget for more wire than a project needed, giving us the excess. Mina felt this was an *optimal deal* and was annoyed that it would end with Merchant's death. This also annoyed Squeem greatly because he would, once again, have to find a new wire provider. Mina felt bad for him for a record-breaking two seconds.

She often would drop into Fruit's office to watch us hound Merchant.

"We need to get visuals of his penthouse. Imagine the dirt we would find," Mina said from behind me. Her hand resting on the back of my chair. My skin burned where her top fingers brushed against me.

Fruit grunted from beside me. "Could break in."

"Exactly. I like the way you think, Fruit. We'd full access to his servers, maybe even find the location of Amnea Station—"

"Taro would flip if she heard you right now," Squeem's voice came from the door.

Mina pounded her fist into my chair back and I jumped.

"Fucking *damnit* Squeem. I make the rules around here! Not Taro!" She sat with a thud on the desk next to me, her thigh brushing my forearm. I jumped again. "I'd like to snap those little legs of yours right off."

I turned to look at Squeem with eyes like saucers.

He laughed, "You alright there, Devin?"

Mina shoved at my shoulder. "Worry about yourself, Merscha. Devin knows I'm right. We haven't had such a big break since before I spent those pointless nine months in NUIT."

On the 158th day of the winter cycle, it became startlingly clear that Merchant was indeed a Full Set player.

Mina was in Sarif meeting with the DAG crew up there to get their intel on Merchant. They had worked with him before and had lots of opinions. She'd put on a fabulous disguise before taking off on her hours-long drive. A blonde wig, braided up into a soft bun at her neck; pale blue blouse that flowed as she walked; soft, shimmering makeup on her cheeks. When she dropped me off at Boister, Squeem told her she looked like her mother and Mina smacked him for it.

Back in breezy Frasier, I rolled around Squeem's office in my dedicated desk chair and daydreamed about Mina's blonde wig. Behind me, Squeem rattled off theories about why the Full Set took Limits. He was working on something on his deskscreen; work he could do with his eyes closed.

"Certainly, it has something to do with their energy levels, the evidence points to such. Their essence. But sometimes they take people who aren't Limits, and that's a confusing bit." Squeem's teeth chattered like he needed to get the words out or they'd disappear forever.

I nodded my head and continued rolling in my chair.

"And Larcies — they all have a certain body type from what we've gathered. Tall, lean. Like fashion models." Squeem paused and scribbled *fashion models?* on a notepad. "Never caught a Larcie, have we? And why's that? Interdimensional beings, yeah? No — but it's a fun theory. No evidence of interdimensional beings. Although—"

"How can you tell what they look like?" I asked. "They're always blurred in surveillance."

"We have plenty of people who've survived them," Squeem answered offhandedly, his fingers working furiously over his keyboard.

Fruit's rough voice said over the intercom: "Hounding alert."

We *ran*.

An assistant of Governor Lambnoc, Loyal Death rest his rotten soul, stood at the front desk of Terrion Banks in downtown Lansche.

"How did you know it was Lambnoc's assistant?" I asked.

Squeem leaned over Fruit with his face an inch from the main screen. "Everyone employed by the State is logged in free-use facial recognition. Anyone can use the program."

"Makes our job easier," Fruit added. He pushed a palmful of spitgrass onto his tongue. The smell prickled in my nose.

"Turn it up," Squeem said.

The assistant's voice rose through the speakers, *"I'm here to close an account, name HLGPV."*

He was promptly taken to Merchant's personal office. Merchant greeted him with expectant, open arms, ushering him in and closing the door.

"Damn," Squeem whispered.

"We can't hear them in there?" I asked.

Fruit answered, "Bright White energy."

"The Sarif crew set up street cameras outside. They're good, but not *that* good."

We watched through the windowed walls of Merchant's office as the two men sat and chatted at length. Merchant typed idly at his deskscreen.

Fruit's large finger lifted and tapped on the main screen. Beneath his finger was the glass-glared painting on Merchant's office wall. Squeem yelped a happy gasp. I squinted, trying to understand. Blurry light and shadow mimicked Merchant and the assistant in the glass.

After half an hour, he walked the assistant to the front desk.

Merchant clapped his hand on the other man's shoulder and said, *"My monthly donation to the foundation will be higher in the coming months. A promising deal has been reached."*

As the assistant left, Merchant chatted up the front desk attendant with a big grin, like the day had progressed just as any day. Like nothing out of the ordinary had happened.

Fruit shifted to an adjacent screen and pulled up the recent footage.

The rest of the day and the next was spent on rendering the bank footage to the highest quality possible. It was slow and frustrating work and we were all on edge from the aimless waiting. I continually walked up to the front desk to huff and complain, crack my neck and stretch my hunched shoulders.

The whole thing seemed impossible. Shiny-hand professional child abductors talking in code to this Merchant guy at a bank in the middle of downtown Lansche. And we caught them on tape. And were going to watch whatever they were saying through the reflection of a painting. Really? Were we *that* good?

We were.

Squeem and Fruit met Matey, Taro, and I in the conference room. Mina was still in Sarif and Cassius was driving through the dark countryside of Nessuir. A big, goofy smile stretched its way across Squeem's face as he opened the footage, selecting and enlarging the glass on the framed painting behind Merchant.

"We know from audio surveillance that this assistant to Governor Lambnoc closed an account," Squeem checked his notes, "With the name *HLGPV*. Watch closely with that in mind."

I had no idea what I was looking for. Merchant spoke animatedly while he clicked around on his deskscreen. The reflection of the screen glowed white with icons and boxes and tiny words. Merchant typed into his arm-inset as the screens changed too quickly to follow. He was typing numbers, letters, nodding, speaking quickly and smiling. Taro gasped audibly, catching something I'd clearly missed.

Matey was just as lost as I was. She gave me an eyebrow shrug.

When Merchant stood to shake the assistant's hand and show him out, Squeem stopped the footage. He shook with joy, tapdancing his fingers on the table with wide eyes. Even Fruit smiled.

Taro started, "How many accounts did you see? I counted three."

Squeem answered, "Yes, the assistant's and two more. The names *must* be acronyms. It almost seems too easy."

Fruit nodded in agreement. "Too easy."

"Can someone fill me in?" Matey sighed, "That was very confusing."

Squeem smiled so big his face could have torn, "Yes! Of course. Let's take the footage back." The image on our screens rewound. "Watch. Merchant closes the first account. *HLGPV*; HL for Herse Lambnoc, maybe?" Squeem spoke with quick jolts. "And then he divides the funds between two different accounts with similar acronyms," Squeem checked his notes again, "*MCLEV* and *KBPEV*. If we can figure out whose accounts these are, we have two more names to add to the list." Squeem lurched forward and rested his chin in his hands, sighing with joy. "Mina is going to lose it."

We took Squeem out for drinks and tablefood at the Turrisian café in Frasier. It was one of the few restaurants in town, with cheap décor, chipping paint and gaudy neon signs. The food always satisfied.

Mina joined us, still donning her blonde wig and flowing blue. She pulled a heavy chair up to the table, settling herself across from me. Her booted foot tapped my leg, and I looked away, damning the flush heating my neck. A prickly feeling drummed in my abdomen; not quite high, not quite sick, not quite dreaming.

Squeem beamed as the table yelled out his Merchant-related accomplishments.

"—Noticed the reflection in the glass! Astonishing!" Taro cried, loopy from a share of Fruit's spitgrass.

"Amazing that he knew such a thing was even possible!" Matey cried.

"He spent sixteen *hours* rendering and re-rendering the footage!" I howled, feeling a little drunk myself.

"I'm not surprised; Squeem *is* the genius who invented the hounding system," Mina said, a wry smile tugging at her lips.

Squeem practically burst with embarrassed delight, his hands up in surrender, shaking his head, *no, no, no.*

Another round of drinks came for the table, but Mina turned hers away, adding it to Squeem's haul. I asked for a mint cream soda and Mina ordered one too, gagging on it when she took a sip.

"Absolutely *not*, that is horrifying. Take it away!" she cried and the whole table laughed. It was nice to see her free from the stress of the last few weeks. Hard to imagine her any other way when she was cracking sarcastic puns and playing out nonsense for a quick laugh.

As the group said their goodnights, Squeem whispered in my ear, "She's been watching you like prey, you know." He nodded to Mina, who was taking an obnoxious bow to the waitstaff, pulling off her wig and letting her pinned-up red hair fall in messy pieces around her shoulders. The staff laughed.

"Terrifying…" I muttered, watching her pull the pins from her tangled hair.

"Terrifying," Squeem repeated, regarding me with knowing eyes. He patted me on the back, "Or not. You never know." He held onto me as we stumbled into the cold streets.

Warmth spread into my chest.

In the following weeks, we continued working with Merchant as if nothing had changed, while watching him covertly. I was amazed with his nerve; he had to know Mina was killing people in his evil secret society. He did know it was an *evil* secret society, right?

Fruit frequently reminded me that the whole double-agent business was likely the Full Set's plan to begin with. Naturally, Fruit said this in far fewer words.

Mina's mood steadied as we focused in on Merchant full-time. She seemed to be floating high, but swore she was off viadin for good this time.

The plants in the houseboat were freshly watered, the dust polished from their leaves. A new, spindly fern grew near the kitchen sink. Rounds of birdseed hung from the overhand of the boat deck. The mound of letters on the dining table slowly diminished as Mina made her way through them each night, filing them away in a box of folders.

I sat on the floor in the kitchen drinking a warm cup of Eivian tea, rummaging through my thoughts. The sounds of Kit Lambnoc's passionless voice, *those children's sacrifices are honored for the good of all.* It cut deep into memories of my quiet childhood, ruptured by the death of my parents and the birth of my youngest brother. And the sickening lurch of guilt; Seth's dark, disastrous childhood, for which I was partially responsible. I was the oldest sibling. I should have been more present. Not so damned interested in my inner world and my own feelings. What about Seth's feelings? What if Larcies had gotten him?

Whatever they were looking for, Seth certainly had it.

An angry howl came from Mina as she sat reading letters at the table. The sound made me jump in my skin.

Mina crumpled the paper in her fists and tossed it to the floor. She reached for a pen and said, "Here's my reply, you *manipulative tyrant.*"

I reached for the crumpled letter.

M1

Tidal waves incoming. N says she is 'long past saving'. She will not listen to me. Your expertise is needed. I can think of nothing else while N destroys herself, and my focus must be elsewhere. You know how important my work is. She will listen to you.

I await your response.

"Ridiculous, isn't it," Mina snarled. She put her response in a crisp, white envelope and licked it shut, "For him to think I'm just — what, sitting around? Waiting for him to ask me to fix his marriage? Like I don't have a billion other, more important things to do. Things *he's* having me do."

I sat for a moment, trying to thread pieces together, "N. That's who sent you the last letter. I remember now, *dead before Veishrin.* Who are these people?"

Mina was quiet as she continued going through her mail. The blotchy red of her cheeks subsided. Eventually she picked up her enveloped response and sighed. "I might have been a bit harsh. I think I'll send it, anyway. Just one more thing for him to worry about."

16

Ghost in the Room

Riolyn was so mad that she went to talk to Benjamin herself.

"That soft prat! I'd like to see him burn in that poncy, paradise-themed office of his!" Riolyn stormed around the Eldrid lounge as other students watched us with shifty eyes.

Aeshra sighed from the floor, "Your dad must really have it out for you, May."

"Thanks, man," I grumbled.

"They're all off their asses if they think this is going to work! Out of their minds!" Riolyn continued.

"What did Benjamin say to you?" I asked.

"*'Sorry, Miss Vite, there's nothing I can do.'* Trash sniffer. Washing his hands of the whole thing like he had nothing to do with it. Do they know what they're putting you through? What they're putting *me* through? And what the hell is with your dad? Fucking child abuse, if you ask me."

"Benjamin did seem awfully apologetic last night. He said Seth needed friends."

Aeshra gasped, "Oh *no*."

Riolyn towered over me, fuming. "It shouldn't be your job to look after that nutcase."

The next morning, Uyentra tapped on the door frame with a handful of wildflowers.

"You slept alone last night?" They nudged their nose into the softness of my jaw. "You should have called me up."

I let out the saddest, most pathetic giggle. They purred against my neck as I smelled the flowers; a cold, sweet sort of smell, like wet moss on tree bark. The yellow petals sprouted from misty blue stems and fuzzy leaves.

My arms found their way around Uyentra's middle as I burrowed into their chest, letting their humming purr surround me.

Someone cleared their throat from the hallway. We startled apart. Benjamin shifted his weight from foot to foot. His back stooped from the weight of the heavy trunk in his arms.

Uyentra bounded to him and took the luggage with a laugh. They set it down next to Riolyn's old bed. With one gold-tipped finger, they wiped a line of dust from the lid.

Benjamin cleared his throat again. "Thank you, Uyentra, but I'll take the rest from here."

My joyfriend gave me a hand squeeze. "I'll be upstairs if you need me."

The advisory of Voltenstraus sat on the floor of my dorm room, lining up four pairs of massive black boots in front of the closet. With a handkerchief, he shined the toe of each boot in small circles. Above him, a silvery grey sitting-sack hung from the closet ceiling.

"I want you to know that I'm sorry we put you in this situation," Benjamin said.

"Oh, yeah?"

Still bent over the boots, he said, "Yes. Seth is a handful. He's become reliant on Idrissa, and I'm not sure how he's going to react to this change.

We've given him everything he needs to succeed, but we can't give him the will to do so. Your father has reassured me time and time again that this is the right choice, but I'm ... not sure. I commend you for being marginally pleasant about it."

We sat in silence, equals in my father's nameless scheme.

"I feel like I'm being used for something, but I don't know what," I said, pulling at the lint caught in my leg hair. The blue-green glow of paphador reflected off the velvet of my bedspread.

There was a knock at the door. Benjamin stood from the floor and shook himself off like a dog. "Come in!" he yelled.

Donnie Mace opened the door, looking more like a bodyguard than a brother. His luscious smile was gone, replaced by a sullen, straight line. Seth sulked behind him, a spider camping in a hall corner, praying to be missed by the broom. I couldn't feel the sickening cloud around him; not yet.

Benjamin's words rushed out: "This is your new dorm, Seth. Here is your bed." He motioned around the room, ushering them in. "I put your things away for you. Your clothes are here, and — boots, of course, along here." He slid open the closet door. "Your sitting sack, as well. You still use one, yes?"

Seth's eyes trailed along the floor to the toes of his polished boots. He nodded.

"That was very nice of you, Benjamin. Wasn't it, Seth?" Donnie said, like a parent talking to a toddler. Seth didn't reply. "Look, he even put your schoolbooks out for you. Seth — are you listening?"

Seth squeezed himself in a protective hug, skinny arms wrapped around his thin chest.

Something painful and hollow settled in my stomach.

The thrumming of dark energy began, whispering out of him in brittle waves. I shook my head against it, willing it from my ears. It pushed at my temples, little unwelcome fingers prodding at me.

Donnie and Benjamin didn't seem to notice. They chatted awkwardly in the center of the room.

Seth nudged himself between them, ignoring the shock on their faces. "Goodbye," he said.

Benjamin's bushy eyebrows shot up. "Oh, well, of course—"

"Now, Seth, we're here to settle you into this. You haven't spoken to Mayli yet," Donnie leveraged his slight height advantage, boxing Seth in with his wide shoulders.

I sat silently on my bed, watching. Benjamin curled away from the two brothers with a flinch. The feeling then rolled to me; a deep, hollow drumming of energy. Twice as much; was Donnie full of the dark stuff, too?

But Donnie pulled at Benjamin's sleeve and they walked to the door. Without a word to me, they left. Seth watched as they disappeared down the hallway.

He slid open the closet door. Before him, the silver sitting sack reflected paphador light, iridescent and liquid as it hung. Seth pulled open the side and slid into it, pulling his platform-booted feet in beneath him. He met my gaze and disappeared into the fabric. I rolled my eyes and stomped out of the room.

Seth's boots *should* have clunked when he walked, heavy platforms on stone. Instead, he was as silent as a bat in flight. The grey of his skin was as smooth as the underbelly of a snake. The impossible amber of his eyes, always humid, always emotionless. The translucence of his eyelids, thin and yellowed like old bruises. The top of his forehead was without pigment, bleeding into the mint-colored streaks of hair framing his face. The pale green bangs had white roots, while the rest of his hair was stark black and short.

I knew as much as I did about Seth's appearance because I stole glances at him as he sat in his sitting sack for hours at a time, lifeless like a powered-down robot. His clothes clung to skinny limbs. It was startling how comatose he seemed laying there, sometimes sitting up, sometimes locking himself in the bathroom for far too long for my own comfort. I'd listen, ready to push my ear to the door but afraid to be caught. I wasn't sure what he was doing in there, but I didn't like it.

Coughing. Lots of coughing. And a healthy amount of showering (more than I was doing).

Some days, Seth would be gone before I woke up. He never came to the room if I was already there, how did he *know?* What did he think would happen? I'd remember he existed? Like I wouldn't notice the shame radiating from him if I saw him *move?*

I could smell his shame in the air.

And my stupid father was avoiding me. He was too busy to meet with me; a student needed him, or he had lessons, or therapy, or countless secret meetings with secret business partners in secret locations. I was sick of secrets. I was about to break into his living quarters in the dead of night. What else was I supposed to do? I needed support in this.

When I didn't want to be in my depressing dorm room with Seth's near-corpse hanging in the closet, I stayed with Riolyn and Aeshra.

We sang and danced obnoxiously, ignoring the noise complaints. Riolyn would yell the lyrics to her favorite lesbians-only metal band. Aeshra was a great dancer — he would spin me around, catching me when I inevitably tripped.

But when we eventually tired out at the end of the evening, we always came back to the same subject. Seth; it was always Seth.

"Is he sick? Should we tell someone?" Aeshra asked, like I would have a different answer this time. He snuggled into my side on the bed. His fluffy sweater was soft on my arm.

I shrugged, "Maybe. I'm concerned, I guess. There's a lot going on in there. I mean, why else would he hide in the closet? He doesn't *move*. I don't want to pry, though, you know. I don't know."

Riolyn asked, laying on my other side, "What does your dad think?"

"Avoiding me, still. He knows I'm going to flip out on him."

"It was *his* idea," Riolyn sniffed.

Aeshra giggled and said, "Should we break into his room and tie him up? He'd have to talk, then!"

Riolyn and I nodded, staring sullenly at the wall. Tying up Doctor Harker, King of Voltenstraus, still seemed like a bad idea.

"School was supposed to be fun. This isn't fun," Aeshra said.

"Well, the good news is, the worst is yet to come!" I slapped Aeshra and Riolyn on their thighs.

A week into the roommate switcheroo, Drucilla had the nerve to ask *me* why Seth wasn't in class.

"Why are you asking me?" I said from the top of the auditorium. "I don't know where he is."

Drucilla pointed her blue finger at me and snarled, "Seth has been forced into a room with you, hasn't he? Tell me, Miss Harker: have you cured him like your father suggested you would? Or have you failed to do that as well?"

"I — what? I'm not curing anyone. I'm just his roommate!" I said, flattening my hair with my hands instinctively.

"I see it's time to implement a hair washing schedule, Miss Harker."

"Are you gonna teach us, or what?" Riolyn hollered down at her.

"Get out! Get out of my classroom!"

I put my head in my hands and sighed.

Uyentra helped me with my homework in the library whenever I needed it. They were a constant point of light in their quiet, dignified way. Always complimenting my outfit, never commenting about the grease in my hair.

At a small table near a fireplace, they asked me for a billionth time if I would join them in Nepa for a house party.

"Saturday night, at the sand house. We'll have a lovely time. Bring your friends." They pushed up my sleeve to run their sharp nails over my wrist. I shivered.

"Yeah, okay. I'll go."

After Limits class, I went to my father's office and banged on his door with every bit of strength I had.

"Doctor Harker! Please, open up! It's an emergency!" I yelled. My bleating voice echoed through the entire cave.

When he opened it, he had his pocketscreen pressed to his ear. His eyes narrowed. "Enough. I'm on an important call!" He began to shut the door.

"If you don't talk to me right now, I am going to tell the whole school you wear women's underwear. *Yellow* ones!"

Dr. Harker covered the mouthpiece and hissed, "I don't care! Tell them!"

I shoved the door back open. "I know you are avoiding me and I refuse to be ignored any longer! I am coming in there right now and you're going to speak to me like an adult!"

He glared at me for a long moment. He said a polite goodbye to whoever was *so important* on the phone.

I stepped in. The mammoth painting of my mother hung over me with judgement. I nodded at her, agreeing; *She* was a hot head, not me. I was not here to fight with my father. I was here to get support. I was here to demand an explanation. I was not going to fight with him — I was *not*.

George swept about his office, pretending to get things in order. He shuffled papers on his desk, righted a framed picture of my brother Tom, ran his fingers over a shelf of books.

"Hey, asshat. Quit dicking around and talk to me."

His eyes were closed behind his glasses. "What did you need, dear?"

"What do I *need*? Are you serious? You can't possibly be serious. You dropped me off with a psycho and locked the door as you left. Are you trying to kill me?" I asked incredulously. I took a deep breath. *Don't fight, don't fight, don't fight.*

George's eyes rounded in innocence. "May, are you upset? It's been weeks. Haven't you and Seth settled in together?"

"Uh, *no*, we haven't. Spider boy isn't moving. He hides in a sitting sack like they're his fucking bat wings. Not to mention, the walls shake when he does more than itch his crotch. So, what the fuck is going on? Is this normal? And why are you making these decisions without asking me? I should have some say in my own damn life! This isn't *like* you!" The words spilled out of me.

My father reached to put his hand on my shoulder. It was clammy and cold.

"Please slow down. One topic at a time," He removed his hand from me and began pacing, "Seth's depression is acting up, but he is seeing his doctors frequently, including me. This is good; It's all part of the plan. Idrissa agrees with me on this. You are fully capable of what I ask of you. I would never put you in any real danger."

I scowled. "Why do you have to say *real* danger? That makes it sound like there's still danger. It's sketchy, Dad. Why didn't you at least tell me first?"

Dr. Harker felt a soft, thick paper with his fingertips as though it made of fairy wings. I watched, distracted by the movements.

"Would you have agreed? Of course not. Your instincts would have begged you to refuse rooming with the boy."

"And my instincts are right?"

Pain cut across him, furrowing for a millisecond, undetectable to the average person. A twinge of his upper lip, a flare of his nostrils. I knew this man; I could read him like a novel.

"What are you hiding from me?" I asked.

His pocketscreen rang, and he answered it. I reached for the paper he folded over and over in his hands. With a pen, I wrote: *This is not okay.*

I slammed the door on the way out.

I was angry, red hot with it. When Uyentra stopped by my dorm to whisk me off to Nepa, they could feel it. Seth wasn't in our dorm; he'd been gone all day long, and I was glad to be rid of him. I stomped around the room, slamming drawers and bathroom doors. While I scribbled heavy makeup on my face, Uyentra sat on my bed, glowing with luxury. Tailored pants and jacket, all navy, with green and gold makeup lining their eyes. So opposite to my ill-fitting clothes; baggy pants and a tight T-shirt stretched over my least favorite part of myself.

On the ferry to Nepa, Uyentra's thumb moved over the back of my hand in comforting circles. The water was still, motionless, and grey. Looking at it made me feel sick.

"Where are your friends?" Uyentra asked.

"Riolyn said something about breaking into the corner store to get some smokes."

They laughed. "Imagine having to buy them like everyone else does! The horror."

Uyentra held my hand as we walked down the foggy, golden-lit streets of Nepa. The rickety, sand-filled house sunk into the lake shore; red smoke billowed up from the beach behind it.

"You're nervous, I can feel it." Uyentra squeezed my hand in theirs and a little shiver bloomed up my back. "Your soul is trembling. We can do something else, if you like. There's always pie."

"No, I want to go. I need a break from my life." I was quiet for a moment, running my free hand through my hair. "You like these parties, so they can't be that bad."

Uyentra gave a small laugh. "You'd trust my taste level?"

"I trust yours more than *mine*!"

The sand house was falling apart. Damp, grey wood creaked in the wet air. Jagged stone stairs led up to a half-framed hole where the front door used to be. Kids laid on sparse grass out front, cackling and rolling around. Definitely not sober.

We stepped into the house. Dunes of sand filled the rooms, moved by tectonic events and high tides. I wondered how long these houses had been here; had this house been used for parties in my older siblings' day as well? Had Tom failed to woo a pretty girl here? Had Mina pushed someone off the roof? My parents had gone to Voltenstraus too; had they chased each other through these ruins, yelling foul names as an excuse to interact with each other?

"Can I get you a drink?" Uyentra asked. "What do you prefer?"

"Something that won't hurt coming back up. Not too sweet," I answered. "I'm going to explore."

Uyentra kissed my cheek and disappeared into the house.

Red smoke hung heavily at the ceiling, fogging the room in scarlet. I stumbled in the sand as I crept through a central room filled with drunk teenagers. They bounced and swayed over synthetic music from the Darkling layer. Green and white paint peeled from the walls, revealing grey, rotted wood beneath. This ruin of a house couldn't possibly stand for much longer, especially with the nightly vibration of heavy-bass EBM.

Students draped over stained armchairs, smoking something nefarious. When I stepped around them, they looked right through me. I looked down at my hands to make sure I was still there. That I was still me. Maybe the red smoke was getting to me.

The crisp, yellow wood of the staircase stood out in the dilapidated party house. Was the school keeping this house usable? Did the school know that kids were smoking junklip in here? Did Doctor Harker know?

At the top of the stairs, I was met with an annoyed look.

"Please tell me you're not here to break up the party." Nathali's eyes narrowed in distrust.

"Am I really that much of a fun-suck?"

"Yes, you are. Are you here with Uyentra?"

I recoiled away from a guy as he nearly fell down the stairs. My lip curled. "They talked me into it. Have you seen Riolyn or Aeshra?"

"You and your weird friends," she said absently, watching the drunk student sit on the steps, laughing with abandon. "I saw them slinking around outside. Aeshra is funny; he was wearing a bedsheet." She paused, really looking at me. "Hey, are you okay?"

I closed my eyes, squeezed them shut. "I feel sick. I literally just want to look around, but there's people everywhere. How can I see anything when I can't *see* anything?"

She laughed, "This is your excuse to get out of your sad dorm room! Have a drink, make out with your joyfriend, go play with your weirdos." She pulled the drunk guy from the stairs and pushed him toward his pretty-boy friends. "Hey, have you guys met my sister Mayli? She's *really* fun."

With a snarl, I swerved away and back down the stairs. "She's lying, I'm the worst."

I skittered down the stairs, where Uyentra stood with a drink in each hand. They handed me something purple with a red ice cube in it. It tasted like bitter herbs and honey. I smiled at Uyentra and took a big gulp.

"Goodness, dear," they said, tipping their chin down to look at me, "Don't hurt yourself."

"This place smells like hormones. Let's go outside."

Students from Voltenstraus crowded around the beach fire, throwing sorite dust in the flames to keep them burning red. Riolyn shoved a bag of the red powder into my face with wild eyes. Aeshra danced behind her, circling like a glittering snow fairy. He was indeed wearing nothing but a bed sheet and tight, metallic shorts.

"What inspired your daring ensemble, friend?" Uyentra yelled over the music.

Aeshra swirled his bed sheet cape, crying out, "I'm trying to find a husband!"

Three purple drinks later and I was just as loud as every other drunk teenager around me. Aeshra danced around the fire with Nathali, the two intoxicated princesses at the ball. Corin, Nathali's lame boyfriend, watched them from the sidelines, sipping his fancy drink. Uyentra lounged next to me on a blanket, watching the spectacle with an unhinged smile.

"Just dare me to and I'll do it," Riolyn begged. She knelt on the sand before me with her hands covered in sorite.

"Do what, now? What am I daring you to do?" I asked, head tipped to the side.

"To touch the fire. I'll do it. You just gotta dare me—"

"What? No. That's a not-good-idea," I hiccupped. Was I cross-eyed? Why was everything blurry? "Hey, do I look cross-eyed?"

Uyentra stilled their hands on my shoulders. "Dear, I think it's time we get back to the school."

Riolyn's cheek scales prickled, "But—"

Uyentra's finger traced my collar bone from one shoulder to the other. My ovaries shuddered.

"Good idea, yeah — let's get back. To the room. To the dorm room," I stammered, getting up from the blanket. "My dorm room, o' course."

Uyentra laughed, pulling me up. I saluted a scowling Riolyn as we took off.

I pushed Uyentra onto my bed with a hard shove. They were a glistening shadow of black and gold in the dark room.

They licked their lips, smiling, "Are we certain your roommate is gone?"

"Oh, uh—" I skipped to the closet and slid open the door; Seth's sitting sack hung limply, unoccupied.

My drunken body twirled, hands in the air, hips swaying. I took a running jump onto the bed next to my date. The bed shook and Uyentra laughed. They pulled me on top of them. When our lips met, I was gone.

Disjointed, disastrous thoughts strung together behind my closed eyes.

Uyentra's skin tasted like smoke and candy — George was lying to me — Uyentra's teeth on my jaw — *for the good of all* — shiny hands, grabbing, pulling — water, trickling down the walls —sensuous whispers beneath me — grey, dead skin — Uyentra smelled like smoke and tart candy and...

The bedroom smelled like mint.

I whipped my head back, eyes wide. "Do you smell that?"

Uyentra blinked in the low light. My blue lipstick was smudged on their pointy teeth. They raised a gilded eyebrow. "I don't think so."

I shook my head, stuck in the slow fog of alcohol, "Blood. No, not blood — are you, do you — *fuck*."

Hopping off the bed, I slipped, landing on my ass with a thud.

Uyentra sat up and rubbed their eyes. "What's the matter?"

"Maybe you should go. Seth'll be back soon."

Uyentra hummed and got up. They pulled me up from the floor and turned my head to look at them. I let myself look. Uyentra chuckled and kissed me, long and slow.

"Sleep well, my prince," they said with a kiss to my nose.

I stood there blushing as I watched them go. The smell of candy and smoke left with them. The mint, however, did not.

I tore through the room in my drunken state, tripping and pushing and sliding things around to find the source.

A little gleam of wetness caught my eye from the bathroom.

Just one drop, a glossy circle of black, on the bathroom tile. I stared down at it as my head warred with dizziness. What was I supposed to do? Should I bring it up to Seth? Should I take this information to my dad? Or to Doctor Valentine? Should I let it go completely?

Devil Spit was serious. Was Seth dying? Was his soul compromised?

Maybe this time I would leave it, and then if I found more, I would talk to Dr. Harker about it. Or maybe I would wait till the morning when I wasn't drunk to decide. That sounded like a good plan.

I crawled over to the cabinet and pulled out a rag and some cleaning spray, then crouched over the little drop of tar. It had been there a while; the edges were starting to harden. I wondered how often Seth kneeled over just like this, cleaning up his soul-messes. The thought tied a big knot in my stomach.

A little click came from the dorm and the door shut. Seth walked by silently, catching me crouched in the bathroom in his periphery. He halted. His eyes jumped from me, to the black spot, to the cleaning supplies in my hands.

"Cheers." I held up the spray bottle like I was making a toast.

Seth stared at me, expressionless and hard. His mouth opened. "Your makeup is messed up."

It took me a second to understand what he'd said, or that he'd even spoken to me at all. And by the time my thoughts arranged, he was crawling into silver fabric, not to be heard from again.

I tipped my head up to look in the mirror and I laughed. Absolutely insane.

Knocking.

I turned over in my bed and groaned. My throat felt sickeningly dry. The knocking at the door mocked the pounding in my head. I pried my eyes opened and looked; the closet door gaped open. Seth was nowhere in sight.

My feet touched the cold floor and I groaned again, "Ok, okay, Messer, I'm coming!"

Aeshra was at the door holding a corked bottle of clear, orange liquid. "Get your electrolytes!" He shoved the bottle into my hands.

"You aren't hungover?" I mumbled and took a gulp of the stuff. It tasted like plastic fruit; I gagged and shoved the bottle away.

"I didn't drink too much last night. But *you* obviously did! I'm dragging you and Riolyn to breakfast. You can tell us all about your night with Uyentra." Aeshra pushed the bottle of electrolytes back at me and smiled with his pointy teeth.

Breakfast helped. No more spinning rooms, no more clenching stomach. Just a neck ache and an aversion to light, but was that really so different than normal? I bid my friends a *"See you later,"* and shuffled back to Eldrid #14.

I pushed open the door and stumbled.

Seth sat upright on his bed, skinny legs crossed in front of him, his knees resting on the platforms of his boots.

I smiled awkwardly at him and escaped to the bathroom.

"Okay," I breathed with my back against the door. "Okay. It's fine." I rested my forehead on the cold stone wall and counted to eight, then brushed my teeth for good luck.

When I emerged from the bathroom, Seth was sitting exactly as he had been. His expression was unreadable. He wore all black and would have blended right into the bed sheets if not for his corpse-like pallor.

I cleared my throat and started, "So..."

Seth cut me off. "Why did Doctor Harker do this?"

"This?" I motioned around the room. "Beats me, dude. I don't know what the man is thinking."

"But he's your father," Seth stated, like that meant anything.

I shot back without thinking, "Yeah, well, I guess he spends half the year with you, so maybe *you* should know what he's doing."

Seth watched me like I was a rodent. Unwanted, annoying, mildly disgusting. I sighed and sat on my bed. A low vibration emitted from him; dull, quiet. Not the unpleasant blasts of nausea he normally gave me.

"So, are we talking now?" I asked with a curled lip.

Seth gave a noncommittal sound.

I watched the slow movement of his breathing. His eyes seemed to shift colors, from the beige-blue of last night to a wolfish green today. I asked the first question that came to mind.

"Where are you from?"

After a long pause, he said, "Dedocia."

I sat up straighter and hung my feet off the bed. "Your brother, Donnie — I met him. Do you have other siblings?"

A tiny light lit in Seth's expression, a pinch of white in the abyss. He rolled his wrists around and cracked his knuckles. "I have three brothers."

"Ok, tell me about them."

Seth stood up and began to pace the room. I couldn't help but turn over and watch him. He took long, silent strides across the room. Seth was *moving*.

"Donnie is here. And Caulder, he's like you. Wants everyone to think he's funny."

"Ouch."

Seth ignored me. "Caulder would jump in front of a wild animal for a stranger." He reached for the lamp on his side table and wrapped both hands around the sphere of glass.

I cringed. "Isn't that hot?"

"I'm not sure," he said. His hands moved around the bulb like liquid. Like he was casting a spell with it. I couldn't look away. Was I still drunk?

"Devin is the reason I'm here." Seth pulled his hands away and looked at them with interest. "Well, no. I am the reason I'm here. He set things in motion."

"Devin is the third one?"

"He's 32, I think." He wiped his totally-not-burned hands on his pants. "The oldest."

Seth pulled his hair up into the air like a mohawk and let it fall back down. He seemed to be verging on manic, nervous energy pouring out of him. Subtly, the vibrations came back online. My ears perked up to listen to the sour sounds of darkness coming from him.

"Devin is gone, or — I don't know. Something is wrong with him."

"He's gone?" I pushed off the bed.

"Don't." He turned on me like a cornered animal.

I threw my hands in the air. "Ok, yeah, but what do you mean, he's gone?"

I could feel his heart beating through his skin.

Seth reached for the paphador wall and pressed his slow fist into the stone. "Devin needs help. I cannot get anyone to listen to me."

My stomach lurched as a wave of Seth's energy rippled past. I pulled myself into a protective hug. He could crack the cave open again, couldn't he?

Seth's head fell onto the glowing green wall, and he whispered, "*You could help.*"

Tears welled in my eyes; the kind I got when there was a ghost in the room.

Donnie Mace spent his Sundays tutoring needy students in the library.

A kid sat next to Donnie as he pointed into a big book. Two tables down, Mieda played with her curls, watching him. When she saw me coming, her eyes narrowed.

I pulled up a chair next to Donnie's pupil and leaned over the book. "Wow, fascinating." I slammed the book shut and handed it to the boy. "Bye!"

The student glared me down as they left the table.

"Um, what can I help you with, Miss?" Donnie said, fitting his gorgeous smile onto his confused face.

Mieda didn't waste a second. "You are so rude. I don't think you understand how badly you treat people! This is exactly why father all but *begged* you NOT to—"

"Not important. Trust me." I turned to Donnie, "Did you know that Seth thinks Devin is in danger?"

Donnie covered his face with his hands. He grabbed ahold of the hair at his temples and squeezed for dear life, his magnificent smile gone.

"Is this what Seth has been throwing fits about?" He leaned his head back and let out a mean laugh. "Let me tell you something; Devin is always in danger. It's always something with him. He makes one bad choice after another, but of course none of it's *his* fault. Whatever danger he's in, he got himself there."

My eyes widened. "Wow, you Maces are a fun bunch."

Mieda said, "I thought you told me Devin was cleaning up?"

Donnie looked at her sideways, "I told you he *said* he was cleaning up. What he says means nothing. Supposedly, he had a job and was paying rent," Donnie turned his attention back to me. "Eventually, Devin slips up. Always has, always will. And we are done cleaning up his mistakes. Or at least I am; Seth can do whatever he wants."

Mieda put her hand on Donnie's shoulder and squeezed.

"Devin forced us to come here in the first place. I love it at Voltenstraus, and I think it's brought Seth some stability, but we can never have a normal life now. Devin got the sweet end of the deal, and I can't stand him for it. The fact that he is out of prison, walking free with a job waiting for him; I just can't understand it. Seth has been telling me for weeks that Devin is in danger. It might seem heartless, but I don't really care. He has torn this family apart and the least he can do is pay for that."

I stood up. "Man, and I thought *you* were the nice one."

I knocked on my father's office door. He opened it, his fake-cheery face vanishing when he realized who was at the door, "I am in a session right now. You of all people should know my schedule."

I threw my hands in the air, ready to burst. He was so arrogant.

"Come back at lunch." He shut the door in my face.

I grumbled all the way to Saren's office.

Saren was standing beside his sad little desk, drinking a cup of something and staring at the wall.

"Are *you* going to kick me out, too?" I tossed myself into a chair.

He sat on his desk. "Who kicked you out?"

"Dr. Harker."

"He seems anxious this year. Not that I can blame him. The landquake was unexpected."

I pulled a little jar of glace from my bag and popped it open.

"Why do you need to see him?"

"Other than family time?" I was being sarcastic, "Roommate troubles."

"As a faculty member, I shouldn't comment on students, but seeing that you're a student and I shouldn't be spending off time with you..." He grabbed my glace, taking a big gulp of it.

"Excuse me, do I need to get a drink for you?!"

Saren smiled angelically. "I was going to say, I think you're doing a great job with Seth. He is not an easy person to be around."

I rolled my eyes, taking my glace jar back. "That's the statement of the year."

"I shouldn't be saying this but, some people *might* have made bets on how long you can stand rooming with Seth. Some of them don't think you'll make it."

"What? I won't *make it*?"

Saren laughed and took a swig of glace again. "I'm drinking to your life."

George opened his office door with sweat gleaming on his brow.

"What did you so desperately need to talk to me about?" My father stood behind his desk thumbing his way through a shelf of books. I knew he wasn't really looking at them, just making motions. I glanced over the stuff on his desk and caught sight of a letter.

I don't care what N said to you, I am busy and cannot fix your fucking marital problems. Get a fucking hobby.

Do not contact me again unless you have pertinent information. I am not your thrall; I am not your marriage counselor. I am barely keeping afloat in this curse of a life. The life you forced on me, and on N.

"Wow, someone's angry," I motioned to the note on the desk. "What did you say to them?"

He whirled around and put his hands over the letter, eyes ablaze, "Do not read my things. Now why are you here?"

I tipped my chin up to the ceiling, with my hands palm-up on the desk, "I will allow you to tell me about your feelings if you wish, good sir. Your anguish is obvious."

"Oh, stop," Dad muttered. He sat down with a thud. His red facial hair was recently groomed and his glasses were clean, but the man was a wreck. "I know I can be harsh with you girls, but you just mean so much to me. Especially you."

"You aren't supposed to pick favorites."

George's frigid hand pushed mine off his desk with a smile, "Everyone knows you're my favorite. I am very lucky to have you. Now, one more time; why did you need to see me?"

"Seth is worried about his oldest brother; he thinks he's in danger. And no one is listening to him."

The doctor stilled. "Seth told you this?"

"Yes! He was a puddle of angst; it was very sad."

"Mayli. Why, this is incredible! Don't you see?" He stood up, "It took *far* too long for Seth to open up to me, and I am trained in these matters. He knew he could trust me, *told me* he trusted me, and yet it took years for him to give me even an inch of his thoughts."

"Are you even listening to me? Seth's brother could be—"

"Yes, yes," he waved me off, stopping to gaze at my mother's portrait, "If Seth is telling you his thoughts, this could show real *growth*! This is the best news we've had in years."

I grabbed Dr. Harker's shirtsleeve. "Hello? Open your ears, man! A guy out there is in danger!"

Dr. Harker squeezed my hand again, alight with frantic enthusiasm. "This is why you are working. Your sheer ability to emote is fascinating to me. You truly do care about your fellow beings." He knelt before me like a neurotic knight before a queen. "I will tell you what I know, but you must continue working with Seth. Promise me, Mayli."

I pulled my hand from his grasp and hissed, "I seem to recall you forcing this on me in first place. Don't start begging me now."

Ignoring my response, George went to his wooden, filigree decorated filing system and returned with a few news clippings. He couldn't contain his delight. "The oldest Mace brother *has* been missing. I received the call the week school started. According to Seth's guardian at the monastery—"

"The monastery?"

"Yes, Elle. Or Friar Lawrence, as I prefer to call him. According to Friar Lawrence, Devin went missing the same day of Seth's outburst on the tram — you remember, the one you *so gracefully* interrupted?"

"Shit," I murmured, suddenly seeing the event in a new light. Seth hadn't been lashing out because he was vile, evil, whatever else I'd called him in the past months. He was lashing out because his brother was likely going through something terrible, and he could *feel* it. He could *feel* it?

"Why the fuck haven't you told him?"

"I have forwarded the news to contacts in Dedocia."

"Does Donnie know?" My hands squeezed into fists.

"Backstage has been made aware of the situation,"

My hands slammed onto the desk and papers scattered. "I do not *care* about *Backstage;* answer me, George. Have you told Seth?"

My Father's eyes shifted away from me. I couldn't believe it. He hadn't told Seth; he hadn't told Donnie. Seth thought no one believed nor cared, and Donnie was sure both Seth and Devin were out of their minds.

"Look at me," I growled at my father.

He did look. "Do not tell me what to do, don't you dare. Seth cannot know about his brother, not now. He is making great strides and I will not let his brother's idiotic mistakes disrupt that. Seth's brother is a drug-dealing felonizor who gives not a thought to his family. I will not risk Seth's progress and sanity for someone who cannot be helped."

"Can't be *helped*? Have you lost your fucking mind? You would NEVER say something like that! What has gotten into you? Who *are* you? Because you are not the man I call my father."

He held a glare with me, breathing through flared nostrils.

"You run a school for kids that 'cannot be helped.' I refuse to believe that you'd throw out Seth's brother. Have you even met him?"

"No, I have not met him. But I have read countless legal reports and have sat through hundreds of Mace brother therapy sessions about him. Seth is very fond of him. But Seth blames himself for his brother's actions, *of course.* And to be honest, I do not have much patience for drug addicts."

I rolled my eyes, "Oh, I can think of one drug addict you have a *world* of patience for."

17

DESTRUCTION OF PROPERTY, PROPERLY

"It's time to grab that goldmine of a server."

Mina stood at the front of the conference room with her hair in a braid down her back. Her pastel blue suit cast long lines over her body. Taro held up her hand and Mina grunted an annoyed "*What?*"

"I'm assuming you mean Merchant's server, correct? I doubt he will continue providing wire scrap if he finds out we have broken into his home."

"Do you think so little of my leadership? I know. But that damn penthouse is driving me mad. And to tell you the truth, I couldn't care less about our wire provider. A solid lead on the Full Set is more important."

Matey spoke up: "Why can't someone just break in?"

Squeem cleared his throat and answered, "We had the Sarif crew check out the place; they sent in one actor to bug his elevator and barely made it out in the three minutes that it took. The whole building is Bright White so we can't see a thing. Merchant has personal security in the penthouse. It's like the Edmunds multiplied by three."

"Exactly, so we need ideas." Mina leaned forward onto the table, "Preferably keeping Merchant alive, for now. I won't mind the chase later."

The chase. The Edmunds. The Sarif crew. Was his name actually Merchant?

Fruit grabbed my shoulder, shaking me out of my daydreams. Everyone was looking at me. I felt my face heat up.

"Devin, wake up or I'm going to stop including you in these meetings." Mina said coldly. She looked at me for a second too long and I knew my face was bright red.

"We uh … why can't we cut the power to the building for a few hours?" I threw out the idea mindlessly. Sitting across from me, Matey was staring at the table in front of her, paying far less attention than I was. How come no one ever yelled at her?

Mina scowled. "Have you been listening at all? The building runs on Bright White."

Squeem turned to me. "Bright White Energy can't be shut off by an outside source, as far as we can tell. It's unhackable, transmitted through the atmosphere. Its connectors are infallible. It never fails, no power outages, no matter how cataclysmic an event. We could blow up an entire Bright White city block and we'd be no closer to affecting their power. Which is why the wealthiest use Bright White. They can afford that kind of security."

"For all of their little secrets," Mina added.

She sat down in her chair, setting her palms flat on the white papers in front of her. "But we digress. We need a plan to buy us enough time to get Fruit into Merchant's loft and snag up every bit of data we can find." Mina turned to Fruit and asked, "How much time will you need?"

Fruit was silent for a moment, and then responded in his unemotional voice, "One hour."

Squeem asked, "Are you sure? The elevator bug picked up two servers, but there could be more. There are safes certainly, as well as recording devices, phones, who knows what else."

"One hour," replied Fruit.

We sat with the quiet drawl of the refrigerator, buzzing against the wall in the next room. Mina focused on the papers in front of her and I focused on the lines between her brows.

Taro cleared her throat, "It will need to be quite a distraction to get Merchant's security out of his apartment for an hour. Especially if we're not taking any lives. Which, I will remind you, is our prime objective as a crew. Hounding and killing."

"There's always the whole city block option I mentioned earlier," Squeem said sarcastically.

Mina rolled her eyes but snapped them back up immediately.

Squeem's face grew worried. "I was clearly joking."

"It's a simple idea, really," Mina said, distracted.

There was an immediate uproar; *We can't destroy a city block! Thousands of people would die! The hospitals would overflow!*

Mina shook her hands and laughed, "Children, use your heads. You can't truly believe I'd blow a city block for a few servers. However," mistrustful groans soared around the table. "*However,* I could be persuaded by some proper destruction of property. It's been a while since we've had that sort of fun. If we threw a big enough production, we could get into Merchant's penthouse and render that damn bank useless. No more Full Set account visits."

I spoke my thoughts out loud. "Kill two birds and all that."

Mina held her eyes on me and nodded, "Exactly."

Veishrin was fast approaching, and Mina wanted to celebrate by blowing a few holes in Merchant's bank.

The plan was as follows: we would meet up with the Sarif crew and caravan into Lansche. Squeem and Matey would run surveillance and diagnostics from a van outside the bank. Boister and Sarif actors would create a false hostage situation in the bank, wrecking the place with whatever means necessary while keeping the employees out of true harm. Meanwhile, Mina and Fruit would break into Merchant's penthouse via his rooftop patio.

The plan hinged on the ability of the crew. Every separate piece of the plan was equally important, but if the bank crew failed, everyone else would be put in danger. Let me repeat: the success of the bank crew was vitally important.

So, Mina told me I would be part of the bank crew. I laughed out loud.

Mina set her hard eyes on me. "You have yet to impress me. So far, I have seen you excel at moping, judging from your moral vantage point, and daydreaming. Your inability to be a team player is getting old. I was certain you'd show a bit more interest when you found out what we do here, but alas, you haven't.

"But—"

"*But*, because you can't seem to die, you could be an important asset to the team. So, I'm giving you yet another chance to prove yourself."

"But," I said, utterly confused. "You want me to carry a gun and ... shoot out the windows? Of a building inhabited by hundreds of people?"

"No one will be hurt," she rolled her eyes.

"What about kids who live there? Or the bank workers? Won't they have *lasting trauma*?"

"Devin, stop. Let me remind you that this bank and building are being used to fund abhorrent affairs of evil. These people are abducting children! The information in Merchant's penthouse could lead to us stopping that. So suck it up and help!"

She was very persuasive. But so was I.

I watched her, thinking. I'd been wearing the same three shirts and pants for literally months. My socks and underwear were so worn I felt like giving up on them completely. I couldn't say no to this opportunity.

"If I am going to commit unspeakable crimes with you, I am going to do so feeling confident and comfortable. Take me to get some new clothes and I'll help."

On the day before Veishrin, Mina took me to a store an hour away to buy me some clothing.

Much to my excitement, we wore disguises. Mina had overdrawn, red lips and brunette hair. It was frigid out and her massive parka hid her thin frame. I wore Mina's black suit coat and slicked my hair back like a man that owns a restaurant downtown.

I dragged Mina into a resale shop. The off-white walls, the dusty smell of worn fabric and peeling wood varnish reminded me of home on Brunock Island. I stood in the doorway and breathed in the impoverished freedom of my childhood.

To do this, I would need to channel my old self; the part of me I'd locked away in the deepest shadows of my past. Devil Mace, the flouncy, attention-seeking performer. The young man who'd spend his days building decadent, slanderous tableaus of protest against the wealthiest citizens of Suradelphia, and spend his nights at the Night Palace, breaking icetar in the bathroom of the club and luring gentlemen to his rented room for a paid romp. The man who clumsily led the

Batifban right to a killer's dumping ground; a mass grave he didn't know was there; a pit of bodies covered in his very own DNA.

I would have to be him again: The Devil of Suradelphia.

And that's when I saw it. The most beautiful, pale green dress. Layers of translucent fabric, A-line with little pearl buttons down the front. I held it out to Mina and she raised an eyebrow at me.

"You're the one who said I needed to loosen up." I held the dress up in front of the foggy mirror.

I expected more of a fight from Mina, maybe a fresh, cutting insult. Instead, Mina marched the dress to the cashier and handed it over. "Will you hold this for us? My partner can't live without it."

A group of us stood on a misty balcony overlooking a forest of thin, moss-covered trees. The morning sky peaked between the trees in stripes of grey. Taro and Cassius were sharing spitgrass. Matey yelped and complained whenever their smoke blew her way.

The Sarif crew hid their DAG "theater" in the thick, clouded forests outside of Lansche near the suburb of Sarif. The building itself was an abandoned concrete structure which once housed power diverters before everything switched to paphador.

"Quite the drag, to be pulled from my travels in Nessuir to sit in a car for 10 hours with you folk," Cassius said, blowing smoke in Matey's face.

"If I have to hear about your stupid jaunt through Nessuir one more time," Taro sniped.

Cassius shifted like silk, curling his lips in delight. "You'll what?"

One of the Sarif actors, Jonwalf, asked, "Are you two related?"

Taro and Cassius were outraged. "No!"

I turned to the Sarif actors. "Are you?"

Jonwalf nodded. "Nalk and I are brothers."

Nalk was taller, Orcorne like Jonwalf, with reddish flesh and little tusks. The third, Malfesia, had big, lopsided horns. They were very fit, older, and intimidating, with lilting voices and legs toned to perfection. Nalk watched me out of the corner of his eye; I couldn't tell if he didn't trust me or if he was checking me out. Maybe he recognized me from back in the day. I didn't look that different, really. Especially with the gauzy green dress I wore.

"Let's go over it again," Squeem said, hobbling up the stairs to the balcony. I stepped over to offer my hand and he took it gratefully.

"Taro is in charge of the talking. She's good with impressions and her Lacausian accent is spot on. Cassius and Jonwalf will deal with the hostages. Malfesia, you will do cover and lookout. Nalk and Devin will make the mess. Proper Destruction of Property, as Mina calls it. Essentially, destroy the place. Wreak havoc. Mentally scar pedestrians."

Nalk laughed while I groaned. Was I supposed to skip around in my dress and dodge bullets from the Batifban?

It was too late to turn back now.

We piled into a car and a van; Mina, Fruit, Squeem and Matey rode in the hounding van. I rode with Taro drove, with Malfesia in the passenger. Cassius, Nalk, Jonwalf, and I squeezed together like unborn kittens in the back seat. Jonwalf could sense my nerves and tried to talk me up, going through how my gun worked over and over so I wouldn't feel so out of place. The gun shook in my hands.

"Devin is helpless, love," Cassius said, patting me on the thigh. "It will be a miracle if he pulls his weight today." He was such a fucking know-it-all. I looked down at the gun; my face reflected in the blue metal. Is that what I looked like?

In the rearview mirror, we watched Squeem's van park across the street. Matey gave us an elaborate hand signal that could have easily been replaced with a wave.

"Don't leave anything in the car that you want to see again," Cassius patronized as we pulled on our ski masks and began to get out of the car. My nerves flushed up my neck and pounded in my cheeks. I looked around the car — we wouldn't get it back? Did I leave something in there? I felt the black ski mask on my face to be sure it was there.

The wind picked up like a slow-motion movie and my dress fluttered, getting caught up between my legs. I looked down; hairy, grey legs, with scuffed sneakers on my feet. Pavement; damp from the overnight rain.

A burst of soundless heat hit my back. I stumbled forward. My ears seemed to gape in the stretching silence. Crackling sounds grew from the quiet. I turned to see the DAG car up in flames. Plumes of black smoke rose in the sky. I saw my reflection in the gun again: windswept hair, mask, dress.

Suddenly, I was someone else.

The blue gun was like an extension of my arm, swaying as I walked alongside the other actors. I slid on the wet concrete like a dancer, swaying and spinning. The tall bank windows mirrored our oil-slicked reflection, multicolored and liquid. I was part of a team of the most fearless, compelling vigilantes to ever exist.

Taro winked at me from under her black mask and pushed open the doors of Terrion Banks. The hush in the bank was cut only by rustling paper, the low, reedy tones of background music, the frantic murmuring of bank employees behind their desks as they watched us and our burning car.

Taro cleared her throat and spoke in her best Lacausian twang: "Good morning! This is a robbery."

Chaos erupted in the bank.

Nalk lifted his gun to the ceiling and sent a few well-placed shots into the gaudy chandelier over our heads. Tiny translucent beads dropped like hail all around.

"Cash, if you could do the honors." Taro motioned to Cassius.

He began barking orders at the bank employees and patrons. Jonwalf told the two front desk employees to stay put, then motioned to the rest of the people in the bank. They began to line up against the farthest wall, holding onto each other in desperation. I felt no pang of guilt; I knew they would be fine. This short hour of fear would be over soon, and everyone would be safe. For the good of all; it felt fitting to say.

Taro went to the front desk and sweetly demanded the employees hand over their purses. One of the employees pulled a gun from underneath. Malfesia jumped, skidding over the counter. Her horns clanged against the beaded lights above as she pulled the gun from the employee's shaking hands and tossed it back to Taro.

Taro caught the gun and yelled, "Money, *now!*" She disarmed the gun and threw a handful of bullets back at the employees, cracking the class of the artwork behind them. Both desk employees began to cry hysterically.

I smiled at my reflection in the big, glass doors, and pulled my gun on them. One, two, three, four, five shots. Glass crackled and shattered into a billion pieces, ringing like tiny bells as they scattered across the floor. A symphony of sounds. Was this what the Indigo Abyss sounded like?

Three big bodyguard types raced into the bank from the building beyond. They seemed well-equipped, but they didn't realize who they were dealing with. Cassius headed them off.

"If you want these citizens to live, you'll get the Batif on the phone and tell them this was a hostage situation. I'll pick off someone for every shot they send into the building."

My head tipped back as I laughed.

I skipped ahead, bounding to the first window, and began to shoot. I took my time getting every piece, every little corner. The racket shook my eardrums in the best way, like the club in the basement of the Night Palace.

Nalk was having as much fun as I was. He shot one of the supports for the chandelier over the entrance. The thing hung sideways, creaking like an old church. Thousands of tiny beads rained down on us.

"Oh, dear, here we go," I heard Cassius drone in annoyance when I turned to help Nalk bring down the chandelier. The sculpture of light fell to the floor with a magnificent crash. My body spun whimsically, the glass crunching beneath the soles of my sneakers. Taro clapped from one of the cushy armchairs at the front desk, with her feet relaxed up like a king. Malfesia was holding her two employees at gunpoint lazily as they set stacks of cash in the purses laid out on the counter.

I continued down the wall of windows. Each shattered pane brought a new level of ecstasy, just like the old days. My movements loosened, edging on a high. I hadn't felt like this in years. But this time was different. Now I was a real part of something. For the first time in my life, I could use my deviance for *good*.

Siren-singing Batif cars were rounding every corner, flying to quick stops on the sidewalk out front. I paid them no mind; the golden-framed, wall-size mirrors on the walls looked too good to pass on. I watched myself destroy each, one by one. I had a big cut on my left bicep; How did that get there? All I felt was joy. Blood droplets followed me around the bank, spatting on the glass-covered floor. I'd never seen a sight quite as lovely.

"Devin, it's time to go!" Taro yelled, laughing. "Only you could get lost in thought at a time like this!"

We left the hostages, we left the bags of money, we left the bank a right wreck. Destruction of property, properly. Mina was certain to approve.

Outside, Batifban yelled into megaphones and sirens rang. Adrenaline pounded loudly in my cheeks. We dropped our weapons with our hands up. I could see news crews parked in the distance and drones flying overhead, filming the bank scene.

"Remember, *white hat*," Taro whispered in my ear.

I nodded, searching. At the center, a Batif with a white uniform cap stood next to his armored caravan, kneeling with his gun out. He came forward with the others and they cuffed us, ushering us toward their caravans.

A news crew stood feet away behind a ballistic barrier. Just before they pushed me into the Batif car, I pulled off my ski mask. Flashes of camera lights strobed, and I smiled the biggest smile I possibly could.

I was okay, I was alive. The news would reach my brothers, wherever they were. And I could continue with this new life, a mirror of my old life, but so much better.

My pale green dress had blood all over it and I wasn't upset. It felt like a trophy, a reward. Something I could have forever.

The white-hat Batif who drove us was a DAG member. Even though I'd been told this part of the plan before, I don't think I'd really believed it. The Batif turned the car unexpectedly, diving into an underground parking garage. He told us to get out as he took a pill that knocked himself right out. We scrambled out of the car before it collided with the concrete wall of the garage.

"Is he going to be okay?" I shouted as we ran up the slippery steps to the hounding van. It blew exhaust into the damp air.

Cassius clapped me on the bleeding shoulder, laughing, "They'll be just fine, love."

I couldn't tell if he was mocking me or not.

Squeem drove us out of the heart of Lansche and parked in a neighborhood. The houses were multistory, multifamily, multicultural.

As soon as we parked, the crew started yelling over each other.

"That was flawless!" Nalk high-fived anyone near him.

"We watched the whole thing with our mouths hanging open!" Matey exclaimed.

"Nothing like celebrating Veishrin with my DAG family!" Taro said.

"Fruit was impeccable. It took him *half* the time we thought it would," Squeem bragged, and Fruit might have flushed.

With my cheeks stretched to their smiling limit, I locked eyes with Mina. She was silent at the back of the van, with a strange twist to her lips. Was it a smile? I pushed my shoulders back and raised my eyebrow, daring her to do ... something. I'm not sure what. But whatever it was, I wanted it. I wanted it all.

18

The Family Cocoon

Seth's spindly legs dangled off the side of his bed. I sat backward in my desk chair, holding my tongue for dear life.

"Lie to him, Mayli. Just this once. If he knows, he will dissolve into a state. I don't want you to have to clean up that mess."

So here I sat, alone with a person sitting on the edge of insanity, and it was up to me to keep him safe. To keep the school safe. To keep the cave from turning into a pit of molten paphador. It was up to *me*.

Seth's legs bounced against the mattress. His skin flushed with blood under the grey surface; his hair was clean. His small body seemed to fill out his clothing.

"I went to talk to my dad," I started.

Seth straightened on his bed, stilling his legs. "Okay."

"He takes whatever is going on with your brother seriously. He doesn't have any more news about him though." I stopped to watch Seth take a slow breath. "He said he believes you."

Long moments passed; I had to count to twenty-four and then start again to stop myself from talking.

Finally, he nodded. "Thank you."

And that was that.

Veishrin was my favorite holiday. With the week-long break from school, I would finally be home again. I could see Tom again.

My father's car was musty after four months parked in the backend of the cave. I'd never seen the garage before, if you could call it a garage. A hollow space behind the Voltenstraus kitchen, where trucks delivered food and supplies every so often.

Mieda groaned as she stepped into a puddle. Her wet, flimsy slipper squished on the stone with every step. I shivered, discomforted by the thought of socks and puddles. The space between toes, crawling with cold, moist disease. Would I ever get over this?

Doctor Harker tossed his bag into the trunk and pressed the car on. "Five hours to Monount. Best we leave now and have some daylight left."

I nestled into the seat, wrapped in a musty car blanket, and fell asleep.

The jostling of the car shook me awake. Outside, early evening fog crept down from the foothills. I opened my window and breathed in the smell of home: madgeflower, spurge, pink olia.

We drove through town. Squat, black houses with pale woodwork dotted the curving road. Charged stones topped each home, stacked like little obelisks, to protect against the violent electrical storms of spring. Fields of flowering spurge and dilly sprawled for miles. Lines of trees broke the horizon, clustering around the thin creeks diverting from the crystal-pink mountains to the South. This was my home, and it was magnificent.

Brigmot, the family home, perched atop the cliffs of Monount Valley proper, surrounded by the other four original manors, three of which had fallen into disrepair. The circle of disheveled, vacant homes and outbuildings was an incredible space to grow up in. Every day was a new adventure as a child, but I'd grown bored with it in my teens. Being gone for a few short months was enough to rekindle the wonder. I couldn't wait to spend hours climbing through the (definitely haunted) ruins downstream. My grandparents' things were still in the house, stagnant and dusty and waiting to be prodded.

As we pulled up to Brigmot, the front doors opened and my Queen Mother stood at the center. She wore a ridiculous, long, white thing that glittered in the setting sun.

"Is she getting married?" I mumbled. I never understood her need to get dressed up for the smallest of things.

"She's showing you how much she loves you," my father replied with a smile. He seemed to glow as he watched her.

The dirt drive was wet from the midday rain. I hung my head out of the window to check for puddles before stepping out. Nathali waved obnoxiously before getting out to unload our bags.

Mom yelled something into the house, and Tom sprung out the door. Dad was already up there kissing and twirling mom.

Tom tried to hide his smile as he pulled out the rest of the bags.

"You're all dressed up, too," I smiled wryly at him.

He scratched at his cheek with his shoulder. "It seemed like an occasion. You've been gone for a while."

I waved at my mother from the entryway. "Hey, mom."

She winked at me as my father had his head buried in her neck. I fake-gagged and followed Tom up the stairs.

In my attic bedroom, Tom sat at the window as I tossed things near their proper place and filled him in on my new life.

"It's so light up here! I mean, sunlight, yeah, but the *air*! The cave is so..." I shook my entire body out to rid myself of the feeling.

"I'm glad you've survived," he smiled. "I knew the environment would be tough. So, tell me about your new life."

"I don't even know where to start." I dumped my bag of clothes on the bed and into the laundry basket.

"Do you have friends? How are classes? How many hearts have you broken?"

"First off, I've broken no hearts and you know it. But I am dating someone." Tom had a momentary look of shock. "Yes, it's true. I've caught the eye of the most magnificent Baskian in school. Their name is Uyentra, they are gorgeous, and they are a *Marionette*."

Tom swiped his hair out of his eyes and said, "You're sure that's a good idea? With your soul the way it is."

"Whoa, what's that supposed to mean?" I took in the purse to my brother's lips, the set to his jaw. "Don't piss me off, man." I stabbed a finger at his chest.

He held his hands up. "No, it's just — It's fine. I wasn't expecting it. I..."

"You what?" When he didn't answer, I said, "Why does everything think I'm undatable?"

"No, that's not it. Your partner has good tastes. I'm just ... protective, you know?"

The silence grew. I picked through dirty socks and missed the hamper with every toss.

"So, they're a Marionette?" Tom scratched his scalp.

I nodded, feeling sore. "Yeah. And they like my soul. A lot." I rolled my eyes. "If you want something to get weird about, don't waste your time on Uyentra. We've got much bigger issues."

I spilled the entire story to him. About Seth Mace on the tram. About Seth Mace cracking fault lines into the main entry. About Seth Mace moving into *my* dorm room and asking for *my* help. And the answers Tom had for me were illuminating, but less than reassuring.

Suffice to say, we were late for dinner.

Sunday and Monday were supposed to be easy days. My original plan was to pal around with Nathali and see if we could get Tom to join us. I wanted to crawl around in the old family houses and visit the underground tombs of our ancestors. But the conversation with Tom the night before overshadowed it all. I needed to talk to my father.

After a breakfast of pear tarts, which I could do without, I snuck up to the family library.

Dr. Harker sat at his desk in the office off the library. A system of clear screens rose out of his desk. Through them, I watched him. He was hunched over a thin sheet of paper with a monocle to help him read the microscopic words trailing the page. It was a transcript; I'd seen them before. Long, thin sheets with tiny writing filled to the edges of the page. Impossible for me to read with how crowded they were. It was something about the family business that I'd been kept out of so well. They printed out of a machine under his desk and they printed at all hours.

"Who the hell is typing out those things? Day and night. That's some dedication."

My father looked up from his reading, his eyes unfocused and watery. He settled and said, "Ah, I was hoping you'd come find me. I have some jobs for you if you want them."

"I don't," I said sharply.

He watched me for a moment, his expression unchanged. "What is it, then?"

I was leaning against the archway into his office in my pajamas. "Tom told me some interesting information last night."

George rose a single brow. "Do continue. The anticipation is too great to stand."

My glare was nothing to him. We looked at each other for a moment before I continued, "You roomed with mom at school. That's what Tom told me."

George sat back in his chair and put his hands behind his head. "I see. So now you think you know what this is all about."

I knew immediately that I'd misjudged the situation. In defeat, I said, "Tell me where I'm wrong."

"It's true that your mother and I roomed together. And we hated each other, or pretended to. I was obnoxious with my humor and such. Anything to get a rise out of my classmates. *Anything* to get a rise out of Narien. She was opinionated and always the activist. I pushed her buttons. But my affliction was different from Seth's. And I did not put you two together for the same reasons that your mother and I were."

He was telling the truth, but I still was missing pieces. "Why were you and mom dormed together?"

"*Dormed* isn't a word, Maysolpheta," Dr. Harker admonished. "It was a simple error. My roommate moved on to Nepa and instead of moving a first year in with me, I was moved in with another singlet who happened to be your mother. We had past animosity, but that didn't matter. A room was a room, and they needed the space for new students. We did our duty, living together."

"But Tom said mom saved your life," I pressed on.

"Yes." George stopped for a moment, tapping the tips of his fingers on the transcript in front of him. A slice of sunlight cut across his face, catching like fire in his red beard. "She helped me see that I needed professional help with my mental health. But Mayli, this is not the case with Seth. He is being helped with his mental health; that is not your responsibility. And also, I am no matchmaker. I see no worse idea than the two of you becoming … one." My father shuddered at the thought, thoroughly disgusted. "Absolutely not. Nightmarish. In truth, Idrissa needed a break from Seth and you are that break. You consistently handle every stressful situation thrown at you, and you will handle this one as well. It's in your blood."

"So, that's it then."

"I understand the connection Tom made, but he is wrong. I am not trying to recreate my school days with you." He looked down his nose at me. "Now, if you will — I have reports to read. Come back for lunch and we'll eat together." And with that, my father turned back to his monocle, holding the thin transcript up to the light. He ignored me as I left.

Nathali and I ate lunch cliffside, ignoring our father's request to join him. We watched the town below move in slow ripples. We visited the barns, using my twin's Faunate power to call the gallies in from the pasture. I buried my hands in their wooly coats, massaging clods of dirt and filth. They whinnied in joy, throwing their maned heads back and singing at the sky. The peace was so overwhelming that I almost forgot my twin could actually talk to these lovely creatures, while I just had to let them listen to my nonsense.

On Monday, Nathali and I explored our grandparent's estate. As we sifted through old, mouse-eaten books, we retold the crazy stories we'd invented as children.

Monount Valley was inhabited by my Vauveric father's ancestors for three generations. They'd come across an underground Gate to this layer while on the run from *cosmic evil*, whatever that was. It was a fitting place to hide.

They'd found Voltenstraus, too; ruins of some great battle, a forgotten cave-dwelling, and a permanently closed gate somewhere near the school. And, to top it all off, they'd found Idrissa, an ancient Non-Eater encased in the glow of the *King's Sleep*. Sae woke for them and the story blossomed into legend.

Idrissa explained that they'd found the Nepatin layer, Nessa, and the closed gate to Develtic. Sae was the only surviving being from Nessa, the last of the Nepatin species; a lab-race created by the Dwavasc a thousand years before. Which meant Idrissa was old as *balls*.

In the three subsequent generations, more gates were discovered — tiny, unknown ones hidden in rock walls and under gnarled trees. For a forgotten layer, Nessa sure had a wealth of entry points. But the Develtic gate had been lost again, this time on purpose. They didn't want that place found, no matter the cost. And, without a Gate Reader on the layer, the gate would remain lost.

Sometimes, I thought about the beings on the Develtic layer. They couldn't all be bad; that wasn't possible. There were rumors of people so deeply entwined in evil that they couldn't be removed from it without ripping apart their souls. Rumors of a hive-mind, where no one thought for themselves, and the idea of *self* did not exist. Some said this wasn't a bad thing; individual wasn't the only answer.

It was all speculation, anyway. The Develtic layer had been closed for more than a thousand years. We knew nothing about the fate of that planet. But it didn't stop me from wondering.

"Thank Mess you called; these people are driving me insane," Riolyn's voice scratched against my ears in the best way.

I smiled at the warmth hiding in her tone. "Maybe next holiday, you guys can come here. You could stay with Nathali. Or, there's always the barn."

"Oh, please, don't you have a mansion?" she laughed.

"Yes, but I need that extra wing for all of my frivolous antiques. You would love my vintage, Vauveric hat collection! Where are you guys staying?"

"Aeshra picked out a fancy hotel. School is paying for it. It's nice as hell."

Saren's voice added, "Riolyn has ordered room service six times already. I keep telling her we need to be a little more concerned with our spending."

"Whatever, that school is loaded. They aren't going to miss the money," Riolyn scoffed.

"Where's Aeshra?" I asked.

There was a rustling of movement. "I'm picking over Riolyn's leftovers. She didn't eat any of her fruit; the *scandal*."

"Have you guys started on your uncle's house?"

Aeshra said through a mouthful of something, "It's a wreck. Riolyn really did a number on the place, eh girl? Psycho, that one."

"I think I'm missing some key information," I replied. I had no idea what Aeshra was talking about.

Riolyn answered like it was nothing. "I burned the house down."

My eyebrows shot to the roof.

Aeshra was still chewing. "Yeah, well, she had to get out of there somehow. And the jerk's in jail for life now, so it's a win-win."

No one knew what to say after that. I had figured Riolyn had been in a bad situation and I had definitely let my imagination run wild with the possibilities. Aeshra had told me that they didn't know where Riolyn was until they'd gotten word that she was coming to Voltenstraus. Had my best friend really been held hostage in her uncle's house? Was *that* what they meant?

"We'll have to revisit *that* story after Veishrin," I said.

"What about you? How is Monount Valley?" Saren asked.

"Oh, the usual. My brother thinks my dad has some grand scheme to relive his years at Voltenstraus through Seth and I. My dad roomed with my mom, I guess."

"Sounds weird. Like, he thinks that's why your dad moved Seth in?" Riolyn asked.

"I asked him about it and he said no. He was telling the truth; I can tell. He said Idrissa needed a break from Seth and lucky me, I'm the break." I rolled over on my bed to look up at the red beams crisscrossing the ceiling. Painted animal scenes decorated the spaces in between.

"Still, I feel like the Idrissa thing was an excuse," I admitted. "Not a lie, but an omission of truth. That's my father's special skill. But, if he can omit the truth, so can I. George still doesn't know I'm in Palm Lifting lessons."

Saren replied, "He doesn't want you to learn Palm Lifting?"

"No, never has. Always said it wasn't the correct power for me, like Erytoa made a mistake. Might be right."

Riolyn scoffed, but Saren and Aeshra remained quiet. I let my eyes wander over my pink hands, imagining my blood-like energy cupped in them. Something *was* wrong with me.

Finally, Saren spoke up, "Take care of yourself, Mayli."

It sounded more like a warning than a goodbye.

On Wednesday, we built the Family Cocoon.

This was something I was good at; something I enjoyed. Nathali and I spent the day in the kitchen, concocting layers of flavor over the stove. The layering process was key; if you placed the wrong food on top or next to a clashing flavor, the spices would mix into a gross, mushy blob.

We pulled out the six-foot long pan, shaped in the silhouette of a prone body, and set it on the floor. It was much too long to fit on the countertop. Then, at the head end, we placed layers of whisp and soft spread. Next, herbed black rice at the neck, and traditional longbeans, rootmash, red gravy and roasted bulbs in the torso. Stonefruit in the pelvis, mashed welu and sweet beans in the thighs. Tom poured spice cake batter into the legs, and Nathali and I spread candied pear overtop.

Mieda also made a pot of vinegar syrup to pour over. It was mostly pomegranate, sweet and bright, but thick and red just like blood; perfect for reenacting Uyenl's massive head wound.

Uyenl, the anti-guardian, the *Dementric*, the dark Undergod. An innocent guy who was possessed by a darkness, much to his dismay. Totally undervalued in modern worship, in my opinion.

The cocoon shell was all up to my mother and father. They spent hours rising the dough in big rolls, butter cut throughout so it would be compact on the inside and flaky on the outside after a successful bake. My siblings and I laid thin sheets of dough over each section, creating a person-sized, edible cocoon. We'd bake the thing overnight and in the morning we'd have a glorious, flaky feast to break open and share.

When the sun hit my face through my attic window, I went down to check the cocoon. Off the kitchen was the kiln room, with a little window in the door that I had to stand on a footstool to see in. The yellowed glass kept me from seeing much of anything.

Mother joined me in the kitchen to rush around in a panic, touching up last-minute details. Her long dressing-gown was thick with pearlescent beading along the bottom, waving in big swoops as she moved from one end of the kitchen to the other. Always at her side, her IV stand hummed. The skin around her chest-port was yellowed and wrinkled.

"The drinks! We need to make the drinks. Mayli, where are the mulling spices? I asked you *yesterday* to set out the mulling spices," On and on she went, reminding me of my flaws.

But she stopped when her IV stand beeped. She lifted her head to stare at the wall.

"Mom?"

She snapped her attention to me. "Scrub your armpits. And don't embarrass me with your wardrobe choice."

We were joined by my uncle and aunt who lived in town, and their children who were closer to Mina and Tom's ages. They brought a cocoon of their own, symbolizing the Undergod Messer, ours dedicated to his brother. We placed the two cocoons head-to-head on the long dining table.

The table was set with sauces and syrups and mulled teas and pear cider. We decorated the room's dark, intricate paneling with boughs of flowering ghostvine, its pale, drooping petals like sheer fabric hanging off a corpse. Pastel candles glowed in their woven hangings against the ceiling. The tall windows cast long lines of midday sunlight across the body-shaped cocoons on the dining table.

"Who wants to read the story?" my father asked, opening a ripped, ancient copy of *The Contents*. The indigo cover was soft and worn in his hands, with silver and gold filigree and decorative lettering in a language that no longer existed.

Mieda reached for the book, snagging it out of my father's grasp and running her long-nailed fingers over the gold-dipped pages, clearing her throat.

"*Erytoa* so loved the mortal *Messer* that she made known to him these forbidden Whims, burrowing them deep in the soft spot of his temples, so that he may live through catastrophe and become equal to her. The gentle song of *Erytoa* wove into *Messer's* mind-seams, lighting him with whispers of the notions of the Faunate Undergod. Sweet smells of honey and ghostvine thick in his nostrils, he set to work on the cocoon, collecting his sweat, dead skin, and secretions. Mindless, he worked through the night to create a chrysalis of perfect form.

"Unseen to the Undergods in the final hours, *Messer* made a second cocoon for his younger brother, his first love, his family in single being. *Messer* was light of heart and as flawless as a mortal could be, but his brother *Uyenl* spoke the *shadowtongue*, plagued by devil-call, and was not meant for divinity.

"*Messer*, lost in his trance, forced *Uyenl* into his cocoon and closed him within, unable to recognize his brother's terror. The two brothers slept long in their deific vessels, through wind and flame and the flood of the *tarfire*. *Erytoa* woke *Messer* with her song, and he burst from his cocoon an Undergod, slick and black like the *tarfire* that had consumed the worlds. *The Mess* saw *Baheeba*, felt *Baheeba*'s weight all around, and held *Baheeba* in his long-fingered hands.

"But *Uyenl* was trapped in his cocoon, deeply asleep and engulfed in the unholy sounds of newly taken souls. *The Mess* reached into *Uyenl's* cocoon, puncturing his brother's head with his sheer-like talons. *Uyenl's* blood spilled like a spring into the new world as *The Mess* pulled him out of his chrysalis tomb. *Uyenl's* rebirth of pain and terror opened his soul to a devil, binding the two in an unfailing avowal.

"*Erytoa* was ashamed of *Messer's* mistake; to bring a dark soul into the new world was a boundless sin. *Uyenl* would now need the *essence* of beings to survive in the cleansed world, but no living being would give such a vital life force to a creature tainted by enduring evil. As *Uyenl* withered and fell into madness, *Messer* pleaded with his love. The Faunate Undergod looked unto *Uyenl* as he was; a dying creature deserving of understanding. *Erytoa* knelt before the dark Non-Eater and presented him with the veins of her soul. *Uyenl* drank and, as *Erytoa's* given essence touched his soul's lips, he transcended."

"Thus is the story of the two-family cocoons, and the Undergods they harbored." Mieda slammed the book shut and motioned gleefully to the feast before us, shouting, "Let's eat!"

We stood and reached our hands into our respective cocoons, tearing at the crisp, flaky dough to reveal the steaming meal beneath. Nathali and Mieda held the big pot of vinegar syrup together, pouring the thick, red sauce over Uyenl's cocoon head, letting it drip onto the table.

That evening, long after the feast, I escaped to the kitchen for a late snack. Nothing was more exciting than the prospect of delicious leftovers and I had to follow my Whims, just like Messer. Because you never knew which Whims were brainless wishing and which were holy whispers.

My mother sat in the dark kitchen, thumbing her way through a catalog of old wax chips and drinking straight from a bottle of Lastrights. Her chest port was snapped shut; no dose of much-needed medicine. I stopped at the doorway and held my breath, but it was too late.

"What are *you* doing down here? Where is your father?" my mother asked me scornfully. Her eyes were fogged, jumping from me to the doorway like she expected George to appear.

I stayed put, frozen. This scenario never ended in my favor, *never.* "I just wanted a snack," I replied, watching her with shielded eyes. She could decipher any single tone, any emotion that played on my face with incredible accuracy. When she was drunk, this gift of hers turned for the worst.

Narien ran her fingers along the rim of the bottle before spitting viciously, "You and your father, waltzing around like new puppies. You *disgust* me."

I faltered. "What? What does that mean?"

Cold bumps rose on my arms. I pulled my sweater higher around my neck.

"You know exactly what I am talking about. You're just like him and the first one; *destroying* my children," My mother snarled, tipping the bottle of liquor over to pour herself a new glass. She laughed, watching the bottle roll over the counter.

"*Nurien*, enough!" My father's voice boomed from behind me. I jumped in my skin, cursing. He was in his night clothes, his glasses low on his nose.

Mom laughed sickly at Dad's use of her Eivian birthname. "Here he is; your Tyrn, come to rescue you."

George pushed past me to caress my mother's hard face. "Love, I am *your* Tyrn. Leave Mayli alone, you are drunk. Go lie down; I'll join you in a moment."

My mother stumbled up, shoving the bottle over the counter. It hit the floor with a shattering crash. She put her hand on my fathers, dripping with ill sarcasm. "Yes, my king. Wipe your little princesses' tears for me.

Wipe her rancid soul while you're at it." The last bit dripped like venom from my mother's mouth.

My father was horrified. "Narien!"

"Hush, hush. I'll be gone," she said, sweeping the floor with her luxurious robe as she left.

I stared at my dad. "Rancid soul?"

He swallowed. "She doesn't mean it."

I swallowed too, with visions of liquid blood-energy dancing in my mind. Maybe she didn't mean it, or maybe she was right.

My mother loved throwing parties even more than she loved insulting me.

And I loved embarrassing her almost as much as I loved self-decoration. I drew red dots around my eyes. On my lips, glossy black, and no eyebrows at all. I put red eyedrops in my eyes to really sell the madness. I pinned a red medical cross to the breast of my dress and wore a little nurse bonnet atop my head. My mother would *not* approve.

If my soul was so rancid, what was the point of acting any different?

The music from below vibrated the attic floor in low, hollow booms. It was always a party for something; every holiday, every birthday, every possible reason. My mother couldn't help herself. It was a wonder she could do it all *and* drink herself to oblivion. It was her way of bringing people together, seeking entertainment in the delightless world she inhabited.

My introverted father had suffered through more parties than any spouse should.

Nathali came up to get me. Her dress could have been strung from the wings of fae, iridescent and endlessly glamorous.

She took my hand and led me down the stairs. We spun like lovebirds as we descended through the house and into the basement.

The music was so loud I worried it would crack through the worn stone and unleash the earth upon us. Nathali led me to the drinks, and we talked to each other through facial expressions, wondering if we should risk alcohol or not. Deciding against it, I grabbed us two sweetwaters, and we made our way into the caverns below.

The lights were like moonstones, pastel and ambient, leaving lightless spaces in between. Every room was at capacity and people were bouncing off of each other. We danced together, hopping like restless souls waiting to enter the abyss.

My dress, my eyes, my vibrant hair caught a few compliments from strangers and I didn't know how to say thank you.

At midnight, my mother unleashed the *tarfire*. It flooded the basement in thick streams from grates in the floor and sprayed from pipes in the ceiling. Black and minty like the stuff from Seth's sick mouth. I shuddered and held myself to shake off the disgust. Drunk partygoers danced in the stuff, slipping and falling over each other, laughing and crying and howling like wild animals.

My father waded through the crowd toward Nathali and I. He stepped through the murky faux-*tarfire* flooding his basement. The feet of his pale grey trousers were soaked and his messy red hair and shoulders were splattered in the stuff.

"Another ruined party dress, I see." He motioned to me.

"Everyone's outfits are ruined; tarfire spares no mortal," I smiled.

"You're actually pretty well-off, dad. Have you been avoiding the party?" Nathali asked, knowing the answer.

"Yes, well — everyone loves your mother's theatrics, but they don't have to clean it in the morning," he said, looking scornfully around at the dancing crowd.

A man with broad shoulders pushed their way to us, putting their hand on George's shoulder, "Sir, I hate to interrupt, but there's been a bit of an upset. I assumed you'd rather know sooner than later."

My father raised an eyebrow in annoyance. "Is that so?" He turned to my sister and I, "I'll be back. Oh, and Mayli — your eyes are bleeding."

He didn't come back.

I fought my way through my mother's drunken mess of a party well after midnight. I was so damn tired, my body ached. I smelled like sweat and sticky alcohol; some idiot tipped their beverage down my arm. Mieda had escaped hours earlier for a hot bath. Nathali was still down there, enjoying herself. And Tom? I had no idea.

Sleeping on a night like this would be difficult with the bass reverberating through the old manor. Maybe I'd force myself into a bath like Mieda; that sounded alright. If I snapped a chill-pill, I could turn on some harp music and imagine what sunflowers would look like if they grew on the moon. How would they evolve? Would they even be sunflowers anymore? Moonflowers?

Trudging up the first landing, I heard a commotion in my parents' bedroom. The doors were swung open as Doctor Harker talked to himself in quick, angry bursts. He was still wearing his black-spattered party outfit. Big swipes of *tarfire* stained the floor.

"Everything alright?" I stood in the doorway.

"You should get to sleep. You look tired with that red in your eyes."

"So do you." I stepped into the room. "What's going on?"

He began pacing the room again, picking up his travel bag and closing the clasps. "I have to go. Tom will take you back to school. Something disastrous has happened."

"Disastrous? Like, *lives taken*?" I asked, legitimately concerned.

"Not until I get there," dad hissed under his breath.

I walked over to him. "So, you're taking lives now?" I asked, eyebrows raised in skepticism. "Where are you going?"

"You know I can't say."

"But *I know* where you're going. You know that I know. And we still can't say it? Not even to each other?"

"*No,*" He growled. "No. I will not sell your soul to something you do not understand."

And that was that.

19

THE PRODUCER

The ten-hour drive back to Frasier went much faster with a group of chatty, adrenaline-rushed criminals. After delivering the Sarif crew to their DAG theater, I sat across from Mina in the van and listened, enamored, as Squeem regaled us with the tale of Mina and Fruit's penthouse adventure.

"The cloaking pins worked, even in the penthouse," he said.

Mina pulled a hard, white square from her shirt with a snap. The elastic fabric of her shirt stretched over her body like synthetic flesh.

"They clipped onto the window-cleaner tethers and scaled the building. I haven't been such a wreck in years, watching them climb."

Taro kicked her feet against the back of Fruit's passenger seat. "Fruit's quite the athlete when he wants to be."

He grunted and tossed a crumpled paper over his shoulder; it bounced off the top of Taro's head.

"They rode the maintenance lift from the fourth floor up. That was easier to watch. But the best part was the data — we're talking three servers full of data," Squeem squirmed in his seat, barely watching the road. "It's likely not all pertinent, but there's going to be *something* on there. I just know it."

"I have a question," Cassius said, with a devious look toward Mina. "Did Backstage approve this little exposition?"

Faces turned toward Mina. She sat with her eyes closed, head back against the side of the van.

"Mina?" Taro chirped sidelong.

Mina sighed in resignation. "No, they did not approve."

A long moment of silence. And then, outrage.

"Why the hell not?!"

"Are you kidding me?"

"We're going to get shuttered!"

Mina threw a halting hand into the air and the van quieted. "It is my job as Director to interpret the script and choose the direction of the crew. Our prime objective is hounding and killing, and we cannot hound and kill Full Set members that we do not know exist. We were justified in our actions. As Squeem said, Fruit copied three servers worth of data, *as well as* phone transcripts *and* video backlog. Backstage will send us a warning at the very most."

With her head back against the van wall, Mina let her eyes droop. Her long legs stretched out past the center of the van, coming dangerously close to touching me. I tucked the skirt-edge of my dress around my knees. My thighs stuck to the faux-leather beneath me.

Mina stirred again. "Merchant is going to know what happened. If he doesn't, he'll be dumber than we thought. If we don't catch up to him within a month, the Full Set will take him out themselves. He's a liability."

After a quiet hour of rest, Matey pulled up footage from the bank.

We howled with laughter, watching Taro, in her expert Lacausian accent, fling her hands out with glee and announce to the bank, "This is a robbery."

I caught glimpses of myself on film, shooting out windows, mirrors, chandeliers.

Cassius laughed and yelped, "Rewind it! Watch Devin!"

There I was in the background, staring in awe as blood dripped in long lines down my arm and onto the floor. My mouth upturned into a big, nasty grin. My head snapped up, and I turned, dancing on glass shards beneath me like it was party glitter.

Mina made an odd, pleased sort of grunt. It was almost predatory. Electric nerves nuzzled deep into my abdomen.

"You're one of us, boy," Cassius said.

Later into the night, while Cassius, Taro, Matey and I drifted close to sleep, Mina, Squeem and Fruit flicked through Merchant's data. They spoke in quick, hushed bursts.

"This is a goldmine. A fucking *goldmine*," Squeem and Mina repeated over and over, pounding their fists, clapping, throwing their hands to the sky.

Mina traded places with Squeem to drive the last three hours in the dead of night. She had to be tired, *so* tired. But Mina was the Director. The leader. The serial killer.

We drove into the back room of Boister and left the van to deal with later. Fruit had already sent multiple copies of the wiped information to other theaters and Backstage. Everyone shifted sleepily to their cars in the silence of dawn. The sun was close to peeking over the lowest dips to the east. Graciously, Mina gave everyone the day off.

"I'll be in the conference room, if anyone cares," Cassius yawned and disappeared into the Boister hallway with a pillow and blanket in hand.

Mina and I climbed into her car. Her reddened eyes and drooping eyes clashed with her hair. She started up the car and pulled out onto the road, following behind Matey. I watched with confusion as Mina trailed Matey home, but when Matey stumbled out of her car and threw us a lifeless wave, I understood; Mina wanted to make sure she got home safe.

I leaned against the car door, floating just beyond the bounds of sleep. As the sun broke the horizon, light gleamed off silver between us; the long-bladed knife Mina kept in her car. She'd stabbed me in the hand with that knife on the first day.

Mina's hand drifted over the knife, but she didn't pick it up. Instead, her fingers draped across my leg. I was too tired to stop the sigh from leaving my throat.

I pulled her in a sleepless daze through the woods. And when she jumped onto the deck of the houseboat, she wrapped her arms around me. Her lips moved against my ears in a whisper.

"You're one of us, boy."

She pulled off my jacket and laid in on the kitchen counter. Her long, sculpted hand clasped onto the minty fabric of my dress, circling the pearly buttons with one finger. And when she pressed her body into mine, our lips met with such force that the boat could have capsized and I'm not sure we'd have noticed.

I fell asleep as soon as I hit the couch. Mina was gone when I woke. It was an anticlimactic ending to the shortest affair in my life.

"Matey brought breakfast cakes; they're in the conference room. We're going to watch our news coverage," Taro said from her spot behind the front desk. "Squeem picked you up?"

I nodded and leaned over the desk. "Haven't seen Mina since we got back."

Taro's eyes darted to Mina's office door. "I think she's in there."

"Working?"

"Or fielding angry calls from Backstage."

The conference room was alight with laughter when Taro and I entered. On the big wallscreen, a newscaster stood in front of Terrion Banks, waving fanatically at the boarded windows behind them.

"Devin Mace was one of the six criminals arrested at the scene. Mace and the other culprits rounded up bank employees and civilians, forcing them into silence while the group shot out windows, destroyed priceless artworks, and gathered the bank's extensive funds. They were halted by Lansche's brave Batifban and arrested. However, the group forced their batif driver off the road and into a building, rendering him unconscious. The group escaped unhindered, while our brave batif lies in critical condition. He is under the care of top medical professionals, and is expected to pull through."

I stood at the door with my mouth gaping, my feet stuck to the floor.

"Many will recall Devin Mace, who went missing nearly five months ago in Pwero Ver. Mace, once coined the Devil of Suradelphia, was one of the founding members of the Tough Ponies, a social terrorist group based in Suradelphia. The group disbanded after Mace was sentenced for the murder of forty-four men, all of which were found in a construction dig site behind the group's headquarters, the Night Palace. Mace's conviction was overturned when new information entered the courts, but this information was never released to Beselian citizens, and many still believe Mace was the culprit of these horrifying acts."

Cassius spun in his chair to look at me with gleeful eyes, "Oh, Devin, do tell us — did you kill those men?" He laughed at the hilarity of it. "Little Devin, a *killer*. How outrageous!"

The newscaster continued over repeat footage of me pulling my ski mask off. "Take a look at Mace's deranged smile. Does he look innocent to you? With a smile like *that*?"

I walked out of the conference room and into the bathroom. In the toilet stall, I cowered with my head in my shaking hands. What if the news got wind of Mina — they'd know I was caught up with a real serial killer. Caught up in a few different ways.

Hours later, I sat at the front desk with Matey and Taro, letting them walk on eggshells around me. My pocket buzzed, and I pulled out my wordsearching screen.

Lightning at Teme'te. Package en route.

I turned to Taro, "Hey, check this out—"

Cassius burst through the front doors with a bag of greasy takeaway food, yelling, "Incoming! Incoming!" He ran through the lobby and into the restroom off the main hall.

Matey, Taro and I looked at each other.

"Indigestion?" I joked.

Taro's eyes moved to the front door and she gasped.

An attractive, angry man with auburn hair and a red, well-kept beard stormed in. He was carrying a luxuriously made travel bag and a sport coat was sling over his arm.

"Where is she?" the newcomer snarled, slamming a hand on the counter. He looked from Taro to Matey and stopped on me. His nostrils flared and he let out a hiss of breath through thin lips. Something in his eyes told me I was the last person he wanted to see. I shrunk back, terrified.

Matey squeaked, "In her office, sir!"

The man turned on his heel, growling a low "*Her office*" like it was a terrible joke. He opened Mina's office door, and she looked up, shock spreading over her face. He slammed the door behind himself before I could hear what was said.

I turned to Matey and Taro, catching the breath I didn't realize I held. "Whoa — who was *that*?"

Matey's voice shook as she replied, "The Producer."

Taro sent an alert to Fruit and Squeem, telling them to get up to the front desk quickly. Squeem limped in as fast as he could, with Fruit trailing behind him. Cassius poked his head out of the bathroom to take stock of the situation. At that moment, Mina yelled from behind her closed office door, "*Vile creature? Really?!*"

"Who's in there?" Squeem asked right before another voice was heard from the office, yelling: "*Do not raise your voice at me!*"

Squeem's eyes went as wide as ours. "The Producer? What is he doing here?"

"*Absolutely not!*" Mina yelled again. Seconds later, the office door opened.

The Producer straightened himself, running nimble fingers over his clothes and fixing his crooked glasses. He picked up his travel bag and suit coat and returned to the lobby. Mina stood behind her desk, panting with anger. Her eyes shot to me and held there for a moment. I shrugged, dumbstruck. Remembering her hands on my chest, gripping—

The Producer cleared his throat, "I will be staying to watch over this theater's productions. I will take up in the conference room, and later today I will hold interviews. I will be questioning *everyone*." His green eyes landed on me, boring into my soul and burning with disdain. He took off through the hall door and vanished.

Taro turned to me, asking incredulously, "Do you two know each other?"

"Of course not!" I yelped, because I didn't know him. Right?

Squeem's interview was first. After, he showed up at the door of Fruit's office, pale-faced and avoidant.

"Are you okay?" I asked.

He dodged eye contact with me, turning from the room, "Yeah — I need to get back to work. Fruit, you're next."

Fruit stared at his hounding screen, watching two women argue out the windows of their hovercars in Rasa Ver.

"Fruit, *now*," Squeem banged his hand on the doorframe. He was definitely not okay.

Fruit signed out and left without so much as a grunt, pushing past his friend. Squeem locked eyes with me for a split second, narrowed his eyes, and looked away.

A shiver of warning moved up my spine.

I escaped to the front desk and lamented to Matey and Taro, "He was acting weird, like he didn't trust me. *Me*! The one who was kidnapped by a serial killer!"

"You're taking this too personally; I doubt it has anything to do with you," Taro said, clicking away on her keyboard.

"Squeem adores you. He's probably stressed about the Producer being here," Matey said.

But as each crew member returned from their interviews, I grew more unsure. Nausea rumbled in my belly. Taro slumped down in her seat, citing a headache when I asked. Matey's meeting was short, but she went home afterward without a word to the rest of us.

Cassius gave me a strange, insulting moment of consideration before throwing his jacket over his shoulder. "Nessuir calls. I'll be glad to be rid of this place." He stooped to pick up his gnarlskin duffle. "Devin, love; it's your turn with the Wolf."

Taro shuddered beside me.

I sat down at the conference table, running my hands through my over-long hair. The Producer had arranged various papers in short stacks in front of him, leaving a little square of space for his hands to rest. A lapscreen sat up next to him on a rolling chair. My hounding profile was on screen.

"Would you like a drink?" The Producer asked. His voice was like too-stretched silk.

"No, thank you. Sir."

He took an empty glass to the sink. He wiped the glass with care before filling it halfway with water, tasting it and then dumping it out again. He refilled the glass for a second time, then came to sit at the end of the table among his stacks of papers. He thumbed through papers as if I wasn't there.

I sat straight-backed and terrified.

Stroking his beard, the Producer turned to his lapscreen and looked at my profile. "You are Devin Mace, correct?"

I cleared my throat, my voice lost momentarily. "Yes, sir."

The Producer continued looking at his lapscreen, "How did you come to know the Dight Actors Guild?"

"Um, I ... I'm not sure. It was by accident. Sir," I choked out. How *did* I get here?

His eyes shot to me. "By accident?"

We looked at each other for a long moment. When I tried to push my shoulders back, nothing happened.

"I think so," was all I could answer.

The Producer watched me with a crippling intensity. His green irises contracted as he looked into my eyes. Almost like he was trying to find something, if only he could flay my eyelids from my body. It was deeply uncomfortable.

"How do you know the Director?"

My heart jumped in my chest; did the Producer know? Was I that easy to read? Did he look into my mind and see Mina and I kissing with furious heat in her floating kitchen? That had happened, hadn't it?

"Mr. Mace," The Producer brought me out of my thoughts with the arch of a thin, skeptical eyebrow.

"Sorry— We bumped into each other in Pwero Ver and she ... took me."

"Took you?" He asked, and when I failed to speak, he said, "Stop thinking, just answer."

My thoughts tripped over one another, "In a hook market in Pwero Ver. I thought she was going to kill me, but she didn't."

He turned back to his lapscreen, "I see that you're listed as Understudy. Although I'm sure that will change after your stunt on Veishrin. The Director loves an irreverent display."

Lines etched across my forehead. "Irreverent display?"

The Producer silently clicked through my hounding profile. "The one where you outed yourself to the entire Endless World."

There were new video clips from the bank heist archived there, but below them I caught glimpses of my old self. Namely, my court case. It was all there for anyone with access to see. *Anyone* at DAG could watch recordings of my court case, my prison outbursts.

"What do you know about this Theater's productions?" the Producer had his eyes back on me before I realized it.

"To hound and kill members of the Full Set," I repeated the words I'd heard Taro say so often. Anything to prove myself to this mysterious, red-bearded man.

"And what do you know about the Full Set?"

I scratched my neck. "They take Limits kids."

"Are you using drugs now, Devin?"

My voice cracked in outrage. "What? No! Not in years."

With two sharp claps on the door, Mina was in the doorway. She had her shoulders thrown back, puffed up in a masculine display. Her hair was tied back tightly, and she had her shirt buttoned up to the top button.

"What are you doing?" Mina hissed at the Producer before turning to me. "Don't tell him anything, Devin. You don't owe him anything."

I was truly confused. "Isn't he in charge?"

Mina threw her head back, ready to retort something pompous, but the Producer interrupted her. "Mina, stop this at once. We must work together, especially after that absurdity on Veishrin."

Mina rolled her eyes, stomping her foot. "A single server of data alone would have been worth it, but we grabbed *three*. It was a good call."

The Producer straightened the collar of his tweed sport coat and cleared his throat. His tone softened to a practiced politeness. "Tonight, I will come to your residence. We will have dinner and talk about our plans. What better time than tonight?" He loosened his posture, leaning back into the chair. Was this guy trying to come onto her?

"No, I'm busy tonight," Mina said, crossing her arms over her chest.

The Producer threw his head back in a sarcastic laugh, "Doing what?"

Looking at me, Mina asked, "Devin, want to go on a date with me tonight?"

"Uh…" I glanced from Mina to the Producer in absolute horror.

"Perfect, I'll pick you up after work." Mina turned one last time to the Producer. "See? I'm busy tonight. We'll have to catch up another time."

He scowled. "Pity."

20

SETHBOOTS

Tom raced around the foyer counting our bags. "Is this everything? Mieda? Don't you have a pillow?"

"It's in the car. Please, calm down. You're kicking up dust," Mieda said, waving her hand in front of her face like she was being attacked by a cloud of bugs.

My mother shuffled into the room and dug her nails into my forearm.

"A londi roll, dear." She handed me a paper package with a shaky heart drawn on it.

"Oh, okay. Just the one?"

"Do you *need* more than one?" Her voice cracked, the veil of kindness already slipping.

"I meant for the others. But, come to think of it — might need two to satisfy my *rancid soul*."

Mom swept her hair from her red eyes and tugged at the port in her chest. "I'm sorry, dear. You know I can be a vicious drunk. I don't remember what I said, but I feel it was ... without cause. I worry about my children, and about my husband. And, now he's gone," her voice broke into silent sobs.

I reflexively patted her back with my hand. "Alright. You don't need to worry about me, though."

"Don't I? I can't help but think Mina's soul must be tarnished in some deeply destructive way. I am to blame for that." She wiped her wet eyes as I held back a yawn.

"Some people just have tendencies, you know?"

"You weren't there when Mina was a child. Your father and I treated her disastrously. Teaching her things no child should know. We didn't know what we were doing, we just wanted to save the *worlds*. We thought she was our answer." Narien broke down, sobbing into my overshirt.

I wrapped an arm around her small body and waited for the wave to recede. Over her shoulder, Nathali watched from the car outside. I let my sad smile curl with unease.

Tom pushed me into the car frantically. "I can't be late. We can't be late."

"You're in charge, right? So, who cares if you're late? The party doesn't start until you get there."

"This isn't a *party*, Maysolpheta! Dad runs the school, and dad is gone! It's up to me to keep things running smoothly. If I can't, I sure as hell won't be given the job when he retires!"

"Tom — do you even want this job?" Nathali asked from the back seat.

Tom slammed his hand on the steering wheel. "What do you think?"

"She has a point," Mieda said as she pulled her slippered feet up onto my shoulder-rests.

"Enough! No more talking. Silence for the rest of the drive."

"Thats five hours!" my sisters and I revolted.

The rain fell in a wash of grey on the cave.

Tom hadn't been to Voltenstraus for years and he was excited to walk through his childhood memories. I was too exhausted to care, and escaped to the Eldrid dorms. In the basement, Riolyn and Aeshra were strewn across the lounge.

"When did you guys get back?" I sat down next to Aeshra on the couch.

"Last night. Three gates in a day is too much." Aeshra rubbed his forehead and mussed his white hair.

"Which gates?" I reached over to fix his hair.

"Crown of Inadex, the Ash Tunnel, Voltenstraus gate. Too much. The Ash Tunnel was absolute hell; Votia is *not* a fun place. Those people are so damn serious," Aeshra said.

"I've never seen so much snow in my life," Riolyn added.

The skin under her eyes seemed dry and tight, and she looked like she hadn't slept the night before.

"Hey," I asked, "Are you okay?"

"Saren should be back by now, but he's not."

"He said he'd be back after us; I'm not worried." Aeshra shot me a look, "He had to pick some stuff from an old family home on Nirth. We're trying to sell off that house and be done with the other layers. Nessa is home now."

"He should be home by now. Class starts tomorrow," Riolyn said, pulling her feet onto the couch beneath her.

I put my hand on Riolyn's knee. "He'll get back tonight. I have class with him in the morning, and I know he wouldn't dare miss it with how much he gushes on Dwavasc literature." I rolled my eyes and Aeshra laughed with me. Riolyn didn't respond.

When I knocked on Eldrid dorm #14, Seth opened the door.

I dropped my stuff bedside and flung myself down. Seth crept back over to his side of the room. He was fidgeting by his closet, moving spare pairs of boots around with his toes. My eyes widened in shock. I peeked through low lashes to watch him.

Seth always wore boots, *always*. When he sat on his bed reading, the boots were on. At his desk doing homework? Boots on. At night, when he crawled into his sitting sack, what was on his feet? Big, platformed, black boots. Aeshra called them Sethboots.

Tonight, though, Seth nudged the closet door open with his bare toes. His feet were pale and grey, like a corpse in the water.

I had to look away. A nauseated sort of intimacy clutched at my chest.

I braved to ask: "How was Veishrin?"

Seth let out a little scoff. I could hear him wrestling something gently in his closet, the sound of soft fabric moving against skin, and metal hangers clanking. There was a whoosh of air as he dropped into the sitting sack.

The closet door closed as Seth said quietly, "Goodnight."

I stared at the closet door, mulling over the sadness in his voice.

Tom showed up at breakfast looking all too pleased with himself.

"Mayli, introduce me." He pulled up a chair and sat across from me with Aeshra and Riolyn on either side. Riolyn shifted as far from him as she could.

Rolling my eyes, I motioned to my friends. "This is Aeshra and Riolyn. Why are you wearing dad's clothes?"

He cast me a friendly scowl. "Well, I didn't have much time to pack, did I? And what about your partner? I'd like to meet this Uyentra," He added the last bit with an embarrassingly mischievous tone.

Riolyn spoke up, scales raised. "Wait, who are you?"

"This is my brother, Tom. He's here while George is out on 'important' business. Or whatever."

"Nice to meet you, Tom," Aeshra smiled, flashing his pearly little fangs.

"Do you know if Saren got in last night?" Riolyn asked. "Saren Vite, he's a teacher here. Looks like Aeshra."

Tom closed his eyes to think. "No, I don't think so. But I haven't gotten acquainted with much of anyone."

"Bummer," Riolyn mumbled, pushing food around her plate.

"Mayli, your partner. When can I meet them?"

I turned back to Tom. "Uyentra doesn't eat breakfast with us. They've got a free-period first hour, and it's none of your business, anyway! Now go bother Mieda and her precious jerk boyfriend."

Tom just laughed and patted the top of my head as he left.

Aeshra turned to me. "*That* is your brother? I think I've found my future husband!" He fanned himself before turning conspiratorial. "He looks quite a bit older than you."

I groaned. "Oh Mess, not this."

"So..." Aeshra smiled wryly. "He would have grown up with Mina."

I rolled my eyes as far back as they could go. "Yeah, they're *terribly* close."

"I just want to know what she's like!" Aeshra whined.

"Ask him yourself. I'm sure he'd love to tell you all about it, he's so damn friendly."

"So, do we just sit here until class is out? Do we call Benjamin?" I said, eyeing my classmates in Saren's Dwavasc Storytelling class. Still no sign of Saren.

When no one moved, I huffed and made my way to the wallscreen by the door. I found the com interface and pressed Dossier Access.

"Dossier, this is Zeel."

"Oh, hey Zeel, this is Mayli Harker calling from room 322. Saren Vite hasn't shown up to teach class."

"Still? Let me call around and find him for you. Does the class need a chaperone?"

"Eh," I looked around the classroom, "Nah."

Behind me, my peers yelled, "Yes!"

Zeel laughed and agreed to send a student aid. By the end of class, she hadn't been able to locate our missing teacher.

After an early dinner with Uyentra upstairs, I came back to the Eldrid dorms to find Benjamin standing awkwardly in Aeshra and Riolyn's doorway.

"Hey, Benny, how's the search going?"

Riolyn sat on her bed, curled up like a python. Aeshra stood next to her, bouncing on the balls of his feet, shivering with nervous energy. Relief washed over both of them when I slipped past Benjamin into the room.

"Baffling," the Advisory mumbled, wringing his hands. "We've reviewed the tram records. He hasn't ridden through yet."

Aeshra added, "You tried his number?"

Benjamin sighed. "Yes, out of service."

"But, if he's on the tram underground, that would cause a service outage," I said, nudging Aeshra's arm with my elbow.

Riolyn shook her head, throwing her chestnut hair about. "They're monitoring the track. No one's on it."

"Okay." I stopped to think, brows scrunched together. My two closest friends at this school were unraveling. Riolyn was flushed with hard, blue scales, and Aeshra had drifted to lean against the wall, clutching at his chest. "Well, you guys said Saren had a lot to do before coming back. Maybe it's taking longer than expected?"

"Yes," Benjamin pulled his head up, rallying his last bits of inadequacy into something that almost formed a whole person. I wanted to shake him. Kick him. His tan suit was the same color as his skin. He looked like an absent-minded, senile man who'd forgot to get dressed that morning. "It would be better if your father was here to help."

"Yeah, well he's not, pal!" My resolve broke. I flung my body toward my superior, my hand grabbing his disgusting *tan jacket*. "Now's your chance to *advise*, Advisory Benjamin!"

My eyes widened. My hand was flickering with a wet, red energy. I slackened my grip on his jacket. Benjamin's beady irises bored into mine with hatred.

"Manhandle me again and I will have you removed from this school."

He shook off his distress and fled.

I peeked at my friends, at Aeshra's horrified expression; at Riolyn's dejected annoyance.

"Messer's crack, Mayli. What is wrong with you?" Riolyn hissed, sliding off the bed. She pushed me from the room and shut the door.

I stood in the hallway, squeezing my fingers into my palm. If I did it hard enough, would the energy drip off like real blood? The glowing energy cast dodgy red on the stone surrounding me.

"Mayli."

I flinched awake, scrambling to cover myself. It must have been dawn — too early to be awake.

Seth stood in the bathroom door, a thin silhouette. "Your friends are upset. In the lounge."

And he wasn't joking. Aeshra walked back and forth, franticly rubbing his eyes. He was speaking in run-on sentences: "I can't lose him, I can't lose him too, everyone is gone, *everyone* is gone, I can't lose him."

Riolyn took on a brave face. "He will come back. Maybe it just took a bit longer to get things settled in Nirth. Saren will come back. Aeshra, look at me."

He looked at her for a split second, his eyes red and raw with tears. Then he was right back to pacing and mumbling, "I can't do this, I can't do this, I can't do this—"

Tom stood at the center of the lounge, very out of his element. He'd been dropped into the hogpit and there was no easy way out. I tiptoed over to him and pulled him into the hall.

"Any ideas?" I asked.

"I don't know!" Tom slumped against the cave wall. "Squidzy said she needed to come check on him; that he had panic attacks. I was dumb enough to offer help. I don't know anything about mental health prevention! What was I thinking?"

"Chill, man. Everything is alright. Aeshra and Riolyn have been through a lot, and when Saren gets back, things will be normal again. Well, until something else happens."

Tom growled, "Fantastic. Dad is going to be thrilled with my handling of this."

"Whatever. Dad is barely a dad sometimes."

Tom didn't like that comment one bit.

On Wednesday night, Aeshra was moved into the sickward under the care of Dr. Valentine.

Two nights later, Riolyn divulged the post-trauma of the Vite family.

In the darkness of her dorm room, I huddled against my friend. The tiny paphador lamp at her bedside lit her face. "I think they're going to have to drug Aeshra. He hasn't been lucid enough to eat. I was lucky to only have to worry about myself all those years, I guess. Didn't realize it 'till now."

"When you were at your uncle's?" I asked, pulling the covers around us.

"Yeah. That was easier than this. It wasn't scary after a while. Boring, depressing, but not scary. I forgot that family comes with good *and bad*. Now I'm worrying about myself, Saren, and Aeshra."

"Saren will be alright. Nirth and Votia are both pretty safe. He will come back. I'm worried too, but I'm almost more worried about Aeshra."

Riolyn took a staggered breath. "He has been through so much. He was there, saw it all happen. Fuck, you don't even know. My uncle killed *everyone*. Big family reunion and he killed every single person there. He just *snapped*. Aeshra wasn't dead, but everyone else was. His parents, my parents, grandparents, aunts, uncles, cousins, everyone. He saw our uncle take me, dragged me out by my fucking hair. I wasn't a blood relative, so I guess he thought he was doing me a service."

"Holy shit."

Riolyn continued, unaware of her shaking body. "All Aeshra had was Saren. They thought I was dead; everyone else was. Saren was the one who got Aeshra out of there alive. He was late to the party, walked in on *that*. If something has happened to Saren, Aeshra won't make it. He's not strong enough."

"He's stronger than he thinks. My dad will know what to do. He has to."

"Yeah, he has to." Riolyn shifted beside me. "Come on, do your thing." She began to unbutton her shirt.

I grumbled and pulled my hands out of the warmth of the blankets. We'd spent the off moments working on my Palm Lifting. It was the only thing we could do in between classes to keep our mind off Saren and heavily medicated Aeshra.

We turned toward each other and I placed my hand, open and flat, on her chest. With my eyes closed, I imagined my energy moving through me, pooling around my eye sockets and in the bowl of my skull.

"Whatever you're doing now is working," Riolyn said.

I sighed, resigned to my fate, "It works better when I imagine it flowing like … a river. But it's supposed to be light energy. Not liquid. I don't know."

"Who cares how it's *supposed* to be? You have magical powers, for fuck's sake. You're already past normal."

We settled into the act. Riolyn's breathing softened, her lungs lifting with each inhale. It was good. It felt good.

I focused on the feeling of her scales beneath my palm, and my sounds of the cave died away. I could hear the colors inside her. My energy sought out the tears in her aura, knitting them back together in stitches of blood red. Riolyn's wounds weren't physical, but they were just as painful. I would help my friend heal. Maybe then I could help Aeshra too.

And Saren, when he came back home. Because he would come back.

Seth had stayed out of my way, not that I expected anything else. The uneasy trust that blossomed before Veishrin vanished. He spent the nights hanging in his closet like a silver bat, as far from me as he could.

When I left Riolyn's dorm on Sunday morning to grab some clothes for the day, I opened the door to find Seth sitting expectantly on his bed.

His boots were back on, thudding against the bed frame as he moved his legs back and forth.

"Hey," I said with a confused smile.

He stopped kicking his feet against the bed. "Hi."

I went about my business, grabbing some clothes from my dresser, not caring what I picked.

"You seem tired," Seth said. Was he trying to have a conversation with me?

I laughed sarcastically. "Yeah, I am. Rough week."

"Yeah," He agreed and awkward silence followed. He started kicking the bed frame again.

I went into the bathroom, passing through Seth's disturbing, vibrating energy. Behind the closed door, I took a few deep breaths to center myself. I brushed my teeth, pulled my hair back off my face and covered my eyelids with orange.

When I opened the bathroom door, Seth was standing at the closet like he was thinking of hiding in there again.

"Was there something you wanted to talk to me about?" I leaned against the doorframe.

One knee jumped in a nervous little tick. Seth turned a bit to face my direction, but he didn't look at me when he spoke. "I, um, I need ... would you help me with something?"

A shiver of excitement ripped through my chest. "Yeah! I mean, yeah, sure. I'll try."

He turned to look at me, "I need to use a deskscreen. They are ... frustrating to me, overwhelming."

"Ok, yeah. Where do you want to go?" I asked, masking my nerves and excitement with easy confidence.

Seth pulled an overshirt from his closet and closed the door with his booted foot. He hugged the black mass of fabric tightly to his chest, asking, "Where is more private?"

"Well," I took a moment to think. There were places in Nepa like the university library and a little net café, but I doubted Seth would agree to go into Nepa with another breathing person by his side. That was too personal. "The Eldrid lounge versus the library. The lounge is smaller, less people, but closer together. They'd want to see what you're looking at — especially you. Because you don't normally ... well, yeah, anyway. The library might have more people, but it's more spaced out."

"The library, then," Seth said to the floor. He pulled the shirt over his head.

"Now?" I looked down at my ratty pajamas. "I can't go in public like this." I grabbed the clothes I'd pulled for myself from the pile on my bed and ran back into the bathroom, changing as quickly as possible. I was afraid Seth would change his mind and disappear. I was going to *help* him. I hadn't had something so positive happen all week.

Seth was standing at the door with his spidery fingers on the handle, waiting for me. I gave him a clumsy smile, and he opened the door. I pushed my shoulders back and led the way through the Eldrid dorms to the main entry. We stepped over the crack in the floor; *Don't comment, don't say anything, don't —*

"Oh, when did that get there?"

A shockwave of dark vibration boomed through the entry. I reached out to steady myself, my fingers brushing a centimeter from Seth's shirtsleeve. That hum of dark energy pushed us apart. He squeezed his eyes shut and continued through the building like he hadn't just dropped a bomb in the school foyer.

Our walking together caught lopsided glances from our peers. At times, I had to glance to make sure he was still there; Seth was startlingly quiet. It's like I was being followed by a ghost, or someone stuck in another dimension.

The library was on the fifth floor, and being early on a Sunday, it was quiet. There were a few groups of whispering students and tutoring sessions going on at the long tables; I could see Donnie near the center of the room.

Baheeba, let him not notice us.

I led Seth to the far side, near the books on biological sciences. A short row of desks spanned the section; their thin, floating screens sat dormant. Seth stood, watching, unable to proceed. I motioned to the far screen, nudging him toward it with my proximity.

In my periphery, Donnie shifted; he *had* noticed, damnit. There was no hope of him staying away, not with the long glance he gave us.

"Alright, so ... shall I?" I flopped down into a rolling chair and logged in, but I wasn't sure what we were doing in the first place. "Do you want me around? I mean, do you want me to leave? Or should I type? I can be the lookout, fist fight anyone who looks over."

Seth breathed heavily through his nose once before shifting into a seat, leaving a chair in between us. I couldn't say I wasn't thankful; It felt like my eardrums were being strummed like mandolin strings.

Seth looked at the lightless screen and fidgeted. This boy parted crowds of chatty teenagers, ripped a canyon into solid stone, made people vomit from being around him on a bad day. But he couldn't use a deskscreen.

His voice cracked. "I need to look up some news. About my brother."

"Oh, the missing one? He's been found?"

A little scoff came from his lips. "Sort of."

I opened the net. "His name is Devin, yeah? What layer?"

"Dedocia. Besel."

I audibly gasped at the picture that came up, "He looks like you."

It was striking: an older version of Seth, smiling widely. Same narrow eyes and grey skin. Longer hair, all black, and wearing something the exact shade of Seth's green bangs. Spots of blood spattered his jaw. He looked so damn *happy*. I'd never seen Seth with a smile like that.

The headline complicated things, though.

Infamous 'Devil of Suradelphia' escapes bank heist!

"He *is* my brother," Seth hissed, but there was no malice in it. The small bite of humor felt like a glistening, bloody gift from Uyenl himself.

The smile on Devin's face made me smile, too. He had crooked canines just like Seth, pointy little things.

"Devil of Suradelphia? Quite the title for such a pretty boy."

Seth leaned toward the screen and began to scroll with one finger on the surface of the desk. He moved with languid grace. I caught glimpses of words as they passed.

Devin Mace, once tried for murder—

Quiet life of freedom wasn't enough—

Property destroyed, but no hostages injured—

Why was this proven criminal let free?—

Seth stiffened and turned. I looked over my shoulder and jumped.

Donnie just couldn't keep his damn nose out of it. A forced smile stretched his gorgeous lips. How long had he been eavesdropping? I hadn't heard him approach. We locked eyes and he shaped his smile into something friendly.

I put on a gnarly grin, baring my teeth. "Hey Donnie, what can we help you with?"

"Good morning, it's nice to see you two up and around." He glanced over Seth's shoulder. Seth's body emitted a shudder of discomfort. The surrounding chairs shifted to the left and my own fear spiked.

I looked Donnie right in the eye as I reached over to Seth and exited out of the article.

Seth turned around to face his brother. "Good morning. We're busy."

"Hmm, I see that. It wouldn't have to do with our Veishrin day celebration, would it?"

Seth answered in a *full sentence*. "Not ours, no. Although I would have liked a bit more mention of Uyenl in ours."

My eyes flooded with a rush of tears and I blinked hard to will them away. The base of my skull began to tingle. I rolled myself farther from the two brothers; away from the electric illness in the air.

Donnie's nostrils flared, "If you are looking up Devin *nothing* good comes from that. He isn't part of this family anymore."

Seth held up one menacing finger, venom in his voice. "It is none of your fucking business what we are doing. Do not ask again."

The two brothers glared at each other in a stand-off that vibrated the cave. Dark, misty colors rose from them, in between them, connecting them, pushing at them. My insides roiled with fear; my animal-side told me to run. The very air seemed to rumble with fear. I wasn't imagining it either; students across the library were noticing.

Donnie tipped his head down and said, "If the Undergods cared one bit for Uyenl, they would have left him to die in the tarfire."

A crack of sound shot through the room, shaking the paphador lamps.

"That would have been convenient for his brother, wouldn't it?"

Above us, a paphador crystal dislodged and fell to the floor, shattering. Donnie turned on a quick heel and left the library.

Seth watched him go as he said, "Devin is not a killer, and he's certainly not a bank robber."

"Whatever he is, he sure looks like he's having a good time," I joked. Seth didn't laugh.

When I got back to the dorm that night, a pair of Seth's boots were laying at the end of his bed and his bedsheets were rumpled up in messy lumps. Normally he was so damn neat. Without thinking, I reached for his boots to put them against the closet doors, where he normally kept them in a tidy row.

I ran my fingers over the tarnished buckles, scuffed from years of wear. My fingers hooked inside the top opening and I gasped. Seth's boots were ungodly heavy; like they were made of cement. I could hardly pick them up. How in the hell did he walk silently in shoes that weighed forty pounds each?

And why the hell were Seth's boots so heavy in the first place?

21

SLICE OF A DREAM

"This was a bad idea."

"You think?" I stabbed the shredded tree fungus on my plate. My fork shrieked against the ceramic.

Mina snatched one of the tiny bowls of herbs, sprinkling them over her soft noodles, and scowled, "What was I supposed to do? I couldn't have the Producer coming to my boat *tonight*!"

"But a date? Really? Do you think I want to date the person who abducted me? Shot me, stabbed me?"

She pushed away from the table, standing abruptly. "Oh, fuck this." Mina stomped in the direction of the restroom, still holding the bowl of herbs. Turrisian music drifted down from the rafters of the tiny restaurant.

I wanted to laugh at her and her childish reactions. But Mina stopped dead at the center of the place and whirled back around to look at me. Harsh red flushed her cheeks. There, smack in the middle of a family establishment, Mina yelled.

"I didn't *force* you to kiss me, Devin! That was real, whether you like it or not! Devin Mace, the *Devil* of fucking *Suradelphia* kissed *me*, Mina Harker: Besel's favorite serial killer! So don't you tell me I'm wrong. Two monsters can go on a date!"

The bowl of herbs fell to the floor as Mina marched to the restroom, slamming the door shut behind her. Tiny green leaves scattered over the edge as the bowl spun across the tile. A waiter snuck to the mess, crouching to clean it, huddled like a mouse in a cat's den.

I closed my eyes and breathed through my nose, stood, and left the restaurant.

Fog lifted from the rain grates on the cracked sidewalk. I stumbled through town, hoping for a glimpse of a drug deal behind a store, or a lonely soul with an extra smoke. A group of rowdy teenagers stood outside the fuel station howling at a streetlamp like it was the moon. Maybe Fruit would give me some of that spitgrass he chewed all the time. Was he still at work?

The moon huddled close to the horizon, a glowing cut in the fog. In the distance, *Boister Energies* loomed. Lobby lights glowed through the floor-to-ceiling windows; inside, the Producer paced alone. I wouldn't be going there, then.

Directly beneath the moon sat the Kajiun temple, big and pink and fenced with barbed wire. I strummed my hand along the fence, humming with the melody of clanking metal.

The fog swirled in ghostly shapes around the temple. It towered in the haze, its top peeking out of the fog like an ornate, jagged mountain. Metal spindles hung like icicles from the boughs of the roof and off slanted buttresses. The pink plaster crumbled away, revealing creamy stone beneath. Overgrown grass and frasiora fern crept on the walkways. When the cold winds of winter ended, this place would be covered with thousands of tiny, neon-green blossoms.

I stood before the locked gate and sighed. "I know you're there."

Footfalls crossed the street behind me. Mina pulled her sweater up over her nose like a half-mask. She said, "I'm sorry for that, back there."

My fingers brushed green frasiora pollen from the posted sign: *No Trespassing: Historical Site. Property of Boister Energies.*

"Do you own everything in this Mess-forsaken town?"

"Not everything." Mina pulled her glove off one hand and pressed a code into the keypad. A click ensued, and she swung the gate open.

"I'm still mad at you," I mumbled.

"And I'm still mad at you."

The stone path fractured beneath our feet. Intricate carvings crawled up the entrance pillars, transforming into the silhouettes of Kajiun figures. Each spindle formed a cat-like spirit, dancing through the air mid-jump. Their graceful movements were captured forever in gleaming metal. As we stepped beneath the overhang, I was surrounded by these ancient sculptures. I closed my eyes, imagining whispers of the Kajiun people, forever connected deeply to the natural world. Quiet, magical peace.

I breathed in the stale, wet wood, and I sneezed.

Mina shoved me playfully and I hit the plaster wall. It crushed and cracked over my shoulder. I sneezed again, twice.

"Wow," the killer laughed, knocking her fist against my chest again. Our eyes met, and I turned away, holding onto my scowl for dear life. I was still mad at her.

Mina removed her hand from my chest and splayed it over the surface of a plastic square near the temple door. She exhaled one long breath over her hand and the whole area glowed. A series of quiet unlockings came from inside the door. Mina reached for the door and opened it up.

"Teenagers kept trying to get in here, so we had to upgrade security."

She stepped inside the temple, her eyes locked on mine like a predator circling prey. The hairs on my back stood, prickling against my new button-down shirt. The privilege of getting to see a place like this was unbearable, heightened only by my arrival by way of abduction.

"Have you ever been to another layer, Devin?" Mina asked.

"No," I answered, blinking against the dark interior of the temple. The place had to be filled to the brim with spirits.

"You're in for a treat, then," Mina replied. She took out her pocketscreen and turned on the flashlight. The single beam of light illuminated a strip of the dusty sanctuary. Hazy benches revealed more carvings and metallic detailing. I heard the scurrying of a rat, the hollow echo of our footsteps. This place had gone untouched by beings for hundreds of years. Except there was a shuffling of dust on the floor, scuff marks and footprints where people had walked many times.

The light from Mina's flashlight moved along the scuffed floor. Higher and higher she went, up a set of old, wooden steps in the center of the temple. At the top of the steps, a shimmer of liquid; a hollow place snagging the air; a slice of a dream. Encased in carved figures and plant life and animals, gilded and impossibly old.

"Is that a..." I couldn't even get the words out.

Mina walked up the ancient steps with careful grace. She moved like a sylph, pulling her fingers out in front of her to grasp at the edges of the thing, "A Gate."

"How... Do the others know it's here? Has it always been here? Have you been through it?" Questions spilled from my mouth. I stayed rooted to the spot, too shaken to move. I had never seen something so magical.

"When we found it, it had a powerful cast over it. Hundreds of years of energy piled on to keep it safe. But I felt it; I knew it was here. One of the greatest achievements of my life." Mina spoke like she was in a trance, tracing her fingers over the fragile frame of the Gate. She pulled her finger away and turned it to watch the moonlight catch shimmers of flaked, golden paint.

"You knew it was here?" The words barely made it out of my mouth. "You found it?"

Mina turned to look at me, smiling so softly. Her eyes glinted in the low light. "Do you want to see the other side?"

I was afraid; I'd never been through a gate before. What if it shredded me to bits? What if my soul was too damaged to survive a Gate jump through the Indigo Abyss?

Mina motioned for me to join her.

"What's on the other side?" I whispered.

With my hand in hers, Mina pulled me up the steps. "Home."

Going through the Gate felt like nothing at all. I stumbled into the black and out again, a mere second of confusion. But on the other side, I fell into great wind and pelting rain. I covered my face with my arms, my shirt soaking through with hard, cold water. Thunder clapped, shaking the rock ledge behind us. Mina clung to me, shaking with laughter.

Through great flashes of lightning, my eyes wandered the dark land — just before us, a lake or an ocean. Pillars of green glowed on the distant shore. Docks, boardwalks, and the shimmering points of light through windows; a seaside town.

The vision disappeared as Mina tugged me back through the gate. We fell back into the temple and slipped down the wooden steps, holding onto each other. Hysterical laughter met with shivering cold.

Mina threw her leg over my thigh, scattering wet dust onto my pants. Water dripped from her forehead onto mine. On the dirty, wet floor of an ancient Kajiun temple, I was kissed like I'd never been kissed before.

Mina Harker was, without a doubt, insane. Never had I been so constantly bombarded with conflicting attention. In the morning, she would wake me up with a kiss and a smack on the cheek. At Boister, she would yell at me for not paying attention to her lengthy speeches about hounding upgrades, only to pull me into the bathroom afterwards and shove me against the sink in a fit of passion.

We were hiding our fling, and that felt the most dangerous of all. The Producer loomed behind every door, watching out of the corner of his glasses-glared green eyes. He knew something was going on. It was only a matter of time before we were caught.

Mina steered clear of the Producer, and it infuriated him. He would extend a hand to Mina's shoulder only for her to move just enough for him to miss. He invited her to lunches, dinners, walks in the *park* (did Frasier even have a park?) daily. Mina dodged those too. The Producer's obvious interest in Mina was not reciprocated in the slightest.

And that gave me a giddy, powerful sort of joy.

I was lounging with Fruit in his office, hounding a teenage kid in Pwero Ver.

"What could this scrawny teenager have to do with the Full Set? He can barely tie his shoelaces," I asked, watching the kid stare at his pocketscreen as he strolled up to a grocery store. He walked right into the doorframe.

"He's on the list," Fruit replied, like it was obvious.

The kid glanced around with embarrassment. No clue that I was watching him from a different part of the country.

The office door burst open and in rushed the Producer. I jumped, sitting up straighter and running a quick hand through my hair.

The Producer took one look at our hounding screens and said, "End this — that child can barely tie his shoelaces."

I gaped. "That's what *I* said!"

The Producer's face twitched in annoyance and I sunk back into my chair.

"We have an urgent situation," the Producer said. "His name is Saren Vite, and he is extremely important. We must find him." The Producer waited a second, then pushed his way between Fruit and I, typing the name into the search.

A very white person came up. He had pure white skin and matching hair. I didn't think before I spoke. "Wow, he's paler than I am."

"He's Sithnic, you fool," the Producer spat.

I had no idea what Sithnic was, though I didn't dare say so. The hounding screens were still searching, darkly flashing through static-dulled video feeds. It was mesmerizing to watch, but it seemed to be taking longer than normal.

The Producer turned to Fruit. "I cannot stress how important this is. Saren Vite is Faunate and belongs Backstage. Any news of his whereabouts must come to me directly." The Producer spun out of the door, heading toward Squeem's office.

"Poor Squeem," I mumbled.

Fruit cocked an unkempt eyebrow. "What do you mean?"

"He was heading to Squeem's office. And he's not ... the nicest," I regretted speaking immediately.

Fruit looked at me like I'd spoken in a different language. I couldn't think of another time I'd see so much emotion on his face. "The Producer is good to us. He is good to me. Smart, too."

"Huh," I grumbled. "Have you ever been Backstage?"

He put a handful of spitgrass on his tongue and bit down. The sweet, musty smell lifted into the room. "One time. I belong here."

Fruit chewed in the silence. At length, he cracked his knuckles and went back to work.

"I think I belong here, too," I said. Above us, screens flickered in the dark room, searching for Saren Vite; an adult Limit lost in the Endless World.

On the first day of the spring cycle, Mina killed again, and I watched.

Cyrus antelopes hollered into the early dawn, searching for mates, waking me from sleep. Mina was curled up at the foot of the couch, burrowed under the other end of my blanket. When the forest antelope claimed their mates, they thrashed their antlers against the trunks of sodden, decaying trees and yowled like rabid dogs.

With mugs of freshly brewed tea leaves, huddled in our shared blanket, I breathed warm air on Mina's cold fingers, and she snapped about the utter disrespect of those *damned creatures* outside with nose nuzzled into the crook of my neck.

Thud. The houseboat rocked.

Mina shot out of the blanket, reaching for a gun tucked between a planter and the wall. My heart began beating so loud I couldn't hear anything else. I threw the blanket off, suddenly claustrophobic on the couch. No one knew we were out here, right? Besides DAG people. And the cyruses.

Someone knocked on the door. Mina disappeared into the kitchen with her gun at the ready. I picked up one of my shoes and followed, wielding the sneaker like a weapon.

Mina pulled the curtain back a smidge to look out and her hard focus was replaced with anger. She pulled the door open in one quick jab and it slammed back to hit the wall.

"What the fuck do you think you're doing, coming out here?" Mina yelled through the open door.

A recognizable voice answered, stiff and antagonizing, "May I come in?"

Mina let out a nasty laugh. "No, you can't come in!"

"I will not ask again," the Producer replied.

With an angry huff, Mina said, "You show up here out of nowhere, no explanation, and expect me to let you into my *home*?" Against her words, Mina took two steps back and the Producer stepped in.

"Yes, I do. I expect you to speak to me about what the hell is going on with this, *this* man. Why is he here?" The Producer looked me over with narrowed eyes, "You've let *him* into your home without a second thought."

I forced my shoulders back and stepped into the kitchen. "What's your problem with me?" My voice went an octave too high and I cringed.

The Producer breathed a fiery breath through his nose and lifted one hand up, crushing the air in his grasp like it was my neck. "You, *you*—" He squeezed his eyes shut. "You have no idea how I want the throttle you. And you—" He turned back to Mina, "Bringing this ... *man* into our fold. You haven't the slightest idea the trouble you've caused." He brought his hands to his forehead and clawed at his temples. "The points at which this disaster touches are beyond your imagination. I expected better from you, Mina."

"You can't talk to her like that," I started, but Mina held up a hand to stop me.

"Ok, we'll talk. Outside." Mina stepped onto the deck with him, leaving me in the kitchen alone.

I held my breath, listening through the thin windows of the boat.

"How did you find him?" the Producer asked, more exhausted than angry.

Mina spoke like she was talking to herself. "It was an accident. He recognized me through my disguise one day. It was a damn good disguise, too. I panicked, fled, but he followed me. I don't know why, but I was angry and frustrated and ... something made me stop. I don't know."

"That doesn't sound like you," the Producer said, his tone strange. Almost kind.

"I know. It was like ... Gate Reading. I knew something was there, but I couldn't see it. I decided to scan him."

"Ahh," the Producer sighed in understanding.

"He's working out so well. He really is. It wasn't a mistake," Mina said.

There were a few moments of silence. I wrapped my arms around myself tightly to stop myself from pacing.

"It *was* a mistake, a big one. Honestly, what were you thinking? Do you know anything about him? Do you know who he is?"

"Of course, I do! So what if he's rough around the edges?" Mina started heating up again. "Dammit. I needed more personal connections, and I found one. Is that so hard for you to believe? I need companionship! Why can't you give a shit about *my* needs?"

"What did his hounding profile say when you scanned him? Did it tell you, 'Dearest Mina, this man would be an excellent choice for an abduction?' Because I know it did *not*."

"Level 12: Classified, Protected Citizen; *that's* what it said. But you already knew that, didn't you?"

My eyes widened. *I* was being protected by DAG? That's why Mina had taken me?

"This is a dangerous situation, regardless of your blasted *personal connection* with him."

The rocking of the boat meant someone had stood.

"You are such a narcissistic psychopath, controlling me even as an adult!" Mina yelled, "You have no idea what I need!"

"Mina, quiet yourself. He will hear you."

"I don't care! You see me four times a year and only for work. You've destroyed all *possibility* of a family relationship. I'm making my own family out here! Devin is a part of us now. You have no say in the matter. Accept what a terrible father you are and move on. I know I have!"

Oh shit. Mina's *father*?

The slow, clunky clicks of connections formed in my mind. The Producer was Mina's dad. The person who'd trained her, who'd brought her up to be a killer. He wasn't trying to come onto her, he was trying to parent her.

"I accept that I wasn't what you needed me to be. I cannot fix that now. And I cannot control you, I don't want to control you," the Producer said, and Mina scoffed. "But ... of all the people in the Endless World, *Devin Mace*? The irony is too much. What do you really know about him? Does he heal faster than possible? Do you know that he is allergic to red water? And what exactly is his species listed as in the hounding system? He was labeled Classified and Protected for a *reason*."

Before I knew what I was doing, I had stepped out onto the boat deck.

"Ah, so you were listening." The Producer pulled off his glasses and rubbed his eyes violently.

I stared at him, dumbstruck, my mouth gaping and my eyebrows to my hairline. "What do you know about me?"

He turned to Mina. "Oh, I wish you wouldn't have done this."

Mina was unreadable too, her eyes darting back and forth from her father to me.

"Do you know who I am? I mean — do you know *what* I am?" In that moment I had transformed from an angry, confused, full-grown man to a lost, hopeful child.

"No Devin, I don't," the Producer said, "I'm sorry." He turned to Mina. "Can I speak to you about DAG for a moment? Then I will leave you be."

They spoke while I stood there, immobile in my heavy thoughts. The sensation of loss, the tangled unknowability, was overwhelming. It would never leave me; it had tracked me even to here, to a rickety, moss-covered houseboat in the Kajiun forest, hundreds of miles from Pwero Ver, thousands of miles from my childhood home on Brunock island. This stranger, the father of a serial killer, the man in charge of the Dight Actors Guild, seemed to know more about me than even I.

What sort of secrets did this man know, if he knew *mine*?

And the age-old question that plagued my life was forced on me again; Who am I?

When the Producer left, Mina slammed me against the refrigerator and growled, "Fuck him, he doesn't know anything." I pushed those questions out of my mind and let her devour me whole.

That evening, Mina killed again, and I watched from Fruit's office.

I, alone with thoughts about my life and Mina's. I was dazed with everything I'd learned, and all the new questions it had brought. Lost in the hazy glow of confusion and wonder, while she slashed up two bodies in quick strokes, spinning and dancing.

I let myself think she was overjoyed, too.

22

OPENING OUT

Uyentra splayed their big hands over my knees as they sat on the low table across from me. "When will your father be back? He chose an interesting time to vanish."

It was late, closer to morning than night, and we should have gone to bed ages ago. But talking to Uyentra was therapeutic. They had a way with words, so you could say. They had nice, big hands, too. Not that it meant anything.

"The doctor is a natural leaving at inconvenient times," I said, distracted by the gorgeous fingers massaging my kneecaps. Uyentra's touch was delicate and generous.

Uyentra's laugh rumbled deep in their chest. "I still can't believe you call him *the doctor*."

"Yeah, when he's being a clinical douchebag," I replied, lounging back onto the couch and hoping Uyentra would follow.

Seth was in the middle of our dorm room, crouched over, which was ... new.

I sunk to my hands and knees, contemplating what to do. I was drunk on infatuation for Uyentra and not thinking straight.

Against all better judgment, I crawled over to Seth and asked him if he was alright.

He turned away from me, bristling like a terrified rodent. It was almost like he hadn't noticed me come in, hadn't noticed me slide up next to him on the floor. That couldn't be possible; Seth noticed *everything*. Didn't he?

"I need you to leave." It was almost inaudible, but I heard it. My stomach lurched with dread.

I rolled my eyes to high heaven, pushing through the nauseous darkness that permeated the air. "I don't think you get it, man. I *want* to help you. But you're being a fucking *baby*." The words stumbled out like a whine.

A deep breath did not help me to steady myself. I was beginning to feel a bit intoxicated, and not just from infatuation.

"Okay, I didn't mean that," I pressed, dimly aware of the strange, limp tingling in my joints, the listless fog around my eyes. "Just tell me what you need and I've got you. We'll help each other out."

I was maybe panting now, I'm not sure. Things weren't making sense. Seth pulled himself from the floor, leaning onto his bed.

"Are you shaking? Or is that me?" I said, watching the room roll.

"*Shut up!*" His blurred form kicked the wall.

"Whoa, man, calm down—"

"The more you talk, the worse it gets! I need you to *leave*."

Was I drunk? Why was my response time so slow? Why was the room all vague shadows and loud thuds?

Seth slammed his fist into the stone wall, and I fell over, laughing, because it wasn't *real*. I was dreaming, or high, or both. But he kept hitting the wall, and by punch four, Seth's knuckles cracked beneath his skin.

The laughing stopped. My eyes focused on the wall. Red spots decorated the wall. Seth didn't seem to notice. He hit the wall again, and again, and again. Blood splattered like a bludgeoning scene. I guess he was bludgeoning his hand.

I laughed at that thought too, swaying with the room.

"You are out of your mind!" I yelled to block out the wet thudding. "I can't *stand* you. I hate how you just do whatever you want, and no one stops you. You skip class, you scare people, you crack fucking canyons into the floor, and *no one cares*! You're over here beating yourself into the wall while I can't catch a break for shit!"

Seth dropped to the ground. Throwing back his head, he let out a horrifying, feral howl. His body seemed to shift and lengthen, bones popping, limbs stretching. Black gunk fell in thick gobs from Seth's mouth, and he wiped it down his neck.

Seth wasn't Seth anymore.

My eyes opened to their widest and then a little more.

The room tilted and Seth went with it, letting air out of his mouth as he hunched on all fours. His eyes gleamed wetly from beneath strands of hair.

A voice tore from Seth's mouth. "You should have listened."

"I — what?"

The very ground under me contracted. I wavered, unable to tell what was real and what was the intoxication I'd succumbed to without a drip of alcohol. Had Seth drugged me? The way the world was moving, it all very well could have been a nightmare.

"Too late now, I fear," he purred, hocking a big loogie of Devil Spit onto the floor. Seth stuck his broken, bleeding hand into his mouth, pulling out a fist full of the black tar as it dropped down his chest. I gagged drunkenly. He'd never get the stain out of that shirt.

"What *is* that?"

"This?" Seth held up his hand and the tar slipped down his thin, translucent wrist. Seth's veins seemed to be surging beneath his skin, black vines rooted into grey flesh. "Surely, you know. They call it Devil Spit, hemacrux. Seth is *full* of it." He turned his palm downward, and we watched as the thick gunk dropped to the floor. It shone like oiled rubber.

"No way this is real," I heard myself say through chattering teeth. I was frozen in place.

"I hoped you'd be smarter," he sighed, reaching out to me, "but we can't have everything now can we." He wrapped his wet fingers around my wrist, knuckle bones shifting beneath grey skin broken in a hundred places.

I pulled away, flicking the hemacrux from my hand. It was slick and oily and smelled like mint. My wrist tingled where the residue remained. "Why was it in the crack in the floor?" I slurred.

Seth threw his head back again, catching and swallowing the Devil Spit that dripped out of his mouth, greedily lapping it up like a drooling dog. His neck, stretched longer than normal, was covered in lines of black goo. "Over-indulged himself, he did. If he'd let me out for a walk more often, we wouldn't have this problem."

I pushed myself to the foot of my bed, watching Seth in pure puzzlement, trying to make out his features through beer goggles. Seth had transformed into a pale, skinny beast with greasy black hair. He looked like a monster that crawled out of a sewer, slurping up all the gunk dripping from his mouth like it was a five-star meal.

Annoyed and repulsed, I changed my tone. "What is going on? Who the fuck *are* you?"

Seth grinned wildly, his black-stained lips stretching over sparkling white teeth. "Mercy — I'll have you call me Mercy." He began to suck the hemacrux from his fingers lewdly. Nausea swept over me as I felt the ground roll under me. Two words rose to the surface of my foggy mind:

Mortal danger.

The door was just —- just *there*, if I could reach it—

Mercy was impossibly fast, easily outpacing an overweight teenager like me. His fingers dug into my arm, talon-like nails breaking open the skin.

"Stupid, insubordinate *child*. You could never outrun this body," he growled, throwing me to the center of the room. I slid across the wet, black-slick rug and slammed into the desk chair. It toppled over me, shielding me. Adrenaline overrode my drunken terror.

I struggled up, shaking myself off, blinking away the haze, "Not a child—"

Mercy laughed, "Are you going to fight me now?"

In my periphery, blood dripped from the fresh holes in my arm. It splattered onto the stone floor. "Rather not, but..."

Mercy hunched like a sprinter, jumping toward me. I kicked one bare foot off his chest, grabbing him by the hair, ripping. His hand, broken and distorted, lifted to my cheek, talons out. They dug in, unzipping the skin from my face. Devil Spit sprayed. I coughed, gagged. Wet flesh hung from my jaw.

Cold mint stung my tongue.

Mercy gripped my neck. My face hit the stone wall, sliding in a line of red. He pushed, claws puncturing my shoulder. Talons scraped hard bone.

"Seth — are you," I coughed; blood sprayed. "Are you in there?"

Mercy dragged me back and slammed me forward. My shoulder snapped.

"Oh, Messer, *oh what the*—"

Blood smeared on the wall. I pounded it with my fists.

Cold breath hit my neck. "Aren't you going to fight? Use your delicious Lifting energy?" Mercy purred, "Are you going to put me away?" It was a sickening, mocking voice.

"No—" I gasped. My body vibrated with painful hate. "Put you — to sleep."

My eyes fell shut. Inside was dark, red, *wet*.

I exploded.

Red energy bloomed, bloody, into the room. A volcanic eruption. It wove into my crushed shoulder bones. Into my face, a hanging banner of flesh.

I slumped against the wall, dead weight. Mercy gurgled behind me, far away. The room teetered. I slipped down the wall into a great puddle of black and red. From there, I could see him.

Seth was on the floor. He convulsed, choking on hemacrux. His features began to soften. I gasped for air. I was a numb, damp rag.

Pounding—in my head, in the room, the walls, the door.

My eyes rolled back, and I slept.

Hot, bright light burned against my eyelids. I rolled away and was hit with an inconceivable pain. My hands found my face, covering my eyes. The sun filtered through in white lines between my fingers. Sun? There was no sun in the caves of Voltenstraus.

Or maybe there was. Over my head was a window, long and curved like half a moon. I could make out smooth, grey stone and strips of paphador. I groaned involuntarily, shielding myself from the blinding light.

Soon, Doctor Valentine was peering over me.

"How are you feeling?" Her tone was overly professional. She might as well have been taking notes.

"Bad." My face throbbed with the vibrations of voice.

"Good." She looked at me for a moment. I couldn't understand her expression: the inkling of wonder on her lips. My eyes adjusted enough to see her bouncing, red curls.

"You are not paralyzed. Your acromion and clavicle were shattered, as is your zygomatic — your cheekbone. We have already operated on your shoulder; it was broken beyond repair. I've replaced that for you. Your right side got the brunt of it. And the bruising on your neck, of course. You needed stitches in your cheek; I've taken care of that as well. And again ... you are not paralyzed."

"Right, sounds great." I cringed against the painful stretch across my face.

"You probably shouldn't talk. You can't seem to control your facial expressions." And there was that illustrious Squidzy Valentine smile I'd been looking for. "I'll go inform your brother that you're awake."

I groaned as Squidzy fled the room, her steps echoing off the stone. I had to be on the top floor with the skylight, not the sunless basement I inhabited with Seth Mace.

Seth Mace. What in all the Abyss happened to Seth Mace? That was *real*?

And then my brother, all six feet of him, rushed to my bedside. His sleepless eyes made my chest ache. Surely, these people knew I was fine. I was fine, wasn't I? Not paralyzed.

"Can I touch you?" Tom looked from me to Dr. Valentine and back.

"Her left hand should be alright," Valentine said.

Tom grabbed my hand without a second thought.

I rolled my eyes at the fussing. "I'd take a foot massage right about now."

"Really?" Tom jumped to reposition, but I smacked him away with my good hand. He cocked an eyebrow. "Still you in there, I see. What do you think about your new shoulder?"

I strained to look — something hard and pink glinted in the sun beneath my flimsy sickgown.

Dr. Valentine rolled forward on her stool. "We should take a look. May I?" She reached forward and unsnapped the shoulder of my sickgown, peeling it away.

"Am I an MMP now?" I said against my own will.

Pale, pink metal molded to the shape of my body. It dipped beneath the swollen, shiny flesh of my collarbone like steel embedded into the trunk of a tree. I shuddered, prickles of distaste grappling at my insides.

Valentine washed her hands in solution while Tom stared at my new parts.

"Once healed, it will feel normal. It should move just as your previous shoulder did. The ball joint will need to be checked once a year, but these products rarely need replacing."

"It itches," I said, watching the muscles move beneath my skin, pushing at the metal device. The shoulder piece moved as well, like it contained muscles of its own.

"It's *healing*. In a few weeks, your shoulder will be back to normal. Your face, however, will take longer."

Tom tore his gaze from the pink metal and rubbed his eyes harshly.

Dr. Valentine handed me an oval mirror. I held my breath.

Clear plastic bandages covered my right side. Beneath, red, yellow, and purple. I pulled the mirror close, trailing the white stitches beneath my eye, contouring my nose. Humid, yellow wetness dotted the surface of the plastic, like looking into an old, dirty greenhouse window. My jawline and cheek were sown together in fragile lines; I felt the hard threads with my tongue.

"Ok. Not great," I said, squeezing my eyes shut, mirroring my brother. My eyelids felt like they were filled with sand.

"The bandages will come off at the end of the year; I'll change them out as they fill up. We need to keep your body's natural healing fluids on the wounds. The stitches will dissolve."

Into my silence, Dr. Valentine asked, "Do you remember what happened?"

I thought for a few moments. "Seth was mad, I think. I felt ... I felt *drunk*, but I swear I hadn't taken anything." I sounded different from the swelling around my mouth. "He punched the wall. Over and over, like — fifty times, wouldn't stop. And his hand was *really* broken. Blood all over the place."

Valentine had a notebook out, scratching down fast words. "And he changed?"

"Into that Mercy thing? He fell on the ground and started growling and coughing up, you know, the black stuff? Thick, oily, like tar. It was..." I trailed off, itching at the skin around my shoulder. "He's got a demon in there?"

Dr. Valentine sighed, folding her notes into her lap. The sun slashed across her face and her neon red hair. "How about we answer questions after your medication kicks in a bit more? And we'll send for our Palm Lifter, Moonie Devince. I think you know her."

Dr. Valentine administered an orange gel into my mouth. I shuddered at the taste of it. My tight, swollen face throbbed with every slight movement, and when I yawned, I yelped at the sudden onslaught of pain.

Dr. Valentine gave me two injections in my shoulder. Then she moved a blue light over me to accelerate healing.

I was left to lie there uncomfortably with Tom at my side, fake-reading a book while constantly checking me over the cover. Where was Riolyn? Was Aeshra still in the sick ward? What colors of light were they using on him? Was my face disfigured? Would this mess up my Palm Lifting?

Where was Seth? *What* was Seth?

I drifted into a fitful sleep.

I awoke in the evening, with the sunlight low in the roof-windows. Dr. Valentine and Moonie Devince spoke by the counter, huddled and whispering. Tom stood awkwardly, hovering in the middle of the room.

I wanted to smile, laugh. At *anything*. But nothing felt funny enough to risk the pain. Was I going to be in this stupid bed for days? Under this nightclub-blue light?

Moonie took the seat next to me; her eyes were dry and tired. I watched her like I had so many times in class, but this time was different. The mood was serious. She closed her eyes, and I did the same, feeling the movement of her energy. It was a lot harder today, like trudging through mind-mud. Our bodies and minds connected, heavy with fatigue.

A splash of ink filled my mind. I jumped back, electrified by it. Mortified.

Moonie's eyes were open, staring daggers into me. "*Oh*. That's new."

"You saw that?" I whispered, glancing at my brother and doctor, chatting in the corner. Tom noticed, started to come over. I smiled against the dull pain and shook my head, *I'm okay.*

Moonie's voice dropped. "I felt it. Liquid, like your energy, but ... more. I'm not sure."

"Should we not Lift?"

"No, it's fine. We'll keep an eye on it."

Moonie's hands rose over me, the healing blue light above. When I closed my eyes, her pale blue energy danced over the surface of the red lake like falling snow. Beautiful.

Physical feelings — how do I describe those? Like sugary-sweet needles poking into my cheek and dragging out thin threads of muscle, weaving together torn flesh. Hard, dead bits of skin turning squishy and alive. The slow dragging of sinew, the melting and reforming of fat. It was unnerving and I would never be able to forget it.

I slept again, dreaming of crunching bones and deep pools of sludge. Of red and green swirling; two life forces meeting in the *Indigo Abyss*. Of Uyenl, the Dementric Undergod, raw and bloody, reaching for my hand and leading me through the emptiness to a sea of deep green sprouting with tiny, white flowers.

"*Oh*", I gasped, sitting up in my bed.

Tom came running. "What are you doing? You need to lie down!"

"I'm good, fine. Where is Valentine?" Things were clicking together rapidly. "I need to talk to her."

Dr. Squidzy Valentine rolled over in a chair. "You really should lay back down."

I ignored her, "Seth — where is he? Is he gone?"

"Shh, shh," Valentine turned to mush, "He won't hurt you. He's safely put away."

"What? No — not that. What do you mean, *put away*? I mean, is he still here? I need to talk to him."

Tom made an outraged sound. "*What*? Why would you do that?"

I scoffed at his idiocy (and maybe mine too). "That thing lives *inside* him. Uyenl showed me — I mean, a dream, but yeah, it's all right there. The hemacrux, the talons — he's a *Dementric*."

"What is *wrong* with you? Mayli, lie down," Tom growled.

I wished he would leave.

Dr. Valentine gave Tom a wry look, and he backed down. She started checking over my shoulder. "This first healing session with Moonie went well. Think you can walk?"

Tom squeaked with indignation "Excuse me?"

"Take a walk, go eat something. You've been up here for days," Valentine said as she helped me up. I got to my feet slowly, dizzy.

"Where are we going?" I asked.

Valentine kept me balanced. "To see Seth. Sort of."

We went through the rounded doors and into a space of shadows and organic shapes. Sitting sacks hung from the ceiling, silvery and velvet. Through the grey haze of scented smoke, turquoise paphador cast a haunting glow over swooping, curved walls. Curtains clung tightly to the ceiling; slivers of evening light peeked through.

A globe-shaped enclosure was anchored to the room's center, made of glass and dark framing.

Inside, Seth Mace sat on the floor. He was motionless, hunched over a round basin. A tightly wound bedroll was pushed under the curved benches lining the perimeter. Just outside of the box sat Drucilla Laverick, watching Seth with nauseating reverence.

"Can he see us?" I whispered as we approached the sphere.

"If he wanted to," a strange voice replied. I turned to see a being cloaked in grey, their body pulsating with divine energy. "You choose what you want to see. Right now, Seth only sees himself."

The ancient being emerged from the shadows, saer grey, stony skin glistening in the paphador. Idrissa's curious gaze was set in drooping, almond eyes. Sae moved with grace, with silky long hair flowing behind sae like a cloak. Saer androgenous features struck me with awe. Maybe fear, too.

I was in the presence of someone truly holy and divine.

Playing out an awkward bow, I said to Idrissa, "Nice to meet you, Ser."

Dr. Valentine swerved to look at the grey figure. "Idrissa, this is Mayli; Dr. Harker's daughter."

"Yes. So, you have awoken the demon, miss Harker. Before you, Seth's dark parasite peacefully slept for nearly five years." The samale had a soft, billowing voice.

"Me?" I stumbled, made meek by the presence of something so powerful.

Most students would never meet Idrissa. Yet, here I was bandaged within an inch of life and touring sae's living quarters.

"I'm not sure what happened, Ser," I admitted.

Idrissa hummed, swishing saer gown in a wide circle to leave the room, beckoning us to follow. Dr. Valentine held my arm, steadying me. Her touch was a comfort in this strange situation.

From my periphery, Drucilla rose from her kneeling stoop. She was stalking us.

My eyes wandered over to Seth. His fingers dipped lazily into the basin, swirling the iridescent liquid inside. His other hand, the one he'd bludgeoned to crunching, bloody bits, was perfectly normal. No bandages. Not a single bruise, not even a scratch.

My shoulder flexed involuntarily.

We made our way toward a rounded door. It opened as Idrissa neared it. Moonie Devince stood there, glossy with sleep, in a comfortable sitting room with pink cushions. Organic forms of glowing blue spanned the walls. The space smelled like burnt vanilla.

I raised my eyebrows at Moonie, wondering what she could possibly be doing in Idrissa's sitting room. She looked right past me like I didn't exist. Something was off; the sleepless, reddened whites of her eyes, the unkempt braids, the wrinkled white thing she was wearing; a dressing gown? That didn't make a bit of sense.

Idrissa lowered into a sitting sack. Moonie positioned herself behind sae with her hands on saer shoulders. The two settled into this state like they'd done it a thousand times.

Idrissa took a long puff from a decadent vapor pipe and a waft of hot vanilla cascaded in smoky billows to the floor. Moonie's eyes closed. *Oh*, I thought, *she's Lifting*. Duh, of course she was. Benjamin had mentioned Idrissa was sick when they shoved Seth onto me.

None of this should have been my problem. It shouldn't be *her* problem either.

Moonie looked undead. How long had she been Palm Lifting Idrissa? Was anyone Palm Lifting her? Should *I* be Palm Lifting her?

"I see an unending curiosity in you," Idrissa said slowly, peering at me through heavily lidded eyes. Sae could have been talking in sae's sleep. "George pushed a curious child into a curious situation. Alas, it was time. Now, what to do with you?"

"George," I mumbled; the weight of his name crumbled inside me like the bones in my shoulder. He wasn't even there.

Drucilla made her presence known, snarling, "She shant miss any more class, as we have a problem completing assignments as it is."

Valentine sent me a sidelong look from under red lashes. Drucilla continued, "Quite frankly, child, if you would have bothered to *leave Seth alone* like you'd been told—"

Idrissa held up one grey hand, mangled with age. Drucilla shut her mouth.

I couldn't help my victorious smirk, batting my eyelashes. "If I could just say one thing: no one gets to call me a child. That demon living inside my roommate called me a child and yeah, I am *not* a fan."

Idrissa sighed while Moonie continued Lifting, "Our time is short, may we please continue? Matters must be tended to."

Drucilla's lips pinched into a sour swirl.

Idrissa continued, "Good. Now, as I believe you know, Seth is inhabited. The creature who calls themself Mercy has opened out again, and with that arises new dangers for our students. Seth will stay in his echosphere until he decides to leave it, and that could be months if this time is like the last. However, I don't see that being the case."

"Why?" I said.

"For the first time in years, he has formed connections outside of this room," Idrissa replied. Sae closed saer eyes and hummed, nodded. "Moon believes he will return to the dorms. I do as well."

My eyes crossed in confusion. Moon? *Moonie*? She remained motionless, Palm Lifting the Non-Eater before us. Could Non-Eaters read minds?

"Wait — my dorm? After he tried to remove my *face*?"

Drucilla banged her blue fist into the couch back. "He will *not* be wasted on such a thoughtless bully as this girl! I won't allow it."

The skin around Idrissa's eyes rippled, shutting tightly. "It is not your decision to make, Madame Adord. It is entirely in the hands of Miss Harker."

Drucilla's presence bloomed like a thunderstorm. The beading of her head covering clanked in tiny plinks as she shouted, "Miss Harker's? Why not her dastard of a father? Or, Miss Valentine here?" Drucilla threw her head back with a cruel laugh. "A medical doctor with no real-world experience? No experience with such *immeasurable* power as this? Don't make me laugh!"

The Adord's blue cheeks heated up to purple. "He is the rarest kind of being! A body with *two souls*, with equal control! He is a treasure of science, the pinnacle of genetic miracles. He must be protected!"

I sat back and splayed my legs, watching her tantrum. When she stopped to breathe, I said, "Man, you are something else."

Dr. Valentine squeezed my hand in warning.

"Be gone, Drucilla." Idrissa's whisper cut through the smoke.

Drucilla bored her eyes into sae, willing Idrissa to combust. When she flew from the room, her jewel-toned robes wisping behind her, she slammed the door with a flick of the wrist. Objects around the room rattled in fear.

"Now, what was I..." Idrissa took a puff of sweet vapor, "Ah, yes. Mayli, you are the sole decider in this. Seth is young like the rest of you; he needs social relationships. He has been alone far too long. With a little prodding from newfound friends, he will ignore his better judgements."

"And you think I should 'prod' him? Because, and this might surprise you — I actually want to *live* through this year."

Idrissa cocked a hairless browbone. "It's merely something I want you to consider. When Seth inevitably considers returning to the dorms, every source will plead against it. Your father, your friends, your siblings. But they do not recognize what I see. You are equal to Seth, and thus you have the power to admit him or turn him away. I suggest thinking this over."

At length, Idrissa puffed flavored smoke into the room, adding, "Mercy will visit again, regardless."

The room hushed.

Why the hell would I agree to rooming with Seth after he tried to kill me? I *wouldn't*. There was no way in the Abyss. In the name of every Undergod: No.

In the quiet, Moonie's breath rattled. Idrissa brought saer hands to rest on hers, whispering, "Yes, Moon. Go, sit."

Moonie, deader than night, slipped away from Idrissa and slung herself, with thoughtless grace, onto the couch. She curled into a tight ball, manicured hands gripping onto striped sock feet. She opened her eyes and blinked up at me. A weak smile settled on her, and she fell asleep.

Things were very bizarre at Voltenstraus.

23

Natural Order of Things

Hounding a stranger deemed 'priority' by the Producer was both entertaining and nerve wrecking.

Saren Vite disappeared the day after Veishrin. After searching for Saren's neurochemical signature all day, we eventually found a trace of him on Dedocia a week prior. As we mapped out Saren's travels, we saw that he had visited four different layers in the past week.

This is where the excitement kicked in. I'd never been to another layer, besides the few seconds with Mina in that rainstorm on the unknown layer she called home (on which she had since remained tight-lipped).

Saren and his companions traveled from the frozen city of Parsells to the warm, wet Quar.

The group stopped in the Sithnic Isles, spending their Veishrin holiday in a decadent hotel on the beach. During the days, they scoured the burnt ruins of a single-family home.

From the Sithnic Isles, Saren and his companions returned through Inilda's Door to Votia, where Saren broke off on his own.

He rode through the white mountains on a tram. He disembarked in the quiet countryside of Sinnia, where spring was just starting to peek through the snow. Without a proper coat, Mr. Vite walked three miles to a lesser Gate, and paid his toll.

The Gate was inconsequential, with thin bars of patina-stained metal bent into layers of twisting archways. Fine, delicate, but nothing like the storied Gates of my childhood.

"Oh," Fruit said with a sudden jerk. "Oh. Teme'te."

"What?"

I watched Saren Vite step inside the Gate, and I understood. That Gate was Teme'te, the very Gate I'd been put in charge of wordsearching. The very wordsearch that had turned up with an alert two days after Veishrin; *lightning at Teme'te.*

Mr. Saren Vite didn't come out on the other side.

The Producer was calling the shots now, and Mina did not like it.

He began to delegate actors for an exploratory search of Teme'te, because: *It's what needs to be done.* Mina argued with him for the sake of arguing, calling his mental state into question at one point. The Producer maintained cold, calculated control over the situation. He was even more terrifying than she was.

Since his arrival, the Producer had stayed to himself for the most part. I wondered what he was doing in there, with his papers spread out and his glasses perched on his nose. He didn't seem to be violent nor quick to action, and the insults he lobbed were precise little stabs as opposed to Mina's all-out flamethrower blasts. He didn't bend to her explosive moods. And when the two of them were going at it, Mina came across as the childish one, no matter how often Mina called him a psychopath.

Because the Producer was often right, no matter how much I wanted to deny it. He was diligent and organized. The Producer was playing the long game, always tending to his perfect plan. Mina, on the other hand, had three or more plans.

Matey, Taro, and Cassius traveled to Teme'te. Mina sent them begrudgingly, even though she knew the Producer was right. Fruit, Squeem and I watched via screen as the crew, donning disguises, bought tickets and wandered into Teme'te. Seconds later, they came out on Votia empty handed.

On a video call in the conference room, Taro said, "There was nothing there, just a gate. These sorts of things follow a natural order."

"Yes, yes, but what did you *see?*" the Producer asked.

"What did we see? Indigo Abyss, like every other gate. There was nothing out of the ordinary."

"How long was the Gatespace?" The Producer asked.

Cassius took over. "About ... three feet, sir. Though she's not wrong, sir; there wasn't anything to it."

Matey interrupted quietly. "We could have missed something."

"Yes, go again. Film it this time," Mina said matter-of-factly, and the call ended.

That evening, Cassius and Matey went through the Gate of Teme'te again. Taro stayed behind to run scans of the area. It seemed like an excuse.

We watched as they entered Teme'te from the Votia side like Saren Vite had. A being can't stop in the Gatespace; the pull to the other side is too great. But, with practice, a person can slow their speed and open their senses enough to see the Indigo Abyss, the Sacred Fabric, the Great Inbetween.

"There," Fruit mumbled, pointing at the screen in front of him.

"What? Cassius, slow down!" Mina yelled.

"I can't, you imbecile!" Cassius yelled back. A second later he and Matey were stepping into sunny, green Nirth.

Mina pounded on the table. "I will pull you apart when you get back here, you filthy—"

Squeem put a hand on Mina's shoulder. "Fruit saw something." He pressed the call button and said to the Teme'te team, "We're going to review the footage now; thanks guys."

The more we rewound the Gate Jump, the heavier it felt.

I'd seen pictures of the Indigo Abyss, of course; we studied it in grade school, even on my backwater little island. Cameras couldn't yet see what a living being's eyes saw, but it was enough to go on. Blue and purple, hazy like an image on fleece. Pinpricks of light, far-off stars, warming the cold dust of space. The realm of Baheeba; the Divine plane of the cosmic Universal Consciousness.

When Fruit slowed the footage to a slug's pace, the camera tipped down just as Cassius' shined shoe stepped into a slick drop of nothingness. My stomach churned. The camera hovered, suspended in an expansive void. Through the grainy film, tiny lights flickered beneath his feet. As he stepped again, he looked up, and the camera followed.

There, stuck to the edge of the tunnel; a thin, shimmery cut, about two by two. A square, buoyant in the Gatespace. And that didn't make a *bit* of sense.

"I don't understand. Is there a hole in the wall?" I said. "There aren't geometric shapes floating in the Abyss, right?"

No one answered. Mina, Fruit, Squeem, the Producer stared at their screens, each of their logical minds turning over rocks and reasons. I could almost see the equations dancing in Squeem's mind. Mina's mouth was just a thin frown, pulled farther to one side.

"Right?" I repeated, staring at the shape too.

The Producer was the first to speak, "We'll send them once more, just to be sure." He scratched at his red beard, the same lined frown on his lips. For the first time, I couldn't ignore the resemblance.

Matey went on her own this time, dressed as a man with a tattered hat and glasses to cover her lack of an eye. She flipped on her flashlight as she stepped into the Gatespace. The outline of the square glittered like cracked glass.

Taro, who'd been hiding at the inn because she was too moody about the "natural order of things," made a discovery of her own. In her scans of the area, she'd found a hollow space beneath the gate; an unmarked maintenance tunnel. It was accessible via a drive-up door just south of the gate.

Mina paced the conference room while the Producer spoke to the crew. "Watch the access door for 48 hours. By then, we'll know if it's safe to infiltrate."

In that time, I manned the front desk and took charge of Matey and Taro's wordsearches. The Producer gave me a wide berth, hunkering down in the conference room with Mina at his side. We didn't have much interaction in those two days. I tried not to take it personally.

Key word: tried.

Is she going to leave me already? I don't know anything about Gates or Gatespaces or glittery squares floating in the Abyss. I'm out of my depth. She would have noticed it eventually, with or without all this Gate business.

I sat at the front desk waiting for her to stroll up and tell me she was leaving me for Cassius; lovely, bitey Cassius, who knew so much more about being an attractive, covert agent for a serial killer and her father. So, what if he was gay? So, what if he was the brother of Mina's dead husband?

She might leave me for Fruit. Fruit's quiet. He works quickly and diligently. He's not affected by Mina's moods, or anything, really. That could be very attractive. And Fruit actually enjoys Mina's father.

Mina's Father. The Producer. He strode around in his fancy sport coats and his tortoiseshell glasses, humming and hawing and scratching his eyes. When would he *leave?* I wished Matey was here; she was afraid of the Producer too. Maybe she and I could talk trash about him when she got back from her fantastical journey of Gate jumping and missing persons. Would I ever be invited on a fantastical journey?

Sunday was my longest, strangest, most exciting day at *Boister Energies* to date.

Mina dragged me up just after 4 AM.

"We have to go! I told you this last night. Why don't you listen? Here, eat this — No, it's not pear; it's spiteberry, just like you like it. I set out your clothes, get dressed. *Quickly!*"

The forest was dark, the drive was dark, Frasier was dark. The sun peeked over the far hills just after we settled into the meeting room with our deskscreens and our burning hot teas wrapped in our chilly fingers.

The Producer was fresh and clean with a pressed shirt underneath his plaid vest. He wore a green-patterned bowtie. His eyes shifted around the room, jumping from window to door to window.

Squeem and Fruit shuffled in, with Squeem's cane clacking against the floor. Fruit leaned over the conference table and grabbed a breakfast cake from the center box. He bit off a chunk, dropping crumbs on the floor.

"Are we late?" Squeem yelped into the silent room. He sat his tea on the table with a thud and it sloshed over the side. "Fruit heard from Taro that they're already there!"

The Producer eyed the mess with an intense side-glare.

"Just sit down," Mina snapped. "They are about to head in." She slid her hand onto my thigh and *squeezed*. I jumped about a foot in the air.

The Producer turned his intense side-glare to me.

Finally, after much grumbling and shuffling from the crew, Taro, Matey, and Cassius were ready to break into the tunnel. They were each packing a wide array of dangerous objects, weapons and otherwise.

From the driver's seat, Taro polished her gun with frazzled commitment. "Who knows what we'll find in there? We have to be prepared for snags."

The first snag appeared right at the drive-up door.

"It's Bright White," Matey groaned.

"They have Bright White Energy on Nirth?" I asked.

The Producer squeezed the pen in his hand until the lid popped off. "Of course, they do."

"Damnit; Squeem, why didn't you come on this little trip?" Matey said, as she looked through the square window at the center of each door. It was pitch-black inside.

"As long as your live feeds stay intact, we'll be fine," Squeem answered.

Taro smacked a metal box onto the doors and an electric buzz clipped through the conference room speakers.

"Hinge jam successful," Fruit said.

Cassius pulled a thick card from his bag and pressed it to the door handles.

"Unlock successful," Fruit said.

Cassius reached back into his bag as Taro and Matey opened the doors an inch. He threw something into the dark innards of the tunnel, jumping away just as Taro and Matey slammed the doors shut. A blast of light flashed through the door windows.

Fruit bit loudly into his breakfast cake as the rest of us were frozen with bated breath. Through chews, he said, "Security signal jammed for forty minutes."

Matey said, "Forty minutes? Will that be enough?"

Cassius grabbed her arm and pulled her in.

Orange hazard lights hung from the roof of the dirt tunnel. The sides of the tunnel were caged in with wire mesh. The crew crept in the direction of Teme'te. At Boister, we watched Matey's camera feed, swinging back and forth. The jagged, short glimpses of their shadows in the unnerving orange light could have been cut from a horror classic. I waited for a fourth shadow to devour my friends.

"This isn't the usual maintenance track. It's thinner, I think," Taro said, scanning the tram track running the length of the tunnel.

"Document it. Document everything," The Producer said.

"Cassius!" Mina yelled. "Hold your flashlight right! We can't see a damn thing."

Cassius yelled back, "I will gladly take an early retirement if you don't *get off my ass about every damn thing!*"

The camera feed shook wildly. Matey's feet pounded on the cement ground, "A door — there's a door!"

A white door, clean and out of place, hung on the tunnel wall, flanked by a window and a garage door. The tram track continued underneath.

Cassius and Taro showed their flashlights through the glass.

"Two cots, medical equipment, a few screens," Matey said.

Mina peered into her deskscreen from a half-inch away. "Get inside there."

I smoothed a hand over my forehead to force the muscles to relax. My eyebrows refused to unscrunch.

As Cassius worked on the door, Taro paced through the dim orange hole, her voice becoming ever-more frantic. "What do we expect to find down here? Saren Vite couldn't have disappeared in the Gatespace. Unless — George, is he a Non-Eater? No, of course not. So, the surveillance footage must have been tampered with. There is no way to leave a Gate without *leaving the Gate*. There are two entrances to each Gate and that's it."

"Taro, *do* shut up," Cassius spat as the door popped open.

"You know as well as I how important it is to maintain some *reality*. We are actors, not miracle workers."

"Yes, yes. Of course, dear," Cassius said. "Alright, again — two cots, very clean space. Medical supplies ... lots of cabinets, three deskscreens. Another door. Well-funded, I'd say."

Cassius switched on his camera to show us the space. A metal bench on rollers stood like silver bones in a bare medbay. White cabinets clung to the metal mesh that kept the dirt contained. Small, unknown tech blinked blue and white.

"Taro, get that door open. Cassius, work on the cabinets," Mina ordered.

Taro got the door open first; a room filled with long, metal boxes. "They're bolted shut. It will take a lot more than we have to open them."

Intimidating shadows were cast upon the walls as Taro's flashlight moved over the room.

"They look like caskets," I said.

"Ahh, Devin. Such a positive fellow," Cassius replied. He used his special card to unlock the cabinets, "The regular ... emesis bags, gloves, syringes. Oh! This one is refrigerated."

"What's in it?" Squeem bounced in his seat like a child before a pile of gifts.

Cassius crouched down into the blue light, turning a glass vial on the shelf. "*Statuestic*. Ring any bells?"

He held up the vial. Its rosy contents sloshed against the glass.

"I've no recollection of it. It's an injectable?" the Producer asked.

"I don't know. Should I pocket one?" Cassius asked.

The Producer rubbed his eyes behind his glasses, "No, it could degrade without reliable refrigeration. We can always come back with better preparation."

Mina said, "Where is Matey? She's the one with a medical degree."

Matey's voice came through, "Hey, guys, I found something... I don't know. Just come down here."

"The signal is starting to come back online," Taro said. White light bounced off the many vials of *Statuestic* in the refrigerator. The camera angle changed as Cassius rose. He followed Taro through the brightening tunnel. The thin track curved ahead, out of sight.

I looked down at my hands in my lap. I was clammy, jittery. Little rumbles of nerves vibrated my breastbone, clenching and flexing. Mina sat next to me with her fists in a single ball on the tabletop. She pounded it on the table absently. The sound beat like a metronome.

Taro's voice crackled through the speakers. "Slight Hands, what is *that*?"

Mina gasped. My head snapped up.

"Oh, *fuck yes*," Squeem yelped.

It was hard to see with Cassius running, tossing the camera around. White beams of light, bright points in shadow, metal gleams from below and—

"Matey, get down from there!" Taro cried.

Cassius stopped; his panting echoed in the mic. The camera stream steadied.

"Is that a—"

The room went quiet.

An unmistakable gleam. Silver, like water, fogged with sacred Indigo. Light and darkness, reflecting one another in perfect harmony. A Gate. *A whole Gate*, shimmering in the underground.

My mouth dropped open. "What's *wrong* with it?"

Jagged snags sliced the surface of the Gate. It gaped, a wound in reality; like someone had taken cosmic scissors and cut right into the Sacred Fabric. I wrapped my arms around my middle.

A flight of stairs perched over the strange Gate. Matey crouched at the top, swaying on the hanging landing.

"Matsil Valentine! Get down here at once!" Taro screeched.

"This I — Te — 'te!" Matey's voice was lost, crackling like a weak fire.

"What did she say?" Squeem said.

Cassius ran to Matey. He stood at the foot of the steps with the camera just high enough to see Matey over the lip of the landing. Above the distorted Gate, a little door, about two by two, hung in the air, attached to nothing at all. Matey pulled it open.

The conference room was lit with noise. Yells and yips and gasps of *No! Yes! What?!*

Matey held onto the doorframe. "I have to close it! It's going to suck me in!"

"Wait! Wait—" Cassius stumbled up the stairs. He crouched next to Matey, holding onto her, and pointed the camera into the open door. Clouds of blue and purple swirled in a cloudless abyss. The Gatespace of Teme'te. Right above another Gate. Two Gates, stacked on top of each other. It didn't make a bit of sense.

"No, can't be — there's no way. It isn't *possible*. Tell them, George. *Tell them*," Taro sputtered. She sounded on the verge of tears. "The Natural Order of Things! The universal rules!"

My sinuses prickled. I wiped my eyes, overcome with it. If I'd stayed at home that day, if I'd stayed out of the Green Sun Hook Market, I'd never have known.

A smile ghosted the Producer's lips, "What did you call it, Mr. Mace? A hole in the wall? Very good. Very good."

Cassius and Matey shut the door together. They made it down the swaying stairs and stood in front of the second Gate. It glittered in long cuts like a broken window.

Matey's voice crackled through. "Boss, we are going to throw in a transmitter."

Mina and the Producer answered "Okay" and "Yes, good" together. Mina growled at him under her breath.

"Surveillance system will be back on any moment," Squeem said.

Cassius handed Matey a small, white, tube-shaped device. She pressed a button on the top.

An extensive set of layer maps opened on our deskscreens. Votia, Nirth, Quar, Ahk, Dedocia, Ma'dra, and a seventh map, unnamed and unknown to me. A flashing dot blinked at the Gate of Teme'te on the Nirth map.

Fruit said, "Acknowledged."

Taro and Cassius held onto Matey. She put her hand into the torn Gate.

The flashing dot disappeared.

"You'll have to toss it in. It's not reading," Mina said. Her hand snaked into mine below the table. I rubbed circles on the back of her thumb.

Matey gave herself a good shake before reeling back, stepping forward and throwing the device into the Gate like she was playing fastball.

Seconds passed.

"Acknowledged," Fruit answered.

Cassius and Matey high-fived, jumping and laughing.

Taro said, still shaken, "Where is it?"

My eyes scanned the maps. The little white dot blinked up at me and I laughed. Of course, of fucking course. Maybe this *was* the Natural Order of Things. It seemed that cosmic forces were mocking me personally.

"It's in Suradelphia," Squeem said. He was laughing too.

"They've got to have a Gate Reader for something like this," Mina said. A still of the torn Gate under Teme'te lit up our deskscreens.

I stood to get myself another hot beverage. I needed *something* to do. I said, "How many Gate Readers can exist at one time? Isn't that rare?"

The Producer placed a finger on the book before him and looked up, "Rare, yes. But we must remember, the Full Set takes Limits. They surely have found a Gate Reader in their time."

"But we have a Gate Reader too, so—"

"Oh, do we?" The Producer turned to Mina, and she slammed her mouth shut. He shook his head and turned back to his book: *Leviantha's History of Magical Corruption.*

Squeem tapped his fingers frantically on the table. "That hole in the wall, if that's what we're calling it; that thing was made by *someone.* It's been documented before — Gate readers making Gates. But that hasn't been documented in centuries. To create doors *in* the Gatespace, though. I can't wrap my head around it."

Mina walked over to me and stood a little too closely. She leaned with her back against the counter. "Hard to believe, but how else do you explain this?"

The Producer said, "Perhaps it's the product of a different Limit that we aren't considering."

"Firewalkers can manipulate objects in space. Could they manipulate the Gatespace?" Mina asked.

"Doubtful. I've never read about a Firewalker manipulating a Gate," Squeem answered.

"Mr. Mace, what do you think?" the Producer asked.

My eyebrows shot up. Was this a cruel test of some sort? I stood in silence as the heat from Mina's body electrified my right side.

"I don't know much about Gate Reading, or Limits really. But ... Gatespace is all the same, isn't it? If someone can open a door into the Gatespace, why couldn't they make an exit too?" I looked down at my hands, "But ... the act is corrupt. Cutting holes in the Indigo Abyss to abduct people? No Undergod could get behind that."

"Hmm, yes. This is a new level of disregard for Taro's precious Natural Order of Things. Corrupt is a good word for it."

A vibrating, clanging noise came from the Producer's pocket. He pulled out his pocketscreen with furrowed brows. He answered with a tight, "Yes?"

The Producer's face fell into a sickly, pinkish yellow.

"Why wasn't I notified immediately? I put you there as my substitute and I expected you to at least respect the position!" he yelled into the phone. Mina glanced at me with wide eyes.

The frantic voice on the other end might have been crying.

"Do not take that tone with me! I am out here mending mile-wide cracks put here by — dammit, Tom! I put my faith in you!"

Mina ran to her father. "That's Tom?"

The Producer waved her off, taking three deep breaths. Finally, he said, "How badly is she hurt?"

"Who? Who's hurt?" Mina cried.

Her father never answered.

24

THE GOOD DOCTOR

Riolyn was not pleased.

Actually, to say that Riolyn was not pleased was the understatement of the millennia. When Tom turned her away, she took a chair from the Dossier and threw it against the door.

"You think I'm overreacting now? Just wait until I unleash my crazy side! You people won't know what hit you!" Riolyn yelled. "Where is she? I will break down every door in this building!"

Benjamin sighed and pushed past Tom to let her in.

Riolyn was at my side like a magnet to metal. "Messer, look at you — what are they doing to you? These lights — these lights do nothing; you know that right? Nothing. You have *stitches* in your *face*!"

"You should see the other guy." I smiled, stomach churning as the muscles in my cheek pulled tightly.

"Where is he? I'll kill him myself!" Riolyn stormed through Dr. Harker's rooms, opening doors and knocking on walls like she'd find a hidden passage.

I stumbled, pushing past Tom to head her off. Tom sat down, huffing. My hands flew out to my sides in front of Idrissa's door. "Hey, man, stop."

"He's in there? Let me see him, let me kill him, I'll do it, let the coward burn—"

"*No*, no. Let's go back downstairs, I'm ready to leave this place anyway." I turned to Tom. "That's what Valentine said, right?"

Tom wanted to lie; I could see it in his eyes. He wanted to tell me that Valentine had said I needed to stay with him up here for a month, or maybe that I had to go home, back to Monount Valley, and live the rest of my life cloistered and celibate. But he didn't lie. He nodded, turning off the blue healing lamp that Riolyn swore did nothing. Just scientifically proven fake news.

"See, we can go! Let's go back to our dorm. Is Aeshra feeling better?" I asked.

Riolyn glared at me, scales raised and bright. She slung my bag of clothes over her shoulder and yelled at Idrissa's door: "Coward!"

I hoped Seth didn't hear.

The whole school knew.

They knew Seth had attacked me, just like he'd attacked those two kids years earlier. He'd lost his mind, or maybe he'd opened himself up to a demon. Maybe he was doing *dark rituals* (which was what, exactly?), or sung the ancient songs backwards. Whatever it was, it was *his fault*, his evil, and he deserved to be hated and ostracized because of it. He couldn't be trusted. He couldn't have friends. Because Seth Mace was Dangerous with a *capital D*. He deserved his punishment.

The punishment bloomed across my face. Purple, black, yellow, green beneath clear bandages. Because I'd poked at Seth when everyone gave such clear signals not to. Someone had warned me, right? My father had warned me, hadn't he? He'd said, *leave him alone, Mayli.*

Before he dropped me into the predator's den.

"So, he didn't attack you?" Riolyn asked. "Everyone is saying he attacked you." She sat on my bed, glaring daggers at me.

I pulled at the hair growing on the backs of my fingers to resist itching my new, metal shoulder. "No. Well, yeah, he attacked me, but it wasn't Seth. He's a Dementric."

"So, he *did* attack you," she repeated, folding her arms over her chest.

"He's a Dementric! The demon attacked me."

"But he let it out, right? Someone said you have to let the thing out."

"No, *no*, Mess, I fucking *hate everyone*. Shut up and let me explain this."

Riolyn kept her arms crossed.

"Seth's got a demon living inside him; that's what Dementricism is. Not like a possession, where you can pray it out or whatever. It's stuck in there. You know, like Uyenl, the Undergod. Something major happened when he was born, and the demon attached to him. In Uyenl's case, he was reborn into the new world. Anyway, he's got all that Devil Spit because his soul is so torn up by the demon."

"So, why did the thing come out, then, if he didn't let it?" Riolyn asked.

I threw myself on my bed in frustration, wincing as my shoulder hit the mattress. "I don't know. They moved him out of Idrissa's room because Idrissa was sick, so maybe sae was keeping the demon under control."

Riolyn shrugged, picking at my blanket. "I just don't get it."

I rolled over, letting my swollen face rub on the bed. The mix of dull pain and itch was unsettling.

"The night he changed into the demon — which is named *Mercy*, by the way. That night, I felt like I was drugged. I couldn't see straight. I don't know if it was the Devil Spit or what. He was literally bursting with the stuff, dripping it all over the place. Absolutely disgusting."

The silence took over. The blue-green paphador cast a glow over the room. I watched the iridescent wall, thinking about that night. If I had stayed with Uyentra a little longer, maybe Seth wouldn't have changed. If I'd left earlier, maybe I could have helped Seth get through it.

"The room is so clean now. When I came in that night, everything was black. Devil Spit everywhere. And blood," Riolyn said. She pulled a thread from the blanket and tossed it to the floor.

I ran my fingers over the edge of my shoulder, close to my skin tone, but shinier, pinker.

"He was so strong; he literally crushed my shoulder bones. Man, check this out," I hopped off the bed and pulled Seth's massive boots from the floor. "Feel how heavy this boot is."

"Why are you touching his stuff?"

"Come on, just pick up the shoe," I replied, forcing it toward her. It was even harder to hold with just one good arm.

"What, are you his friend now?" Riolyn said, not bothering to disguise her revulsion.

"What? No! It's just a boot, man. Come on. Friends? You can't be serious."

She reluctantly took the boot, her arm dropping against the weight. She sighed. "Why does he even go here? My cousins said Voltenstraus had all kinds of people, but I didn't think this is what they meant."

We settled into my bed, curling around each other to stave off nightmares. It almost worked. But Riolyn's question filtered into my strange, hallucinogenic dreams. Disgusted faces, whispering about the evil that lived in Seth Mace, and how only someone equally as damaged could befriend such a dark, splintered soul.

Not that I even wanted to be his friend.

Dr. Squidzy Valentine scooped a gloved finger into a pot of clear goo. "The gel has no odor. It is oil based." She held up her finger to the class. "The oil will break apart the bandage's glue. This way, we can remove Mayli's bandages without pulling the delicate skin beneath."

The entire class leaned in as Valentine brought her lubed-up fingers to my face. I winced against the cold gel. She massaged along my jaw in quick circles. I closed my eyes to keep them from bouncing over the unwanted audience.

She pulled up the very bottom of the bandage. It slipped easily from my skin. The silent class watched as my bruised, torn flesh was revealed.

"*Fuck.*"

I snorted. My eyes caught Riolyn's toward the back of the class. Her cheek scales were bright blue, flushed with disgust and framing her wrinkled nose.

Valentine tipped her head back and sighed. "Miss Vite, watch your language, please."

She pulled her rolling table to her side with her foot, her pink striped socks peeking out from under her work pants. She dried her hands with a disinfectant towel. Valentine picked up thin tweezers and brought them to my cheek.

"Mayli's stitches will dissolve within the next few weeks," Valentine said to the class. She tossed the plastic bandage in the trash and unwrapped another. "The wound will continue to clean itself, and by the end of the year, Mayli's cheek will be back to normal."

Valentine pressed the new bandage to my skin and quizzed the class on the four stages of wound healing while I dipped my toes in the bleak underground of my thoughts. Like: why had I consented to being the class prop?

Because it was such a great subject to learn! Why, wound dressing on a *real patient*! Marvelous! Such a brave kid, that Mayli is! Such an inspiration! She's so very *strong*, so *unaffected* by her hardships. We should all strive to be more like Mayli; the student who was beaten to the edge of death and survived to tell the story! Although, we don't *really* want to hear the story; no, we'd rather make up our own version of it. It's more about personal interpretation, anyway, isn't it? More about how we can use another person's *sad story* to feel good about ourselves.

I let Valentine do it. I acted like it was all well and good, and then when it was done, I excused myself from class to have a big, wet cry. No one would notice the puffy redness around my swollen eyes, anyway.

I let Valentine do it because I let Seth do it. And I let Seth do it because I had a rancid soul.

Nathali's easel screeched across the floor as she pulled it across the room and parked it next to mine. She didn't wait for a hello from me. "They're saying Seth attacked you, and now that I'm seeing you, I believe them. I'm so sorry I didn't take this seriously. I should have visited you."

"It's okay, seriously. I'm fine. Moonie is Palm Lifting me every day. And Tom was hovering, so be glad you missed it." I pushed a thin stick of charcoal across my paper aimlessly.

"So, this was Seth, then? How is that possible? You look terrible—May, your face," Nathali said. She traced a single finger over the clear plastic on my cheek.

"And here I was thinking I looked great." I pulled her closer to me and whispered into her pale gold locks: "Seth is a Dementric."

"What?" she replied too loudly. "Seriously? That is ... actually, that makes more sense than what people are saying." Her eyes turned pensive. "You saw him change, then?"

"It was insane! His entire body changed, like he was being stretched out. Still his face, but... different. And, Devil Spit everywhere. It was gushing out of his mouth like a fountain. Everywhere. Felt like I was drunk, room spinning and all that. Tasted bad, too. Weirdly minty."

"You *ate* some?"

"Not on purpose!" I pulled my shirt neck down. "Check this out — new shoulder. My old one was crushed into dust."

Nathali gasped and grabbed at me, feeling the new metal part of me. "It's warm! Almost feels like skin."

"So their name is Mercy. *Mercy*, how fuckin' ironic."

"The demon?"

I nodded.

She looked me over, raking me for more damage, more new parts. "Have you talked to Seth since?"

"No," I said, finally. "I saw him in Idrissa's room. He didn't see me."

Nathali let the statement sit before saying, "I wonder what the hell dad was thinking?"

"Yeah. I don't know. But I'm going to find out, even if I have to cut it out of him with those stupid scissors."

Riolyn sat on her bed, watching as Moonie situated across from me. The floor was hard and cold beneath us, and oddly comforting. Moonie's quick grace was gone. She placed one trembling hand on my shoulder and began her work.

When she was done, I rotated it with a dull ache.

She repositioned, lifting her hands to my face.

I reached out to touch her. "Hey. How are you doing?"

Her eyes barely opened. "It's been a long day."

"Are you still Lifting Idrissa? Is that what this is about?"

"It's just difficult, with Seth there. I mean to say, it's difficult for Idrissa. I get on fine with Seth." Moonie stopped to let out a yawn. She seemed to be missing the magical glow that so often followed her.

"Are you trying to keep Idrissa alive? I mean, damn, I don't need these sessions if it's just one more thing you have to do. I'm fine, really."

"You do need them." She smiled, looking over at Riolyn as she frantically nodded her head in agreement. "Once Seth is moved, Idrissa will stabilize. They might move him back to Dedocia."

Riolyn said, "Fucking *finally*. They need to get him out of here before someone else gets hurt. He's unhinged."

The dull ache in my shoulder moved to my chest, throbbing beneath my breastbone.

With an apologetic smile, Moonie placed her hand on my chest. Icy, powerful blue glistened in her eyes.

"Deep breaths, Mayli," she said.

Riolyn and I shot up from my bed, sticky with sweat in the humid cave.

Someone was banging, *pounding* on the door.

"Who the hell?" Riolyn hissed, pulling the blankets over her head.

But I knew. I knew that frantic knocking from years of explosive outbursts brought on by plans gone awry.

Doctor George Alton Walls Harker was at our door, beating the poor thing into submission at 5 AM. Too early for the door. Too early for two angry, traumatized seventeen-year-olds. I slid out of bed, wrapping the topmost blanket around myself, tripping on it and landing at the door.

I cracked the door an inch and glared out. "So nice of you to join us."

"Let me see you." George's eyes widened as the clear, squishy bandage on my face came into view.

My father reached for the door. I slammed it shut. "If you won't leave me alone, at least let me get dressed."

George banged his fists once more, frustrated. "Yes, well. Come to my office immediately. And *hurry*."

Riolyn lay sideways in the bed with the covers strewn all around her, her chestnut hair sticking in all directions. "Let's set fire to his office," she grumbled, rolling onto her stomach and throwing a pillow over her head.

I didn't like his tone. His little "*And hurry.*" Like I was in trouble for something. Like I'd covered myself in frosting and baited a feral dog into my dorm room. No — that was *him*. Not me. He shoved me into a locked room with a demon. He let that demon run its blackened, wet fingers over my shoulder until the bones exploded.

So, I took my time getting dressed, choosing something outrageous. Something to infuriate him. Show him how little I cared for his damned plot.

"Are you going to pick wildflowers?" Riolyn laughed at my floor-length plaid dress.

"No. I'm going to tell that man what I think of him."

"This is what you took an hour and forty-five minutes? Mess, child. What is wrong with you?" My father scowled, but there was no anger there, just pain. Guilt, maybe. He pulled me into a feather-light hug, avoiding my shoulder and cheek. Anger singed at my edges.

And melted away like an afterthought.

Had anyone *hugged me*? I'd been prodded, crushed, probed, and stitched. I'd been wrapped, cleaned, paraded before my classmates. I was supposed to be strong, but I didn't feel strong. I felt like a toy.

George cried against me, his face in my hair, "I'm so sorry for what happened. My love, my Mayli. I wasn't here. I'm so sorry."

His smell and the scratch of his bowtie on my chin were comforting. I couldn't be mad at my father. He always meant well. He had a plan, and I just needed to let it pan out. When was he ever wrong?

We stepped through his office and into his rooms. He sat on the wooden pew, ignoring the pillows that slipped out from behind him. I stood over my father. His hands held onto his knees; the veins bulged beneath his pinkened skin.

"Say it again. Say you're sorry."

His fingers jumped, clenching to the brown fabric of his pants. "I'm sorry. This is my fault. I knew the risks, and I still put you with him. I didn't think he would open out. I thought he was done with that."

I pulled back to look at his stupid face. "You thought he was *done*? With what, being a Dementric? Uyenl's nuts, Dad, you are out of your mind. Come on, man, no one is just *done* with that. Did you get lobotomized while you were away?"

His eyes squeezed shut like little cracks in stone. "But, love, I believed things would be different. You have an effect on people. I thought — I *knew* it would be the same with Seth. And it was working. You said it yourself: he was talking to you. Asking you for help."

"So, let me get this straight. You thought, *Hey, Mayli is great with weirdos, so let's put this demonized psychopath in her dorm room. My best idea yet!*"

"Mayli, please, love. I'm sorry." George reached for my hand.

I slapped him away. "No, dude. No one gets to touch me anymore. Not you, not anyone. I'm done being everyone's angry little pet."

"Of course, yes. I understand." He nodded, wiping his eyes. His eyes raked over my bruised face, sullen. But then they moved to the scissors.

Glittering silver, thick and sharp. The sheers sat on their golden tray, disconnected from reality. They seemed to hover in the green glow of paphador.

"What are those things even for?" I asked.

"Hmm?" He glanced at me. His cheeks were wet and red. They reminded me of Harot Rubio, the man I'd tied up in his own apartment. His friction-burned face, squeaking across the floor and rubbing the skin off. My father had put me in that situation, too.

"The scissors." My body tipped down, ready to touch them. I snapped back up. "Whatever, never mind. I don't care. I'm just going to focus on school now. Everything else can fuck right off. Just me, class, Palm Lifting, my friends. That's it. I'll see you when school's out."

I headed to the door, leaving the silence behind me.

"Mayli."

His voice cut right to my core. Hard, shocked. *Dark.* I stopped, but didn't turn. "What?"

"You said Palm Lifting."

I turned. The scissors were in his hands.

"Yeah, so?"

"Are you Palm Lifting?"

"I mean, yeah — a little bit, but I suck at it — it's fun, though, and the class is fun—"

"Mayli."

My mouth closed.

"You are not Palm Lifting. You are forbidden from Palm Lifting." His cold voice sent terror into my bones.

Terror. In my body, riding up my spine like a tram on a track. Vibrating, pummeling me. I closed my eyes, shaking away the nausea. And there, in the darkness of my lids, I could see it. Wet, glowing red energy spreading through me. He knew nothing of my power. Because I was *rancid.* I was rancid, just like Seth Mace.

"I've been Lifting for months. And I am going to keep Lifting. I have a gift and I'm going to use it. You can forbid me all day long, but it won't matter. Don't act so shocked, you knew this would happen. You can go on hiding all your pitch-black soul behind the blinding light of your *Greatness,* but I know what you are." I got down in his face and yelled, "He crushed my shoulder, George! I had to get a *new* shoulder!"

He removed his glasses, no longer hiding his anger behind the frames. "Do you have any idea what you've done? Seth Mace opened out because of you! His demon would have stayed put had you not started Lifting! He's being sent back to Dedocia to live the rest of his life in a *cage,* Maysolpheta!"

I pulled the scissors from his hands and pointed the blade between his eyes. "Don't put this on me, man. Maybe you could have stopped it, I don't know. But *you weren't here.* You were off doing your more important, more secret, more exciting job. While I was getting beat into a bloody heap by the person you forced me to live with."

When my father started crying, I let him. The scissors clattered to the floor. Because, yeah, he felt bad. But I was traumatized for life, and it was his fault. *His fault.* Not mine.

Moonie was so weak. She slumped over on my bed, drifting on the edge of sleep. I couldn't possibly take anything more from her. So, instead, I would Palm Lift her.

And Uyentra came by to help, to gift us with their glistening, golden energy, because mine wasn't even close to enough to heal Moonie Devince, the most powerful kid in school. Riolyn even sat with us, offering her energy. And she shouldn't have been able to do that at all. Because she didn't have a Limit.

But I took Riolyn's bright, fiery sparks and Uyentra's luxurious threads of gold and pushed it all into Moonie so she could have a bit of peace. So that she could know what it was to be cared for by people who didn't need anything from her.

"There's something new in you," she whispered. The blackish green disease, she could see it.

"Yeah, it's gross. Sorry."

"*No,*" she stopped me. "It's beautiful."

"You mean the sickness? The gunk?"

Moonie's hairless brows knitted together. "Not gunk. Power."

Uyentra curled their body around me and hummed, "I feel it too. Something is different. Not bad, just different."

My eyes locked with Riolyn. She shrugged. "You're the same to me. But I'm not special like these two." She laughed, dodging the pillow Uyentra threw at her.

"Okay, okay, but for real. Be honest. Do I feel like Seth, now?"

Silence. I sucked in a breath.

And my friends laughed.

"Dear, you're *joking*. You feel nothing like Seth Mace." Uyentra buried their face in the softness of my hip, shaking with giggles.

Moonie took my hands and said, "You feel whole. Now, Lift me."

I couldn't sleep that night, even while wrapped in a pile of my friends. Every time I drifted off, I remembered that Aeshra was stuck in the sickward, drifting from nightmare to nightmare.

My father had put a dangerous boy in a room with his favorite child, the one he so arrogantly believed could charm the demon right out of the Dementric. I could have — no, *should have* died. And now I was whole?

The dark halls glowed an icy, paphador blue. The cave seemed colder in the dead of night, without students awake to warm it. Water trickled down the walls. I wrapped my arms around myself.

The thunderous ache in my chest pushed me forward.

I snuck through back access passages, spiraled up five stairwells, unable to stop myself. My hands pulled at the wooden doors, and I was hit by a cold burst of air.

In the center of the sanctuary, I knelt before the iridescent pool, just like Seth had. Panic welled inside of me. My reflection swirled, watery and pink, green, and lavender. My heart felt like it could explode. The pain was poison. It was time to suck it out.

If it could work for a boy with a Demon inside of him, it could work for me.

The tears started flowing.

He'd betrayed me; my own father. Why had he told me that I was given the wrong gift? That I could never be a Palm Lifter. That I was *wrong*.

Had my gift really forced Seth's Demon out? Was I truly the reason for this disaster? Did I really have a rancid soul?

I faced my horrendous reflection. Makeup ran down my cheeks. Stitches poked out of swollen flesh beneath the clear bandage on my face, and the grease in my hair stuck my bangs together in thick clumps. I was a mess.

Deep breaths. I just had to put my face in the pool. I wouldn't suffocate. I would live through it. It would feel wet, maybe. But I had my jacket; I would wipe it off. I would be clean again.

I knelt, holding my breath, and pushed my face into the cold, milky pool.

Emotions shattered in my skin. I screamed into the water. Bubbles burst from my mouth like an underwater vent. Pain glimmered before my eyes like a vision, light dancing off each separate feeling. I pulled my face up, gasping, gulping in air.

Franticly, I wiped at my eyes, at my throbbing face, begging to get the stuff off me. Get the feelings away. They *hurt*. The wetness *hurt*.

"What are you doing?" came a soft voice.

Through wet lashes, I saw him. Seth knelt in front of me, his hands dipping into the pool, and he was looking at me with the kindest, purest eyes I'd ever seen.

25

EYES

"We know he spends a lot of time at the balcony restaurant, so that would probably be the ideal place to nab him," Squeem said as he took off his rumpled overshirt, sweat glistening on his forehead.

It was an unusually hot morning in Frasier, signaling the end of the cool season. Sure, we'd have a few more weeks of breezy days, but summer was just over there.

"How reliable are these reports?" Mina asked, fanning herself with a napkin. She was in a foul mood today and had been since the Producer's abrupt leaving.

Taro said, "Cassius has already been to check on it, on his way back to Nessuir. The resort is Bright White, but his signature is all over it. Merchant is there."

"And who approved Cassius to go there? Because I know I didn't," Mina snapped.

Squeem cleared his throat. "I did. It was the best course of action, since Cassius would already be in the area on his way to Nessuir. And before you jump in, just remember: as your second in command, you've given me decision-making abilities for when you can't."

"I don't recall being unable to make decisions."

I could feel myself curling up, sinking into my chair. Mina looked at me. Her expression didn't soften an ounce.

I gathered my courage. "Your mood has been rather bleak, dear."

Mina's eyes narrowed, and I resisted the urge to cower.

Before Mina could respond, Squeem sat up straight in his chair and took her attention away from me. "Was it the wrong choice, then? Truly, Mina. Because I wouldn't have imagined asking Cassius to check on the location of the man we need to eliminate as soon as possible to be a problem."

"I don't appreciate being out of the loop. But, no, it wasn't wrong," she said with as much contempt as possible. She stood up, "Come on, Devin. We'll need to get ready."

"For what?" I asked.

Mina whirled around, the shell-beads on her thin top hitting together in angry taps. "You'll come *with* me, of course."

Taro spoke before Squeem could get past his confusion. "Do you think that's wise?"

With a growl of annoyance, Mina said to me: "Well, don't you want to? You need a vacation. Especially with my mood being so *bleak.*"

No one dared argue with her.

The Chessier Resort was on the Northwest coast, just east of the land bridge that connected Lacause and Besel. The proximity to the ocean and being situated in the humid, rainforest-like woods of Northwest Besel made for a spectacular setting. The Kajiun Forest went right up to the edge of the rocky shore.

I had come here once when I was in my early twenties. My "working friends" and I had just come into a heap of money after moving into a new territory, and we didn't know how to spend it. A fancy resort in luxurious Chessier seemed about right.

We only made it one night in the hotel before we were forcibly removed. I vividly remembered jumping from the high-ceilinged chandelier, missing the couch and crashing to the floor laughing. They'd always loved throwing me from high places, because I couldn't seem to break a bone.

Couldn't die, maybe.

But things were different this time around. We had a job to do, or at least Mina did. We'd ordered a room ahead of time, up on the fourth floor with a big tree pressed against our balcony. That's how Mina wanted it. I assumed she wanted to climb down the thing as an escape, and I dearly hoped she realized that *I* wouldn't be attempting such a feat. Just because I maybe couldn't die didn't mean I wanted to try. Not anymore.

Our first day at Chessier was magical. I spent the whole time in the room, because I was a wanted criminal for the "attempted bank robbery" and all the priors. We ordered room service, big sandwiches and fruit with cream. Thick, vine-covered trees surrounded the balcony in all directions. Massive birds flew through the canopy overhead, cawing and nipping at each other. Flat, blue beetles skittled across the mossy tree trunks.

"I have to go down for a bit, see if I can catch a glimpse of Merchant," Mina said as she pinned a dirty blonde wig to her head. She wore a bronze tan like she'd spent the last six weeks on a yacht.

"You look weird like that," I said, looking up from the beetle walking along the edge of my shadow.

"You prefer me the other way? Business suits and red hair?" Mina did a little spin in the sheer white thing she was wearing.

I smiled. "Yeah, and pale."

Mina laughed. "Pale like death, my prince."

She kissed me before she disappeared for the rest of the evening. I wasn't jealous, not really. I knew she'd be gone for hours, scoping out the bars and restaurants, shops, pools, and whatever else this gaudy place had to offer. Merchant was here, somewhere, and she was going to find him. She was going to kill him.

I settled down on the balcony with a fancy, non-alcoholic drink from the dispenser in our room. Warm flits of sunlight gleamed through the treetops, dancing along the floor. Soft music played from somewhere below.

With my drink in one hand and a pen in another, I set out to understand.

Mina's father knew things about me that no one besides my siblings knew. Had I known him before? He despised my past as much as I did, so maybe he was there? Maybe he had been around when we lived in Suradelphia, or maybe, Mess forbid, he'd known my parents.

The Producer knew I was allergic to sorite, the mineral in red water. But that could be explained if Squeem had done a report on my reaction to that tanker weeks ago. He also knew my species was labeled as Unknown, and he could have just noticed when looking at my file.

Although Mina had said she'd scanned me on that first day in Pwero Ver. I was already in the hounding system as Classified and Protected. *Why?*

My parents had never told us about our ancestry. They had no documentation, and no extended family to ask. When I was young, I didn't know that knowledge of species was something to question; everyone looked different on Dedocia and that was the norm.

Questioning where we came from when I was older just brought more unanswered questions. My father would laugh it off, claiming that we were *obviously* Dedocian; my mother would scold me for being too curious.

Long after my parents had died, things became clearer: we had been in hiding. The odd set of events that led to my parents' deaths was questionable, and my siblings and I had been whisked away by a stranger to live in a high security religious order. I had to accept that while I probably wasn't Dedocian, I needed to believe that I was. Because some questions are dangerous to ask.

The last thing, the most surprising of all, the Producer knew I healed quickly. In the Producer's own words, *"Does he heal faster than possible?"*

The answer to that question, without a doubt, was yes.

The sun had set when I heard the keycard nick at the door. I was sitting on the balcony in candlelight, listening to insects sing through the trees. Two voices laughed as the door opened. I couldn't see but for the strip of light closing with the door and the bare flicker of the candles outside.

Mina stumbled in and she seemed pleasantly drunk. She pulled another person in behind her as she giggled.

My brain halted. I crossed and uncrossed my arms. I knew what was coming.

Mina saw me through the darkness and ran to me, laughing. She draped herself over me. "Dear, I brought us a friend!" She didn't even sound like herself.

My heartbeat pounded in my ears. She smelled like burnt matches and wine.

The other man wasn't pleased. "I wasn't expecting to share."

"No?" Mina lilted in response. She flipped on one of the lights and Merchant was standing there awkwardly in the entry of our grand hotel room. This lay definitely wasn't going the way he wanted.

Mina pushed Merchant onto the bed with too much force for a thin, drunk woman. He startled, choking on his own spit. Mina straddled him, her sheer white dress pulled tight around her thighs.

I set my glass on the table and stepped into the room. Realization hit Merchant when he saw my face.

"You — you're that Mace kid. Am I being robbed?" Merchant reached for something inside his blue waistcoat, but Mina grabbed his hand first.

"Stay put. No, you're not being robbed. Sit back and enjoy!" Mina slithered off him, playing the part of a wanton damsel. Mina dragged her hands into the man's jacket and pulled out a small gun, kissing it and tossing it aside. "You won't be needing this tonight."

Merchant was deeply confused and drunk. He stared as Mina rolled her body in fascinating, liquid patterns, removing the pins from her wig. The man's lust and confusion spun like a revolving door.

Mina caught my eye and glanced at my dinner knife. I picked the thing up as she pulled her wig off, revealing a snagging nest of red hair. "Ah, much better. Hello, Merchant."

Merchant's breath hitched, and he reached for his chest.

"Don't you *dare* have a heart attack," Mina turned sideways, sinking into his belly. She spread her legs and pushed the man down with her foot on his chest. Mina motioned to her overnight bag. "Devin, my hairbrush, please. And the knife."

I found the paddle brush in her bag.

Merchant's eyes were wide with terror and his breath caught in ragged gasps. Maybe he really *was* having a heart attack.

Mina crawled over Merchant like a lanky cat. She perched on his chest. The poor fool spat into the air as he enunciated *"Please. Please,"* over and over. Mina gave him one loud slap on the cheek to shut him up. She ran her delicate fingers over the softness of Merchant's jaw, pushing into his flesh. He made disgusting, gurgling sounds in his throat.

"Come sit behind me, babe. He's a big man; it'll take both of us to keep him down. And you can brush these tangles out of my hair while I chat with him."

Excited and humiliated, I climbed onto the bed. I sat behind my lovely girlfriend, both of us weighing down the man she was about to kill.

I began unraveling the swirl of a bun wrapped around her scalp. Over the rumbling, groveling chorus from Merchant, Mina hummed approval. I ran my hands from the edges of her ears to the long ends of her hair.

Mina's hair ratted around the nape of her neck, so I started there.

Speaking softly, Mina began her questioning. "Merchant, dear, I heard you wanted to meet me, so I've decided to come find you. Tell me, have you worked with the Full Set long? I was surprised when we uncovered that bit."

Merchant tried to clear his throat, but Mina pressed her fingers into the squishy bits around his Adam's apple and he choked. The sound of it made me shudder.

"I won't talk," the man protested feebly.

"You will." Mina's voice dropped a cruel octave. "You're going to die tonight. No point in withholding information."

I let her hair pool in my hands, feeling the weight of it. It shone like threads of silken copper. I continued brushing as Merchant squirmed beneath us. The man really was a beast; he probably could have thrown off the both of us if he hadn't been so frozen in terror.

He tried again. "You don't know who you're dealing with here. You'll never win."

"Oh, stop it," Mina snarled. She dragged the blade across Merchant's forehead, cutting through each furrowed wrinkle. The man shrieked like a domesticated bird.

"No, please, *please,* I can give you anything. I have money — so much money. You can have it all, just let me go—"

Mina leaned back into me and I wrapped an arm around her waist as she poked the thin blade into Merchant's left nostril "Again you surprise me, Merchant. Groveling? *Money?* Did your little Boys Club even bother to train you? You should know these kinds of bargains have no hold on us."

Big, round tears fell from the man's eyes, dripping down his temples into his ears. Again, I shuddered. Mina noticed and took the time to squeeze my hand across her belly.

"You're upsetting my love, Merchant."

Merchant wheezed. "They will take him from you. They will take everything you care about until you have nothing but them."

Mina put her head back onto my shoulder and hummed. The knife resting on Merchant's neck bobbed when he swallowed. He watched us. Something in his eyes told me he was speaking from experience.

"Is that what the Full Set did to you?" I asked over Mina's shoulder. Mina turned and planted a lingering kiss on my cheek, breathing me in.

"It doesn't matter what I tell you. They will win," Merchant said. "They have the masses on their side, they have the governing forces, and the general population will bend for them. They have morality, and they certainly have science on their side. Anything you think you're doing to stop them is nothing, not even a hiccup. *For the good of all.*"

Mina's head jerked up as Merchant finished his monologue. "They have *science* on their side?"

Merchant shook his head. "You are missing so many pieces that you aren't even in the game."

Mina's hands raised up and she slammed the knife into Merchant's chest. Merchant jolted, struck. He looked down and howled in terror. I jumped off the bed, overcome, ready to vomit.

Mina leaned over Merchant, screaming: "What is Amnea Station?"

Spit flew from Merchant's red face. "You disgusting swine of a woman! Finish the job!"

Mina stabbed Merchant again, red beginning to spill over the pink bedspread. He howled and howled.

"What is Amnea Station?!" Mina yelled again, right in his face.

"In Sura," he coughed. "Now kill me, you whore!"

Mina stabbed him again, and I dropped to the floor. My hands and feet were numb and tingly. That man was going to die.

"What do I have to say to make you kill me?" Merchant's voice bubbled in his throat. "The things I've seen would drive you to madness, too. The people we take, and the *children*—"

Oh god, I heaved and heaved on the floor, unable to hear anything but the blood rushing in my ears. The floor tumbled beneath me, and I rolled onto my side. Mina was stabbing and stabbing. Sprays of blood littered the bronzer on her cheeks and forehead.

Merchant wasn't moving much anymore.

Mina sat up, gasping. Her eyes were glazed. She reached over the dead man and grabbed a pillow, pulling off a pillowcase and pressing it onto the man's face.

After a few minutes, Mina crawled off the bed, clenching and unclenching her whole body. Every muscle flexed, jittered, and unwound. I watched from the floor, laying on my side, as she took three deep breaths. She picked up the desk chair and walked it to the balcony, chucking it off into the trees with an angry yell. Then she stepped over to me and offered me a bloody hand.

I took it without a second thought.

We cleaned each other up in silence. When Merchant's body stopped twitching, Mina pulled the pillowslip off his face and dried it with a hairdryer. It was horrifying what she did to him.

"If it bothers you so much, please stop looking at it," Mina snapped as she folded up the dry pillowslip and stowed it in her bag.

"I can't stop looking. It's disgusting. I'll have nightmares about this forever," I said, staring.

"That man aided in the trafficking of people and who knows what else," she placated softly. "You knew I was going to kill him, didn't you?"

I continued staring at Merchant. "Yes, but, his eyes. You couldn't have left his eyes?"

Mina laughed, handing me a piece of paper. "Here, put this on the door."

On the piece of paper, she'd written: "*For the good of all.*"

"I don't want to wear a disguise," I said as Mina handed me a jar of temporary hair color.

We had cleaned the room to the best of our ability, leaving only the bed and Merchant's body untouched.

"That is a terrible idea," Mina said. "You'll be ID'ed as soon as they roll back the surveillance footage. You're already in trouble enough as it is with the bank. I don't want a murder on your hands as well."

"It is on my hands, though. All they have to do is run my DNA and they'll know, so what's the point?"

Mina shook her head. "I don't think you understand. What if you decide to leave? You won't be able to pretend you were forced to work for me if there is video footage of us waltzing away from a crime scene together."

"If I decide to *leave*?" I couldn't understand what she was saying.

"If you decide to leave DAG. You aren't in too deep to back out. Not yet." She turned away from me, tugging on a long dress, something the real Mina would never wear. Her hair was twisted up, ready for a wig.

"Why would I leave? I thought I already told you that I'm in this. DAG makes me feel something, like belonging. Like I'm finally doing something. And," I wavered as Mina continued with her back to me, "you make me feel something, too. I'm not leaving."

Mina scowled and put her head down as she hunched over her bag. "You do know that was me over Merchant last night, right? That was *me*, the real me. Unabashed, true, walls-down me. I'm a killer. I *enjoy* killing people."

"Your parents taught you that. It's not your fault."

She laughed cruelly, "No, you don't get it. My parents taught me how to *focus* my evil. I don't blame this on anyone but myself."

I could feel a tightening in my throat, the sting in my nostrils. "But don't you still deserve to know happiness? Love?"

"I know love, Devin. I love *hurting people*. Watching them bleed." She pulled out the stained, bloodied pillowcase; her trophy for the evening. Merchant's wounds were imprinted on the thing like a holy shroud. "I don't deserve to know love, not anymore. And I don't wish this curse on anyone. But it is mine, and I know the reality of it."

I grabbed the pillowcase and held it up. "You are more than this!"

Mina snatched the pillowcase out of my hands again and held it to her chest like a child squeezing a comfort animal. "Don't you realize you can't romance the murderer out of me? Love won't change me, Devin. This isn't a fucking fairytale."

I paced the room angrily as Mina pinned on her dirty blonde wig and covered her shoulders and cheekbones with fake tan.

She refused to apologize as we left the hotel room with our bags in tow. Her disguise was good, but not so good that she wouldn't be recognized under investigation. I refused a disguise at all to prove my point. I wasn't going to vanish on her. I was a part of the Dight Actors Guild and I was a part of her.

As we walked to the lobby, Mina put on her most business-like tone to brief me. "We're going straight to Suradelphia. That's where Merchant said we'll find Amnea Station. Our tracker is still active. It could very well be a trap, but I'm willing to risk it. This would be a good time for you to bow out."

Nearing the front desk, I pulled Mina close and whispered, "You can't tell me what to do. I'm not leaving." I made a show of things, running my hands along Mina's back and moving the blonde hair off her exposed shoulder, kissing her there. The front desk attendant averted her eyes.

"We're in a hurry," Mina giggled to the employee in a voice that wasn't her own, "but something strange is happening on the fourth floor. You should send security up there."

"Oh! What do you mean?" the front desk attendant asked awkwardly as I pulled Mina into a slow, wet kiss.

She pulled away and answered, "Fighting, maybe? I don't know, we were busy."

With that, I tugged my bronzed, luxurious girlfriend by the hand, and we caught a cab to the tram station. I couldn't wait to get that stupid wig off her.

26

THE OTHER PLACE

Seth had an animal's eyes. Orange, grey, and yellow lines crisscrossed to create a warm, dead ochre. His shoulders poked up like dull spines, sharp bones hiding beneath his black T-shirt. He hunched over the bubbling spring, swirling his hands in the liquid. Both feral and restrained.

Comfortingly unsafe. *Like my father.*

See? It was little thoughts like those that kept me doubled over, crying into my armpit. Wrapped up in my own limbs. Choking on emotional spit while Seth Mace twirled his skinny hand around in that ... disgusting ... glittery ... *fuck.*

I fell backward onto the cold floor, sprawled like a dying lizard, out in the open and ready to become a meal. Seth breathed in and out slowly, like I would catch on. I didn't want to. This wasn't a fucking *teachable moment.* And screw him for thinking it was.

Maybe I was confusing him with the doctor. Maybe not.

His voice startled me. "I'm sorry for the effect the essence is having on you."

I groaned, rubbing at my eyes with the striped sleeve of my shirt. Of course, it was a pool of essence. A *spring* of the stuff. That made absolutely no sense, so of course that was the answer. Impossible, so why not?

"I fucking hate this place," I said. "Toss in some Non-Eaters and a few breakfast cakes and you've got yourself a metaphysical shitshow."

Seth gave something verging on a laugh, like he understood.

We were both out of our minds.

Propping up, I watched Seth watching me. He wasn't crawling out of his skin like normal. Calm had smoothed the hardness of his eyes, softening the scowl lines between his brows and the frown lines around his mouth. He seemed younger, healthy, unafraid.

"It's essence? Like, someone's *power*? But this stuff calms you down? How? Is it a Dementric thing?"

He closed his eyes and breathed out for a long count. "It has a calming effect, yes. Or, rather, given essence gives a person what they need. As far as whose it is; I'm not sure. Whoever lived here before. A Nepatin tradition, according to Idrissa."

I watched him breathe: in, out, in, out. I didn't want to cry. I hated crying. I didn't want to breathe deeply either; didn't want to feel my insides moving up and down; organs and bones and whatever else was hiding in there. I didn't want that. I wanted to keep going forward. I didn't want to be stuck. If the essence thought that I needed a release of emotion, it was wrong.

"I think we should talk about what happened."

"You *do*?" I asked incredulously.

"Yes. I wanted to apologize. I felt myself losing control. I should have forced you to leave or taken myself out of the school completely. You could have died. I'm not sure why it *didn't* kill you." The boy opened his eyes to look at me, snapping them shut as soon as he did. "Doctor Harker is sending me back to my home layer, so shortly it won't be a problem. Still, I'm sorry,"

I stood up from the ground and groaned, shaking my body off like a wet dog. I walked to the white and green walls. I traced my finger along cracks in the glassy tiles.

"It's too bright in here," I mumbled. My hand scratched my neck. "It's old and bright and full of bullshit."

Seth didn't reply.

An edgy, sharp feeling twisted through my middle. Circling, clenching. I looked down at my foot — my boots were scuffed and greyed. I pulled my foot back and swung, kicking the wall. "Fucking dipping our faces into other people's bodily fluids. Oh, *sorry, ancient beings'* bodily fluids. Such a gift! No. I hate this place."

I paced the little room, tossing myself about, unable to stop. "That crack you made downstairs? Time to break this place open, Sethboy. Time to let it rip." I whirled around and pointed one finger at him. "And before you get all, '*Oh poor me, I'm so evil, I have to leeeave!*' Let me just tell you, sonny. You're not going anywhere. You're going to buckle down and see this through. And I'm going to help you."

Seth took one of his hands out of the pool and rubbed the essence on his jaw. "You aren't making sense."

I threw my head back and laughed. "Welcome to the family, Mr. Mace!"

Seth's skin drew tightly around his mouth. "You would have me stay here and endanger everyone? I've been here for years; it's evident that my time has come."

"It's evident? What are you, a fucking scientist?" I was at the doors, pounding on them. "Get out of your glass ball, man! Put down the beaker and join the party, because we are all *nuts* and it's time you were, too."

"Mayli."

Something dropped. Oh, *I* dropped.

I was on my hands and knees, panting. The room was so bright. I rested my forehead on the cold floor.

"You wanna know why Mercy couldn't kill me?"

Seth stared at me. His eyes were round.

"Because I'm as messed up as you are. I've got a rancid soul and I'm ready to air it out. My energy is *blood,* man. A big, wet mess; dark red. There's no light in there." I let the words fall from my mouth in big, wet syllables. "Just. Like. You."

In the pure white of Seth's personal shrine, he transformed. Not into his devil, but into someone who, for the first time, understood.

"You don't have a demon."

"And yet, I've got the energy of someone with one."

His rigid body unlocked. He sat back, "You think…" Seth squeezed his eyes, shaking his head, "I can't say the words. It's dangerous."

"Aright. I'll say it. Screw everyone's ideas of what we *can* and *can't do.* My energy — which, by the way, is supposed to be *wrong* — stopped your demon. And I'll do it again. Let me at him. I'll pulverize that sticky pervert."

Seth laughed, shocked. Then stifled it and said, "This is not a good idea."

"We'll plan for it — for next time. Hit it head on, you know? It'll be fine. It'll be good." I wrenched open the sanctuary doors. "Thanks for the essence," I added with some awkward finger guns to really sell it.

The guy was moved back in by the end of the day.

I suffered through another morning of Dwavasc storytelling with no Saren Vite.

Oesh, debutante cult leader and Mieda's best friend *ever*, was assigned to fill in until the Saren situation reached some sort of end. Oesh was no Saren. She took her professionalism to the extreme and it was hilarious. I told her what a great job she was doing just to watch her squirm.

Riolyn wouldn't talk to me at lunch.

With Saren gone, Aeshra under observation, and Seth Mace moving back into my dorm, she decided I was the one in the wrong. I pretended everything was fine, went about my hotwrap just like always, hoping she'd get bored and give in. She did not.

But then, Grant Tallis busted our asses in Intro Defense.

We were practicing safe landings, jumping from the two- and three-foot lifts, and Tallis didn't care even a bit that I was recovering from a shoulder replacement.

I stood at the top of the three-foot landing and yelled at Tallis, "What part of 'it hurts' do you not understand? It's a *new* shoulder, man. I'm not landing on it!"

Tallis, inflexible with rage, clipped back, "Dr. Valentine does not agree. You need to strengthen — to work it." His expression broke, and he squeezed his arms at his sides. "I have never been forced to work with such an expectant, *arrogant* rich girl!"

"Excuse me?" I howled back, "You're *joking*. I'm arrogant because I was *crushed* into smithereens?"

Riolyn let out an audible scoff. I shot my eyes to her, and she said, "You kind of asked for it didn't you?"

Literal *Ooohs* from the class.

My jaw fell open and dropped to the floor. "Uh, *what?* Are you two on the same team now?"

"I'm just saying." She had the audacity to shrug her totally fine shoulders. "If it's not handed to you on a golden plate—"

"Will the both of you just shut up?" Grant tried to interject.

"You're just saying what? I'm a rich girl who was begging to be attacked? Beaten within an inch of my life?"

"You keep bringing up how hurt you are," Riolyn roared back. "So, why are you inviting that psycho back into our room?"

"Detention, both of you!" Grant yelled over us.

"What does that even mean?" I yelled too, not quite sure who I was yelling at. My eyes raked the room. Everyone was staring.

I didn't know what detention was, and that supposedly proved what a spoiled rich kid I was.

Turns out, detention is when you have to do whatever menial, terribly boring task a teacher asks of you until you feel sorry for your actions.

"Jokes on you, Tallis. I can make anything fun," I said, pushing a lightbulb off the edge of the table then catching it before it hit the floor. I was hoping for a laugh. Riolyn didn't react.

The odds of catching another bulb were against me.

We'd been given the task of testing and sorting lightbulbs, weeding out the spent ones. Tallis had given us two overbright lamps that we had to shield our eyes from with every new bulb. There were probably a hundred bulbs in the box between us, and we were expected to sort all of them. So far, all of them lit up. I had the inkling that this was just some garbage punishment he dreamed up in an awkward, torturous, wet dream. I didn't spend too much time thinking about what kind of dreams Grant Tallis had, but I was sure they were awkward and torturous.

I had to do everything in my power not to toss the whole box down the auditorium steps.

"Grant is such a fucking menace," I groaned. I screwed in another bulb and shielded my eyes from the blast of light.

Riolyn ignored me.

"Dude, you're going to have to acknowledge me eventually."

"I don't have anything to say to you, *dude*."

I let out a slow breath, ignoring the sting. "You just did."

Riolyn slammed her hands down on the table. "You know you almost died, right? You could have died, Mayli. That guy practically ripped your face off. I had to peel you off the floor when I found you. You keep reminding everyone that you had to get a shoulder replacement, but you can't seem to remember *how* you got it."

Stunned, I met her fiery glare. I wasn't the bad guy here.

"I know what happened. I remember clearly enough."

"And yet, he's moving back in. He should be locked up. He was *going* to be locked up!"

"Seth has a Demon living inside him," I said.

"Oh, right, and so it's your responsibility to give a shit? It's your responsibility to get you and everyone else you care about killed?"

"I'm not allowed to care about him too? I shouldn't even have to explain this to you!"

We went on checking lightbulbs in the silent echoes of the auditorium. Heat radiated off my friend.

"Whatever happened to you hating him? It was you and me against the world, and now … what?" Riolyn picked up a big, round lightbulb and threw it into the center of the auditorium. It clashed with the waxed floor and shattered, spraying glass in every direction.

"Hey." I put my hand on Riolyn's forearm, feeling her scales beneath my fingers. "I'm not afraid of him. I think I might be able to do some good. And stick it to my dumbfuck dad, too."

Riolyn gave me the side eye before throwing another bulb. I picked up a small yellow bulb, and tossed it too.

"You're fucking stubborn, you know that?" Riolyn said.

"Me? You are the most stubborn person I've ever met!"

"And you're not going to change your mind about this Seth thing? You're going to get hurt again."

I tossed another bulb into the center and watched it break. Tiny pieces of glass sprayed in all directions. "He's alone, I think. The demon thing is a bit out of my skill level, but I don't know. I feel like I can handle it."

"People have a right to want to stay away from him," Riolyn said. "He deserves to be alone."

"Maybe. I don't know. It's got to be hard, going through life with everyone thinking you're going to hurt them."

"He hurt you, though."

"Yeah. And I stopped him. Didn't know I could, but now I do."

"There's no changing your mind on this?"

I rolled a bulb between my hands, watching dust rub off onto my fingers. I shook my head no.

"I'm not helping you with him," Riolyn growled. Her eyes flitted slowly over the auditorium under us as she took a deep breath and said, "You know who I really hate? Grant fucking Tallis."

With a wry smile, I took another bulb and tossed it. "Yeah, fuck that guy."

It didn't take long for us to break every bulb in the box.

Grant gave Riolyn and I detention twice a week for the rest of the school year. It's like he'd expected us to fuck up the detention like we did. It was worth it just to have Riolyn seated equally at my side at meals like two royal heirs before their burning kingdom. And what did Tallis know, anyway? Maybe next time we'd take the detention seriously. I almost wanted to, just to prove him wrong.

We visited Aeshra. I imagined every scenario possible: prepared myself for the worst, so I could be pleasantly surprised.

Moonie sat in the hallway outside the sickward, resting her head on the cave wall. Her glittery eyelids reflected blue and green paphador.

"Hey, Moon," I said.

She opened her eyes and nodded. "Thanks for having Seth back."

Riolyn scowled, "Why?"

I shot a *Chill, dude!* look at Riolyn.

Moonie put her arms back behind her head. Her chin thrust out and she said, "You do know it's nice to help people, right? Considered the right thing to do. Not that it matters to you."

Riolyn was taken aback. She smiled a big, toothy grin and bent down, clapping Moonie on the knee. "You want to see Aeshra with us? Use some of that healing magic on him? Since it's so nice to help people and all."

Moonie rolled her eyes but led us into the sickward anyway.

Aeshra sat up on his cot under his healing lamps, bright orange and pink. Homework was piled on his blanket-covered lap.

"Come to gawk at the unstable boy?" he said, fanning himself with his pale hand.

He did look better, more alive, but the shadows beneath his eyes were deep. The skin of his cheeks clung to his cheekbones.

"At least they don't have you hooked up to anything anymore," Riolyn said.

"Mayli looks like she should be in here with me. Seth's little monster do that to your face?" He smiled weakly, his grey, dry lips stretching and cracking.

I nodded. "It's not as bad as it looks. I always felt like bruise was a good color on me, anyway."

"That's gross," Riolyn said, shoving me. I wrapped my arms around her, and she shoved some more.

Moonie slid into place behind Aeshra. She raised her silky hands to his cheeks. Aeshra sighed. He closed his eyes and leaned back against her. Moonie's dark flesh seemed to glow in contrast to Aeshra's starkness. If I looked hard enough, I could see the energy flowing from her. I might have been imagining it.

What a spectacular place to exist, I thought. Her power was unlike anything I'd known.

"Do you want to help?" Moonie said, eyes closed.

It took me a moment to realize she was talking to me.

"Like I know what I'm doing," I replied sarcastically.

Moonie didn't open her eyes. "You've missed class and you need practice."

She wasn't wrong, I did need the practice, but it seemed a bit egocentric to believe I could help Aeshra at all. "I don't want to interfere with your Lifting," I replied.

Riolyn scoffed. "Just do it. It's not going to hurt."

Moonie puffed a breath onto the back of Aeshra's neck and he twitched out of his reverie. Moonie spoke softly, "I'm going to have Mayli join us."

Aeshra nodded and smiled so innocently.

I nodded and closed my eyes to focus on my points of energy. My mind creaked open, rusted like a metal box at the bottom of a lake.

My lake of blood sat placid, but the Something New was there. A streak of inky green, snaking across the surface. Slippery and unable to hold. Moonie was inside me, too, watching. Her energy frosted the shore.

A sudden wave shocked me. My eyes prickled with tears.

Moonie opened her eyes and said, "Maybe not today. You need to heal a bit more."

Riolyn and Aeshra were none the wiser, but something in Moonie's glowing eyes tugged ominously at me.

After twenty minutes of silence, listening to Aeshra and Moonie's slow breathing, the rise and fall of their chests in unison, the Lifting session ended. Moonie stretched and pulled the creamy sweater back over Aeshra's shoulders, squeezing him before hopping off the bed. She left without much of a word to us, sweeping herself away in a dart of black, beaded fabric and remnants of pale blue energy.

"Man, she's something else," Riolyn growled like a predator.

"I thought you were trying to snag Valentine?" I laughed. Aeshra smiled slowly, still high.

"I am! I'm just saying, Moonie's cool." She leaned onto the cot and gazed longingly at the door.

"She wears nice clothes," Aeshra said. He was close to sleep, drifting between worlds. "News of Saren?"

Riolyn shook herself free of her daydreams. "Nothing."

I went to the side table and pulled out a jar of salve. I dipped a finger in and swiped it across Aeshra's cracked lips. Dry skin snagged at my fingertip.

Aeshra smiled. "Did Seth make you that cold? Frigid."

I scowled. "Seth didn't make me anything."

Riolyn and I stayed, poring over homework on the bed next to Aeshra while he slept. Our Post-Gate Rebellions essays were due tomorrow, and I wanted to show Drucilla that I was a cognitive being. That I had more vocabulary than sneers and bad words. Riolyn tapped her fingers on her paper, staring at nothing. She was unfocused, unusually so.

When Riolyn and I packed up, Aeshra stirred. He rolled onto his side and spoke in a traveled whisper, "Everyone makes you something."

Riolyn rolled her eyes, acting like everything was fine. "He talks in his sleep."

Something was off with Riolyn.

In the morning, after Seth's first night back in the dorm, I met Riolyn in the hallway. She was bouncing off the walls, jumping on the balls of her feet like an overactive puppy.

I raised an eyebrow. "Ready for class?"

"So ready."

"Didn't realize you were so into health class."

She laughed almost like a different person. Bubbly, rounded at the edges. Not the sharp, snarky friend I knew.

I focused on Dr. Valentine's lecture about wound care. Riolyn, at my side, tapped her hard fingers on the desk we shared. It was distracting.

Tapping, tapping, frantic tapping. It was a manic sort of pattern. Like she was speaking in code, but I didn't know the language.

I was missing something. What was I missing? What was Valentine talking about? She was pointing to the wallscreen, to a picture of a mottled arm. I read the words again; *burn wound care.* The importance of assessing the burn, knowing the differences between minor and severe burns. Riolyn tapped the desk with both hands now. Something was going on.

And then class was over and Riolyn was jumping up, eyes wide and bright. She clapped her hands together, shaking her body like an excited animal.

"Alright, let's go!" she said, abnormally energetic.

"Wow, never thought I'd see you so excited for Drucilla's class," I said.

"Huh? Oh, no, just..." Riolyn shook herself again as we headed for the second floor. "No, I hate Drucilla!"

We sat on the floor outside the auditorium doors, waiting for them to open. Seth wasn't hovering around in any dark corners as far as I could tell. Thank Mess, too. Riolyn had enough going on without having to see him.

Riolyn jabbered breathlessly about nothing.

"I just want to get in the water, you know? The lake — that fucking lake. It's right outside! Who makes the rules again? Your dad? Yeah, fuck him. He's wrong." She tossed her legs out in front of her, nearly tripping another student as they stepped by. Riolyn didn't notice. "I need to get in that lake. A bunch of assholes won't let me go *swimming*. I'm a *Margrev*! I need to go *swimming*! You'd think they'd know that. I need to go *swimming*!"

My hands clutched onto my elbows, and I leaned further away from my friend.

"I'm sure you can go swimming when the weather is better. It's cold, dude. No one's stopping you from swimming."

She didn't hear a word I said.

"If they'd just let me in the water, I could cool off. It's so fucking hot. My scales are so dry." She scratched at her arms. "Need to get in the water. Doesn't make sense! Who is sitting there thinking, *Yeah, this is a great idea. Put Riolyn in a cave. A fucking basement cave.* Who the fuck is thinking this through? Where *are we*?"

"Hey, hey man, slow down." I moved in front of Riolyn and put my hands on her shoulders, clenching down with fingers pushing at her totally normal, not dry scales. "What's happening? Do we need to skip class?"

Riolyn caught my look and held it, pieces falling back into place. "What? No. I'm alright." She took a deep breath, and then added, "Maybe I should see your dad early this week."

I nodded slowly, eyes watching hers. "Yeah, good idea. Maybe go now. While it's fresh."

Riolyn went to meet with Dr. Harker and didn't come back until the end of the day.

While I ate food by myself on the floor like a weirdo, Nathali slid up next to me and whispered, "Dad wanted me to tell you he's sorry."

It was laughable, really.

"Have you ever swam in the lake?" I asked Seth from my spot on the floor. I was folding the laundry I had been putting off for literal weeks. I was tired of having wrinkly clothes.

From his sitting sack in the closet, Seth said, "Of course not."

"What do you mean, of course not? Are people not allowed in the lake?"

He didn't move his eyes from his book. "*I'm* not allowed in the lake. Others are."

I leaned back against the bed, groaning. Why was everyone so difficult? I kicked over my haphazard pile of unfolded clothes with my socked feet, pushing the fabric around and huffing when a bra strap got caught on my toes.

"Why do you ask?" Seth asked from his dark hole.

"I'm just trying to figure out what the deal with the lake is. Riolyn had a bit of a ... I don't know. Meltdown, I guess? She was going off about people not letting her swim in the lake."

Seth still had his book open, but it didn't seem like he was looking at it anymore. His eyes were lost in the space in between. He said, "Donnie swims in the lake with his girlfriend. So does Moonie."

And then he was back in his book.

That just wasn't enough for me. Dammit, it made me so *angry*. The way Seth dodged every single question, the way he refused to divulge even the smallest detail about himself. If he trusted me enough to continue rooming with me, to possibly unzip his Demon in front of me, why the fuck couldn't he *talk* to me?

I glared at the laundry pile. Why was it so hard for me to do *the stuff*? The stuff everyone else did. If I could conquer basic chores like folding laundry and showering regularly and keeping my schoolwork organized, then maybe I could work on the things I so desperately wanted to do. I could dive into my ideas and create wonderful things that would make everyone see how magnificent I was.

I groaned out loud at the thought.

Seth ignored me. He was reading *Plants as Beings*. I wasn't sure what that meant exactly, but the guy was really into plants. I knew he spent a lot of time in the greenhouses in Nepa, and that's where he'd been the day he came back and cracked the floor open and threw up a river of hemacrux inside of it.

"So, where's Uyentra?" Seth asked out of nowhere.

My eyebrows knit together, "Uh, right now? Not sure. Probably in Nepa. It's *skalds* night at the diner."

"You didn't want to go?" he asked.

I fished around in my sock pile for a match. "Nah, as nice as getting drunk at the sand house sounds, I'm not up for it. Wouldn't want to go without Riolyn and, anyway, I don't eat meat. I'll spend time with Uyentra tomorrow."

Seth nodded, head back in his book.

I looked at the socks in my hand. *Mundane bullshit*. Nothing fun about folding laundry.

"A while ago, you asked why I was at Voltenstraus," Seth said, playing at nonchalance.

Torn between wanting to give him my full attention and not wanting to scare him off, I just nodded and kept on with the laundry. Suddenly, laundry seemed to be the easiest thing in front of me. I just had to put the shirts with the shirts, and the pants with the pants, and the underwear with the underwear, and keep my eyes off Seth Mace.

But then he said, "I killed some people. Before."

I choked, spitting into the laundry. *Play it cool, Mayli*.

My voice croaked. "Oh yeah?"

No, it was totally cool, totally *fine* that Seth was … what, a murderer? A demon-possessed *murderer?* My face needed to show that it was totally fine. My bruised-up face.

I felt my insides shiver; that deep, disturbing clench in my abdomen that I got when my nerves kicked in. And Seth was like an animal; he had to know. He had to feel my nervous energy vibrating in the air. His Demon, Mercy, was probably egging him on about it in his head right now.

Seth stared at his book. I couldn't even feel that odd magic that so often poured from him like a violent shadow.

Harnessing a thread of bravery, I asked, "You killed them? Or the demon?"

He sighed, bored. "Is there a difference?"

"Definitely."

He shifted in the silvery fabric, shaking his head. "I let Mercy out. I let it happen."

"What do you mean?" The floor was cold, pricking against my shins. And I was alone with a supposed murderer.

Stiff discomfort flickered over Seth. "I've gone over all of this with your father."

"You brought it up, man. I think you're making yourself out to be a monster. But you're also a seventeen-year-old kid."

Seth put his book on his lap and peered at me from the ill-lit closet.

"I had been fighting Mercy for a long time, and my... then-therapist wasn't so good for me." Seth took a moment, staring at his bony fingers as they moved in his lap. "So, when Mercy wanted to walk, I guess I let him. To be free from living. And when Mercy was done and pushed me back in place, I felt great. It was like the months of exhaustion and agony were gone."

My innate desire to validate reared its ugly head. "Alright, that's not ... so bad. You didn't do the killing. Or I guess your *body* did. But it wasn't you."

He slipped out of his sitting sack, his boots clunking against the floor, "I destroyed my family. My brother took the fall for me and I got to come to this sacred paradise while he sat in prison. *That* was me."

Seth ended up in the bathroom with the door shut. But a second later he rushed out again.

I managed an eye roll. "You're very dramatic."

"You don't *get it*, do you? I killed forty-four people, for fuck's sake. I should have been strapped into an acid bath, I should have to spend the rest of my life in a windowless cell, I should—" Seth leaned against the bathroom door and smacked his head back with a painful crack.

"Well, as long as you're not going for forty-five tonight," I joked.

"What the fuck is wrong with you?" He threw his hands up.

"Just trying to lighten the mood. You had to be ... what, twelve when it happened? You couldn't have even known."

"No." Seth cracked his knuckles. "It felt so good after the first time that I just let it keep happening. I didn't know *what* had happened, but I knew it was evil. I felt *incredible*. And my fucking therapist felt good about it too."

"Sounds like the therapist was the problem."

Seth straightened, tremors rippling through the floor as he did. My body geared up for a fight, red running beneath my skin on instinct.

He picked up his jacket, checked the pockets and headed for the door.

"I can't be here," was all he said. And he didn't come back for days.

When Aeshra was finally let out of the sickward, he wanted to party. Riolyn, still jittery and full of bad ideas, totally agreed.

I knew it was the worst possible plan. And I went anyway. I was angry with my father, angry with the itchy bandages on my face and the hard, uncomfortable metal that was now part of me forever.

We met Uyentra, Nathali, and Corin at the sand house. Nathali was already pleasantly drunk when we got there.

"I want to get in the water!" she howled, holding Aeshra's hands on the beach, swaying to some nondescript, garbage music playing in the house.

Riolyn was hopping next to us, up, down, up, "Water. That's *exactly* what we need."

I shook my head, "What is with you idiots?"

No one was interested in my thoughts. I hated them all.

Uyentra caught my eye, holding up their drink and downing it. Was that a wink? Did they wink at me? I didn't know, I couldn't see. Everything was unfocused.

I crawled over them and planted a kiss on their soft nose, "When did you get so attractive?" I breathed into their neck.

"You're just noticing?" They laughed, pushing me off and into the sand. Pieces of sand stuck to my hands like little bugs. I shook it off, disgusted.

Corin scoffed from his seat next to us while he stared at his pocketscreen. Why didn't I have one of those?

"Ugh, this stuff is so gross." I brushed off the sand on my sleeves and my shoes. Sand in my shoes; the thought gave me a full-body twitch.

"Sand is gross?" Uyentra laughed some more, taking a handful of sand and letting it slowly sift through their fingers like soft rain.

"Everything is gross," I explained. Not so eloquent, but it was how I felt.

Uyentra took my face in their hands while Nathali, Riolyn, and Aeshra hopped around like punk kids at a basement show. The three of them looked funny together, given how different they were. Uyentra and I stared into each other and I could feel them reaching into my soul, searching.

"I feel the Something. Do you feel it?" Uyentra asked quietly. The short, black fur across their cheeks stood on end, glistering in the firelight.

I nodded. "Always. I'm a black hole."

They nibbled at my ear with sharp teeth. "Ahh, that would explain it."

I downed my drink and went into the house for another.

When I got back, the beach trio was in the water, splashing and yelping. They were in their clothes. Their now *wet* clothes. So very wrong, so disturbing that I didn't want to look at them. But I looked; I had to look. I had to get over this phobia sometime, desensitize myself to it. So I stepped closer with a neon-colored beverage in hand.

Nathali was floating on her back, bemoaning life's trials to Aeshra as Riolyn stood hip-deep in the water, staring out over the bonfire near the house. She looked quite drunk. I watched Nathali dip her head under the water and come back up, gasping for breath. She laughed, cackled almost.

"My brother is missing," Aeshra said. It was out of nowhere and he was giggling and the whole thing felt very uncomfortable.

"*We* could go missing," Nathali replied, dipping into the water again. Every time her nose went under, I felt my lungs pull, my chest tighten. And then Aeshra started doing it too, laughing and sputtering dirty lake water.

"Save us, Mayli!" Nathali called, laughing, coughing on water. I felt my seams ripping as I watched them play. They had water all over their bodies, dripping off their faces, wet clothes clinging to their skin. I couldn't breathe. And then I looked over to Riolyn.

She was zombie-walking to the fire, her hands out in a state between wanting to feel the warmth and needing to shield herself. I watched as she picked up a piece of driftwood, entranced. It poked into the flames and caught fire.

"That's what she did to our uncle. Just lit him up. Lit the whole house on fire. She's a hero," Aeshra said.

I walked over to her, felt the fire hot on our faces. Riolyn's trance was broken.

"Hey, don't burn this. Toxic chemicals and all that," I mumbled, pulling her away, taking her hand and guiding her to the water. She put the fire out, tossing the driftwood away.

"Thanks," Riolyn said.

When Seth did come back, he talked. He told me about his brothers; about Donnie and his impossible need to dissolve conflict in the name of harmony. About Caulder, who was funny and soft and chose to stay on Dedocia to be a slice of home for Devin, who never came home anyway.

Devin, the brother who'd taken the fall for Mercy's crimes, even though he was the least likely person to harm another. Devin, who was closest to Seth, who was so full of promise, who loved him more than any person in the world. Devin, who was out of prison and off drugs and on the right track. Devin, who'd recently been caught on film robbing a bank with a team of criminals.

He told me about the place he went when Mercy opened out. *The Other Place*, he called it. And sometimes when he went there, he wasn't alone.

27

CRICKETS IN THE BASEMENT

From the passenger seat of Squeem's van, I watched the emerald skyline approach. It was the oldest city in Besel: Suradelphia. This place was never my home, just a momentary reprise between traumatic events. The last time I was here, I was being carted off to prison. Maybe I hadn't committed the crimes, but they were still, certainly, my fault.

Steam rose from peaks of aged factories, slotted between modern high-rises and rounded, green government buildings. The most-ancient Kajiun forest loomed outside the city limits. A barrier of stone cradled the woods like protective arms. The last reservation of the remaining Kajiun people hid inside. Those forests were off-limits to outsiders. For good reason, considering what our descendants had done to the great Kajiun city of Suradelphia.

A story as old as time; someone bigger and meaner came along.

"Look at that," Squeem sighed, awed over the foggy green city. The final sun gleamed off silver and gold peaks of the oldest architecture. "Matey's family is from here. Yours too?"

"We moved here when I was a teenager," I replied. Sweat clung to my skin as I shuddered, both repelled and drawn to Sura. Was it my home? Maybe it was; part of me submitted to the idea. Part of me longed for it. "My brother Caulder is still here."

"What does he do on a Tuesday night?" Squeem asked. We neared the city's edge, laid low before us like a gift. The van slowed at the highest part of the slope. Soon, we would descend into Sura proper.

"He calls me. Or that's what he did before I ended up with Mina," I responded as the skyline drew nearer.

"You didn't just 'end up' with Mina," Squeem replied crisply. "She abducted you. Not that I don't like having you around, but ... perspective."

"You're the one that said we were good together," I grumbled.

"I said it wasn't the *worst* idea. And you probably are good together. Again, perspective. Mina is better than the monsters we're trying to take down, but only just."

The van pulled onto a rounded exit into the heart of Suradelphia. The rest of the crew huddled together in a tight circle, poring over plans. An energetic silence crackled in the back of the vehicle.

I searched the skyline for the Landornian Monastery; a brick building flanked by mid-range apartments and a multilevel casino. New buildings crowded the area, overshadowing what *might* have been my old home. Inside, layers upon layers revived: of relationships, memories, trauma.

"See that casino? Red, with the white sign?" I pointed.

"*Scarlet Tower*?" asked Squeem. "Yeah, I see it."

"We lived right next door. In a Monastery, if you can believe it. Raised my baby brothers in there."

"Mina mentioned it. Said you lived with Landornian monks. Must have been nice to have a community to lean on."

"Eh, I should have done more leaning. It was an unconventional place to spend my teens and early twenties. I was a mess, though. Probably would have been, no matter where I was."

"How did you end up there?"

"We lived on Brunock Island. My parents died, or were killed. After, my brothers and I were whisked away the very next day. The Monastery had offered to take us. I'm still not sure who set it up. Why would Friar Elle, a whole ocean away, hear about four orphaned boys and say, '*Yes, of course, I'll help!*'"

"Monks are supposed to help people, aren't they?" Squeem asked, glancing at me sidelong.

I laughed, "Sure. It was just so *fast*. When we got there, we didn't belong. I sure didn't. Brunock was warm, but the Monastery was so cold. Everything falling apart. No heat, just blankets and freezing, stone floors. I used to light a bunch of candles and huddle up next to them. Elle kept us away from the rest of the monks at first. I remember being so *angry*."

"Your parents had just died.".

"Yeah. Seth was all of a day old when we left home. I remember carrying him onto the boat, bundled in a black blanket. His hair — he has a patch of white hair right in the front. He looked like a rat, with black hair and that white spot. I remember *hating* him, thinking, '*Look at this wrinkly, ugly thing I have to carry around.*'"

Squeem was quiet. I kept on.

"He was hungry but wouldn't take a bottle from me. I remember feeling that everything was his fault; he'd killed our parents. Donnie was *five years old;* he took Seth from me and fed him the bottle. Looked at me like I was dumb."

"You were a child, too. I wouldn't have known what to do either."

"I still feel like a child," I said. "I should have told them everything would be okay, and that *Seth* was okay. I should have just lied."

Squeem pulled off onto a side street in the Rastian district. Upscale, modern buildings; lofts and banks and restaurants. At our front, hazy brick buildings with fogged windows and steamy, grated streets. A distant rumbling beneath us. The differences in neighborhoods in the city had become even more stark than I'd remembered.

Squeem turned to the back and said, "We're just about there."

"Alright, let's go over the plan. Fruit, Matey, and Squeem will monitor from the car. Where are you parking?"

"The multilevel garage across the street from the office building," he replied. "Do you still want to go in by the side door?"

"The big shop windows near the trash expellers in the alley. We should be able to get in those with little trouble. The building is high security, especially for an office building. Taro, Devin, do you have your cloaking pins?"

"Wait, you don't want *me* to go in there—" I started.

Mina shut me up with a hand wave. "Yes; you, me, and Taro. The best kind of practice is to be thrown right in. You did well at the bank job, so this is the next step."

I looked to Taro for comfort, but she was stifling an eye roll. I couldn't tell if she was annoyed with Mina or me, but it made me feel even more inadequate. "We need to get moving," she said stiffly. "We have no idea what we're looking for and we can't spend the entire night searching."

Squeem crawled to the back and hopped on the computer next to Fruit, leaving me alone and nervous in the front of the van. "Surveillance shows there's a cleaning crew, same time every night. They normally go through a door toward the back around 8:15, and whatever is back there isn't hackable. I think that door is where you need to start. The door is keypad locked, so we'll work on opening it remotely, because I haven't been able to see the code reliably."

"When does the cleaning crew leave the building for the night?" Taro asked.

"They don't, as far as we can tell. I've never seen them enter or exit the building. It's got to be something to do with that door." Squeem pulled up surveillance of the entryway on the computer.

Mina nodded, handing out palmpods, internal earpieces, cloaking pins, and live feed cameras. I attached the cloaking pin and camera on my chest and wrapped the palmpod around my hand. It was sticky, gel-like and clear with a pale green screen across my palm. I tested it out, using my middle fingers to press the pad. Three low tones sounded in my earpiece.

Taro was dressed and ready first. "Say we get the door open. What then?"

"We go through it." Mina said, lacing flat boots up her legs with zipper pouches on the calves. She wore two small packs, one on her waist and one between her shoulder blades. No big weapons, just a big, serrated knife and a silenced handgun. For such a terrifying mission into enemy territory, we sure were packing light.

"Do I need a weapon?" I asked, hoping the answer was no.

Taro pushed a pair of boots and a plated vest toward me. "You'll wear these. You aren't trained in combat. You can carry the medical supplies."

"I agree," Mina motioned to Squeem. "Hey, wake up asshole." She smacked him, and he turned groggily, before handing me a tightly packed bag. "You wear it at the curve of your lower back. Make sure it doesn't move around." Mina helped me strap it onto my middle. "Huh, you aren't as skinny as I thought you were."

She ended with a loud slap to my behind.

We turned on our cloaking pins. Fruit checked to make sure they worked as we exited the van and made our way down the foggy, grated street. I still couldn't believe we were in Suradelphia.

"How do the cloaking pins work? Can those people over there see us?" I eyed two street-sleepers suspiciously. They certainly seemed like they could see us.

"I don't know, Devin. Why don't you try waving at them to find out?" Mina sniped.

"Don't be rude, Mina; he's asking important questions," Taro said. "We're cloaked from surveillance and scanners. We could walk into a health scanner and wouldn't register. We're essentially invisible to tech. Another masterful invention of our friend Squeem."

"Yes, yes, thank you, carry on," Squeem sounded over our earpieces.

"Technology like this has to give us a leg up on the Full Set, doesn't it?" I asked.

"Certainly, but they have a lot of tech of their own. If we could grab a sample of some of it, that would make today a big success," Mina answered as we rounded the street corner.

The street was quiet, lined with corporate offices on one side and green space on the other. A massive parking garage took up half the block next to the park. Our van disappeared into it.

An office building with yellow lights illuminating the front glowed brightly in the night. The words Nerova Beauty were spelled out in neon. Matey's tracer, blinking on our scanners, was hidden somewhere inside. Somewhere in this luxury cosmetics office was the other side of a being-made Gate. A Gate torn right into the Indigo Abyss; a feat I didn't even know was possible.

Mina stuck a little tab on the front door of the office building. "I've placed the first sensor."

"It's active," Squeem replied.

Condensation gleamed on the asphalt as the temperature dropped. Our boots gripped at the ground below silently. Taro's were a beautiful teal color. I wondered where they got such expensive tactical footwear.

"Devin, where are you going? Pay attention!" Mina grabbed my arm and pulled me down a tight alleyway.

In the wet alley between buildings, the drainpipes were flooded. I hopped away from a big, rushing puddle that swirled down into the depths of the undercity. There were two dumpsters on either side, and a plain, metal door with a keypad and a line of wide windows.

"We're going to open an upper window remotely to test the security," Squeem said.

A window overhead slid open. No alarms sounded; no security forces rushed out. Mina and Taro looked at each other. Mina started tapping her foot, waiting for Squeem to reply. The window shut again.

Mina sighed. "All clear?"

Quiet, before: "...All clear," Matey replied.

"Where's Squeem?" Taro asked.

Fruit chuckled. "Indisposed."

"Listen idiots, we need to get moving. Open the damn window before I have to come back to the van and do it myself," Mina threatened. "What is Squeem doing?!" Mina snapped after another few seconds of silence.

Fruit laughed under his breath again. "He's taking a piss into a jug."

"Fruit — what is *wrong* with you? Like you can't open a window," Squeem yelled. Mina glared at me as I tried to stifle my laughter.

The window opened, and Taro was the first to jump inside. She checked the corridor and Fruit and Squeem said the surveillance was clear. I was up next and Mina boosted me up. I didn't fall on my face on the way in.

Taro crouched, one hand on the floor with her other hand in front of her nose, looking at her palmpod, which was lit up in the center like a screen. I looked at my own palmpod and saw nothing but pale green gel and a few circles.

My chest tightened. Why was I here? Wearing tactical boots and bulletproof vest, carrying a bag of medical supplies I didn't know how to use, adorned with cloaking pins and live feed cams and palmpod. What if I pressed the wrong button and opened up a channel right to the Full Set? They'd swoop in and spoon feed us poison.

"Devin, you alright there? Your heart rate is spiking," Matey said in my ear.

Mina shot her eyes to me, fierce and full of adrenaline and ready for a fight. I wasn't going to slow her down.

"I'm not prepared for this," I said.

Mina put her hands on my shoulders. "You are. You will be fine. Taro and I won't let anything happen to you. I bet you won't even need us once we get going. You're a natural."

Maybe she was right, maybe I would be fine.

"I don't feel fine. I feel terrified."

"Devin." Mina squeezed my arms. "Remember when I nabbed you? I had to skewer your hand to the dashboard to keep you from escaping."

I looked at my hand. It was normal.

"You have fight in you. You're not going to mess this up."

We breathed together. I nodded. Pushed my shoulders back.

Taro stood up. "The scanner shows Matey's pin under us, a bit to the south. I'm going to look for a stairway, something to get us downstairs."

My eyes widened. "You're going alone?"

"She's fine." Mina squeezed me again. "She's made for this." Mina turned back to Taro. "Devin and I will find Squeem's door. We've got a good twenty minutes before the cleaners go through it, so we can get in place." Mina took her hands off my shoulders and gave me a quick kiss.

The front lobby was pristine and elegant, with crystal fixtures and glass tables. Whimsically sculpted flowers hung from the ceiling. There were conference rooms around the front, a lobby with yellow armchairs and fluffy pillows, and a corner office.

The deeper we crept into this corporate monstrosity, the more it felt like a cage. The back rooms turned from gaudy, business gush to grey, ill-lit cubicles with light boxes framing unhelpful phrases like "The Customer is King," and "Royalty is our Policy."

Squeem's voice flooded my ears. "You guys are getting close to the door."

"Taro, where are you?" Mina asked.

"Coming up with nothing downstairs; it's mainly storage. I'll make my way back to you."

"The cleaners are right on schedule, so you have a few minutes," Squeem said.

He quietly directed Taro through the building to us. His voice was comforting, like soft rain on the boat deck. Tomorrow, after this show was over, I would sit on Mina's boat deck all day, drink rootbrew and watch the rain.

Mina pushed open a door at the back wall, the word *Management* scrawled across it. We stepped into a long hallway.

"You're almost there," Matey said into our ears.

Mina placed her keycard on the handle on the first door. It clicked open to reveal a windowless office. I stepped around her, continuing down the hall. The second door reeked of imitation floral. At the back, a central door was flanked by a custodial closet and a trash can.

The door read: *Warning: hazardous electrical equipment.*

"Is this it?" I asked, glancing over the keypad next to the door.

"Yep," Matey answered. "We can see you in the camera feed."

I turned around and jumped; Taro was crouched behind me, staring down into her palmpod. Above her, a bent-up camera blinked at me.

Taro said, "My scans are inconclusive. Fruit, will you run a frequency update?"

"We think the Gate is back there?" I looked around at the hallway; the carpet was scuffed with wear, dust clung to the white walls. "It doesn't make sense. The cleaning people don't even *clean.*"

Taro scoffed at my feet.

Mina tugged at my sleeve, and we began back down the hallway.

"Let's take what we know. We know the torn Gate under Teme'te connects here. Matey's tracker is still active, unmoved. We know that a tram track runs through the torn Gate. We know that people are being taken from the Gate of Teme'te, as we've seen with Saren Vite. So, somewhere under us, is a tram track, and the other end of the torn Gate."

Mina and I dipped back into the windowless office. She scanned the room with her palmpod, looking for some breakthrough, some easy sliver of a clue that would nudge everything into place. But it just looked like an office to me.

"If we can figure this out, we'll be that much closer to understanding," Mina said.

Taro said from the door, "We need to work fast and grab as much tech as possible."

"And the less we touch, the better. We don't want them to shut this place down, whatever it is."

"Cleaners are finished and coming downstairs," said Squeem. "They're two minutes out. Going silent on this end."

Mina sent back a single tone via palmpod in an affirmative. She crouched next to Taro behind the door of the office. I tried to take deep breaths in the corner of the room. I didn't want to mess this up, but I was so *scared*. Two minutes had never felt longer.

I smelled it first; the metallic tickle in my nose that could only be heavy cleaning products. In the glossy, clean glass of the non-committal artwork on the office walls, I could see them go by.

Five cleaners, women and men with five service carts, trailed in a line toward the back room. Their grey and white aprons were starchy, untouched by dust or dirt. Their bodies moved like well-oiled machines.

Mina watched them, her lips a stiff line. Motionless, she waited like a widowspider as the cleaners passed the office door.

The hair on my arms stood alert, prickling in the cold vent air and the stinging smell of cleaning products. The back door opened with a soft click, and when it shut behind the cleaners, a heavy, metallic thud vibrated through the floor.

Mina's eyes darted to Taro and then to me before sending four quick tones to Squeem and Fruit, telling them to remain quiet. Taro added one long and one quick tone to signal that they were on the move.

Mina crept to the door silently. Taro followed, staying down and alert. Taro leaned back on her heels and pulled out a thin, folded sheet of metallic fabric from inside her sleeve and handed it to Mina. She unfolded the strange material to reveal a translucent, mirror-like object. Mina knelt at the door and slipped the mirror underneath.

Taro sent three quick tones, telling Squeem to speak. My palmpod vibrated, and I looked down to see a live feed from the mirror Mina slid under the door.

"Fruit is having a hell of a time getting any read on what's behind that door. The power conduits shifted energy for a second," Squeem asked. "Did the cleaners get through?

I cleared my throat before answering. "They're through, but the door made a loud noise when it shut. That's when the energy spiked. Mina's looking under the door with ... something. I just see concrete."

"She's using the lucid? I don't have a connection. Don't move, you three."

We waited, crouched in the hallway, while Squeem and Fruit tried to reconnect. Mina didn't like waiting. She scowled. "We can't wait here all night. We need to keep moving. Let's get this damn door open."

Taro moved her palmpod over the area. "The handle is a scanner, and it's not affected by our cloaking. If we touch it, it'll see right through us." She maneuvered her hand over the keypad a few times. "Six of the keypad numbers have skin oils on them, so we need to compare those with Fruit's combination guesses."

There was a moment of silence before Fruit's quiet voice replied, "Sending now."

A long list of number combinations rolled over our palm screens. I groaned, overwhelmed, but Taro smiled. She started poring over the numbers.

"I'm not getting through," Squeem said after another few minutes. "The system won't budge. I think it's Bright White Energy past the door."

Mina growled, "We have to make do, then. We've done it before. Taro?"

Taro held up a finger. "Almost. Running combination probabilities."

My stomach ached. *I shouldn't be here.*

And then Taro was wiping her gloved finger on a white, papery sheet before pressing an eighteen-digit code into the keypad. A low hum sounded, and the door unlocked. Mina slid her thin fingers under the door and popped it open. Cold, wet air blasted our faces, like we'd entered a cave system.

Taro continued scanning the doorway, looking for any reason not to go in there. I held my breath, hoping she'd find something.

"Come, dear. We've got criminals to undermine." Mina kissed my nose before slipping into this new adventure. She stepped through the door without looking back.

I peeked in. Towers of electrical equipment clung to the back wall. Blinking lights, warning signs, piping and wires. It was very convincing, but Taro laughed at it, regardless. Fake electrical equipment, and for what?

An elevator door with no buttons stood sharply just past a panel of blinking, whirring fans. Beyond that, a stairwell descended into cold shadow. Taro scanned the room while Mina shined a light down the stairs. The hair on my arms stood like antennae, warning me off. Chilled air rose from the hole in the floor.

I didn't want to go down there.

Mina cracked a lightstick and tossed it down. It hit the ground with a splash, the sound echoing far beneath us.

"It's the old tram system," Mina said before taking her first step down.

Taro squeezed my shoulder. We followed our leader; our killer.

It took a moment to acclimate to the pink glow of the lightstick. The air was thick with humidity, like the cool season in a rainforest. Soft drips and sloshes filled the darkness. Mina picked up the lightstick as Taro snapped one of her own.

"There are more stairs over here," Taro said. She stepped into the water. "It's only about an inch."

Grey water slopped onto my boots. I circled my foot, drudging up filth.

Two frosted bulbs were fastened to the concrete, clouded with dust. Opposite the wall, a clear barrier contained stagnant, green water. I stepped up to it, squinting through the muck.

"It's the flooded tram," Mina said, standing next to me. "A great place to hide."

The ten-foot walkway was sparse. The smell of wet, dusty minerals and algae fogged my senses.

Mina hummed as she looked things over, bouncing from one foot to the next, practically thinking out loud. Her burgundy jacket dripped as the humidity rolled off its waterproof fabric. She was a flash of red, copper, and pink; completely in her element.

I ... was not. The entire thing felt like an apocalyptic dream. Secret tunnels beneath my city? And how did I end up back here in the first place? Dearest Mina dragged me here, didn't she? No, this was my choice. I was terribly out of my depth and *my* choices brought me here.

"We need to continue," Taro said as she tapped against her palm, sending messages to Fruit and Squeem. There was little chance they would receive them.

"Ingenious, don't you think?" Mina said as she looked out into the murky water, her short nails tapping the glass. "Building underneath the flooded tram system. It would have cost a fortune, completely unnoticed on the surface."

"I can't imagine the lower levels are watertight," said Taro, eyebrows raised. "The Full Set likes things clean."

"I guess we'll find out," Mina said, spinning toward the next stairwell, floodwater spraying around her. She was so *alive*. The serial killer, an infamous symbol of evil.

It felt like a gift to see these sides of her.

My ears popped as we continued down. I cracked my jaw to alleviate the discomfort. The green, slick floor shone in the glow of Taro's lightstick. How could any creature, even bacteria, live down here? I had to pick up my feet with purpose to keep from falling. Mina and Taro might as well have been figure skating.

Another two floors of flooded tunnels and the air started to change. Humidity was replaced by cool, conditioned air. The stale stench dissipated, and a low hum of motors grew louder with each passing step. The floors were clean and clear, the walls free of growth.

A bright white light perched atop the final door. We'd met our destination.

Mina went to the door as Taro tapped furiously on her palmpod.

She unfolded the lucid mirror and slid it under the door. A nondescript, grey image filled our palmpod screens. More concrete, a tinny shine of metal from a great distance, the spatter of white light; the scene was unreadable. All was silent behind the door.

Mina's gloved hand hovered over the door latch; simple and silver and square. She looked at Taro, then at me, before turning the handle. The latch clicked and the door gave way.

"That's *it*?" I said.

Soft light illuminated Mina's face. The glow caught the wetness of her lashes. She was beautiful, and she was going through the door.

Taro followed, her steps unheard. A middle-aged woman, the strongest, the *smartest* of us three. Competent, agile, perfect.

I, on the other hand... My attempt at total silence was laughable. As I entered the cavernous space on the tips of my toes, the door slammed behind me. Mina and Taro turned at the brilliant *thud*, glaring. I flushed.

At once, a clicking sound began.

The sound bounced, echoed in the vast, concrete hollow. The ceiling rose high above us, shadows cast in sharp cuts across grey.

Click ... click ... click, three seconds apart and monotonous.

"Any ideas what that unsettling *clicking* is?" I asked, into the blank space around me. Mina was at the elevator door, scanning, searching. Where were the cleaners?

Taro was — where was Taro?

The space was gargantuan. White sheets of weatherproofing plastic adhered to the walls. Strips of bright white light lined the perimeters of little rooms, windows, doors. Glass cubicles surrounded stark white, metal cabinets and metallic, body-sized boxes on wheels. Like the ones under Teme'te.

Click ... click ... click ... click.

I walked up to one of these boxes. It was cold, and the window at the top was dark. Anxiety rolled through me in a hair-standing burst.

Taro stood motionless, scanning, eyebrows bunched together. Had I ever been that focused before? Was that something a person could learn? Mina was hunched over a screen stand across the room. She fished around in her pack, pulled out something small. She fit it into the screen and stepped back, stretched her body. Her neck cracked.

Light glanced off the metal at her feet. My eyes followed the gleam; a thin track ran the length of the room. Both ends curved out of sight.

I didn't know what to do. Following the track seemed the best course of action.

*Click ... click ... click ...*like the call of a giant, mating bug.

On my palmpod, I followed my memorized directions; draw a circle, press the menu button, open the app, check the location of Matey's tracker, follow the compass. It was easy — *supposed* to be easy. Except, none of this was easy.

The further I walked along the track, the closer I got. With Mina and Taro just out of sight, the flickers of Indigo caught my eye. A Gate, like the one at Teme'te, hung in the air like electric silk. Below, a little, white tube lay on the ground. I reached down to pick it up.

The crackling of sound began in my earpiece, "Hello, anyone? Mess, this is a *nightmare* — does anyone read?"

"Squeem?" I replied, holding the tracker in my hand. Its light blinked at me like a smile.

"Devin? Is that you? Oh, thank Mess," Squeem laughed. Matey's cries of relief muffled in the background.

"We're five stories down, under the flooded tramline. I just picked up Matey's tracker."

Fruit spoke up, "Tracker movement acknowledged."

Back down the track, Mina called for me.

"I need to get back to Mina and Taro. There's a lot of weird stuff down here."

"Ok, go, but come back to give me an update in a few," Squeem replied.

Click ... click ... click ... click. The incessant noise was louder than before as I walked along the track. Whatever made the noise was back here.

In the main room, Mina was hooked up to another computer. "Where'd you go?"

I showed her the tracker, "Got ahold of Squeem. The other side of the Gate is back there."

She smiled, grabbed my hand with the tracker and pulled me into her. Mina nipped at my bottom lip, slipping the tracker out of my hand. "Good work, Devil Mace."

Taro was pulling up the lid of a wooden crate. "Hey, Devin, would you help me with this?"

"Yeah, okay," I stumbled away from Mina. As I got closer, the woozy feeling began. Dizziness hit with a hard slam. I fell to the floor, groaning, crawling backward, sliding on the polished cement.

Mina ran over, crouched next to me. "Hun, what's going on?"

"*Hun?*" I laughed, wincing away from the split in my temple.

"Red water — lots of it. Why would they be shipping this?" Taro said as she peered into the crate. "Go check those metal boxes, Devin. We need to scan this stuff."

I nodded, more than happy to get away from the container. I pushed myself further away, uncorked my canteen and chugged. The cold, clear water rinsed away the nausea. My fingers wiped the hair from my eyes; longer now, from months of living on a boat on the other end of the Kajiun forest. I smiled at the thought.

Click ... click ... click...

The closest cubicle smelled bare, sanitary. Soft chirps and hums sung in the glass chamber like android birds. I ran my gloved hand over the white countertops, over the sink space, the warm wires connecting to the metallic box. A vent at the top of the room opened and a whoosh of air pulled in. The space was clean, sparse, steady. It might have even been comforting. And from here, I could almost ignore that incessant clicking.

I opened the deskscreen and it was logged in, lying in wait. A messaging system at the top of the screen blinked, awaiting a reply. The draft, unsent, read:

Do not open the control container until it's delivered to the Venus facility. The specimen is likely not dangerous, but it does react strongly to sorite-based liquids.

My eyes blurred with tears. Deep in my bones, I knew.

The metal box was person-sized. I leaned over it, holding my breath. The container's window was fogged. I knew what I'd see behind the fog, if I just *looked*. But I didn't want to look.

I didn't want to see that stark-white face.

I forced my eyes open. The face — a blur of pale flesh, eyes squeezed tightly shut in discomfort. My own body froze in place, clammy hands freezing cold at my sides. Fingers trembling. They'd locked him in a metal box, a sarcophagus, and here he'd stayed. What were they going to do to him? Was he alive?

"Oh shit, oh Mess." My voice cracked. I banged on the glass wall.

Mina and Taro looked up, eyes wide, *angry.* How could I be so careless, so stupid, making such a racket? But my face must have told them otherwise. Mina jumped up, began to run.

Click ... click ... click, click, click.

The clicking sound pulsed through the floor, quicker now. Beneath my feet, a resounding hum burst. The glass walls shook.

Clickclickclick—

Without thought, I unclipped the latches on the sarcophagus. Fog rolled out as I pulled up the lid. And there, in a cold, metal box, with frost clinging to his eyebrows.

Saren Vite.

The clicking stopped. Silence loomed. Mina swung into the room, a whirl of red. She gasped.

A steady trickle of pink fluid flowed via clear tubing into Saren Vite's chest port. A shroud of red fabric draped over him. I hung my head, overcome with nausea.

Outside, alarms switched on and swelled.

"Statuestic, in the IV. Pink. Just like we found at Teme'te," Mina said. She turned into the room, moving like an orange light. As she looked for a way to unplug the box, I clung to myself, heaving into the sink.

"Sorite," I coughed. "The sheet — on him."

"Push through it, just a little longer," Mina said, searching around the box. "We need to get out. No idea how long he'll have once we dislodge him."

A high, metallic screech ripped the air.

A loud bang, a gunshot. Taro was shooting at something.

Mina cursed and pushed me aside. She tore the tube from Saren Vite's chest.

"Get him out, Devin!" Mina yelled, running from the glass room.

My vision greyed at the edges. Nothing made sense. Who was Taro shooting at? I staggered to the box, my stomach rolling. My hand reached in.

Fingertips grazed Vite's shrouded chest. I doubled over, coughing, sputtering, gagging. The fabric felt like red water. I couldn't touch that—I couldn't get him out.

I banged my head on the box, yelling, "I shouldn't be here!"

Then I pulled myself up and wrapped my arms around the man's middle.

Pain burst behind my eyes. I lifted Saren up. The red fabric heated, irradiated. I cried out, dragging the man from the casket. Saren thudded to the ground. He was dead weight and cold, *so cold*. The fabric draped over him like a funeral shroud, sending stabs into me with every touch.

Saren stirred in my arms. I pulled the red shroud from his shoulders and threw it as far as my weak arms would let me. He was growing warmer. He *groaned*.

Mina and Taro were shooting, yelling, throwing things. I couldn't see what was happening, but I could hear it. A jumble of noise.

I dragged Saren Vite from the cubicle, barely able to keep myself from vomiting. I had to keep going, I had to save this man. He was innocent, more innocent than I'd ever been.

"Devin, get him to that stairwell!" Taro shouted as she crouched behind a wooden crate. Across the room came a loud, simpering call, like a chorus of crickets in a basement.

My vision swam, eyes fogged with tears. Something moved on the ceiling. A person — was it a person? With a hollow face and long legs that bent back in the wrong direction. A glowing middle with hot lines like veins stemming from it, wrapping themselves around fleshy, metallic arms. A cleaning apron hung from their middle.

"What the fuck is that?" I yelled.

The creature cried out. It hopped through the air and landed on Taro's crate.

Taro shot up at the thing, hitting its face. Purple liquid sprayed, rained down. The creature let out another yowl as Mina ran up behind it. She sunk a knife right in its spine, thrusting down, *sawing*. She tore something off, a piece of the creature.

"There's four more! Some kind of MMP. *Damn!*" Taro slid from the spot behind the crate and shot up at the ceiling.

Mina's voice rang, "Get Saren out of here!"

That's when the hyperventilating started.

Two Melodic Mechanical Persons crawled above us. Their swollen eyes swam in dead faces. Their sounds, harmonic and terrifying. Ice grew in my lungs. These creatures were nothing like the common robots I'd seen on screen programs.

"Aren't they supposed to look like people?" I yelled, pulling Saren Vite's dead weight behind me. Away from those *things*.

An MMP shot down from the ceiling, landing on hands and feet. It let out a sad growl. This one looked soft, female. Her sunken eyes reached mine. Stringy hair hung around her face, dirty and snagged. A dark object floated at the center of her transparent chest cavity. It emitted blue light.

The creature moved toward us. Frozen, I slid to the floor with Saren at my back. He was shuddering, grumbling.

"Devin, move!"

Someone shot at the MMP, hit her neck. She fell and began to crawl. It was like staring into a mirror image of myself, or who I used to be. But instead of running on cheap drugs, this bot ran on murder program.

The MMP was shot again, this time in her shoulder. Purple sprayed the air.

A mellow cry slipped from her mouth. She reached for my foot. I skittered back, shoving Saren farther behind. Her flesh-and-silver fingers gripped my boot, metal nails like talons. I searched inside for something, anything. Power. Limit. Light. There was nothing.

I threw my head to the side and vomited.

Around us, circling, waltzing, flying, Mina and Taro fought like Undergods.

I let out a pathetic squeal as the MMP's other hand reached for my calf. She latched on, tearing into my muscle. Her facial overlay was emotionless. Her soulless lips didn't quiver. But she opened her mouth anyway.

Mina flew through the air, red, copper, pink. She landed onto the MMPs back, serrated knife poised. The bot sank, hissed. Let out something almost *real*. Like a long, long breath.

Voice euphonic, the MMP said, "Deactivate us. They will not."

Mina plunged in the knife.

The MMP fell onto my legs. She shivered and sighed, Mina sawing at her back. Her eyes closed and did not open again.

Behind me, Saren stirred again.

I pulled him against me, laughing. "A dead bot on my legs and a resurrected man at my side. My brothers would never believe it."

I wiped my eyes, and then wiped Saren's, too. His eyelids fluttered. His lips twitched; a little, groggy sound slipped out.

With a wet, tearing squelch, Mina pulled the MMP's spine from her body. Purple liquid dripped from the false bone, thick like blood. A miserable imitation of a person.

At my side, Saren Vite opened his eyes; unfocused white irises streaked with grey drifted. Sounds like gravel scratched at his throat. I gave him a weak smile, knowing he couldn't see a thing. Not yet.

Mina and Taro pulled the MMP from my legs. My feet tingled, numb from the weight. They turned her over. My sight drifted from Saren Vite's fluttering eyes to the object glowing in her chest. It seemed to sing, emitting a pleasant hum. The object floated in the clear cavity, suspended. A few inches long, curved slightly. Dark brown. Fleshy. Five little toes tipped with five little toenails.

The dark, delicate foot of a child.

"What the fuck?" Mina swore.

Taro gasped, dropping next to me, "Is that a—"

My hands clapped over my eyes. My thoughts blinked away, too stunned to form. Who — who would do such a thing?

A chill brushed my arm. Cold fingers gripped weakly at me. I quivered, looking down at him. Saren Vite. His odd, white eyes searched mine. His mouth opened, forming one hoarse word.

"Seth?"

My heart stopped beating.

28

THE SAND HOUSE

The *Other Place* was Seth's own personal corner of the sky. He called it a pinpoint of darkness in the vastness of blue. When Mercy took over, Seth left his body to float in his umbral room, overlooking the sun, the clouds, the Endless World below. In the *Other Place*, Seth left behind all suffering.

I'd asked him if the Other Place was real. He wasn't sure.

The problem with vacationing to the *Other Place* was the chaos his body created while he was away. Seth couldn't affect what Mercy did; not when he gave up complete control. So, he clung to shreds of self for as long as possible. Let it rip his soul up, let it overflow him with Devil Spit, the hemacrux.

It was a harsh existence for a seventeen-year-old. A constant, painful strain to subdue his inner Demon. The *Other Place* was a nirvana of easy safety. Nothing could be more tempting.

"I never want to open out. Never on purpose," he would say. He would swear it up and down. Swinging in his sitting sack, jittering about, talking too fast. "I would never do that. Never again."

I would watch, nod my head. Dig my nails into my thighs, because he was *lying*. He didn't even know he was lying. Maybe Seth didn't want to hurt anyone else, sure. I believed that. But he was hurting, and eventually he'd let Mercy slip out again. He'd talk himself into it, or maybe Mercy would do the talking. Eventually, Seth's Demon would open out.

Seth's moods shifted rapidly in the coming weeks. Often, it was like living with his corpse. He didn't move, didn't speak, didn't leave the closet.

Some days he spoke quickly, letting out as many words as possible in as short of a time. He'd go to class and even answer a teacher's questions. He'd walk through the gardens in Nepa, telling strangers facts about the plants they were treading on. He'd chat with me about *whatever.*

I would nod, play along. And inside, I would prepare.

Late afternoon, after Friday free hour, I headed back to our dorm room. Riolyn, Aeshra, and I had planned to go into Nepa to meet Uyentra's group for dinner. I'd spent the day bargaining with myself over whether it was time to give in and take a shower or not. If I let it go too long in between, people would start to notice. If they hadn't already.

Seth was in the bathroom. I could feel his energy swelling, hear him grumbling, arguing with the beast within.

I sat on the bed, kicking off my shoes. Maybe I wouldn't have to take a shower tonight; was I really that gross? And Seth was in there. He probably needed it more than I did.

I looked woefully at myself in the shine of the wardrobe, running my fingers through my roots. My reflection tilted and rolled. I shook myself, squeezed my eyes.

A fog hummed beneath my skin. I stood and nearly toppled, reaching for the bedpost. I hadn't been drinking, right? No, of course not.

"Hey, man," I called toward the bathroom. "Hey!"

The sizzling sound rippled through the door like a gust of wind. The tone grated me raw.

I steadied myself and knocked on the door.

"Seth? Just want to know you're doing all right."

He laughed — was it a laugh? It didn't sound right. I tugged a hair clip from my scalp and pinned the lock.

Seth was sitting on the sink counter with his head down, breathing roughly. Mint green bangs hung in his eyes. A pair of scissors sat at his side. Big ones, like those my father worshipped in his upper room.

I knocked on the doorframe and Seth looked up. Tears refused to leave his eyes, welling up right on the edge.

"What's going on?" I asked.

He shook his head silently. The hum around him deepened into a low growl.

I knew what was coming.

"*No.* Not today, man. You've been doing great. Breathe through it, right? Should we go upstairs? The recovery space?" I stepped toward him, talking too fast.

He slid down onto his feet and put his hands up in defense. They hung in the air like fragile, grey fences. The crisp color of his eyes had deadened to red-rimmed dust. He started to cough. Drops of black spattered his palm. He picked up the scissors and handed them to me.

I stepped toward him, opened my hands. "Not today, Seth. *I mean it.*"

"Go, please. I'm sick," He coughed hard this time, wasn't stopping to breathe.

I couldn't just stand there. I lifted my hands to the sky, letting the scissors clatter to the floor.

Seth's eyes opened wide. "Wait, no, Mayli, no—"

I was going to stop Mercy. I had a gift, and I was going to use it, damnit.

A red wave surged in me. My palms hit the force over his chest; I couldn't touch him, but it was enough. My energy, scarlet and aching, collided with his, prismatic and jade. The swell of healing power burst through my hands into Seth's body. Our powers met, tangled in a burst of red and green.

A hollow pulsation thundered through us.

"You idiot!" Seth shouted as black spilled down his chin. He slammed his blackened fist on the counter.

The ground shook — the wall *cracked*.

I stepped back, "Oh, no."

Seth moved quickly; his eyes pure black now. I skidded from the bathroom and fell on my ass.

"Ugh, why is this happening?" I groaned, scrambling away.

Seth grabbed at his chest as his body lengthened, twisted. Our eyes met; Seth was still in there, grappling for control. His other trembling hand reached for me.

Mercy latched onto my ankle and *pulled*. The bones popped.

"No, man — I'm not getting another new bodypart." I swung my other leg and kicked him in the jaw. Hemacrux splattered. The room seemed to tip sideways.

Mercy's blackened mouth screwed into a wicked grin. "Come on, *Maysolpheta*. Use that luscious power on me again. Our last meeting was too short, don't you think?"

I spit at him, "Not your *toy*," I twisted away, raising my voice to the Undergods, "Help! *Help*!"

The Demon chuckled, "I thought you'd have a plan this time around. It doesn't seem that you do."

Too-long hands stretched, reached. I looked — the scissors, *fuck*. Shiny silver sheers were sprayed with black droplets.

I thrashed, reaching for one of Seth's too-heavy boots.

Mercy's grey fingers wrapped around the blade slowly. Reverently.

"That's not yours, asshole!"

The boot came down on his hand. The scissors clattered away as Mercy yowled. He turned, black eyes glaring. Pain burst in my temples, clamping down like teeth. He got to his knees and sunk his blackened fingers into my scalp. He pulled me up onto my knees.

"Seth, no." I closed my eyes, searching for his energy. "Please don't let Mercy do this."

Seth was in there, awake and terrified. I could see him, tear-streaked cheeks and black-slick chin. He was frozen in fear.

My own energy coiled like a frightened snake. The red lake was gone, dry. The Something New, the inky green gunk, marbling the blood red, heavy and wrong. My thoughts formed a question; *Can I use you?* It shivered, cowered. *Great time to bow out. Excellent.*

Why wasn't it *working*?

Mercy's hand was on my neck. Not squeezing, just testing. Smooth fingertips traced the column of my throat. I shuddered, stomach rolling. His narrow eyes tracked as my skin rippled in distaste. My body rejected him down to the very bone marrow.

Mercy's voice softened to a distracted murmur. "Such a surprise, this gift. A Palm Lifter, just for me." A curious finger dipped into the hollow of my collarbone, fingerpainting with my sweat. "Is there where you keep it? I want to find the source."

My facial bandages had unstuck at the jaw, flapping unnervingly. Beneath, my skin burned hot. I opened my eyes and watched the demon, the *monster*.

Seth was in there, and he wasn't fighting back. And my energy was on fucking vacation.

The squeeze slashed one final breath from my lungs. Mercy's silky hand tightened and constricted; he was a better snake than I. My eyes bulged. I gasped silently, pointlessly.

I was going to die on my knees, eye-level with the devil.

There was a noise at the door.

"Uh, hello? You ready?" Riolyn opened it, clueless.

Her scales erupted to blue, and she was on us. Riolyn skidded into the room, sneakers squeaking on stone. *"Messer's tits, the fuck?"*

She jumped on Mercy's back, punching the back of his head. He stood, lifting me into the air with my throat in his hand and Riolyn on his back. The three of us spun in a ball of disoriented limbs.

Breathless and purple, I motioned to the scissors. Mercy dropped me as Riolyn dove to the floor. Silver streaked from Riolyn's hands and through the air. I gulped down a breath and caught them.

Mercy dropped to the floor, coughing. I took my chance.

I sunk the blade into his forehead. A silent stab through grey flesh and teenage bone.

We locked eyes and I heaved. Grey, orange, brown — Mercy was *gone*. What had I done?

But *Seth didn't die*; he didn't even flinch. He slumped down with an exhale, sending a tremor through the cave. The scissors stuck out of his face. Blood seeped down the side of his nose.

Riolyn eyed him, panting. "What *are you?*"

Seth reached up, bone-tired. He pulled the scissors out with a wet squelch. The wound knit closed.

"I don't know," he replied.

Riolyn paced in long steps through the lounge. Her ripped sneakers smacked on the floor, silenced every few feet by the luxurious rug in front of the couch I sat on. Seth was back in the dorm, hiding from the bruises around my neck.

"Who gets stabbed in the face like it's nothing? He shouldn't be here," Riolyn said as she turned to cross the room again.

Aeshra pulled his arms around his knees and slid deeper into his chair. His eyes peeked out, watching.

Riolyn continued, "Let's go to Nepa. We need to get out of here. I can't be stuck in this cave right now."

Tender parts of my jaw throbbed as I repositioned, looking over my shoulder. Every sound echoed right to my core. What was that sound? Shadows gleamed like shiny pools of essence waiting to swallow me whole.

"At least go to Dr. Harker," Aeshra sighed, burrowing into his sweater.

"No, we need to get out of here. Now. It's late enough to party at the sand house. We can stay there all night."

"Riolyn, quit moving for three seconds," I snapped. "He's right, we need to tell someone what happened. And I don't know that I'm in the mood to *party* after all that."

"Screw that. We don't answer to anyone. We need to get drunk."

Riolyn reached for my hand and pulled me up. I didn't have the willpower to fight with her. Saren was missing, Aeshra was a basket case, and Riolyn had just had to defend her best friend against a Dementric. She was bound to cope with this trauma somehow.

So, hand in hand, the three of us left the Eldrid lounge, stepped over the cracked entry floor, and headed into the night.

The dark sky cradled pockets of stars, shimmering across the glassy surface of the lake. Nothing like my lake, dry and fearful. The air was still, calm. We hopped on the ferry, Riolyn talking incessantly about getting fucked up. Aeshra stared at my neck when he thought I wasn't looking.

This wasn't the last time I'd feel like this; I knew that. Life had a way of throwing knives at my back every time I turned around. And wasn't this my fault anyway? I'd told Seth to move back in. I welcomed him to sleep a few feet away from me every night. I watched his moods fluctuate every day. I assured myself that I could talk him out of another attack.

Because I was such an incredible talker.

Riolyn took us right to the sand house. I didn't even bother to find Uyentra; if I did, they would know something serious had happened and try to intervene. Maybe Riolyn was right, maybe a stiff drink in a ruined house full of ruined teenagers was exactly what I needed.

Yeah, right.

The fire on the beach wasn't big enough for Riolyn's liking. While Aeshra and I huddled in lawn chairs drinking polysacc, Riolyn scoured the beach for every burnable object she could find; handfuls of paper trash, leaves, driftwood, a fabric bag. She piled them high in her empty seat. Every once in a while, she'd run inside to take a shot, then bolt back out with newfound energy and continue her mission.

Aeshra lifted his chin and eyed my swollen neck. "Your face was just starting to look normal again."

"Yeah."

"Riolyn said you Palm Lifted him?"

Nodding again, I said, "I think so. I couldn't touch him, but I felt it work. But then... It was like the Lift split. Seth got some, Mercy got some."

"Why did you do it?"

"I don't know," I mumbled, drawing with my show in the sand. "Palm Lifting is about healing, but I don't think you can Lift a demon out of a Dementric."

The sand house quickly filled with students. Music pulsed in time with the throb in my ankle. I took off my shoes and buried my feet in the cold sand. After a while, when Aeshra was pleasantly drunk, his body moved to the music playing inside the house. I watched him, pleasantly drunk myself.

Nathali was in front of me, talking, pointing. I had to focus on her lips to hear what she was saying.

"May, hello? What the heck happened to you?"

The question rang in my head. "What do you mean?" I slurred.

She crouched in front of me and pulled at my shirt, "Your clothes! And — holy shit, your neck! What happened?"

My head tipped down to take it in. My lovely hand-dyed shirt had a gaping rip from neck to chest.

"Got in a fight," I answered, rolling my head to look at Aeshra. He was asleep.

"A fight? With who? Mayli—"

"Get a move on, princess. We've got it covered," Riolyn stood over the both of us. Something in her hand was on fire. Was it a stick? An umbrella?

Nathali stood, "You've got it covered? What the hell are you doing then? She's *hurt*."

I tried to stand, too. "I agreed to come—"

"Sit down. Get your shoes on, I'm taking you back." Nathali bent to pick up my sneakers.

Riolyn was a blur of moonlit scales and fire. She started ranting. "This place is just like everywhere else. Always trying to control us, to put us in our place. Get us medicated. We don't need to be medicated!"

The music from inside the house pounded out deep, erratic beats. Louder, louder.

Riolyn threw her arms wide, with the bonfire cracking and hissing behind her. "I know how to solve problems. I've done it before. I was locked up in that room for years, and I stopped it!"

Nathali pulled on her arm, "You need to sit down too, you're drunk!"

But she didn't move. The flames were tasting the side of her hand and she didn't move.

Aeshra was up now, fire reflecting in his round eyes.

"You want to see how I stopped it? You want to see how I got out?"

As Riolyn moved for the sand house, Aeshra sat up gasping.

"What is she doing?" Nathali asked with panic.

But it was too late. The house was aflame.

29

THE DEVIL OF SURADELPHIA

Like an installation artist, Mina laid the MMP's bodies in a line on the cement floor. At their feet, five severed spinal columns stretched. False bone gleamed white and wet. Purple fluid leaked onto the floor in glassy pools around their bodies. Alarms rung overhead, unending.

Taro and I pulled a sleeping Saren onto an automatic lift next to the stairwell.

"Someone is going to show up sooner than later," said Taro. "We need to leave."

Mina waved her off. "I'm almost done. Just wish I had some wax."

I watched her finesse the placement of an MMP's hand; the one who'd spoken to me. *Deactivate us. They will not;* her words swam circles in me.

The dark-skinned, floating foot in her chest cavity continued to glow. Pale blue, like the moon on dark water. My eyes skimmed the others — a bone, a finger, a strip of skin, a kneecap. Each one refracted colored light.

"Should we take those body parts?" I asked. "The ones in their ribs."

Mina bent down and dislodged the clear container holding the little foot. She snipped the connecting wires. The MMP's veins faded from pale blue to black. Mina unclipped a roll of fabric from her waist, unfurling it to reveal a large bag. She held the object up for a better look, the glow casting a moonstone shimmer over her face. She dropped the box in the bag and slung it over her shoulder.

"Ready to go. Taro, you've scanned everything? Lots of footage?" Mina stepped onto the lift next to us.

Taro's eyes bounced over the immense space for one last time. "Yes, I've got it all. According to my scans, this lift should take us to the parking garage."

I sat on the lift, holding Saren Vite against me. He'd fallen unconscious just after waking. No way to ask him if he'd said *Seth*, and if he had ... did that mean he knew Seth? How could this man, wrapped up with the Producer, know Seth?

Mina smacked the lift button and the motor clanked into gear, grinding in tandem with the alarms blaring above us. The MMPs floated on their pools of purple, four still glowing in different colors; white, pink, gold, peach. The fifth was dark; I doubted they could bring her back.

Up five floors we drifted. The alarms quieted the higher we got, and after the third floor our view was obscured by a concrete shaft. The smell of the air dulled as we rose.

"What time is it?" I asked, covering Saren's bare chest with my jacket. Bruising stained the skin around his leaking chest port.

Taro answered, "Nearly four."

"At least we'll have the sunrise to watch on the drive back," I said. "It was always beautiful over the Kajiun forest."

Mina gifted me with a smile, her lashes grazing her cheeks. Her elbow nudged into my side. "You did good, kid."

I had to look away for fear she'd see my watering eyes.

The lowest level of the garage was lonely, shadowed and covered in oil-spills, but we didn't care. The three of us hollered and smacked hands as soon as the double doors opened wide. Nightbugs hissed to silence. Mina helped me carry Saren Vite as Taro called the van on her palmpod. Within minutes, the van cleared the corner and screeched to a stop before us.

Squeem hopped out first, stumbling to steady his legs, a wide smile on his face. Fruit wandered over to take hold of Saren and drag him to the van. Matey followed last, on the edge of tears. Joyful, I think.

"He's alive. But we're not sure what they've been doping him with," Taro said as she walked with Fruit to the van. After Fruit sat Mr. Vite down on the bed of the van, he took Taro's hand and gave it a long squeeze. She squeezed back.

I averted my eyes, certain I'd seen something I wasn't supposed to.

Squeem was talking to Mina. "Five MMPs? What sort of programming? Wait. Hand over the copychips so I can start rendering them."

She unloaded a flip-pouch of chips into Squeem's open palm and swung around in an ecstatic dance.

"I can't believe we did it. This is the biggest break we've ever had! I can't wait to shove this in the Producer's face." Mina pulled a small gun from her back and pointed it up toward the ceiling of the garage. She shot it once, *bang*. Mina spun, twirling like the first version of her I'd seen; the one on the yacht, flinging around the hand of a victim. Joyous, free, completely out of her mind.

And here I was, doing nothing. While Mina and Taro fought death-programmed robots, I'd sat on the floor and cried. Vomited even. Always a loser, never the hero. Meanwhile, children were having their *body parts removed.*

"Show them the foot," I said, eyes glazed.

"Oh, that." Mina pulled the bag from her shoulder, reached in and tossed the clear, glowing container to Fruit.

Matey gasped.

He caught it. "Huh. A kid's foot."

I nodded. "All the bots had them. Not feet, but ... parts. Powering the bots, I think."

Squeem took hold of the container, yellow in the face. "A Limit kid. That's why they are taking them? To power MMPs? It doesn't make sense."

I walked over to Squeem. His distress caught something in my chest. The entirety of the situation, the horror of it. My body slotted next to his against the van; the cold metal shocked my spine, reminding me to breathe.

He turned to me. His brow hairs were wild, sticking in odd directions like he'd been scrubbing his face with nerves while we were gone. "You saw a lot today. Are you going to be okay?"

I wanted to laugh, because no, I was not okay. I would never be okay. I wasn't like these people: strong, resilient. I was a *coward*. But I stepped away from the van, gave him a winning smile and said, "Are *you* going to be okay?"

Again, Mina was dancing with her gun. I turned to watch her.

She swung her leg out and began to pirouette around and around. My mind wandered to our first moment together in the Green Sun Hook Market; she could have been a professional dancer, the way her body swam through the air. Instead, she pointed her gun at the wall — *Bang*. The ceiling, twice; *Bang, Bang*. Cement clattered to the floor. *Bang*; a parked car. *Bang*; the wall again. *Bang*.

Squeem slumped against the van with a low gasp.

Blood rushed to my ears. The thumping, thudding sound of my heart. Red streaked down the side of the van as Squeem slid to the floor.

Suddenly, the parking garage was very loud. People were shouting, running, holding Squeem. I ran to him, too. His breath was heavy, coughing. Mina stood in place, her eyes round like brown planets.

"Where is he hit?" Matey called.

"Back," Fruit answered, "Move him?"

"Mina, *help*!" Taro cried.

Sirens. The sounds of car engines in a cement tomb. Deep rumbling.

"They're coming," I yelled, frozen over my friend. Squeem was yellow and blotchy, gasping. I took his hand. Both of us were trembling.

Batifban sirens screamed ever closer.

Mina woke to action. "We need to get Squeem out of here. *Now.*"

Mina began to hoist Squeem up. He managed a world-shattering cry, and that set Mina off too. Painful sobs echoed with the sirens, nearly on us now.

"Squeem, baby, I'm sorry, I'm so sorry," she hammered on, crying and trying to get Squeem in the van.

Matey slapped her hands away. "You're making it *worse*, slow down—"

Two Batifban screeched around the curve. I stared into their strobing neon lights; blue, pink, yellow. The colors stirred me. I stood.

I reached for Mina and took her hand one last time. Her eyes locked with mine, brown irises, pupils blown wide. I took ahold of her pale face and kissed her.

"Get him out of here," I said. And let go.

Walking towards the Batifban was the easiest thing I'd ever done. It felt like floating; my feet didn't touch the ground. The sirens fell silent to my pounding ears, and the guns over car doors looked like beacons of hope. Hope for the DAG crew, *my* crew. My friends. They would get Squeem out, they would save him. I could make sure that happened.

I put my hands in the air, the universal sign of submission.

"I'm ready to pay for my crimes. Just tell me what you need me to do," I called, my voice calm, my hands still with confidence.

"Get down! Get down on your knees! Arms up where we can see them!"

I knelt, head down.

"Devin!" Someone called behind me. I shook my head, sending a prayer to Uyenl that they would understand.

A Batif ran over with their gun pointed out. They slid a metal link around my neck, shutting it with a silent click. My wrists were secured behind me, cool metal slipping on my veins. A stiff bar attached the neck link to my cuffed wrists. I smiled into my chest. I was going *home*.

As I was ushered to the transport car, I saw the DAG van squeal away to safety. They would be okay. Squeem was in good hands; the best hands. He'd live, and Mina would be safe, and so would Taro, Fruit, Matey, Cassius. Everyone I'd grown to care for over the past months. The Dight Actors Guild would go on.

The Batif asked, "Are you Devin Mace?"

I watched my crew's van disappear; my friends.

"Devil Mace. That's what they used to call me."

30

THE SHORE

Orange, red, white, dancing into the sky. The smell of burning wood and plastic. The screams of students. The sand house, up in flames.

My eyes blinked, blurred.

"Water, get water!" Nathali's voice was close to me. She yelled, "Is there a hose?"

I'd never seen something devoured. I couldn't look away. The beautiful ruins of a house, too close to the shore and filled to the brim with sand. Gone. Flames ate the walls, the frame. Heat enveloped my body. Why wasn't I sobering up? Where was Riolyn? Had she just set the sand house on *fire*?

Aeshra pulled me up, his hair glowing hot in the firelight. "We need to help." He was shaking me. "What do we do?"

I stared at him, putting the words together. "Uh. Yeah, who deals with fire?" I slurred, "Firewalkers?"

"Ok, do we have any of those?"

"Corin. Nathali's boyfriend," I said, spotting my sister. We locked eyes — she nodded.

Nathali set off for Corin.

"Go find help," I said.

Aeshra nodded, bouncing on his feet, psyching himself up, "Okay, okay, I can do that." He took off down the shore. I watched him go. Something heavy had settled into my stomach. I didn't know how to move around it.

Students were using whatever they could find to carry water from the lake to the house, splashing it at the flames. Little cups, a bucket. It wasn't helping.

My eyes scanned the scene. There she was—cobalt scales dusting sepia, chestnut hair raised like an angry dog. Riolyn stood motionless. The flames glowed before her, a fiery aura. I shook her by her shoulders like Aeshra had done to me.

"I don't know what happened." She stared over my head at the flames.

"Focus. Now we have to fix it. Someone could get hurt," I said. Our hands met halfway, clinging to each other. I pulled her along. "We need to find something to carry water."

The scales on the back of her hand stood, scratching my palm like little blades.

A wall of sound exploded from inside the house. We tumbled into the sand, curling into each other for protection. Sparks flew, sizzling on the lake. Students screamed while *stupid fucking music* still thumped somewhere. Madness.

Riolyn was crying into my chest.

Nathali's bright hair caught my eye — she dragged Corin up from the beach like a true hero. She dusted off his jacket. Together, they took a deep breath.

My sister turned to the heavens. Energy bloomed from her, crisp and green. It rose into the air like a cloud of moss. She cried out, divine music springing from her lips. Her Faunate gift; a cry for help. Winged creatures took to the sky.

An alarm sounded in Nepa; Aeshra's work. The birds called with it, sweeping over the lake and to the cave.

Corin Verner walked into the flames.

Riolyn and I scoured the beach. Corin was searching for students. I knew he would be okay — his power was made for this. But it was unsettling. Awful. Riolyn shook with it. She gasped for air, running along the water, frantically searching for something, anything, to help.

Minutes passed; I don't know how long. A ferry pulled up to the dock.

Varali Garima and Drucilla Laverick jumped to shore, their long skirts ballooning in the air. Their hands raised in unison. The two Firewalkers tremored with limitless power. Lake water swelled.

"What are they—" Riolyn started.

Sloshing orbs of water rose into the air and slammed against the house. They hit like wet bombs, water spraying and sizzling. Grey clouds built above. Within seconds, rain threatened to fall.

"No, *no*," I squeaked, so *pathetic*. My body clenched; tendons strung tight. I flung my jacket over my head.

A creaking sound forced me to look. The brittle top floor of the sand house shifted and dropped. Corin pushed through the doorway with someone else.

The soft patter of rain fell on my jacket. I scratched at my eyes, trying to breathe. Things blurred — was it *me* or the rain? I fumbled blindly in the sand, forcing breath from my lungs.

Another *boom* of water hit the burning house. I willed myself to find my friend.

Riolyn was beside the ferryboat. Her voice rose over the rain. "What are you doing here? This is all your fault!"

A thin silhouette stood on the boat, drenched in rain. I would know that spidery boy anywhere. Angry energy spiked in my blood.

Seth's voice carried through the storm. "I want to help!"

"No one let this psychopath off the boat!" Riolyn threw her arms out like a shield.

I pulled myself up from the beach. My ankle throbbed; I'd almost forgotten it.

The wind slammed whitecaps against the ferry, tossing the boat from side to side. Seth coughed into his hands. He fell forward and spit up over the side of the boat. Black oil bubbled on the surface of the water.

"Shit," I cursed. "Not now."

Riolyn stepped back in terror. I pushed past her. Black slid down Seth's neck and he threw his head back, gasping for air. A howl ripped from him, an animal sound.

"Seth, look at me," I yelled. "This can't happen here!"

"Let him die in there," Riolyn grumbled behind me. Her voice wasn't as sure as her words.

He doubled over, shaking, His body jarred, creaked. He shook his head at me, black eyes consumed by the shadows.

"Not here, man!"

Seth took a running leap off the boat and into the lake.

Maybe the screams had never stopped, but I began to hear them again. Students stood on the beach watching as Seth thrashed in the lake. He was a trapped animal; shrieks muffled by mouthfuls of water, shrill babbling between gasps of air.

Water on his face. Flailing arms, grey, splashing. Black shapes floated around him and *on* him, dragging him down. The sunrise streaking through the clouds, casting the scene in red.

I watched, paralyzed.

"Is he *drowning*?" Riolyn said. "Someone, help him!"

No one moved.

"Aren't you going to do anything?" She waved her hands in my face. Her flesh had greyed like the storm. She was *scared*.

The water moved like a serpent, coiling around him.

"I — I can't, the water—" I stammered, unable to look away.

Riolyn huffed and turned to the frozen crowd. "He's drowning! Do something! Drucilla?"

My brain moved slowly, listening. No one came forward. Was Drucilla afraid for Seth? Was she afraid *of* Seth?

Riolyn began stripping off her jacket. "I can't believe *I* have to save this asshole."

She dove off the dock with a silent splash.

Things clicked into place. Riolyn was *in the lake with Mercy.*

I ran to the edge and watched my best friend dart through the water. She circled Seth like a predator. He splashed and coughed at the surface, awful gargling sounds coming from his throat. His body shifted, stretched, oscillating between Seth and Mercy. The two snapped at each other like seadogs. A rippling hand reached for Riolyn. She dove under and disappeared.

My eyes slammed shut and I skimmed the pathetic, dry lake of power in me. The green sludge at the bottom winked up at me with embarrassment. I snarled at it. *Fuck you, trashbag. Get off your belly and work.* Trickles of red rose through the cracks. The lake was filling, replenishing. I took a bit of it and pushed.

Seth tipped backward. His head dipped under. Riolyn had a hold of his ankles, pulling him to shore. His ever-changing body slumped like a corpse.

A swell of cheers rose from the shore. I cared about *both* people down there. I shouted over my shoulder, "Shut up! This isn't a dance recital!"

Riolyn's slim form leapt from the water like a fish. Up and back down, spiraling deeper than we could see. Seconds later, she was pulling Seth ashore. He was unconscious.

Drucilla pushed me aside with a snarl. "Stupid girl." She bent over him, hammering on his chest. Devil Spit sprayed onto her pristine Adord robes. She stumbled back, horrified at the filth.

Black bubbled at the corner of Seth's mouth. Someone in the crowd gasped.

As I lifted my palms and stretched them flat, I felt the raw, red energy beneath my fingernails. Another person gasped, whispers swelling, the shuffling of feet on sand. I cursed them, wanted to yell *Fuck off!* But I maintained focus, drawing my power. Its heat burned between my eyes.

Palms hovering over Seth's chest, our energy collided; red and green raising from a lake of blood. The Something New tugged deep in my belly, a flopping, wet shadow. The energy in me pulled at Seth, weaving itself into his lungs and drawing out the water and hemacrux, blocking his air. I puffed out a breath, sucked in another, and squeezed my eyes shut tight, willing the liquid up his throat and out of his mouth.

Seth coughed. His narrow eyes fluttered. Our woven power fell with a great splash; my internal lake stilled.

Senses returned; the smell of burning wood, plastic, melted power conduits. Next was sound; the cackles of steam and snapped wires. But under the sounds of a recent fire was something else; gasps, frantic whispers, movement on shore behind us. I turned to look, blinking away the fog in my sight.

Standing with the crowd, just over there. A man so void of color that I swear I could see right through him. Sithnic, without a doubt, with skin like snow and eyes like marble.

Saren Vite.

He stood in front of the smoldering house frame, smoke coiling through the air. His eyes were bloodshot. Gaunt in the cheeks, thin as hell. Aeshra was wrapped around him, shaking them both with his sobs. And right next to Saren — I rubbed the fuzz from my eyes. Red hair pulled back into a ponytail, long sweater, even skinnier than Saren.

I straightened. Shook my head. But she was *there*, holding onto Saren's arm like he would disappear any moment.

Seth propped himself up, made an odd sound.

"Mina?" I think I said.

She looked me over, eyebrows scrunched together, and followed my body down to the person next to me; the Mace boy at my knees. Her head turned lopsided, like a confused puppy. Her mouth opened, might have said, "Oh."

And she started crying.

31

Necros Universal Institute for Tyrants

NUIT was a fine place; as fine as you'd expect from a prison dealing with "holistic reform."

That's what they called the major changes ricocheting through the place. After Mina had escaped, select inmates had taken up the challenge and attempted the same. One man, life-sentenced for fraud and attempted homicide, got out. That was bad news for the rest of us.

For the time being, outside period was held in a small, mesh-covered yard with high cement walls. Most inmates skipped the outside period altogether because of the constant inclement weather, but I used the time to read whatever book I'd checked out for the week. The selection was sad. Suffice to say, they had not a single book about Narien Evroldengaud.

I wasn't allowed to write letters until I'd been in for at least four months, with good behavior.

The pale blue inmate's uniform washed out my grey skin. I could stand next to the never-ending cement and all but disappear. I fondly remembered photos of Mina in a uniform identical to mine. But I was here now, and she was out there, surely crafting new batches of trophy wax.

To say I missed her did not encompass the truth of it.

I'd chosen to be caught. And it was probably for the best, as I wasn't much good to anyone on the outside. I'd had a few exciting months with Mina Harker and the Dight Actors Guild, but that was over. Now, I needed to keep my head down so I didn't attract the attention of the wards and Batifban stalking the halls.

No one liked me much here, but it was nothing compared to last time.

Last time, I was convicted of killing forty-four men; of crushing their skulls with my very fingers. Like I could even *do* that.

This time, I was just a loser who'd turned myself in for skipping town, shooting up a bank and breaking into a cosmetics office.

Oh, and for setting a bomb off in downtown Suradelphia. Just like the old days.

The evening we infiltrated Amnea Station, the parking garage and office building had blown to bits. I was blamed for that too. And it made sense, because while I hadn't crushed forty-four skulls with my bare hands, I had been in a terrorist organization back in the day. We might have been known to place bombs. Just little ones.

There were rumors that I'd been spotted with Mina Harker, but the dashcam footage was inconclusive. Squeem's blood on the scene had no matches in the database.

I prayed he was still alive every single day.

I'd never know if Squeem made it or not. That kept me up late into the night. Mina had shot him in the back, and as little as I knew about anatomy, I knew that damage to the spine could be lethal. That's how Mina had deactivated the MMPs.

What if Mina had deactivated Squeem, too?

On cloudy, wet afternoons like this one, I would sit on the covered, metal bench farthest from the alarm. Every time there was an altercation, the alarm pushed flashbacks up. MMPs skittering across the ceiling, jumping down on us, screeching like giant bugs. Their glowing veins. The glass cubicles and metal coffins meant to hold beings in transport to whatever hell the Full Set had dreamed up. Little glowing body parts floating in glass chambers, instead of hearts, lungs, what *should have* been there.

The worst part of this whole endeavor was that I would never see my family again; the stunts I'd pulled over the last months made sure of that.

Caulder had stayed in Suradelphia for nothing. Donnie and Seth were who-knows-where. And Saren Vite had recognized me *as Seth,* hadn't he? Or had I imagined that? I could have; the whole thing was a blur; nothing but alarms and screeching and thunderous booms.

The longer I stayed in this grey, lifeless building with these lonesome psychopaths, the worse my memory got.

I would never know what happened to my friends, to Saren Vite, to Squeem or Mina. I made the choice to give myself up. I was bound to this for eternity. The loss thrummed deep in my bones.

So here I sat, with my back to the mist and a mediocre book in my hand. And I didn't regret even a second of it.

32

VISITOR

Thick, oily blobs of hemacrux washed ashore as the wind rocked the waves.

Seth sat on the very patio chair where I'd watched the sand house go up in flames. His head lulled in his hands while Dr. Harker spoke to him in hurried whispers. Sitting on the sand next to them was Riolyn, her glorious scales lying flat in submission.

Leaning against the patio table stood Mina, my estranged, serial murdering sister. I couldn't tell if she was listening or not.

The crowd had gone, ready to sleep off our recent catastrophe. Saren went with them, back to Voltenstraus, surely forced into the infirmary with Dr. Valentine ruling over him; colored lights and all. Aeshra held onto him for dear life as they boarded the ferry.

Next to me, letting lake-spray mist over her like perfume, was Moonie Devince. Her dark skin glistened, wet in the clouded sunlight. She stood still, gazing out over the water.

I hid beneath an oversized raincoat.

"This is an interesting development," Moonie said, stretching her hand over the water. Tiny droplets spattered her lacquered nails.

"Mina and Saren? Yeah."

"Hmm, that too. But I'm talking about your ability to Lift Seth." She flicked the water from her hands and faced me, eyes bright with curiosity. "Seth told us you Palm Lifted him. Twice, now."

"It wasn't very successful," I replied, watching Nathali pace the shore to keep herself from staring at our older sister.

Uyentra caught my eye from the steps of the blackened sand house. They smiled sullenly, encouragingly. Corin walked through the ruins of the sand house, kicking aside smoldering wood and snarling at the ash on his pants. He might have been a hero, but he was still a prick.

"It's odd you had any success at all. I've tried to Lift him; it's too painful of a process. And, not to offend you, but you're no prodigy. You're a fine Lifter, but this is something else. This is an addition that isn't documented, at least not in the books I've read. There's something else going on."

Moonie toed off her velvet boots and sat on the dock. I caught a gleam of gunmetal as she dipped her feet into the cold water.

"You've never Lifted Seth before?" I asked.

She shook her head. "Seth's devil is a drove of pure corruption; energy so dark it cannot be pierced by neutral power like mine. Only a Non-Eater, a being of transcendence, can affect such a state. This is why Seth was given to Idrissa in the first place. But Seth's devil has drained Idrissa to the edge of eternal sleep."

I cursed, shaking off my raincoat and bending to sit with Moonie.

"I think it has to do with your visitor," Moonie added.

"My *visitor*?"

"The darkness, the mass in you. Whatever it is, it's physical." She splashed her feet on the surface of the water. I realized that one of them wasn't a foot at all, but a perfect, metallic replacement with articulated toes and ankle. A metal prosthetic, like my shoulder. Moonie only had one foot? Why hadn't I known that?

She turned her head to the side, like she was listening to something. I didn't hear anything but the wind, crashing waves, and Dr. Harker barking something at my oldest sister.

A moment later, Moonie nodded and continued. "Did you ingest any of Seth's hemacrux?"

"Ugh, yes, do *not* recommend. Tasted like tar and toothpaste."

Moonie nodded. "That could be it. I can't understand why it would allow your energy to weave with Seth's, but it certainly seems that way." She leaned back on her hands and swirled her feet in the water. "Well, Idrissa would like to spend some time with you over the last month of school."

"Sae would? Sae said that?"

"We need to tell Dr. Harker," she said, standing, followed by, "You don't like the water, do you?"

I coughed up a sore laugh. "No. That's why Riolyn had to jump in after Seth. I couldn't do it. I guess I would have let him die."

"I very much doubt that," and she gave me this *look*. "Have you found your points of power?"

"I think so; between my eyes."

Moonie squatted down and dipped her hand into the grey water.

She stood in front of me and pressed two wet fingertips to either side of my nose, between my eyes. I shuddered, horrified by the water on my face. As I pushed through the feeling of terror, I could see it; a boiling well of red swimming in my soul, escaping in a slow seep of molten power. My power.

I let the water drip down my cheeks for a second before frantically wiping it away.

George's eyes were on me as I strolled up beside Moonie, who was carrying her boots in hand. She set them on the table. His tired eyes caught the tender bruises on my neck and welled with tears.

"Dear. Oh, Mayli. I'm sorry I haven't spoken to you yet. This matter is of grave importance," he said, standing to wrap an arm around my shoulder. I burrowed myself into his side, feeling the comforting scratch of his tweed vest on my cheek.

"Idrissa wishes to meet with Mayli over the next weeks to hone her Palm Lifting," Moonie said.

"Oh, does Sae." He stiffened at my side. "Well, you can tell Idrissa—"

"Dad, chill out," I mumbled into his armpit.

"I didn't want you Palm Lifting in the first place," he growled.

I pulled away to see the venomous look he threw at Moonie, who took it in stride. Seth watched with quiet interest. Riolyn leaned back on the sand, dazed in a post-arson stupor.

Mina, of all people, broke the silence. "If she can Lift, why stifle that? It's a gift. The opposite of what the rest of our family does."

My father wrapped two arms around me, holding me in a protective clutch.

"That's exactly it. I didn't *want* Mayli to know her gift. A practiced Palm Lifter saves life from the brink of death — sometimes beyond death. Our family *takes* lives. For a Palm Lifter to take life is a disastrous invitation to evil. It shreds the soul of the Lifter, leaving them but a fraction of who they were. It takes everything from them but their very breath. And now that is all but inevitable for Mayli."

I rolled my eyes. "Sounds like another decision made for me, without any consideration of what *I want*."

"Of course I didn't give you the choice! You would have chosen to *fight!* You'd rather invite a devil in for rootbrew than to be a *passive healer,*" He laughed to the sky, glasses sliding off his face, absolutely mad. "Why do you think I forced you to live with a Dementric? Mercy has marked you as territory now. Another demon can't slide in and take you. Uyenl abound, any other power would have been a gift, but *Palm Lifting*? A punishment, a damned *punishment* sent from Erytoa straight to your mother and I. It's begun, and it will be the nail in your coffin."

Silence.

Violence tingled at the base of my neck.

"You — you *gave me to a demon*?" My eyes snapped from person to person; everyone was stunned. "You handed me off to Mercy, as, what, protection? No, man. I'll stay with Idrissa."

The doctor, my father, sighed. His fists clenched at his sides.

Mina held my gaze. "Good choice. And Seth will come with me, back to Monount Valley."

My father sighed again. Louder this time.

Riolyn, barely out of her daze, asked, "What are you going to do in Monount?"

"Fill him in on some things. Get to know his demon. Get some use out of that monster."

"And then?" our father grumbled.

"And *then* I'm going to break Devin out of prison."

The doctor wanted to sigh again; a third, louder time. Really drive it home, just how insubordinate and stupid he thought we were. But Seth's head snapped up first.

With the most physical expression he'd likely ever mustered, Seth yelped, "*Who?*"

But Wait, There's More!

First off, thank you for taking a chance on *The Cave and the Houseboat*. I've written a special gift for readers like you. Ever wondered what wild turns led to Devin earning his Devil of Suradelphia title? And what's the real story behind young Mayli's first encounter with Mina? Find out in *Red Feathers and the Night Palace*, a free prequel novella! Sign up to get it here: https://BookHip.com/HMKNPPV

If you enjoyed *The Cave and the Houseboat*, I would deeply appreciate if you left a review wherever you purchased the book. Reviews make a huge difference to help new readers find the series. Not just for my book, but for all books! It means a lot to authors when their readers take a moment from their busy lives to leave a review. Thank you!

About the Author

Behind the scenes of this novel, Moose Shoemaker might have been refereeing a spat between the cats and the dog, or perhaps rescuing the chickens from misadventure. But in the quiet moments, between teaching art, single-parenting a delightfully spirited child, and laughing in the face of dyslexia, magic happens on the keyboard.

Follow Moose's socials for a view into her life and writing process.

instagram.com/moosewrites/

facebook.com/moosewrites